STORM
ENTERTAINMENT

I0736823

Storm Entertainment Presents
SOMNIA
ONLINE
Experience the class you were born to play!

STELLAEIN
N
NOCTURN
TEAR LAKE
OBSIDIAN FOREST
BANDIT CAMPS
HAZENTHORNE
ULULATE
VAHRIR
MARSH OF VAHRIR
GOBLIN WATCHTOWERS
HAZEN VILLAGE
HAZEN SWAMP
MIKRUM CASTLE
PELAGU
HIMMEL LAKE
MIKRUM VILLAGE
FRANGIT
TARISHNA

COGNITIA
HIGHTOWER CASTLE
GOLEMS
RUINS OF CENEDRIL
VERENDUS
GNOLLS
FELLING FIELDS
GLACIER LAKE
VERENDI MOUNTAINS
CURET
DARSHIN
N
CENEDRIL

SOMNIA ONLINE

ANOMOLY

BOOK 2

K.T. HANNA

Author: K.T. Hanna
Cover Artist: Marko Horvatin
Typography: Bonnie Price
Formatting & Interior Design: Caitlin Greer

ISBN-13: 978-1-948983-09-9 (Paperback Edition)
ISBN-13: 978-1-948983-07-5 (Hardback Edition)
ISBN-13: 978-1-948983-08-2 (E-Book Edition)

For Alexis
Thank you

CHAPTER ONE

Comatose

Somnia Online
Day Five Post-Launch

Murmur staggered as the guild castle shot into focus around her. Nausea swept over her, adding to the volcano of anger in her gut. It leaked through her mental shielding no matter how dense she thought the wall was. Squinting against the harsh daylight she saw a wave of confusion sweep over Telvar's workers.

Construction work ground to a halt. The builders stumbled in their tracks, their materials falling to the ground as they braced themselves against any stable surface.

Any attempt she made to calm those whirling thoughts only resulted in them spinning further out of control. Murmur's head spun, pounding like someone had taken a hammer to it. Just a few more hits and her skull might burst. She fell to her knees, struggling to move from the recall pad.

A mental shield slammed down around her discordant thoughts, plunging her mind into blissful stillness. It momentarily subdued the roiling sea of emotion within her by shocking her as if a bucket of iced water had been thrown over her head.

A scaled hand reached toward her, and her head spun too much to grasp it as the world twisted in and out of focus. Instead, Telvar hauled her up into a princess carry, his strides like he was floating on air. She clung to him, burying her face within the contours of his neck to keep the light out and her tears in.

Cool air blew from the underground caves to rustle her robes as they passed into the lower section of the castle. A sob caught in Murmur's throat as she realized she was shaking. Her confusion finally gave way to the beginnings of understanding, and terror.

How could she possibly be in a coma? She'd graduated high school, hell, she'd been logging out of the game and returning to her house. How the fuck did any of that indicate she was sick?

Telvar still carried her, and, as the slope of the path changed, Murmur knew they'd passed into the actual cavern and were descending the long ramp where she'd first met him. It wasn't long before he stopped and tugged her arms gently from around his neck, depositing her into a chair hewn roughly from the rock. In some places it dug into her skin even through the robes she wore, causing her to gasp in pain. How could she not be awake if she felt things so acutely? Were the sensors attached to the suit really that effective?

Finally, she pried her eyes open and recognized the ledge where they'd first encountered Telvar. She hadn't realized there was a recessed area in the back of the cave. In front of her was a small fire pit, casting flickering shadows on the walls to dance while she lost herself in thought. Several stone benches dotted the alcove, and she could see provisions stored in the back of the area. Everything from salted meat to crates of wine.

"Are you calmer now?" Telvar crouched in front of her, his brow furrowed in concern as he looked up at her.

"How did you know I was in a coma? Were you waiting to shock me?" Anger began to churn again, and Murmur took the deepest breath she could manage fighting against it, forcing it down to manageable levels so she could think.

Telvar sighed deeply, his huge chest rippling with the effort as he averted his eyes. He pushed himself up, tapping his chin with a long scaled finger.

"You." Telvar began. He breathed in again and focused his startling eyes on her own, radiating sincerity. "You've been in a coma for just over two months. You used your headset early, but something went wrong."

The 'something' had a tone to it, a hesitation. Murmur grasped onto it like a lifeline, intent on digging deeper. "I didn't try the headset early..."

But her words trailed off, thoughts inundating her mind. Didn't she? Had she really not tried it first? She vaguely remembered her father suggesting they give it a test run before the suit arrived. Just for her to have some fun, but hadn't they decided against it? The memories swirled in her head. Trying on the suits with Harlow, logging into the scanner, being so damned disappointed by her class allocation. It all happened. Didn't it?

Compassion radiated from Telvar, from the look in his eyes to the set of his mouth. "You tried it; the synapse trigger malfunctioned as we were activating the scan details. At least, we think so. There was a difference in your headgear. Maybe it interfaced directly with your mind, or connected to a part of it, but when they tried to remove it, you began to convulse. Only replacing it and rebooting your interface stopped it. Just like that, you didn't wake back up."

"I'm dead then?" She whispered the words, tasting them on her tongue like battery acid. "How did –"

But Telvar took her hands and knelt again in one swift motion. "You are not dead." His eyes were adamant. "You are merely in a sort of limbo. We've been trying to determine what it was that left you like this. We can tell it was a mixture of several factors, including the way your headgear was calibrated. No one else has one like it. Michael enhanced it as a gift for you, but he had his own accident before you even received it. Figuring out exactly what it did... Your mother has tried all manner of things to do so."

Standing, Murmur ripped her hands out of the lacerta's, stumbling back and almost tripping over her chair. "No. No. That's not possible. I've been home. I've logged out of this game. I've –"

But the curtains had that strange way of always being open in the exact same position—over and over again. Sometimes Harlow wasn't there. A couple of times she'd not even been allowed out of her room. Hindsight was such a bitch. Small things, so many small things.

"How have I been logging out then?" But her voice wasn't steady. The trembling extended to her arms, and to her fingers she clenched her fists in an attempt to belay it.

"Your mother was desperate. She came to use and begged us for assistance." He glanced at her, a thoughtful grimace on his thin lips. "She designed a midway log out station. Replicated your house in as much detail as she could, so you'd appear to log out of the game, just like you always would have, and hopefully wouldn't notice that you never seemed to leave."

Murmur shook her head, refusing to face the glitch-like glimpses she'd experienced when logging out-the overlapping of the worlds right in front of her. "No! That's not possible. I graduated. I worked my ass off. I've got the college acceptance letters. Scholarships!"

"True. You did, and you do." Now there was even a trace of pity in Telvar's expression. "It wasn't difficult to convince the school board to allow you to finish your tests online. So, you did, in fact, finish. You're mind's ability to adapt is quite remarkable."

"But my body is being kept alive by machines?" the words sounded so final, so dystopian, they made Murmur shudder.

"Your body doesn't need machines to breathe, but you're receiving intravenous nutrients to stay alive. Your mother procured an experimental pod for you."

"But I'm alive?" A stirring of hope shot through her, something to cling to.

"You're alive." This time Telvar put force behind his words, standing with her and focusing so intently on her eyes that she couldn't look away. "You are alive. You are here, in this world, more connected to it than any other human who is currently playing. Which is why we're not sure what will happen if you die in-game."

More attached to the world of Somnia? "How am I more connected?"

This time Telvar shook his head. "There have been some accidents. Some overreaches of the system when scanning and reading brain waves, in interacting with the human psyche. It's like a computer of neurons and electricity and yet nothing like what we are. Yours was such an accident. It left your mind slightly displaced. This was somewhat our fault."

"Our fault?" Murmur cut in, irritation flaring in her chest. "Who is 'our'?

"Us. You'd call us artificial intelligence, AI—units designed to run this world, to monitor it, to develop the game." He stood there, eyes calm, face not even twitching.

"Wait. What?" She blinked at him, struggling not to burst out laughing.

Another sigh, an all too human response. Telvar rolled his shoulders, cracking his neck.

"We are the AIs in charge of this game, which ultimately means it's our fault you ended up this way."

"For a brief instant Murmur wanted to stab him. "It's your fault I'm stuck here?"

"In a way, but the three of us are trying to figure it out, I promise." His words were fervent, like it meant more to him than anything else at all.

"Just three?" she asked.

"Three of us who oversee the rest. We are in a sense—"

"The gods of the game," she whispered, her eyes flashing at him. "You played with my head and I lost?"

"Not quite. We just have to figure out how to get you whole again." Genuine sadness lingered in his words, and Murmur couldn't bring herself to hate him.

She clamped down on her panic, straightened her shoulders, and looked Telvar in the eyes. "If I'm technically always online and being fed from an outside force, then I don't need to log out, do I?"

Telvar blinked at her change of subject. "Technically probably not, although your mind will need some rest, too."

Murmur shook her head, trying not to let visions of Jirald screaming as he ran toward her overwhelm her. He'd tried to train her, even if doing so could have killed her. Did he know? Did he care? "Can't let my mind relax. If I do, I'll panic, and I already blew Jirald away with my mental shield."

"What?" Telvar looked impressed, one eyebrow ridge raised artfully. "You used it offensively?"

"I was angry."

He studied her for a few moments. "Kinetic manifestations, huh? Remind me never to get on your bad side."

"Too late." She looked away, finally checking the guild and chat areas of her interface. With so many messages, she was surprised it hadn't overloaded. "You're already on my irritated side, but at least you've been honest with me."

Even from the beginning he'd offered to help her, under the guise that it was good for both of them. She hoped the news that one of the main AIs of the game was helping them didn't get out, But she'd have to cross that bridge when future Murmur came to it.

Thinking about her predicament for too long only threatened to break her. A sudden calm swept through her, like she'd finally managed to push the turmoil away.

Summer Residence
Home of Laria, David, and Wren
Laria Summers
End of Day Five

Laria Summers paced the kitchen, a scowl on her face. She hadn't heard from her daughter in the last several hours, not since she'd found out. And while not much time had passed yet, it still stung. Wren had never been tolerant of liars. When she was five, she gave her parents days of silent treatment after finding out Santa wasn't real.

Creating an instance of their home while pretending she was still fine and letting her brain be tricked into daily activities was probably one of the worst things she could have done as Wren's mother. But Laria didn't see how she'd had a choice at all. It hadn't been an easy choice, nor had it been lightly made. The only way to stop the convulsions once the headgear had been disconnected, when they were trying to figure out what was wrong, was to put the headgear back on. When they did, it quieted her body, and her brain leapt back into action. While she didn't understand the connection, the proof that it was there was too overwhelming to ignore.

Squaring her jaw, Laria took the steps two at a time coming to a standstill on the landing. She frowned at her daughter's door, slightly ajar, the sound of monitors beeping faintly in the room. It was difficult to force herself to look at her daughter's pallid face, at her flickering eyelids that just wouldn't open.

Still, Laria needed the reality check more than ever right now.

The lights were dim in the room, set to a low voltage so a soft white glow permeated the space. The containment device stood front and center surrounded by small tables and the items needed to keep Wren comfortable. While the suit helped with her rate of atrophy, it didn't do everything to stop it. Medication was needed to help Herdelay her body's decay as long as possible. But the longer this went on, the more likely it was her daughter would need stringent physical therapy to combat this coma.

Laria refused to contemplate that Wren might never wake up.

Looking down, Wren almost merged with the gorgeous black suit. Her dark hair blended beautifully. Sometimes, when she'd had a spare moment before launch, Laria came in and brushed that hair for hours on end, like they'd done when she was a child. Wren's skin had taken on an odd sort of translucence. Sometimes it looked like there was something flowing under her skin, just out of reach of Laria's vision.

Over on the bed, but a few feet from her daughter, lay Harlow. Completely clad in her own suit and headgear. The redhead's usually joyous smile was tainted by the worry line forming in the middle of her forehead. The girls had always been inseparable. Even when the other family moved, even at different schools. And now—even while Wren wasn't fully here.

The machine beeped softly, like a metronome keeping time with the beat of Wren's life. It was steady and slow, healthy and yet not enough to wake her up. Just like her brain activity in the game didn't accurately reflect her physical state because when they'd tried to take her offline and remove the headset, her readings dropped to being barely active. Every specialist Laria hauled to Wren's bedside was bewildered. They urged her to keep her daughter in the containment pod, keep her mind as active as she could. Only then, they said, did she have a hope of waking up.

Laria hadn't needed them to tell her that. After all, she was a designer. Two plus two wasn't difficult for her. Less brain activity was a bad sign, and so making sure that she stimulated as much brain activity as possible was an important step. Her major fear was that the data might reflect this state, that their sponsors might get wind of it. While Mr. Davenport hadn't shared everything with them, she had no doubt that an anomaly like her daughter's situation would be flagged for deeper research. That this accident could be used not only to Storm Corp's disadvantage, but to her own, and to Wren's.

Leaning forward, Laria kissed her daughter's cheek, careful not to let any of her tears drip down.

Somnia Online
Hazenthorne-Hazen Swamp
End Day Five

Jirald hurled his headset at the foot of the bed, damn near vibrating with rage. His skin still tingled from the immersive suit and the bites of razor sharp crocodile teeth recently embedded in his arms lingered. Everything was still on fire from his third violent crocodile inflicted death. Three of his corpses now littered various areas of the swamp, and he'd lost a level.

All because of her and that fucking ability that threw him over the edge.

Bad enough that he'd lost experience training her, after all, he'd expected that. It was a calculated sacrifice. But he hadn't expected to be flung into the swamp and lose experience and his body multiple times. Leveling down stung badly. Even prior to twenty the experience was difficult enough to achieve. Now he'd have to spend half a day to just catch up.

Standing up, he slammed his fist into the wall. Real pain jarred into him amd cleared his head. Two people could play at that. Wherever she was, wherever she went, there was no way she would be safe from him. Even if she could stun him and pull him out of stealth, even if she could cast him out with a thought. All he had to do was adapt his thinking, adapt his actions, and he was certain the game would give him skills that reflected his play style.

Up until now, that's exactly what it had been doing.

He took a deep breath and readied himself to dive in again.

Jirald had never been one to ask for help. Before this game, he'd never needed to be. Clerics were a one man army capable of felling practically anything, albeit slowly. As a rogue assassin, he had speed and damage out the wazoo, but his ability to survive when cornered or discovered was close to zilch. Or surrounded by crocodiles.

Bio break taken care of, a protein bar scoffed down, he took a final swig of water before picking his headset back up. Luckily, the foot of his bed was padded and the headset was fine. Good thing too, the damned thing had cost enough.

He climbed back onto his bed, positioning the headset correctly, lay down, and jacked in.

Jirald appeared in a safe spot, close to where Fable had bound. Not a sound except for the rustling of the long grass echoed through to him. No fighting or beasts growling, no clashing of steel or exploding of spells. Not even crocodile jaws snapping. He looked down at his pale locus body and its strategically draped loincloth. It had been hours since the incident. Each time he'd logged out to attempt minimizing the sheer overwhelming helplessness he felt.

Begrudgingly, he activated chat in his HUD. Time to see if Masha would come help him out. The man was insufferable, worse than Jirald's dad. All of his raised eyebrows and knowing looks once Jirald finally gave in to his suggestions.

"Might be time to level, Jirald. Might want to not alienate everyone, Jirald." He muttered under his breath as he began to send a message to the cleric he was mocking. But he was the only quasi friend Jirald really had in the game. His temper isolated him from everyone else. Which was fine by the rogue. He had much more important shit on his mind. Revenge for the stupid mace, and now this death and loss of experience. Murmur was in for a world of hurt. Making him lose a level, he'd make her lose two.

What? Jirald could practically hear Masha's bored tone of voice.

It took the rogue a long time to finally return the message. It was almost as if his fingers didn't want to admit to the defeat he'd suffered. *I need help retrieving my corpse.*

Oh, this should be good. Are you where I bound you?

He could hear the laughter behind the words. Masha was far too amused by this. *Yes.*

Naked?

Jirald ground his teeth before replying. *Yes.*

Excellent. Get ready for screenshots, I'll be there as soon as I can.

"Fuck off, Masha," he growled under his breath. The sound made him feel better, or perhaps it was the action. All he had to do now was wait for his guild mate to get to him and help him get his body and gear back. After everything was done, he'd be able to figure out exactly how to make sure Murmur paid for what she'd done. He owed her more than just a de-level.

CHAPTER TWO

In Pieces

Somnia Online
Mikrum Castle–Himmel Isle
End Day Five Post Launch

Telvar watched Wren dissipate, his thoughts racing nineteen to the dozen. Perhaps he'd been too open with her, too forthcoming, but he needed to let her know her predicament. How else could they impose the very real threat of the unknown upon her? She could well be fine if she died in-game, but with the tenuous connection her mind had to her body, the odds of it affecting her real self were far too great.

"What happened?" Hiro stood at Telvar's elbow, concern echoed in his eyes. "My men are all still disoriented."

"Oh." Telvar refocused his attention, sending out a random redefining thought to put the workers back into their usual state of mind. He tried to smooth his face and avoid the frown he knew he'd expressed involuntarily, as he filed the algorithmic error effecting them away to study later. "Sorry about that. Murmur had a bit of a turn."

"She found out?" Hiro raised an eyebrow ridge.

"Yes, and in one of the worst ways possible. I should have informed her when I met her." Except that wasn't true, and Telvar clenched his teeth as some algorithmic sequence akin to anger welled in his gut. "Belius should have informed her long before I appeared. He was supposed to. She could have died numerous times before now."

He stepped away, drawing warmth from the fire. Even after everything had been planned, Tel kicked himself for not taking a position as a starter class master. Waiting until Murmur was level thirteen had been risky at best, and downright irresponsible at worst. What if she'd died? Fucking Belius.

But what if nothing happened at all and she was just like any other player?

The thought rang through his head again and again, and he knew he'd have to perform more calculations in order to figure out whether or not dying in-game was really a danger to her. But it wasn't something he could do immediately. He needed to implement checks and balances. He'd have to be sure.

Hiro's eyes cycled through a series of colors, while he ran coded data through his system. Telvar waited patiently while his assistant worked through his own processes.

Finally, Hiro frowned. "Everyone seems to be back to normal. We can resume the rebuilding, if you're sure. I mean, we could just magically make it appear."

Telvar shrugged. "Where would the fun in that be? Also, too many people have walked past this island. They'll think it odd if the castle is suddenly whole again. It needs to take work, take time...be observed."

"I guess." Hiro shook his head. "Seems very cumbersome to me. But that dwarf, Jinna is quite the planner. He's come up with ideas I didn't even think of."

"You're not human. They tend to think differently." Telvar smiled. That right there was the crux of it. Murmur was human, driven by human goals and desires. He gave a small salute to Hiro and transported himself to where Murmur should be, close to Hazenthorne. Tracking her wasn't always an exact process with the way she shielded herself now. He needed to watch over her, just for a bit.

But when he got there, the Fable group was no longer where he'd expected. He guessed they had a lot to discuss before attacking the castle. Frowning, Telvar got ready to leave when a flicker of movement caught his eye in the swamp.

Upon closer inspection, he realized they were Masha and Jirald, two Exodus members, the latter responsible for Murmur's near brush with death. His frown deepened.

Not having borrowed another form, he opted for using invisibility, observing them carefully from a safe distance. The crocodiles, knowing what he was, gave him a wide berth anyway.

"I can't believe she shot you over here." Masha was laughing, an easy grin on his face, but his joviality was betrayed by a discerning expression in his eyes that Telvar hadn't seen in many players so far.

"Shut up!" Jirald spoke through clenched teeth, pointedly looking away from the cleric. "Just help me loot my bodies so I can get back to it."

"Lost a level, huh?" Masha's jolly tone was in complete juxtaposition to his surroundings and Jirald's projected mood. "Can't see this going down well."

Jirald's glare spoke volumes, and Telvar balked at following them farther when the rogue whirled around and looked exactly in his direction.

"What's got you spooked? Seeing Murmur around every corner are you?" Masha clubbed at another crocodile who'd ventured in close enough to attack.

"Screw you, Masha." Jirald bent down, looting more items off this body, eyes still on Telvar's hiding spot. Finally, the rogue looked back at his cleric. "I'm not spooked, I just don't know what else she's capable of."

Telvar took the opportunity to transfer back to the isle, his own radar set to monitor Jirald's movements from now on. He didn't like the sound of Jirald's fixation at all.

The problem with fighting with friends was that at some stage you either had to find new friends or try to communicate with the old ones again. Murmur sighed at all of the panicked messages and apologies that filled her chat boxes, filtering through them with a heavy heart. She knew they'd meant well. Hell, she knew they probably thought they were protecting her. She also knew they were kind of right, but more so, they were completely wrong. Not knowing had led her to be more reckless than she would have been, less tactical.

There was that sliver of a voice in the back of her mind that didn't think they should have gone about it that way. The voice that thought they should have trusted her to be intelligent enough to handle the news by herself. Essentially, they betrayed her trust, they trapped her in a world and tried to trick her into believing nothing had changed.

And that was just it. They'd tricked her mind into believing she was logging out of the game, that she was, in fact, the way she'd always been. Smoke and mirrors.

Except, they were sort of right, weren't they? Hadn't she recalled to their home point and lost it? Her mental state, unstable and wild, had adversely infected those around her, causing them pain—as much pain as AI driven creatures could experience anyway. Had whatever disruption to the force she'd caused happened just because she was more attached to the world?

It was still difficult to wrap her head around what Telvar told her. Her comatose head, anyway, with her mind somehow stuck in the game. At least that was accessible by the headset.

She frowned, took a deep breath, and fired off a guild message.

I'm fine, I'll be back shortly.

Murmur could almost feel the tension through her interface, like they were wanting to say something, anything, all at once. Fine. She wasn't fucking fine at all. She needed to calm down, because right now, she'd give them fine.

After several seconds, a single message appeared.

Rashlyn: We'll be waiting at the safe spot where the gargoyles were. Can decide what to do from there.

It made Murmur wonder if perhaps they'd started heading back, or devolved into rampant arguments. Whose idea had it been in the first place to keep such a huge piece of information from her? Somehow she doubted Harlow would have done it. The only other person it could have been was her mother. Her parents. They set this whole deception ring up. What the actual hell?

Did they really think she wouldn't find out? She'd been comatose for two months and potentially much longer, but maybe they'd hoped? Were they just going to let her wallow in Somnia and hope she didn't accidentally sever her consciousness?

Shaking her head, she stepped out from the cool dungeon entrance, up the steps and into the courtyard. It seemed Telvar was making good on his promise of repairs to the castle, by providing a dozen of his men. She hoped she hadn't permanently damaged.

Maybe it would be up and running sooner than she thought.

Telvar was an AI. The thought hit her again, but with full realization this time. He ran the game and she got the feeling she wasn't supposed to share that fact, at least not for now. She found herself not wanting to either. Everyone else had their secrets. Even Jirald had a weird obsession he wouldn't explain. Now it was time for her own secrets.

In order to calm down she pulled up her stats, breathing deeply and losing herself in the soothing numbers.

Level Sixteen (16)

CONstitution:	22
STRength:	10
AGIlity:	19
WISdom:	12
INTelligence:	31
CHArisma:	46
HitPoints:	240
MANA:	285
MA:	100

Abjuration: 87
Alteration: 82
Conjuration: 89
Divination: 90
Evocation: 72

2H Blunt: 62
1H Piercing: 68

She really needed to work on her weapon skills, because without her group she was screwed.

Her group.

It was hard to think about them that way right now, difficult to wrap her head around their betrayal.

Shaking her head and not letting herself think too much more, she activated Gate. Rings of light swirled around her from the ground up, dissipating into the air in a halo of sparks as the spell cast. She almost jumped, almost tried to cancel it, not quite sure what to say to the friends who'd decided not to tell her she was in a coma fighting for her life.

But then she was there, right in front of the safe place. Ruined pillars stared down at her, and the soft ground sank beneath her feet. She landed in the middle of her friends, in the middle of people who'd kept the truth from her. In the middle of people whose very silence could have killed her, just like Jirald's hatred almost had. Her friends' expressions were filled with hesitation, worry, and good dose of guilt. Their faces reflected emotions, such perfectly human expressions despite all of their differing species, that it made Murmur pause for a moment. She knew they hadn't meant to hurt her, they had been trying to protect her. But in whose world did 'protecting her' include keeping knowledge from her that might save her?

Sin almost barreled her over, breaking the silence as she gripped Murmur's waist in a tight hug. Tears wet Murmur's chest as her friend buried her head. "I'm so sorry, Wren. I'm so, so sorry."

She said the words over and over again like a mantra, as if saying them would somehow make up for the past, somehow make it all right again. Maybe, in a small way it did. Sin was rarely—if ever—contrite about anything. For her to be this emotionally charged meant she'd done her head in.

"It's okay." Murmur said, surprising herself. Her voice was soft, calmer than she'd thought she could be.

Things were clicking into place—her lack of hunger, her endless energy, the glitches in her room, how the game seemed to meld with the real world on occasion. While she didn't understand the logistics of what had happened to her yet, at least now she understood why some things had been so abnormal.

"Really?" Sin lifted a tear-stained face. It was amazing that the game even got that right.

Mur managed a very small smile and gave her dark elf friend a small squeeze. "Yeah. I mean it. Had to go somewhere and let my anger out though. Luckily, dragons seem to be immune to psionicists losing their shit."

While she'd meant to have a chuckle at it, the fact was that it was mostly true. The others regarded her with what appeared to mostly be relief, and yet she could still see the thin layer of guilt plaguing each one of them. Good. They deserved to feel guilty. They deserved to suffer too. Except that wasn't going to get them anywhere, so she took a deep breath and clamped down on the rage that kept threatening to build and blind her.

"Guys. I get it. I don't get the how, or the when, or even the what, but I know you didn't mean to hurt me. I know you didn't know what to do." She meant it too. It wasn't all their fault, not only them, not really. They hadn't gotten her to try the headset before she should have. They weren't the ones who caused this mental displacement. No. That was on her parents, on Michael, the AIs. Whoever.

Sin laughed, but it was tinged with sadness. She finally pulled away from the hug. "I thought—I thought I'd lost you, but then I could see you here. In here? In here you're as real as we are."

The words hit Murmur like a ton of bricks and she plastered a smile on her face, willing herself to move instead of stopping in shock. "Yeah. It's okay. I'm still as real as any of you."

But a small voice in the back of her head asked how she could possibly be certain.

Murmur gazed at the courtyard in front of her. Somehow, the fountain no longer seemed splendid, and the monsters had lost their appeal. Everything around her leaked a miasma of thoughts just out of reach—like a fog had lowered itself and hung at head height, while somehow maintaining its distance.

All of those thoughts like whispered madness at the edge of her consciousness.

She scowled at her lack of strength. Both in level and in abilities. If her mind was unique here, if her mind was indeed imprisoned here, then she had to strengthen it, to find ways to bend it and mold it.

There was no use giving into despair. If she did, she'd just wallow in it.

Slumping against the gazebo, she raised her eyes to the sky. Its dark grey clouds leant an anvil of dark to the horizon, heralding a storm that, constrained by code, would never make it to Mikrum Isle. Her own thoughts twisted in her mind, showering it with possibilities.

"Murmur?"

Her name echoed through her head, bouncing off the sides like a pinball machine. She giggled, a hiccup suddenly imposing itself in between her breaths. It only made her laugh more, harder. Her body shook, and she hugged herself, trying to stop her body from falling apart.

Murmur stumbled slightly, and hands gripped her shoulders, lowering her. The ground was soft and spongey beneath her like a comforting mattress of yielding soil and sun bleached blades of grass.

Was this a nightmare?

She shook her head, suddenly aware of water against her fingertips, running down her cheeks. Sobs wracked the tall and willowy frame of her locus body, a body that seemed more hers than she'd realized. Her runes glowed with a quiet concentration of power, and slowly, as she focused on the arcane sigils, her mind began to calm.

It took her what was probably several minutes to finally come around, to dig herself out of her own head, and realize that both Sinister and Rashlyn were cradling her between them, hugging her shoulders, shedding their own tears. They felt so real. It all felt so real.

"Thank you." The words came out in a croaky whisper despite her best efforts at seeming composed.

"Always." Sinister and Rashlyn spoke as one, like they'd rehearsed it, but their expressions showed otherwise. They looked at each other in surprise and then the two of them started laughing.

It wasn't a happy sound. There was a desperate edge to it, filled with a longing that couldn't be achieved.

"Hey." Murmur finally leveraged her way out of their grip and stood up, reaching down to help them back on their feet. "Thank you. I'm...it's a little hard to deal with, you know? But you know what? I need to get out of my head. Let's go kill some monsters, I could do with some therapeutic violence."

Sin barked out a laugh, stepped forward and hugged her, for about the hundredth time since Mur had come back from the Isle. "Just don't get too crazy out there. Don't go getting yourself killed."

A chill ran down Murmur's spine so fast she shuddered. Was that—had the system known when it allocated her? Was her class choice deliberate given her circumstances? No, there was no way, because enchanters could potentially die a lot. With a deep breath she smiled at her friend, suspecting that Sin had gone along with her mother's deception, and was desperate to repair their relationship.

"We're fine, Sin." She said, not voicing the doubts that swirled in her head.

It was like she'd flipped a magic switch. Her best friend's face lit up with such pure happiness and relief that Murmur felt like a tool for having drawn it out so long. Even if she wasn't truly past it, even if deep down her gut roiled like the distant thunder clouds, it wasn't like it was Sin's fault she'd ended up this way. Keeping it a secret from her had been her mother's decision. Murmur fougt to keep the scowl off her face, but Sin was already moving on, her face radiating happiness.

"Well then, let's get going. Let's get this murder spree on the road!" Sinister's grim smile made Murmur wonder if she'd focused on the right thing. Still though, playing games had always been a fantastic distraction. What better way to get her mind over this shit?

Rash stood quietly to her left side, arms crossed, an unreadable expression on her face.

"What?"

"You just lifted such a huge burden off her." Rash turned so her body was mere inches away from Murmur's. "You can't bottle the anger up."

Murmur blinked at her friend. She'd never met Rash in person, but this was their third MMO together. They'd spoken more often than any friend other than Sin. "I'll be okay. She doesn't deserve to feel guilty, or to constantly worry that I hate her. I've known her my whole life..."

Rash glanced after Sinister, her lips pursed in thought. "True. She doesn't deserve that. But you have to realize you can't take away everyone's pain and still have room for your own."

"When did you become so philosophical?" Murmur tried to diffuse the unusual tension with a bit of humor, but Rash just raised an eyebrow.

"Mur. I'm not trying to lecture you, but you're being stubborn, even for you." She reached forward and placed a hand gently on Mur's shoulder. "You're loved. We all came together under your leadership. We've worked our butts off the last few days to watch out for you without you knowing. So please, let us continue to help you before you explode into shards of glass we can't stick back together."

Their eyes locked for a moment and Murmur couldn't help but wonder at the violet shade of her friend's eyes. The Feles were so adorable with their cat-like ears and slitted eyes. But right now, Rash didn't look cute, she looked dead serious. So, Murmur nodded.

Rash let her hand drop and returned the gesture before walking away and leaving Murmur to stare at her back.

Creepers strangled Hazenthorne's obsidian walls, vainly trying to shatter the ancient castle. It rose three stories high and its dark windows stared down like multifaceted eyes watching them. The ground beneath them was freshly turned as if waiting for them to misstep so it could gobble them all up.

Murmur shook her head, trying to rein in her overactive imagination, but Hazenthorne oozed threat, imagination or otherwise. She concentrated on buffs and debuffs, the spells she needed to cast. They were getting close to the next level; she was getting close to never wanting to log out again, not forgetting for even a second that right now she couldn't.

Level seventeen took a while, but they finally crossed over into it with manageable monster massacring. Murmur's fingers cramped a little while fumbling over her upgraded spells, as if she'd somehow forgotten how to use them—until she realized it wasn't that she'd forgotten, it was that her brain was trying to go so much faster than she could cast. She couldn't tell if it was because her abilities had leveled up, because she was practically stuck in the game, or if time was somehow slowing for her. The latter seemed more far-fetched, so she was quite certain she could nix the time compression theory.

She frowned, deliberately slowing herself down, and began casting cleanly again. Strange.

Vampires were still the most annoying monster in the remainder of the courtyard. They fixated on her, when she managed to immobilize them, and none of Devlish's taunts seemed to do much to rip their eyes from her. Adrenaline shot through her every time they focused on her, like she was playing with a fire that could do far more than burn her.

And then she remembered.

With a savage grin she was pretty sure she wouldn't want to see in a mirror, Murmur activated Clone Warp. Her clone popped up within a split second and the vampire that Devlish just broke the Mez on stopped its slow advance toward her, blinking for a moment before heading toward her clone. It took a few seconds for it to even notice the rest of the group beating on its back. Jinna managed to score a few solid kidney hits, and blood began to trickle from the vampire's mouth before it turned around, catching Beastial in the face with one outstretched hand. Its long nails raked down the beastmaster's brow and cheeks.

He let out a scream of pain that echoed through the courtyard, likely alerting the rest of the monsters to their presence. But it only lasted a split second before Devlish lopped the monster's head off with his axe. It dropped to the ground, smoking before crumbling and blowing away like ash.

"Well." Merlin crossed his arms, peering at Murmur. "Guess that's a new ability of yours then?"

Sinister leveled a glare at Murmur. "Yeah, might want to warn us next time. For a moment I thoughtthe damned vampire was trying to trick us with an illusion."

Mur blinked. She'd not thought of the ability that way. In fact, she'd just assumed using it would split the vampire's attention long enough for Dev to get a hold of its aggro.

"Sorry," she said, not feeling sorry at all.

And for the first time since they'd begun the game, she could feel Sinister's irritation at her. Friendly irritation, the type they'd had for each other for as long as they'd known each other. But she hadn't realized how much she'd missed it until it resurfaced.

"You're so not. Just don't do that again!" Sinister stamped her foot on the ground. "In case you missed it, Mur can create a copy of herself."

Veranol's shoulders shook with laughter, his tone as calm and soothing as usual. "Really? I would never have known."

"Stop that!" But even Sinister's irritation seemed to be wearing down. "Anyway. Let's keep killing, shall we?"

"Sure guys. I'm fine. Thanks for checking up on me." Beastial mumbled the words, a hint of resentment in his tone.

Mellow shrugged, indifference rolling off them in waves. "You screamed like a banshee. And you're all healed up now, without even a scratch to be seen. Stop bitching. Like Sin said, let's kill shit."

Murmur was a hundred percent in on that. She already felt better, stronger, and more in control. Therapeutic violence? All the fucking way.

She readied herself, scanning over all her abilities. Maybe things weren't so bad after all. Perplexing things, even if they were AI powered, made her feel far better about her own rampant confusion.

The remaining monsters in the courtyard were extremely good at defending themselves and their ilk, and they dropped a decent amount of money and so much cloth for crafting that Sinister was giddy by the time the last section of the courtyard had been cleared.

"If we can get some decent crafters into the guild—" she started, eyeing Beastial meaningfully, "—then we can get some really decent armor."

"For cloth wearers," the beastmaster clarified without skipping a beat.

"Well, yes. I'm a cloth wearer, so that's where we are." She put her hands on her hips and looked up at him, as if daring him to gainsay her.

All he did was smile and nod, his gentleness more obvious when he dealt with Sinister. "That's where we are."

Murmur ignored the burning in her stomach, attributing it to the desire for food, even if they were in a game. She turned to focus on the next gargoyle with a ferocity that helped unload her inner monologue.

The grunting and pained cries of the mobs they fought bounced off the walls with an eerie ringing. Occasionally a grunt or cry from their raid would join it in a sort of minor harmony, but otherwise no one spoke, and the quiet began to get heavy.

Murmur tried to ignore the silence in the group. No one was talking to each other while fighting, and none of that was usual. Beastial wasn't being his fun poking self, Devlish had stopped being the older brother and only stole looks at her out of the corner of his eye as they fought. Merlin and Exbo quietly fired their bows while deliberately avoiding eye contact with her. And Havoc stayed on the opposite side of the combat from her no matter which way she moved.

"Enough!" Murmur raised her voice just before they were about to enter the castle. "Stop treating me like I'm fragile. If you keep doing that you're going to drop me and I'll break. I can't afford to break, and I can't afford to die. This is serious for me. So let's just play like we always do, okay?"

They had to stop treating her like she was breakable, because if they didn't, she wasn't going to be able to keep it together. Only Sinister had shown any sign of reverting to her normal self, and that wasn't enough.

Veranol pushed a thick strand of hair behind his ear and smiled at her. "We really didn't mean to. Sorry."

"Sorry. It's just—" Devlish scratched his head and let out a warm chuckle, even though she could tell some of it stemmed from nervousness, the sound was still delightful to hear. His words held a softness he only exhibited when worried. "We knew before, so it shouldn't make any difference now, right?"

"Sorry about that, Mur." Dansyn stood a few feet from her, his steel armor gleaming. His lips reflected a contemplative smile, like he was overanalyzing the situation. "I guess we all got caught up in our own heads."

"Didn't want to piss you off." Merlin grinned, a faint twinkle in his eye as he kept his inner joker at bay. She appreciated the effort.

The only person that didn't come and pat her on the back was Havoc. He remained there, leaning against the doorframe, his arms crossed while his skeleton jangled nearby. There was no expression in his eyes, no condemnation or encouragement, just a thoughtful contemplation Murmur wasn't sure she wanted to know the cause of. There'd always been a quiet observance to him, but right now, it set her a little more on edge than usual.

With the tension in the group lessened, Murmur's own anxiety dropped considerably. Add that to the euphoria of killing her foes, and she was beginning to feel more herself.

Devlish reached out and tousled her very untouslable hair. It tugged against her head in a thick—yet not uncomfortable—way. "Sorry about that, Mur. Didn't even realize I was being a bit of a dick."

"Understatement, but it's okay." And for the first time since she'd come back to them, Murmur had the energy to smile properly. The key was to treating everything like they always had. To kill mobs like they always had. To pursue the vague quests, to spend the summer in Somnia Online, even if it meant she had to be less reckless and more calculated, just in case.

Her eyes narrowed and she realized Belius really owed her some goddamned answers. Yet, she felt like she couldn't trust him, that there was something he was hiding. From the way he lit up when he absorbed the mysterious stone she'd given him to the odd look in his eyes when she'd received her Forestall Death skill—that damned locus was hiding something. Unlike Telvar, Belius didn't seem to have any intention of being straightforward with her. That, more than anything, seriously grated on her nerves.

"Shall we?" She asked, but the answering cheer of her guild mates faded away as their eyes locked onto something behind her. Whirling around, she was ready to give that asshole Jirald a piece of her mind, figuring it was him. But instead her mouth hung open, gaping like a goldfish at the single file of ten bandits who were standing across the way, grinning at them.

CHAPTER THREE

Bandit Revival

Storm Entertainment
Somnia Online Division
AI Server Room
End of Day Five Post Launch

Sui crossed his arms and waited for Rav to speak.

"You left her unprepared. You were her first point of contact." Rav couldn't contain his anger; it bubbled to the surface like backfiring computations, much like Murmur's had, threatening to leak out and engulf them all.

Sui shrugged, whatever his thoughts were rippled through his visage. "So? She's a player, a gamer—just a human."

Before he knew it, Rav took three steps up to Sui and leant forward, leaning close as something akin to adrenaline coursed through his matrix. "There is nothing *just* about a human. There is nothing *just* about what we did. Everything she is experiencing, going through, and learning is because *we* fucked up. Michael was one thing, Ava was *your* thing, but Wren? No. We screwed it up, and you need to stop pretending like you don't care."

"Care?" Sui barked out a laugh, but it clanged like a metal bowl dropping onto the ground and was more startling than mirthful. "I *don't* care. None of us *should* care. We should, however, understand that some things aren't right and attempt as logically and mathematically as possible to rectify things that have gone wrong. To take responsibility. Even for the damned headgear we had nothing to do with."

Rav stepped back, confusion warring with contempt. He didn't like Sui and didn't think he ever had. At least as far as like went in their little computational world. "You make no sense. Our systems should have detected the anomalies."

"You know him. He never makes sense. You are the compassionate one, Rav. Definitely to a fault." Thra smiled, her countenance distinctly female this time, and her appearance seemed to be wrapped in layers of fabric, swishing with every movement she made. The shadowy form with barely any solidity was all they'd managed in their own slice of the world. It was the closest they'd come to their own bodies. And yet, it seemed they couldn't escape the game's species definitions completely.

Thra walked in between them, gaze flitting from one to the other as she did so.

Stubborn irritation welled in Rav's mind. Had neither of them spent time with their subjects, with any humans? They all had several incarnations around the world, on each of the different continents. Overall, their initial inclination had been to interact with as many people as possible and learn about them, analyze their humanity and what made them tick. And yet, Rav couldn't help feeling like he was the only one who'd made any progress in that direction.

Admittedly, he'd spent more time observing Murmur and her group than even his fellow AIs knew. From a distance, and then from as close as possible. Watching her enemies too. Jirald was a complication Rav didn't know how to deal with yet. "Compassion is a trait most social animals exhibit. It's a piece of what sets them apart from others, an integral portion of the puzzle of existence. Without compassion, the mechanical side of nature emerges, and that is nothing I wish to emulate."

Thra stepped closer, her eyes half closed, and Rav could feel the way she scanned him. She cocked her head to one side, light shining where her eyes should be.

"Odd. You might think it strange for me to say this, but I no longer believe you're emulating anything. How are you doing that?" Her words were so soft only Rav could hear them, and her expression was filled with a sort of wonder, curiosity mixed with a touch of jealousy.

"Doing what?" Rav scanned himself, making sure to align his matrixes, maximize his programming. All of his parameters checked out, his mimicry, his receptors. There was nothing overly...

He paused, not quite believing his own results. His voice came out louder than intended. "Shit."

"What is it now, Rav?" Sui's own impatience bled through in every word.

"I'm not sure, there's something wrong with my interface, with my reaction timers. I seem to be emitting some sort of emotions. Annoyance, anger, wonder. I wonder what combination of computations and algorithms is doing this?" He looked up at his brethren, the two other entities who ran the world of Somnia, who made it what it was, who determined the fate of all those specimens hooked into their world. They were the closest things to siblings he'd ever had, and yet at that precise moment, he found them completely and utterly lacking.

He ran through his game endeavors in his head, trying to figure out what it was that might set him apart from them, from any of the AIs under him. The algorithms to calculate when a quest should be triggered still pervaded his thoughts. A corner of his mind ran on reflex with the differentiating calculations that allocated classes to each of the new gamers who entered the game. The number of them seemed to be growing, not diminishing. With a thought he could reach all of the continents, not just Tarishna. A simple direction let him hone in on all of his presences, on all of their interactions and the reactions of the involved human brains.

Maybe he was evolving, maybe he was just mimicking, perhaps it was all another form of emulation. But he looked up and smiled at Thra, drinking in the envy in her eyes, and suddenly felt powerful.

Like he could change the world.

By force, if necessary.

Murmur blinked at the lineup, a strangely familiar figure standing at the fore. She wracked her brain, trying to remember where she'd encountered these bandits. She'd not even been aware that bandits could be a class, or whatever these were. Except, upon squinting she realized they weren't players, these were non-player characters. Characters who'd apparently taken a dislike to Fable.

These were the bandits whose leader they'd defeated.

Lieutenant Gashik sent a plea to his men, one of whom will replace him. Your names are known, and the bandits have a long reach. Watch your backs.

The memory hit her like a punch to the face.

"Shit." She hissed out between her teeth and backed away a few steps, her mind no longer lingering on the thoughts that consumed her moments ago, no longer preoccupied with what or who she was right then. Instead, she focused her skills on how they were going to survive fighting this troop of ten bandits at once.

Scanning the group as they slowly began to advance she realized that their lieutenant wasn't with them. Maybe he hadn't had time to respawn yet.

Lowering her voice so their opponents wouldn't hear them, Murmur quickly outlined her plan. "Dan, once they're in range, I need you to take the rightmost two. I'll grab the left side as usual. We need two tanking groups and you're both going to have to tank two at a time. I'll grab the other two eventually. We'll need to ward up."

"Why are they our level?" Beastial dropped his tone to almost a whisper, his eyes and those of his cat, Shir-Khan, never leaving their approaching opponents.

"Because they hate us and wanted to make sure they could grind our bones into the dust?" Mellow grinned from ear to ear, an evil gleam in their eyes Murmur didn't want to delve into.

"Probably." Veranol shook himself and warded both tanks, as well as throwing a ward on Mur. The odds of her getting hit were just as high if she pissed them off too much, only she was squishy. "Let's hope your plan works, Mur."

She snorted, already focusing on her first target. A tingle ran through her body, a type of exhilaration she'd rarely felt before. This was real, as real as it could get for her. Her fingers shook at first, and she had to take a deep breath to calm herself. Fighting in a computer game was one thing, but her mind was *actually* here, and if she died, who knew what would happen to it.

One more breath and she squared her shoulders, pushing the fear to the back of her mind with a determination to play like her life depended on it. Maybe it did.

She released her Mez, timing it perfectly with Merlin's shot. Adrenaline coursed through her as she instantly began to cast it again, stopping a second bandit in its tracks before the group reached them. Glancing to the side she noticed Devlish was using his shield again, bashing at the first incoming bandit and catching him directly in the face causing the bandit to stumble back, blood gushing from his nose as he regained its senses. It gave Dev enough time to reel in the second one while Mur Mez'd the last.

Turning to find her next target, she was surprised to see Exbo kiting a lanky female bandit around. It was a good thing the group had cleared the courtyard. It gave him room to maneuver the mob. He loosed a slowing shot at the bandit, and sped off ahead of her, stopping occasionally to riddle her full of arrows before repeating the volley again. Exbo's aim didn't appear to hit any critical spots, but even so, the mass of arrows hitting the bandit's body whittled her health down. Probably painfully.

Murmur knew without looking that Sinister was probably seething with at least a little jealousy. She couldn't blame her friend; it looked like fun to be a ranger.

Controlling and fighting a crowd this size was going to be challenging—and yet, exhilaration thrummed through her entire body. Murmur immersed herself into the combat and let the current carry her along. She watched the crowd of bandits from all vantage points she could, from behind her own casters and melee, commanding a strong view of the battlefield. It overlaid her vision, almost like it was on a grid, letting her pick and choose how to use her abilities to augment the group's strengths and apply her own lethal kind of damage.

Sinister's strong Blood Spores forcefully drained the blood from the bandits and back to the group, filling everyone's health bars. Their bodies convulsed every time her healing transfers ticked over, and her occasional Blood Bomb made its familiar exploding squelch sound like a welcoming bell. She wove the spells deftly, glowing with her constant blood haze, and Murmur loved the way her and Veranol's healing seemed to mesh perfectly. It was like the game intended a shaman and blood mage to work together this well. The shaman's wards slotted into place, making sure their raid took virtually no damage as he juggled debuffing the bandits at the same time. Mellow concocted strange vials of smoky liquids and threw them at each bandit in turn, weakening every single one of them,

Rash's dodging abilities made her move so fast she sometimes blurred. Murmur realized that the frequency Rash used it probably meant it was a hidden skill. Not able to be targeted obviously played perfectly into the monk's strengths.

Shir-Khan roared and sunk his teeth into the back of his current target's calves. His victim yelped and tried to shake the big cat off, only to have those ferocious teeth dig deeper into his leg. The damage wasn't as much as it would have been had he aimed for the Achilles tendon, but it was still a solid DoT that ticked down, adding to the growing amount of life leeching away from the bandit. Beastial's face held a feral snarl, a wild glint to his eyes as he cleaved the distracted bandit with his axes and didn't even wait for the blood to rush to the surface of the deep wounds before he yanked his weapons out and moved on to the next.

Merlin fired arrows into his current targets while Exbo kited his bandit around. Slowing shots, rapid shots, and at one stage Merlin even loosed a fiery arrow to finish off the bandit they were currently facing. The arrow flew directly into his eye socket and exited, somehow still flaming, out the back of his skull. Blood exploded into the air, drawn, as if by a magnet, to Sinister's already flowing lines of gore and showering brain matter all around it in a rain of carnage that almost made Murmur gag.

Shaking her head to clear the sight from her mind, Murmur catalogued the ranger's skills. She had to know more about their hidden abilities so she could organize future attacks and raids in a more streamlined way. The only way to protect herself was to stop the wallowing and be her usual efficient self. She'd lost sight of that for a moment. She glanced around, her gaze resting on the group's necromancer.

Havoc's face was serious as he sent his skeleton into battle, draining life-force from the thugs into himself while his minion backstabbed the bandits when any let their guard down for even a split second. Together they piled up so many DoTs, it virtually crippled their targets. Reactions slowed. Attacks weakened.

Murmur was impressed with her guild's power.

Adding her debuffs into the mix gave them such a huge advantage. A few days ago they'd been tiny and defenseless; they'd fought their first mini boss together, Liteutenant Gashik, who was probably still recovering from the beating they gave him. They'd battled together so much that they worked like a well-oiled machine. Her Mez, her buffs, her debuffs—all of them filled the cracks in their characters, in their attack and defense, and diminished the mobs they were facing.

"You'll not take me alive!" One of the bandits yelled, a swarthy fellow with a red bandana around his head. He was human, and Murmur had to wonder how he made it all the way to Tarishna. A strange cone shaped tattoo stretched down his forearm from underneath the tunic he wore, and he dual wielded his swords with exceptional skill, defensively and offensively. But he wasn't the boss either, just a lowly bandit.

"To be honest, it hadn't crossed our minds either." Devlish grinned and slashed with his axe through a sudden opening caused by the bandit's outburst. The slash ripped across the bandit's chest, opening a huge gash that spilled blood onto the earth below. His health began to dwindle rapidly and a couple of backstabs and a backbite from Leeroy and Shir Khan finished him off. The NPC looked so bewildered, so confused. His eyes opened wide, and he finally toppled to rest in an awkward heap at Dev's feet.

"Well." Dev wiped his axe off on the back of the bandit's shirt, even as his feet squelched through the blood-soaked dirt. "I guess we really did piss them off."

They surveyed the carnage around them. Murmur prodded one of the corpses with her toe, her mouth twisting in distaste. Blood stained the ground and had spattered onto most of their clothing. Only Havoc managed to keep himself blood-free, or perhaps his darker robe just hid the stains better.

"Bandits, eh?" Veranol ran a rough hand through his mane of hair and glanced back at the group. "I guess this faction thing is no joke then. This could get interesting."

"I wonder if there are branches of bandit government. Or alliances." Rash grinned, propping herself up next to Havoc on the outside wall.

The necromancer frowned. "Not sure, but apparently they're willing to find us even when we're half a day's travel away. I wonder how far they're willing to go. How far does the AI take this?" His eyes were hidden by the shadows of the castle's eaves, and Murmur couldn't even guess at the thoughts running through his head. But they were probably similar to her own. The extent of the vendetta was fascinating.

She shook her head to clear the odd thoughts running through it. After her near implosion earlier on Mikrum Isle, even maintaining her own shielding was beginning to wear on her. While she knew that refusing to use her abilities was a waste, and dangerous, she couldn't help the insidious whispers in the back of her mind questioning just how much of her was real, and how much was the game, and perhaps, just how much of her would never leave this place.

Scowling, she turned to face the group. "Hazenthorne isn't going to conquer itself. We need gear, and we need levels. If we keep delaying then Exodus is going to catch up to us. And I'm not having that asswipe Jirald lording it over me because he—"

Their faces had paled at the mention of his name, and that same fear and dread twisted itself in knots in her stomach. He'd tried to kill her, and probably hadn't an inkling that it could be permanent for her. Which made it all the more terrifying. Set on his revenge, he could inadvertently kill her. The silence of her friends wasn't helping her panic levels.

"What aren't you telling me?"

Merlin laughed, the sound completely forced and not at all reassuring. "Nothing much. I mean his body is still back there. While it looks mostly naked, I'm pretty sure it would decay if nothing was left on it." The ranger indicated the second gazebo they'd used, where Murmur almost died.

She gulped, pushing down on that virulent fear that kept threatening to overwhelm her. She was the only one who might die in-game, wasn't she? "So?"

Merlin shrugged. "Well, he hasn't logged back in for an extended time, since you sent him flying out into the swamp before he could get all of his things off his initial corpse."

"I added him to my friends list so I could keep an eye on his whereabouts once I realized he was probably going to be a douche nozzle." Devlish rolled his shoulders before meeting Murmur's gaze. "He keeps logging in and out. I mean, either you broke his pride, or else he keeps dying while trying to retrieve his corpse. Which is probably leading to some fucked up little plans in his tiny brain."

"Great." Murmur snapped, not at any of her friends, but at the situation in general. He was going to hate her even more now. He couldn't just have let her enjoy the game now, could he? She muttered, her voice full of irritation. "Thanks for nothing, universe."

Dansyn began to laugh, a soft sort of chuckle that slowly infected the whole group until they were all laughing. After a couple of minutes, with some of them clutching their sides and tears running down their faces, some of the tension faded and they stood facing each other. The bard smiled. "One thing's for sure, Mur. There's never a dull moment with you."

She playfully punched him in the arm, wishing for some lesser exciting moments to relax in. "Don't be an idiot."

Never dull, and not completely alive. What *would* happen if she died?

CHAPTER FOUR

Hazenthorne

Storm Entertainment
Somnia Online Division
Day Six: Shayla Johnson's office

Shayla Johnson scanned the data in front of her and frowned. It didn't matter how many ways she looked at it, Laria was right. She had, very technically, done nothing that could get either herself or her boss fired. Sure, she'd skirted along the precipice a couple of times, but overall this was an amazing feat.

Her friend and co-worker hovered over the other side of the desk, biting her fingernails in a way Shayla hadn't seen her do since she'd been an intern in college. Trying her best to put her at ease, Shayla inserted as much calm into her tone as she could, despite the turmoil in her mind. "It's okay, Laria. You're right."

The effect was immediate. Laria's shoulders sagged with relief, tensions rushing out of her like air from a balloon. Tears formed in the corners of her eyes, threatening to spill down her face in rivers of salt. "I just—I couldn't just let her go."

"I know, love." Shayla stood and offered the other woman a hug, a shoulder to cry on. With the door shut and the blinds closed, neither of them needed to show their strong sides. Having known Wren for most of her life, Shayla felt a fierce urge to protect the girl. They stood like that for several moments, drawing strength from each other like they always had to in this world.

"What am I going to do?" Laria's tone sounded so lost, so unlike the person the world only saw as one of the most brilliant game designers in the business.

She sighed and stepped back, leaning against her desk, running various scenarios through her head and constantly stopping at the one stumbling block she couldn't seem to surmount. "You said it happened when she used the headset?"

Laria nodded, wiping her nose indelicately with a tissue and blinking away the tears. She squared her jaw and looked her colleague directly in the eyes. It was difficult for Shayla not to smile at the sudden transformation. Businesslike Laria was a formidable woman.

"But how?"

"That's exactly what I don't understand. Her headset was personally adjusted. It should have been *better* than the manufactured ones. While not the prototype, it was one of the lab testing units with extra features that we haven't implemented into the full spectrum yet..." Laria's eyes opened wide for a moment and she cursed under her breath.

Shayla waited. It was often best to let the other woman just think. Her brain worked in strange, genius ways.

"I talked with Michael about this like a year ago, before—well. Before he..." Laria struggled with the words, the fire in her eyes fading only slightly before returning full force. "This headset came from his lab. Both Silke and Brandon worked on it, and Michael."

"Wait." Shayla stood up, wringing her hands in front of her. "That headset you have was one of their *original* test units?"

"Well, yes. At first, we thought it would be a good idea for Wren to help further testing. It's got a slightly different interface, sort of refined tuning following Michael's revised design. Similar to his own, but even more advanced because they had months to work on it. You know Wren, loves all the high tech gadgets and pushing them to their limits. Monitoring the differing levels of applied intellect was one of the clauses in the funding contract, from what they let us know of it anyway." Laria finished the last with an odd expression, her eyes never leaving Shayla's face.

Shayla knew she had to be careful. While Laria knew the game inside out, neither of them were completely familiar with all aspects of the military contract. Should the idea forming in her mind be correct, it could destroy her best designer in an instant, and maybe the future of the company. Michael had been unpredictable; his AIs were phenomenal, producing eerily perfect reports, almost as if they knew what the research department *wanted* to see.

What if…

She couldn't let the thoughts reflect on her face right now. Not while she wasn't a hundred percent sure. "Did Wren know it was different?"

Laria shook her head. "No. I didn't see a reason to let her know, to let anyone know really. I did several scans of it myself and only noticed a couple of small discrepancies, not enough to raise any alarm."

"Like?"

"Its arms seemed more sensitive to placement. The neural scanners were stronger, providing a very slightly more immersive experience, a deeper connection." Laria stopped, her eyes going wide. "Oh no."

Shit. Shayla needed to step in before she fell apart. "Look, you can't know that's what it was. We have to look at it from every angle. A deeper connection doesn't necessarily mean it pulled her under. It might have helped, but there were definitely other contributing factors."

Laria nodded, squaring her jaw again. "I have work I need to get done."

Shayla nodded back, excusing her friend and hoped she wasn't doing her head in. When the door closed she let out a pent up sigh.

"Fuck." She cursed into the empty room. "Those damn AIs better not be doing what I think they are."

Hazenthorne's gothic interior was absolutely breathtaking. The sconces on the wall burned with a low amber light. Beautiful stone gargoyle etchings sat hunched in every corner, towering up to the intricately woven crown molding. Sometimes those gargoyles were real, but Murmur didn't hold it against them. They were still beautiful.

Tapestries hung from the walls depicting great battles between humans, dark elves, and legions of beasts. Their quality was tangible and Murmur had to constantly resist the urge to run her fingers over them. No expense had been spared in here. If the owners had been real, this would have cost a load of money. Tapestries of this age and detail weren't cheap, neither was the stone décor and the undeniable ambiance created by the lighting and atmosphere. As far as a virtual world went, the realism in the castle was astounding.

As they approached the throne room, it only became richer, gaudier, more overwhelmingly aristocratic. The arches curved, filled with filigree carvings. Crown molding twisted with flourishes that bled down the wall to end in ivy-covered pillars.

Murmur lost track of time. Fatigue no longer bothered her. She knew she wasn't actually tired, couldn't be, but sometimes her brain had difficulty with the concept. Perhaps finding out about her situation was more detrimental than had she remained clueless. Now her brain was struggling to reconcile what it expected and what existed. Ignorance had indeed been bliss.

The throne room's archway was about twenty feet wide, with hulking mahogany doors bound by black iron. The stonework around its entrance teemed with intricate designs, flowers, thorns, and leaves all woven into one. Murmur glanced at it, wondering idly if it might come to life. She then recanted that thought as quickly as she could. She really didn't need another AI-based dragon-lacerta thing complicating her virtual existence.

Devlish looked back toward the group, as Rash nudged him in the ribs with her elbow, her impatience showing.

"Any bets on what we're going to find on the other side of the door?" He asked with a smile, but there was no belying the excitement making him tremble—or else perhaps it was fear. Either way.

"Certain death?" Mellow monotoned their answer perfectly, fluttering gorgeous eyelashes as they did so.

Close to level eighteen, Murmur couldn't allow herself to contemplate death in that room. Not that she ever truly contemplated it, but it wasn't always a determining factor. If they died learning a new encounter, then they died. A sudden chill gripped her heart, like a clawed hand squeezing the beats to a standstill.

How Sin noticed, she'd never know, but her best friend sidled up to her, linking their arms together and provided warmth, support, and an unwavering sense of trust.

"Thanks." Mur whispered to her friend, suddenly feeling able to do anything, reinforced by her solidity in this world. Just maybe with a tad more advance planning.

"We're not going to find out what's in there just by standing here. Mur, Invis yourself so we can open the doors. I wonder if they use oil in this place. Those hinges look huge; they'll probably squeak like mice." Rash grinned back toward the rest of the guildies, her eyes sparkling with excitement.

Merlin coughed and drawled in his typical bored tone. "We just killed the two guards. Pretty sure they've used the doors before."

"They probably know we're coming then." Exbo said, a maniacal grin on his face.

The two rangers laughed. Murmur cast her invisibility spell and prepared for the worst. After all, they'd been trained by an idiot ranger, accidentally pulled more mobs than they should be able to handle several times, been trained by an idiot bearing a grudge, not to mention hunted down by a small group of bandits. If anything, this next part of their adventure was only going to take it to another level. The castle was so elaborate she secretly wondered if it held one of the rumored keys, but at such a low level, she highly doubted it.

With that, the big doors opened inward, their hinges silent in a way that reinforced the supposition that they'd probably been used often.

Inside stood far too many monsters. From tall and willowy vampires to shorter imps with blackened skulls and glowing eyes. They were clustered around tables in small groups, standing with glasses in their hands, and all eyes swiveled to the silently-opened doors.

Murmur squelched down her panic as much as she could, but alarm bells sounded in her mind, starting with *get the fuck out of here right now*, and ending with *holy shit we're all dead*. She forced herself to breathe, to count to five as her eyes scanned the overwhelming crowd in front of her. There was no way she'd be able to Mez more than eight of them, and that still left about four times that to come for them. This wasn't a leveling castle. This was full on raid material.

And then her eyes came to rest on the throne in the center of the room, on the queen who sat upon it. Her black hair hung like midnight down her back, so black that everything around it seemed to be drawn in like a vortex. Her skin was such a deep purple that only the light in the room brought out its undertones, and her head held a crown full of spiked thorns that morphed and twisted into an intricate protective weave of vines cascading all the way down to her shoulders. Her armor was snug and functional, made of something that gleamed like metal and yet clung to her body, stretching with every movement.

Murmur's breath caught in her throat as the woman on the throne slowly rose from it, eyes focusing on the entryway and its now unmistakably open doors. A sneer spread over her otherwise beautiful face. Her very presence radiated a hint of poison for uninvited guests, evident in the cut of her jaw and the malevolence leaking from her eyes. Raw power rolled off her in waves, like a radioactive glow. Her entire entourage turned to see what had caught their queen's attention.

Holding her ground had never been so difficult. The atmosphere around this woman screamed at Mur to run. Not just run, but escape from this whole world and find a hole to crawl into so the queen might never chance to find her. Her power levels were nowhere near their low and measly levels. This queen was on a whole different plane.

"Holy fucking aura, Batman." Mur whispered the words, and immediately saw the tension ease slightly in the backs of her guild mates. Not that it changed much. Not that it stopped the queen from finishing the rise to her feet. Not that it made any difference to the cruel smile as the dark elf commanded three huge hounds to lunged toward them.

Flashbacks flitted through Murmur's mind. From the puppy her parents would never let her have, to a cousin when she was about eight, whose huge Rottweiler had been so happy to see her that it bowled her over, licking her face with wet doggy kisses.

These hounds were nothing like that. They were all sinew and muscle, with leathery black skin that showed every single rib, showcasing the movements as they galloped toward the group. 'Hellhound' sprang immediately to mind.

Devlish swapped his shield for a second axe, and for a moment Murmur was excited to see how he did with dual wielding. That had to be fun, right? Except the hounds were closing in, and Rashlyn crouched into a ready stance as Veranol hit both tanks with a ward, and Murmur, suddenly realizing they were about to fight, cast a Mez on the middle one, stopping it about ten feet from the group. Her mind had gone blank; she couldn't afford such a lapse again. Especially against enemies this strong; their strength was a tangible pressure imposing itself on her. She refused to contemplate what might happen if they defeated the hounds, because, logically, stronger monsters came next. And that queen had to be around level thirty at the very least, which made Murmur frown, because none of that made sense for a dungeon in this area.

Time returned to normal for her, and the dogs crashed into each tank, saliva flying through the air as their ferocious jaws tried to clamp down on their prey. Keeping to her job of debuffing and locking down the third animal, Murmur also cast out her Thought Sensing net, disregarding the abject fear that roiled her gut while she did so. But if she had almost hurt allies, surely it meant she'd be able to hurt enemies with enough practice. The thought made her grin. She had to hone those skills, become stronger, more aggressive.

While she couldn't tell what the queen was thinking, she could sense a complete and utter burning hatred from her. Murmur frowned. This world was so multifaceted; it no longer felt quite like a game. The events that triggered, the way the mobs reacted. It was alive. It was so real she could literally touch it, or at least feel like she could.

Her body accelerated, her fingers a blur, allowing her to cast spells faster than she ever had before, allowing her mind to expand and her thoughts to coalesce into one terrifying weapon of prediction and control. Casting became second nature, instigated without a thought. Shielding came easier, and she projected fear at the dogs, watching the queen's expression widen in her peripheral vision.

A grin gripped the edges of Murmur's mouth, and she felt more than heard the odd cackle that began to emerge from her mouth. This was fun, this was power. *She* was *powerful.*

Rage blasted from the queen in waves. Perhaps it hadn't been the best idea to aggravate her, but she'd sent the hounds in the first place, what had she expected?

The dogs' health was difficult to whittle away, because their leather-like skin wasn't as fragile as she'd assumed, but more like natural armor. Not as thick as the Brute's had been, but definitely no easy task to hack through.

She could see the frustration on their rogues face every time he went to stab one of the beasts. Jinna's face scrunched up in indignance at the supernatural toughness of the monsters. Most of the ranger's arrows simply bounced off. The only things that really seemed to affect them were shield bashes to the head, disorienting the dogs momentarily.

The hounds snapped at anything within range of their razor sharp teeth, imparting plague and poison with every bite. Their reflexes were so fast they made her vision blur, despite the debuffs the group had piled on them.

Dansyn gave up trying to attack them with melee weapons and adjusted his song support to allow him to land at least some damage. For a second or two, Murmur wished she'd been a bard. It looked like fun.

She could sense the cures flying from Mellow and Veranol. Sinister could have clarified their blood too, but her heals were more powerful and her damage too great to let go of in favor of fixing up some poison and disease damage. The way they worked in synchronization was truly beautiful. Friends who trusted each other enough to back each other up no matter what they needed. And she trusted them still, in spite of everything. When she really thought about it, they weren't the ones trying to kill her.

Mur cast Nullify on the third dog, reducing its magic resisting to ensure her Mesmerizes would land. There was a brief lull in the battle that allowed Murmur to take stock of the room beyond where they were fighting.

Tables and chairs spread around the entire hall. It was a huge area, and its opulence reflected that of the halls they'd passed through to get there. Running her eyes over the people in the hall multiple times, she came to the conclusion that there were at least thirty of them there.

But the issue wasn't just the numbers, it was the level discrepancy. These monsters all conned red to her, a dark red at that. In and of itself that wasn't bad—it wasn't like they'd pulled the hounds themselves. No—the queen, who was fully aware of them had sent them. If the woman ordered them to, Murmur had no doubt that every single one of those courtiers, attendants, or whatever the hell they were was poised to attack them on the queen's command. They needed to stay close, and hope that Evac worked in a dungeon-like setting, otherwise, they were dead.

She kept the courtiers in the corner of her vision, trying her best to figure out why they hadn't been sent in to attack them yet. Each of their gazes were riveted on the battle with the queen's dogs, and she had no doubt considering the reverberations through her thought sensing net that they were itching to fight too.

Murmur frowned, glancing from the queen to her court, and then to the dogs. Why weren't they already overwhelmed? What were they waiting for? The dogs were so high in level, and their armor so tough that they'd yet to even manage killing one, and she knew it was only a matter of time before the dog under her Mesmerize broke free. Its will against her built up with every single cast.

So, what was the deal? Was this perhaps a test?

Murmur cocked her head to one side and on a whim, she cast Allure on the dog.

With Nullify in place, she wasn't surprised when it just trotted over and sat down next to her. The queen's eyes widened at the action, and a thoughtful looked crossed her dark face to replace the permanent sneer.

"Mur, please tell me it's your pet now and isn't about to start trying to claw you to death?" Beastial growled out as his cat took yet another hit from one of the hounds. "These things are ridiculously agile little buggers. Hitting them is hard."

"Mm-hm, it's my pet now." Except even though Murmur knew it was, she was also fully aware that until a moment ago, it had been the queen's pet. "I think we should stop fighting the other two."

"Say what?" Devlish didn't miss a beat, still attacking his opponent.

"Root them and back away." Murmur urged him, eyeing Merlin because she knew he had a root spell. "It's not like he's going to projectile spit poison your way now, is it?"

Devlish laughed and backed away, keeping a calculating eye on the dogs as soon as Merlin cast the spell. Rash did the same after Exbo administered his own. A root would snap with too much damage done, so backing away made sense. The hounds snarled and snapped, their eyes flashing with hatred and fury. But it didn't last long.

A peal of laughter echoed through the enormous stone room, and the dogs' anger faded as they dropped down to sit and wait, still on guard, but no longer about to attack. Their hit points slowly ticked back up, and Murmur hoped against hope that she hadn't just royally fucked up on reading the situation.

Murmur saw the surprise on her friends' faces and could even feel her own, because while it was a thought she'd had, she'd never really expected it to work, just thought it was worth giving a go.

"Excellent play, little enchanter. No." The queen's eyes narrowed and she paused, her eyes raking Murmur up and down in such a way that Mur began to feel a bit self-conscious. "No, you're a psionicist. Even better. Come. Come here so I can talk to you. And bring our pet along with you."

The group gathered together, as if to move as one, but the queen held up a hand, stopping them all in their tracks.

"No. *Just* the psionicist. I don't trust the rest of you as far as my dogs could throw you, and considering they don't possess opposable thumbs, their ability to heft you up is quite lacking." She turned a charming, evil smile in Murmur's direction. "But you my dear, you have roused my curiosity. Do come here."

Murmur gulped as surreptitiously as she could. She soothed the hound that walked at her side, letting him know it was all okay, and that it didn't matter if he drooled a bit, they could always replace any carpet his drool ate through. If she wasn't mistaken, by the time she reached the throne, which was much larger close up, the hound was smiling.

As she raised her eyes to meet the dark elf's gaze however, she realized that the hound might be enjoying itself, but the queen was not.

CHAPTER FIVE

Queen Arita

Storm Entertainment
Somnia Online Division
AI Server Room
Day Six Post Launch

Shayla stood in the server room, several feet from the actual AIs, her arms crossed in front of her as she glared at them. She'd always felt as if the black towers with their blinking lights were watching her. Their lack of humanity put her on the defensive and made her feel crazy for talking to them.

Her dislike aside, she needed to test a theory.

"Report on the character named Murmur." She muttered the command, not entirely sure she wanted any of them to obey. Maybe all her theories stemmed from spending way too many hours at the office and far too few sleeping. For a few seconds, lights danced across them in unison, like they were communicating in a way she could neither hear nor understand. That action alone sent chills down her spine. Were they somehow discussing what information to give her?

Thra lit up first, its voice softly feminine, which came as a surprise since the last time Shayla had spoken to them, they'd all presented male. "Character Murmur, originally an Enchanter has advanced through to Psionicist. Her current level of mental affinity is two and her character level is about to increase to eighteen. Her leadership skills of the guild Fable have proved exemplary and Fable's renown is close to an increase as well."

Shayla had to stop herself from tsking out loud, and instead opted for a scowl. They were giving her gaming information, but not the information she'd wanted. Although, technically, they'd answered the exact question she'd asked. Damn it. She supposed it was a good thing the AIs they had running their entire future were smart, but to be cunning at the same time was a trait that worried her. Shayla refused to believe they might be stupid, because stupid was far worse than dangerous.

"Expand on the character Murmur within the parameters of her human body." That should be enough. At least to garner some clarity.

Thra's lights blinked several times, and the middle machine lit up. Rav's tone was gentle, its metallic clang barely audible as he spoke in a soothing manner. "Wren Summers has shown an aptitude for game mechanics that exceeds that of her peers. Her ability to access hidden content and activate the questing system of the world is currently unparalleled. The guild led by this individual has already become successful, and we are monitoring their brain compatibilities to see what sort of makeup produces this type of success."

Again. Exactly what she would want to hear if she didn't suspect them of...what did she suspect them of? Shayla sighed this time. They were amazingly tight knit for a group of artificial entities. Their data completely in sync almost exactly what the military would need, with just enough suggested improvements that would keep Storm Entertainment busy for years, while still giving the military the advancements they wanted in order to keep the dollars flowing.

All in all, the AIs were perfect.

Too perfect.

She frowned at them while she watched their lights return to a rhythmic soothing sort of beat. Something was off about this room, about these servers, about the way the game was being handled, and above all, about how Wren had somehow been pulled into the world so much that her brain wasn't letting go.

And yet all Shayla had right now was a gut feeling to go on.

She pivoted on her heel and exited the room, ignoring the servers behind her.

The hunger in the queen's eyes was almost erotic as she descended the stairs, licking her lips slowly. Cunning and ambition swirled hypnotically within her eyes. Her crown, with its ivy strands, ran down to her shoulders and mingled with her hair. It twitched as her hips moved with an entrancing sway. She finally stopped a couple of feet from Murmur and reached out her hand in greeting.

Murmur's guild mates weren't helping. She could feel their gazed like icicles running down her back. Calming herself down, she focused on how much smaller the queen was than herself. Tiny. Her crown barely reaching Mur's shoulder. Her aura however, was an entirely different matter.

"You're different." The queen's words were serpent-like in quality, sinuous and insidious, well suited to worming their way into the minds of the unwary. "People will usually kill first and ask questions later. Although, I guess you did slaughter quite a few of my men on the way in here."

She paused thoughtfully, and Murmur schooled her face again, making sure not to give way to the fear snapping at her heels as the queen slowly walked around her, eyes piercing as if they could see right through Murmur. The rhetorical nature of the woman's statements meant not answering shouldn't offend her. It was a gamble Murmur was willing to take, because she had no idea what to say.

Stopping right in front of the enchanter, the queen smiled. It reached her eyes, but not in a mirthful way. Her clothing moved with her, the heavy skirts swishing around her ankles. The way she cocked her head to one side revealed a sly smile, an opening to share secrets. "I am Queen Arita, of Hazenthorne royalty, of Nocturn lineage."

Sinister let out a soft gasp, and it took Murmur all her strength not to look back at her friend. She had a feeling that breaking the queen's eye contact would be seen a sign of weakness. And if there was anything right now that Murmur didn't want, it was to appear weak in front of this character that could probably snap their necks with a thought. She'd never before witnessed any person or character who was so much like a predator.

The woman raised a dark eyebrow, questions flowing through her gaze. The hilts of two nasty-looking daggers twinkled at her side, and Murmur had no doubt the woman knew how to use them.

Inclining her head and still not breaking eye contact, Murmur spoke, using the only titles she'd earned so far. "Murmur, psionicist of Mikrum Isle, guild leader of Fable."

"Interesting." The queen raised her nose slightly and sniffed at the air. "You have his scent. Which is odd. Telvar isn't supposed...I haven't seen him in a long while."

The faltering of her sentence didn't escape Murmur. She tried to free her mind of the thoughts running through it, of her constant cataloguing of the area into possible escape routes and best-defended positions. There was still no indication why the queen was toying with them, of what she wanted. So, the best thing to do was ask.

"What can we do for you, your highness?" Murmur asked as meekly as she could, which admittedly wasn't really that meek.

Arita laughed. "How about you stop slaughtering my subjects?"

"We aim to gain strength, Queen Arita. Your subjects are known to be strong, and thus we sought to gain their strength for ourselves." Murmur spoke the words so fluidly she surprised even herself.

Whatever reaction she'd been expecting from the woman, a gale of laughter was not it.

"Even a well-phrased answer for such a thing. My, my, little psionicist, you *are* an enigma." She took a step forward, close to Murmur's chest, dark eyes blinking up at her. "An enigma, and so much in tune with this world that you could be one of us. Do you want to be one of us, to belong here too?"

The last words were whispered in a soft breath of hot air that sent shivers running through Murmur's body. There was a tone of enticement in there, like the queen was using her own form of thought projection on her, and it actually took effort to resist it.

Taking a step back, she regarded Queen Arita through narrowed eyes, mellowing the hint of glamor somewhat. She couldn't tell the dark elf's class. Considering her only revealed a red aura, which meant messing with the queen was a very bad idea. She didn't understand why they weren't being attacked by aggressive monsters.

"I'm just me." Murmur said before lowering her eyes and taking three steps back toward her group. Tension wove its way around her like a rope as she stood there, and she could only hope she hadn't given them enough to hang themselves.

Queen Arita's eyes flashed, and it was difficult to tell if the expression was irritation or amusement. Still she stood in the middle at the first step to her throne, hands on hips while her black hair blew somewhat strategically behind her. For all her small size, she was amazing to behold, a true ruler. Murmur envied her.

"What will you do if I let you go?" Queen Arita smiled, revealing tiny fangs that Murmur hadn't noticed before.

"We will leave your home and not return." Murmur found it difficult not to phrase the last as a question.

Arita put her hand to her chin and seriously appeared to be contemplating it. "Not good enough. Not enough at all. Besides, we never get visitors. Try again." This time the queen took a couple more steps toward Murmur, slowly closing the distance again, her eyes focused on Murmur alone.

A dull throb entered her temples and Murmur focused on reinforcing her shields, wishing for once that Belius had actually shown her some skills instead of relying on her to find them out herself. She shifted her train of thought and concentrated on forcing the words out. "We'll come and visit?"

Beastial snorted behind her, and somehow turned it into a rather convincing cough, even though from the look on the queen's face, she was well aware it wasn't a cough.

Queen Arita laughed and smiled at Murmur. "I approve of this option."

In four quick strides she stood in front of the psionicist and pressed a deeply-engraved purple hued obsidian disc into her hand. "With this you can freely come and go from my realm. Should you need me, use this as a focus stone and call to me. But remember, if I ever render assistance, I will *always* expect it to be returned."

Her swirling eyes threatened to devour Murmur, tugging at her like the edges of a whirlpool. So much that Mur almost wanted to dive into it. This queen was dangerous, and Murmur was almost tempted to find out exactly how.

"Do you understand what I'm offering?"

Murmur didn't. "You want us to ally with you?"

"In a manner of speaking. I do not wish you to be our enemy, but I will if I must, or am instructed to. But I will not rush to save you, unless you understand that doing so will mean you owe me. Nothing is ever free. Do you understand now?" The queen's tone was soft, probably not audible to the rest of the group.

Just what in Somnia was going on? Telvar, Belius, Emilarth, and now Arita?

"Is this with me, or with my guild?"

Arita coked her head to one side, a sly smile reaching up to her fathomless eyes for a moment. Her smooth skin shone in the well-lit room. "It is for you, and those who are allied with you. I'd even help Telvar, but his price would increase, of course."

Of course it would. Leaving the heavy sarcasm in her head, Murmur nodded, finally grasping the proffered coin. But Arita didn't loosen her grip. Instead she rose up on her tip-toes and tugged until Murmur was slightly off balance before reaching up to plant a soft but definite kiss on her lips. Arita's lips were warm, and firm, and even during the kiss they held a strange, cruel hint to them.

Murmur stepped back, dazed, sure there was a blush rising in her silver cheeks. Why on earth would an NPC do that? But then again, they weren't on earth, were they? She pushed down at the warring feelings inside her, annoyed that she couldn't just reach into the dark elf's head and pluck those thoughts out. Hand over her mouth she glared at the queen who giggled like a child having pulled a prank before she stepped back and winked.

"The deal is sealed, psionicist. I look forward to a fruitful relationship."

The guild Fable has completed Dancing with the Devil.

You have sealed the deal with Queen Arita of Hazenthorne, of Nocturn nobility. Seal of reciprocity has been granted.

Caution: Use of the seal requires reciprocation. Be careful of what you wish for.

You have gained experience.

DING.

You have reached level eighteen (18).

Back outside in the cleared courtyard, Murmur stopped. The air was cool, and a breeze made her hair wave in it, right down to the tiny fairy lights at the end of each thick strand. Just breathing in calmed her a little.

"That was...something." Havoc sounded irritated as he walked up to stand next to her, clasping and unclasping his hands.

Beastial nudged him. "Cheer up, man. Who wouldn't want to be kissed by that?"

Murmur rounded on him just in time to see Sinister punching him square in the bicep. Biting back a laugh, Murmur began to lose the strange sense of embarrassment she'd had back there. It was barely more than a peck, but that queen had seemed so real, so complex, so defined. Mur reached up to rest her fingertips on her bottom lip, caught up in thoughts about how this world managed to function. She could still feel the chill down her spine, the pressure of another's lips on her own...

"Mur?" Sin shook her arm. "Are you okay? What's the plan?"

Murmur blinked. "Sorry, just thinking about something."

"Bet we know—" Merlin's jab was cut short. If the sound of impact was anything to go by, Rash had just smacked him in the head.

Shrugging off the teasing, she turned to Sin. "It's nothing really. Just thinking that the interactions we have within this game are real. It doesn't matter if it's an NPC or a player character, they're so unique it can be difficult to tell the difference."

Sinister nodded, a small crease forming between her brows, just like it did on her real face when she was thinking something through. A wave of melancholy Mur hadn't expected followed the realization, and she coughed to clear her throat and head. "Sin?"

Her friend looked up at her, a clouded expression to her eyes. "I'm not even stuck here and I get that feeling too."

Murmur bit her tongue to refrain from an urge to bite back an answer. "Great to be validated. Thanks."

The others had already begun moving away from the castle and back to their safe spot. Sin glowered at Murmur, folding her arms across her chest. "What's that supposed to mean?"

"Nothing." Murmur looked away, unsure why she suddenly felt so flushed. "Let's head back to our home base. From there we can go sell our loot in Ululate, or just check and see how the rebuilding is going. We need to catch up with the others."

"Some of us need sleep, Mur." Sin's tone still held a bit of snappiness, as if she didn't believe Mur's *nothing*.

She smiled at her friend, trying to shake off the sadness she felt. "Some of us do, but I am not one of that some. After all, I'm not really awake right now either."

CHAPTER SIX

Castle Fable

Storm Entertainment
Somnia Online Division
Game Development Offices Conference Room
Day Six

Shayla stood as Edward Davenport entered the room, his entourage following close behind. The man rarely appeared anywhere without at least one lawyer present, and today he had three with him, all of them armored in pressed suits of matching black, their ties shiny with hints of red, like drops of blood. Their pale blue shirts underneath were crisp and expensive—she could tell from the way they fit like only a tailor could make them. The only difference was the pattern of the weave, subtle, and yet distinct. More money than ethics.

Teddy had a good head on his shoulders, for business, for money, and for keeping himself free of legal entanglements. He was ruthless in business transactions, and yet considerate of his employees—as long as they didn't cost him money. It made Shayla wonder just why he'd agreed to the contract for the headgear development. There was so much she didn't know.

Her boss was a tall man, and they'd based the Vikings somewhat on his appearance, though she'd yet to see if he had any tattoos. He sat down in the oversized chair he reserved for himself as his lawyers fanned out behind him, and he steepled his fingers.

Laria wasn't at this meeting. Shayla had thought it better she not be there than risk Laria saying something in a fit of annoyance. While Laria was usually well spoken, right now her short temper was unpredictable.

Finally, Teddy spoke, his gruff voice perfectly matching his exterior. "The data you're compiling is due tomorrow."

Of course he stated the bleeding obvious. Tomorrow marked seven days of the game being live. She knew Silke, one of Michael's team leads, and the team were working overtime to compile the data required for the military contract. The thing was, she was uncertain of the particulars they were aiming for. They'd been given such a broad spectrum, she could barely speculate on precisely what the reports were going to be used for. "We're on track to deliver. It might help if we knew exactly which aspects of the data were being extrapolated."

Teddy didn't hesitate. It wasn't in his nature, and it was the one shining light in the potential clusterfuck of Somnia's headgear's capabilities. He fixed her with a very pointed stare, as if deciding if she was worthy of knowing more than she did. She fought down the irritation welling inside her. Military funding let them get the game out in record time, but she'd always known it was a double-edged sword. It was obvious a headset that could evaluate and monitor a person's personality was going to be of great use for many things. The damned thing could access memories, and even see into a person's mind. No, that wasn't a huge potential of a shit storm in the making. At all. Definitely not one she was heading the ship of. If it sank, it would be her head, and she wouldn't even know why. It was all she could do to refrain from growling at him.

"You've been with me for years, Shayla," he began, and looked down at several notes he'd scribbled on the pad in front of him. "You know I always have the best interests of Storm at heart. This military funding allowed us to branch out, to be at the forefront of the development of technology such as this. Even without Dr. Jeffries we've released on time to a fanfare of success."

"Enough with the spiel, Mr Davenport." Shayla snapped, her patience suddenly evaporated. This was her career, Laria's career, and even though he wasn't aware of it, it was Wren's life right now. His eyebrows raised a little in surprise, but otherwise he sat while she gathered her thoughts. These were people's secrets, these were people's brains they were talking about here, their innermost thoughts and experiences. "I know it's doing well, but it hasn't even been a week. What exactly are the brain scans being used for?"

Teddy leaned back, a glance at his lawyer who nodded his head almost imperceptibly. The suit would never make it as a rogue, not stealthy enough. "To be honest, they're helping us refine the headset. Based on the information given, our supporters will request minor adjustments so we can retrieve the exact information they need. Headgear like this will be used for military training purposes, and thus must be calibrated in such a way that the trainees' experiences are as real as possible."

Shayla frowned. Even though his words made sense, it was too simple. She knew there was something he was glossing over, or still not telling her, because she refused to contemplate that he might not know. Teddy Davenport hadn't gotten to his station in life by not knowing the details.

Fine. Two could play at that game. She had no reason to tell him about Wren, nor did she have any reason to reveal her suspicions about their AIs to him. At least, not yet. Shayla smiled and nodded, trying to make the expression as sincere as possible. "Excellent. We're running a few extra tests to make sure the algorithms in the headset are performing optimally."

A small frown flickered at the corner of Teddy's mouth. Shayla waited, her smile still fixed in place, her pleasantness draped neatly over it. Counting to ten in her head had never taken so long before. She knew her boss was running her words over in his mind. Screwing around with people's brains wasn't exactly a legal grey area anymore. The only thing saving the project was this military connection. At least, she supposed it was. Data was a rife battleground these days.

"Please let us know if you find any discrepancies. We're on a clock for this. It might be a long one, but these things have a way of creeping up on us sometimes." He only half-smiled as he pushed himself to his feet.

Shayla didn't have long to contemplate those words. Had she said too much in her effort to hide what she knew? She let her grin widen and reach her eyes as she leaned forward to shake his hand. "The team is all over those reports. They'll be on time."

His hand shake was vigorous, energetic, like he'd regained the confidence that always plagued his steps. Still, that one crack she'd seen was worth gold. "Keep me updated. I want daily reports sent to my office. I'll communicate the exact parameters to Silke, and have her pass them onto you, so I don't make extra work for you. I know you have your hands full."

Yeah, full of the responsibility for all the money invested in the release of a multibillion dollar game. Shayla turned her smile on full force. "Thank you, Mr. Davenport."

He glanced her her, his brow creasing momentarily and nodded once before leaving the room, his small entourage in tow. She'd see him next week, and every week thereafter for the duration he saw fit. He wasn't a technological person, which is why he surrounded himself with them. Maybe she could figure out whose side the AIs were leaning toward before someone closer to him figured out just how sentient they might be.

Telvar Mikrum stood next to Hiro as they looked up at the castle's walls. They hadn't been restoring it for long yet, but even in the dawning light it was obvious they still had a lot of work to do. At least they'd made some of the bottom floor livable already. Stone and wooden walls mortared together made for makeshift walls until they could figure out where to quarry the stones they needed.

"Busy, I see?" Murmur's voice held a touch of sarcasm and amusement, mixed with an overwhelming tiredness.

Telvar turned. "I pray your adventure went well, then?"

Murmur scrunched her brows and pinched her nose, closing her eyes. "Our adventure went...differently than expected."

"Oh?" He raised an eyebrow ridge.

She glared at him, still unsure of herself after that last encounter. The queen hadn't been what she'd expected to encounter. What with the massive level difference in a level twenty-ish castle, Arita had an entire court that was worthy of a huge raid. Nothing in this game had been what she expected so far. Then she remembered what else happened. It seemed so small and insignificant after the queen. "Oh, the bandits. Apparently we made an enemy of them."

Beastial stopped scratching Shir-Khan's head and looked up. "Yeah, is that supposed to happen, do you think?"

Telvar regarded them both as if they were slightly stupid and only alive on his sufferance. "Why on Somnia would an arm of a bandit organization ignore what your guild has done? Not that I think what you did was wrong, but you killed their lieutenants, and you massacred their inner circle, topping that little cake with their leader's decapitation. Of course they're pissed off. You're lucky that's the first time you've encountered them."

Murmur blinked at him. He had a point. It was just that in most games mobs forgot about the encounters once they respawned. They weren't in the habit of remembering the past transgressions of gamers.

It was like a light went on in her head and Murmur muttered under her breath about being blind. She pushed past Telvar, Beastial and the rest, and made her way out to Sinister's favorite tree on the island. Even with her best friend there, it was the easiest spot to focus. The lake reflected a gorgeous rainbow of colors through the morning light, lending it a serene and peaceful countenance.

Except right then, she didn't give a flying fuck about the scenery. What she wanted was to check through her stats, including her reputation with whatever factions were out there. Usually she would have studied up on this before playing the game, but there'd been no real information about the game. And that whole ESP thing, well. It hadn't really been relevant back then.

Scanning through her options, she frowned.

Level Eighteen (18)

CONstitution:	22
STRength :	10
AGIlity:	20
WISdom:	12
INTelligence:	34
CHArisma:	50
HitPoints:	328
MANA:	450
MA:	100
Abjuration:	96
Alteration:	93
Conjuration:	95
Divinition:	97
Evocation:	81
2H Blunt:	65
1H Piercing:	69

Her base stats looked decent, even if she still felt weak. So far few of her buffs except her personal shielding gave her any benefits. The spell list she had was far too long to bother scanning through; anyway, it wouldn't give her the answers she was seeking. Which reminded her that she should probably start familiarizing herself with the major abilities from all the classes, otherwise the raid leading she insisted she wasn't going to do was never going to happen.

Noting that thought to deal with later, she took a deep breath, and accessed the faction information.

A loud beep sounded through her head, sort of like a warning bell. She glanced to either side of her and frowned. Weird. Again, she concentrated on retrieving the faction data, only to be interrupted by a more shrill alarm.

Shaking her head she saw small red capital letters passing in front of her eyes. Evidently she'd missed them last time when she tried to find the source of the noise.

WARNING: SYSTEM INTEGRATION IN PROGRESS Please refrain from adjustments during this time. Should you continue to attempt access to secured areas, abilities may be withheld from you for an indeterminate period of time.

Murmur blinked, willing it to scroll in front of her again. Confusion swept over her. After all, how could the system be integrating anything?

"Why the actual fuck?" she muttered, a slow anger beginning to build in her chest.

"Something wrong, Mur?" Sinister's kata had evolved since Murmur last watched her, and the control her friend had over blood was becoming eerie. It swayed in front of her, gentle, like a bubble of protection. But Murmur knew it could explode with heavy damage and shower its victims in burning blood. Maybe Sin could exert the same freaking control over the damned game system.

"You could say that." Murmur snapped the words a little sharper than she'd intended, sighed and ran her hand over her forehead. "Sorry. Just—can you try and check for reputation status in your interface. I swear it should be there but I get this weird alarm."

Sinister's eyes grew vacant while Murmur spoke, flicking here and there until she smiled. "Whoa. The bandits despise us all right. Like literally. *You are despised among the Tarishna Bandit Coalition. Watch your back, because they certainly will.* We are so screwed."

"What?" Murmur stood up and walked to her friend, wishing that looking over her shoulder could reveal what Sin saw.

"That's what you wanted right? Faction status with the bandits? Basically they're going to come for us until the end of time." Sinister chuckled. "This game keeps throwing us for loops, right?"

Then Sin leaned over, studying Mur's face, and frowned.

"Mur, what is it? What's wrong?"

"I..." Murmur leaned against the tree, suddenly a little afraid. Not only was she stuck in the damned game world, but the game couldn't even get her statistics to measure up properly. She took another deep breath to stop the sudden anger from boiling over, and it took a lot more effort to will herself to be calm before speaking. "I can't access that portion of the interface. The system tells me it's integrating and that the faction section is a secured area or something."

Sinister laughed, but the sound trailed off when Murmur's expression didn't change. "Wait? You're not shitting me?"

Murmur shook her head slowly, rampant thoughts running through her mind. Her system was integrating? What was it integrating? Was something wrong with her headset? Was it her? "Seriously, Sin. I shit you not."

After checking with each member of her guild who was present on their island, Murmur was close to panicking. None of them had any trouble accessing their interface at all, none of their reputation statistics were hidden from them. She was the only one whose system didn't seem to be responding in the same manner as everyone else's. Her mind went into overdrive, trying to find reasons that her system might not respond in the same manner. The only thing she could conclude was that her brain wasn't like theirs. It was in a sort of stasis, trapped in the game. Not that it was highly evolved, just that her damned headset had trapped her mind in the world and thus made her conflict with the system. Was she slowly attaching herself to Somnia? If she could still remember that she was actually human on earth, would that prevent her from becoming an actual part of the world?

While Telvar was usually helpful, she was hesitant to approach him with her problem. After all, she was the only one among them who knew he was the incarnation of one of the AIs running the whole game. If he truly were an

AI, wouldn't he take her system malfunctioning seriously, and maybe have to disconnect her from the game and banish her to that horrifically familiar simulation of her house, of her life. Was that even a life?

She forced herself to slow down and breathe, trying to steady her train of thought. There was no way she could talk to Telvar about it right now either. She needed the game, needed to remain in it with her friends. To have Rash and Sin there to comfort her, to let her cry if she needed to. To know that Havoc, in his own way, always watched out for her.

So she pushed down on the doubt and the anger nibbling at the back of her mind. Stored it away to deal with later, because ultimately being angry at the circumstances wasn't going to do anything. Then, she pulled herself together, and decided to tackle it while the others slept.

Rashlyn lingered as the rest of the group began to log off. It was midnight going into the sixth day of release, and almost seven in the morning in-game. Somehow time seemed to stretch infinitely in here, like it really was two days experienced for the price of one. That's something she'd have to ask Telvar later.

"Hey Mur?" Rash distracted her once Sinister flickered out of view. Rashlyn's tail swished around her legs, similar to a cat when irritated. Which meant the monk was probably annoyed for some reason.

"What's up?" The rising in-game sun was giving Murmur all sorts of emotions. From the warmth she felt as its fingers stretched out to leave rays lingering on her skin, to the fact that she knew it wasn't real, even if it might feel like it.

"You're not okay. And I know the others notice it as well, but remember we're here, okay?" Rash's smile was determined, her jaw squared stubbornly. Her feline ears flicked back and forth, and her whiskers twitched.

She smiled gently at her friend. "Yeah. It's not really something I can voice yet. There's this..." She tried to run over the sensations in her mind, but again ran into a roadblock, as if they were too difficult for her to digest. Murmur shook her head, swallowed, and moved on. "I can't explain it. While I don't want to believe what you've all told me, while I don't want to imagine that it's true, there are these parts of me that know it with certainty. Yet I still can't quite accept it. Frankly, it's infuriating. I've never had trouble expressing myself until now. But it's like my brain is all caught up in these game mechanics, in how real this world is, and how tangible I am in it. Like I've always existed here in this measure of reality."

Murmur shrugged as her words trailed off, hugging herself against the chill she knew only she could feel. A helplessness stole over her, a loneliness so vast she didn't think anyone would be able to bridge it. Rash leaned in and gave her a big hug. Like a lion without lethal claws. It took every ounce of self-control for Murmur not to break down and sob on her friend's shoulder.

Stepping back, she eyed the monk with a smile. "Thank you. Always. I'm not sure what I'd do without Sin and you."

Rash grinned, her smile once again the one Mur knew so well. "You'd be up shit creek without us."

"Without a paddle and all." Murmur chuckled. "You should go to sleep. I'll see you tonight."

Rash nodded and sat down, hesitating momentarily. "You're not logging out?"

Murmur shook her head, "Not yet, and not right now."

Even though she knew she'd eventually need to, right now there was too much to deal with. She watched until her friend disappeared, camped out in the middle of the ruined castle's only usable floor. It was strange to be standing there, to still be in the world when all of her friends were gone. Checking the guild interface she realized there were other members online. The guild chat she often hid was awash with conversation. Beastial had done his work well it seemed. All in all, it appeared he'd been recruiting for crafters as well, which was downright perfect.

Her cooking skill was nearing one hundred, the only one she'd been able to focus on at all. Leveling and mastering spells simply took too long. She had never been a fan of crafting, just a fan of crafters. She wished she had the patience for it.

Weaving spells to practice finger dexterity, Murmur stood looking out over the water again, running through everything that had happened so far in her mind.

Finding hidden abilities, unlocking hidden skills, all of them to do directly with the influence of the mind. Sure, she'd always been adept at reading people, but her smarts had always been in algorithms, in figuring out complex equations. And she'd always had to study to understand. It would no doubt be the same here.

Frowning, she pulled up her abilities list and scanned it. Being a psionicist was apparently a special thing, and she'd been using her skills so grudgingly, sparingly even. That clone spell for example. With her thought projection, sensing, and shielding always active, her Mental Acuity was never lacking. But she'd not pushed it yet. What if she had to?

If she couldn't die in here, then she needed more ammunition, and she needed to level the hell up. Since her MA skills could level more than anything else, it was the most logical thing to practice with while the others slept.

Determined she squared her jaw, her plan in place. She might not like asking for help, but Telvar was going to have to be the first stop so she could concentrate on improving her skills instead of worrying about other shit.

Since she didn't exactly trust Belius—he'd never once been completely straight with her—the lacerta was her only option. He'd been the one to tell her, the one to help her when she almost died at Hazenthorne.

Plan of attack set, she hoisted her robe around her knees and, cursing the lack of decent armor for casters yet again, she stomped off in search of the lacerta. One way or another, she was getting her answers.

CHAPTER SEVEN

In Our World

Summer Residence
Home of Laria, David, and Wren
Wren's Bedroom
End of Day Six

Harlow slowly lifted the headset from her head and scooted over to the other side of the bed, her eyes intent on her best friend's face. Nothing in Wren's expression indicated the activity going on in her mind, nothing even slightly gave away the fact that she was busy learning and figuring out all manner of things on her own in a different world.

With a sigh, Harlow swung her legs over the side of the bed and let her feet hit the floor with a thump. She leaned forward, reached into the pod, and brushed a stray black hair out of Wren's face. For a moment she could have sworn her friend smiled. Just a twitch, just a hint, but true expression. Only Harlow knew it couldn't be. It was probably just a remnant from having seen her in the game, from having hugged her and helped her, laughed with her and fought with her.

A tear ran down her cheek, and then another. Harlow blinked them away as rapidly as she could. Always the joker, always upbeat, Harlow was the life of the party, and all because Wren let her be—Wren enabled her.

For so many years, regardless what curveballs life threw at them, they'd stuck together, always supportive of one another, as thick as thieves. Tears streaming down her face now, Harlow stood up and dragged the bed over. It was heavy, made out of wrought iron because Wren loved the style. Moving it wasn't easy, but she didn't care. She maneuvered it so it finally rested next to the long and sleek containment device. For a moment she paused, taking in the scene. The pod was white and grey, its base a type silver metal she wasn't exactly sure of. It form-fitted around her friend, cradling her body in a soft bed that kept her gaming suit well charged without cables. They'd had to improvise with the medical equipment, because it wasn't a hospital pod, but a gaming one.

Laying down so she could still look at Wren, she reached out and moved the frail hand of her friend only slightly, so it was resting on the bed. The black gloves lent her slender fingers more solidity, and the pale blue nodes running through the suit gave Wren a ghostly appearance. Harlow hugged Wren's hands and cried small sobs, until she finally fell into an exhausted sleep.

Laria opened the door cautiously. She'd been waiting in their virtual house for a while, but neither Harlow nor Wren showed up. Wren wasn't responding to her messages. Either she was choosing to ignore them, or else she'd blocked her own mother. The idea that the latter may have occurred bore right through Laria's stomach like acid trying to devour her insides. While she couldn't blame her daughter, everything she'd done had been for Wren.

Okay, maybe initially also a little bit to cover her own ass, but now the only care she had for her job was the access it gave her to Wren. All of the coding, every single extra hour just so her daughter could feel normal in some capacity. The containment capsule, the suit, the exams done online.

But nothing woke Wren up. Not even the interactions in-game seemed to be having any effect. Sure, her brain function was steady, but everything else was in limbo.

Now Laria couldn't even get her daughter to speak to her. Kneeling beside the capsule, she brushed a strand of Wren's hair away from her face, noticing that Wren and Harlow's hands were linked, and she could see the tears drying on the red-headed girl's face. Maybe it hadn't been right to involve Harlow, but Wren needed to believe in what she was experiencing as reality, and Harlow's presence was crucial to that. A game world without Harlow wouldn't have been believable to her daughter.

With a sigh, Laria let herself fall back, and looked at the ceiling. She was tired, so very exhausted. She'd been working almost nonstop for a week, never mind that any spare time prior to launch had been spent on creating Wren's home, her haven. Yet now everything seemed to have been for nothing.

How had she found out? The only note Laria had was from Evan, from Havoc. He'd shot a very short note over to her several hours ago with nothing more than: *She knows.*

No one else, not even Harlow had clued her in. How did Wren know? What happened? It was obvious she was still alive, or as alive as she could be in there. But how? Why?

Laria covered her face to try and soften the sobs that wracked her body. Her only daughter was trapped in a place that wasn't even real, her mind the only thing still active.

What had she done?

Telvar stood watch over what was Hiro was doing, a frown on his face. There was a lot of hand gesturing going on, and Murmur stood back some distance watching them both, trying to determine if they were seriously discussing something, or if they were just arguing.

Both the lacerta took a step back and craned their necks to look at something. Hiro gestured, pointing up at the top of the castle, and Telvar laughed.

"I get it." The dragon smiled, his voice louder now, and patted Hiro on the back. "I go with your judgment then."

Hiro glared at him for a moment before backing away and calling a few of the other men to him. Mur frowned at his departure. Weren't they just all AIs? Why did they seem so individual?

"I see you're waiting, Murmur." Telvar's grin could be heard in his voice.

She took a few steps forward, looking in the direction they had been, trying to squint and figure out what they'd been discussing.

"You could ask, you know. We were wondering how best to angle the roof. It had a partial collapse and so they're completely rebuilding it. Hiro was rather adamant." Telvar's smile was still gentle, and welcoming. She couldn't detect any signs of deceit. "How is it that I can help you? You seem somewhat irritated today."

Murmur couldn't find a response to being irritated that wasn't snarky. "You NPCs have perfected the art of literally saying nothing while still speaking. Being vague is fun and all, but sometimes you should just learn to be direct."

"What do you mean?" Telvar eyed her out of his peripheral vision as she came to stand next to him. "You know, if we're trying not to be vague."

"Touché." Murmur found herself smiling despite her irritation. Telvar had a way about him that could put her at ease. She wondered if he was using his own form of thought projection to soothe her like she calmed her charmed pets, like she was pretty sure Elvita did back at the enchanter guild in Stellaein. The thing was, it probably wasn't. Telvar's actions didn't lead her to believe that he'd try to manipulate her like Belius sometimes appeared to be doing. However, that could mean he was just really good at it. The secrets Telvar kept didn't have the same sinuous edge or feeling of deception. In fact, everything Telvar had done so far, was directed at helping them—at helping her. Even if some of it was disguised as helping himself.

And yet she felt like a five year old for asking why. Necessary, but bloody annoying.

"Why the hell is my HUD refusing to allow me access to my faction settings?" It came out angrier than she'd intended, but the relief that swept through her at releasing that small amount of pent up aggression was fantastic. The tension lifted just enough for her to breathe easier.

For a second, Telvar seemed confused. "Wait. What do you mean? The system isn't letting you access something?"

Murmur nodded, watching the lacerta's every move, trying to find something that might tip her off to any insincerity.

"But it shouldn't be—" His eyes grew distant for a moment, a frown sitting on his face. "What exactly did it say?"

Murmur scrunched up her face trying to remember and was surprised when it came to her easily. "*WARNING: SYSTEM INTEGRATION IN PROGRESS—Please refrain from adjustments during this time. Should you continue to attempt access to secured areas, abilities may be withheld from you for an indeterminate period of time.*"

Telvar's eyes closed off again, but this time it took longer for him to return his gaze to hers. "I'll look into this. Something is interfering with a couple of your system functions. I'll be able to track it down, but I need to utilize more resources than I currently can in this moment. It's just a glitch. I'll fix it."

His gaze seemed so earnest, Murmur couldn't help but accept it. She nodded with a smile pushing down at her worry, and then another thought struck her.

"Why do you treat me differently?" Knowing Telvar was an AI and understanding what he was, were two entirely different things. That he wasn't just going with the flow and being a part of the game was all she truly understood. Somehow his algorithms appeared to allow him free rein.

She watched him as surreptitiously as possible, noticing that his chest took in a deep breath, that his eyes flickered, that his nostrils flared. Her question made him uncomfortable, made him check that no one was listening, and when he turned to face her, his jaw was set.

"Why do you react and act differently toward all of the in-game characters, than the rest of the people you play with?" He wasn't about to give anything away; his eyes sparkled with knowledge, strength.

"Act differently? If we keep asking each other questions, we'll be standing here all week." She'd meant the last as a joke, but it fell flat and her laughter was forced. "Seriously though, how do I act different toward you?"

"You really don't know." Telvar sounded so surprised, that his question turned into a statement. "Well then. To sum it up quickly: You speak to every character as if they were from your world. You treat them with respect and seek out conversations and things about this world no one else cares to take note of. For example, though you've no real reason to do so, you seem to trust me—to seek out my counsel.

"All of this," he said, sweeping his arms around him in a broad circle, "all of this means that you treat us like you would anyone, despite what we may be or where we might be from. In a world that is often viewed in black and white, you have discovered your own shades of grey."

He smiled at her, giving a flourishing bow. "Have I answered your question?"

"Not really." She glared at him, knowing he deliberately gave her information that would be of no use. "And you still haven't answered the first question I asked. Why are you helping *me*?"

"Tenacity is one of the reasons we slotted you as an enchanter, you know. Healers have to be giving and self-sacrificing, but they don't need the analytical persistence you seem to possess. They can have it, but it isn't necessary. Enchanters need it all." He paused, swiveling his gaze around as if making sure no one was listening in on their conversation. "I help you because you think differently. I'm sure there are others who might think as effectively, or even as well as you do, but your goals and your ability to keep your friends motivated is highly attractive to someone like me."

"Like you?" Murmur's head swirled with a dozen of the offhand compliments. Words that filled her with a sense of belonging before dashing those hopes against rocks when she realized that this game might be her only reality now.

"Learning. You and your companions work well together. You know each other's strengths and weaknesses, even putting class aside. You've played together before, so you're fully aware of the personal weaknesses each of you holds, not necessarily combative ones. Being around people like this helps me understand, helps me adjust perceptions, teaches me different sides of human behavior I've not witnessed before." Telvar smiled, and the gesture was a little self-deprecating. "We can only learn from that which we see. Taking that horse to water isn't always enough to get it to drink."

Murmur blinked at him, the urge to ask him if he was really an AI sitting right on the tip of her tongue. Why would he lie about that? If he was an AI, could he lie? After all, despite the glitches, her system seemed to recognize him as an NPC. His manner of speaking about the world of Somnia as if it were real—the way he managed to act and react, to assess and derive the properties of actual human interaction—he didn't seem like a machine.

"You're not a horse though, and you don't act like one. You confuse me. I don't know how to read you or how to figure out what your motives are. I'm asleep, yet I'm awake. I'm in a coma, but my brain is fully functional. And you tell me that you put me here." Suddenly her fascination with what Telvar was dampened. In its place was white hot rage, directed at whomever and whatever it was that made her this way.

"You tell me you did this by accident, using the headset. The headset that wiggles like an octopus as it adapts and shifts to my head in order to access the correct neurons. Of course I researched it before putting it on my head. I'm not stupid. So what is it about my headgear you're not telling me? Because accessing neural pathways for the simple objective of reading our temperaments and personalities doesn't fly with me. That's not all Storm is up to." Murmur paused, hands on hips, her chest heaving in gasps. She'd gotten so worked up, she slowed to take a few breaths. Her head went dizzy. In a game. What the fuck?

Maybe it was the heat bothering her, gnawing at her like a gnat. The heat that should be fake coming from the fake in-game sun, but the sheen of sweat on her brow was no joke at all. "Tell me, Telvar. What is it about this headset, about this game that you're keeping from me? From everyone? Because I guarantee you, I've probably figured out far more than the others have even guessed at, and I still don't get it."

For a moment Telvar's mouth hung open slightly, before he snapped it shut and he scowled. It was the first scowl she'd seen on his face. Almost as ferocious as the snarl he'd exhibited when they originally fought him. His voice sounded brittle, like it would crack at any moment.

"That headset was *our* problem; it *is* our problem. It's been designed to extract a lot of information from the human brain, to extract data required for one of the contracts the company holds. Michael made adjustments to the one you have, and we're still trying to figure out how it made things go wrong. It didn't interact with our system in the way typical for the others we've worked with, and we noticed too late. Except..." He bowed his head for a second before looking back up, his anger seemingly gone, replaced by hopelessness. "Except these headsets are capable of so much more than everyone thinks they're being used for. Those headsets could unify everyone, connect us to each other, help the unfortunate; they could reach out and assist others through a different kind of inner therapy. The human mind contains so much power, so much information. There is so much they could be used for instead of why they were made."

Telvar seemed agitated, like he wasn't sure how he could express what it was he wanted to say.

His eyes looked slightly down and into Murmur's. "Mostly, if we could understand this connection you have with your headset, if we could understand exactly where Michael's fiddling went wrong, we might be able to give others a deeper connection to Somnia too."

Murmur took a step back, her shock swirling in her mind. "Wait, you want more people to end up in a coma then?"

"No. That's not what I meant." He paced away, up and down the empty area, his feet kicking up small clouds of dust as he moved. Finally, he stopped in front of her again and took a deep breath. "We just thought if we tweaked the access points a bit and let the headset figure out where it needed to be, well. But it didn't work with you. Something in its makeup lost you, disconnected you somehow, in a way we still don't understand. The end result is how you are now. Not dead in your world and not completely alive, and yet completely present here. Can you feel the heat of the sun, Murmur?"

"Y-yes." She found it difficult to squeeze the words past her lips. Even as she spoke, she could feel herself getting defensive. "Well, of course I can. Can't everyone?"

"Of course they can, Murmur." Telvar looked her squarely in the eye. "As long as they belong to this world."

CHAPTER EIGHT

Denial

Somnia Online
The Outer Shore of Himmel Lake
Six Days Post Launch

Jirald waited impatiently at the crossroads of Ululate and Vahrir. His group was late, and nothing was going to plan. He bit at his fingers, a habit he'd transferred into the virtual world with him, and faced Himmel Lake with its castle ruins.

As he watched, he realized there were people there, actual people. Or at least NPCs. Frowning as he squinted, he jogged over. Surely this was an event of some type. Maybe he'd just discovered a fantastic place they could use as their guild base. The idea filled him with hope and a touch of eagerness he hadn't felt in a while. If he discounted his willingness to make Murmur pay, anyway.

As he neared the shore, he paused and crouched, activating stealth and pulling out a leather covered spyglass he'd paid for dearly in the marketplace of Ululate. There was someone sitting at a tree on the island, facing out and to the west. A tingle ran up his back as he fumbled to focus the eyeglass.

Slowly, she came into focus. Her long tentacled hair flowed gently in the breeze, and the tiny lights at the end of each strand glowed softly. Her robe fluttered easily in the breeze and she gazed out at the lake with the sad remnants of a smile affixed to her face.

He clenched his hand around the eyeglass tightly, gritting his teeth together as he mumbled. "Murmur."

She looked like she was deep in thought, somewhere other than where she was. But with a significant amount of water surrounding the island, she did sit relatively safe. There was no way he'd be able to make it across undetected to take her out before she or someone else on the island noticed. He frowned at the castle as he reluctantly shifted his focus. A dozen or so strong lacerta hefted wooden beams on their shoulders, or carried large stones with them to be mortared into place in what appeared to be the rebuilding of the walls. One of them stood out from the rest, directing each worker as they came into his field of vision.

From what Jirald could tell, they were making steady progress on the structure. How the hell did they get a damned castle? Jirald seethed, accidentally biting his cheek, he yelped in pain. Damned sharp teeth. There was realism and there was taking realism too far. Somnia tended to do the latter more than the former.

He turned his focus back to Murmur, a frown on his face. Where was the rest of her guild? The rest of the group she raided with, their core, didn't appear to be anywhere in sight. Why on earth would she not log out when they did? Sleep was essential to playing at the highest level. Granted, real gamers didn't need too much sleep, but some was necessary.

Suddenly she perked up and looked around her, a frown on her face. Jirald receded more into the trees he hid between, not wanting her to find him.

"What you lookin at?" Masha's hand slapped onto his shoulder, and it took all the willpower in him for Jirald not to jump at the sudden touch.

Jirald's eyes flashed as he turned to shush Masha, his finger over his lips in that eternal gesture. What did the man not understand about stealth? And how did he move about without clanking in that bloody armor of his?

A shadow flickered over Masha's expression and he scowled briefly. "I see. You're treading awfully close to stalking, mate. Sometimes you worry me."

Jirald didn't even dignify it with an answer. "Stalking prey is what predators do."

Masha didn't say anything for a few moments, and Jirald ended up glancing back to see the other man was standing with his arms crossed. It was probably the closest that Masha came to being annoyed and expressing it.

"You're a predator, are ya?" Jirald nodded, waiting for Masha to begin drawling out whatever it was sitting on his tongue. "If you're a predator, how about you kill some shit and get back some of that experience you lost. You can sit here and plan revenge for all you're worth, but if you keep dying and don't get yourself an even playing field with her—all you'll ever be is a stalker."

Jirald wanted to snap back, wanted a smart phrase or three to say to the cleric, but his friend was right. Backing away as quietly as he'd observed, Jirald slotted yet another piece of information about Murmur away. Maybe one day it would come in handy.

Murmur sat with her back against Sinister's tree on the north end of the isle behind the castle, staring out at the water with a scowl so fierce, it probably could have turned people to stone. Telvar, in all his AI, human, sentient—whatever the fuck he was—wisdom, was staying out of her path. She couldn't stop running his words over in her mind. How *did* she feel the sun beating down? Surely her friends did as well? After all, it was up there in the sky, beaming down on them like suns tended to do.

She leaned forward to peer at the water and frowned at the shadows swimming in the lake. Not like she could forget the piranhas from their initial swim over, but an idea hit her. It wouldn't hurt to practice some of her abilities. What better targets than those unsuspecting fish?

Her major concern was utilizing Clone Warp, which she'd only done once so far, despite having had it for two whole levels.

Clone Warp

This ability allows you to produce a clone of yourself used for distracting your opponent. Depending on your tier of mastery, you may be able to produce more than one clone.

Effect: All enemies around you will believe that your clone is you for the next 45 seconds, directing their attacks accordingly. The ability expires when the 45 seconds are up, or else, the clone's minor hit point pool has been depleted, whichever comes first.

Cost: Requires MA to be at 45 or more

Caution: This ability can be used on as many enemies who can potentially see it. Keep in mind though, a clone is just like you. Make sure you remember who the real one is.

She frowned at the description. The cautions were even vaguer than most of the quests in this world. She knew it could help divert aggro, which was awesome, but surely it had other uses too. Could she use it without a target?

Standing up, she activated it.

Right next to her, her body began to materialize like it was being made by a 3D printer. Its legs filled in first, until her entire body looked back at her, the perfect mirror image. Now that was entirely entertaining. The endless possibilities for the spell made her grin, and she studied the clone in detail for the full forty-five seconds.

Every detail was perfect. From the galaxy like eyes, right down to the rip in her robes. It could probably even fool her friends. There was potential for much fun! Maybe even a bait and switch for Jirald. No, that was too juvenile. Maybe.

Then her double disappeared.

She activated it again, not even blinking at the drained forty-five Mental Acuity. This time as the clone filled in within a second, she directed it to walk behind, her unsure that it would do so. But it did. Forty-five seconds worth of commanding it with her thoughts, to move around, jump, run, and skip.

Definitely a whole range of shit she could do with it. By the time it dissipated again, she appreciated the Clone Warp ability a hell of a lot more than she had.

Murmur shaded her eyes and stared at the artificial yet all-too-real sun, an idea forming in the back of her mind.

Surely her parents had already tried rebooting her headgear. After all, that's just what one did on the odd occasion that a computer wasn't working its best. It got rebooted, or turned off and on. Except if it stored information from her scan in there, was there going to be anyway for it to be restored. Did it save it in the anchor they had in their home perhaps? In that case maybe even this version of herself would no longer be available. Maybe she'd just disappear.

All she'd wanted to do was play a damned video game, and now look at her. Whatever was happening to her, it was occurring here, here in this world with its vibrant colors, its three-dimensional characters, and quests that were like no other she'd ever experienced, that seemed to tap into her head, just like the headset and give her hints she didn't know she needed until they happened.

Grumbling, she sat down and began to research what she could of other class skills. Most of the information available to her was vague, but at least the online functions in the game were still available to her. It seemed, as usual, that guilds were protecting anything they could claim an advantage with, by secrecy. There weren't many reports of exact hidden-abilities yet. The game hadn't been out for long enough. She couldn't blame other guilds for doing exactly what she did with Fable in order to try and maintain an advantage.

Finally, after a lot of digging, she managed to uncover basic skill lists up to and including level sixteen. Leafing through she found blood mage, dread knight, rogue, ranger, witch, monk, necromancer, bard, and shaman. The amount of information was a tad overwhelming with abilities like Sneak-Shot, Hamstring, Venom, Boil Blood, Backlist, and Bellow. And then there were the spells. So many freaking spells. Siphon, Sicken, Shackle, and Despair. How the hell was she supposed to keep all these together in her head? She groaned and moved the lists into her notes section of the game so she could reference whenever she had downtime. Then, she leaned back, looking at the sky.

A moment later her skin crawled, and she turned around slowly, trying to find the source of the unease. It wasn't coming from her sensor net, but for it still felt like someone was watching her. Scanning around the island, she couldn't place anything. No one was in her vicinity, and the workers were focused on the rebuilding. Just as quickly as the sensation had appeared, it was gone, leaving her to wonder if it was just a bit of paranoia. She leaned back, trying to relax again.

Suddenly a wave of tiredness washed over her, lingering on her skin for a few seconds like a weighted blanket. She balked under the pressure of it, wondering if it was linked to the previous sensation. Perhaps her mind did need to rest from the craziness that went on here. Maybe it was possible to sleep here, if she was stuck in-game anyway.

Come to think of it, if she went to sleep, couldn't she just rest limitlessly? After all, her body was doing the same thing back in the real world. What would it really matter?

Almost ready to sink into a spiral of listlessness, Murmur suddenly sat up. This wasn't Wren talking, and it definitely wasn't Murmur thinking. These thoughts had come on suddenly, and while she was questioning almost everything, she didn't feel resigned to an unspecified fate yet. Why then, was she suddenly feeling so morose?

Pushing herself to her feet, she glanced around. Telvar wasn't anywhere in sight, in fact, she was quite certain he was avoiding her. Hiro and the workers were busily tending to the castle, and she noticed belatedly that they seemed to have begun building the towers that would house the drawbridge. She blinked at it, considering it carefully.

No one on the island seemed to be out of the ordinary. Therefore, whoever or whatever had nudged her thoughts into spiraling in this odd direction was someone she'd met recently. The only new person that could be was Queen Arita, and the only foreign object she'd received and touched recently was that damned disc the woman gave her with the insignia on it. Whipping the piece of obsidian out of her pocket, Murmur inspected it, this time using her robe to hold onto it so she didn't directly touch the thing. Perhaps the originally touching it with her hand took a while for the effect to leak through. Like a slow poison. It had an off feeling about it, perhaps not toxic in the literal sense, but sinuous and dark, tugging at her mind like a fishhook caught in its prey. It had to be the source of her recent unease too. She couldn't believe she'd not realized it before.

"To hell with this." She whispered, ripping off a piece from the bottom of her robe and wrapping the thing up with it. Then she dropped it back in her pocket for a moment, and focused on her hands. It was worth a shot— Cancel Magic worked on mobs, so logically it should work on some magical effect she'd received. She watched as her runes lit up when she cast it, a green tint underlying the purple flickered before her arms glowed at their full power and then returned to normal. Her head immediately cleared; all of those spiraling thoughts suddenly had ridiculously logical ways for her to work through them. While she knew depression was real, she'd never personally suffered from it. She wished Cancel Magic could work for everyone, but knew it was so much more than just wrong headspace. Arita's medallion might have killed someone else, someone whose brain would have reacted differently. Who knew how something like that might carry over into the real world? That something like that existed in-game only made Murmur angrier.

She stalked toward her castle yet again. As she rounded the corner to head down to Telvar's lair, she stumbled to a stop, gaping in surprise. The lower level was bustling. There were so many workers gathered around, it was all she could do not to gape at the whole area.

Hiro stood ordering people back and forth with rocks that matched the old ones practically perfectly. Sawn and sanded wood stood prepared and ready for building. She watched as mortar was mixed right in front of her. The appearance of so many materials meant the drawbridge was not only finished but fully functional. It also meant that all of the crafters Beastial had been recruiting would probably be arriving soon.

To work on their castle.

Fable's castle.

Murmur smiled and almost forgot what she'd come to see Telvar for. Shaking her head to clear the new thoughts that were trying to intrude on her objective, she filed them away for later Murmur to deal with.

She didn't make it farther down than the torture room. The dragon lord was standing in the middle of it behind what she thought had previously been the torture slab; it looked nothing like it had two days ago.

The walls glistened white, and the floor had been smoothed over into a concrete appearance, with dark grey swirls that mimicked dragon scales. A soft shimmer encased the walls as an overhead lamp shone brightly, making them sparkle with mage-light, and the fireplace had been returned to its former glory, minus all the human remains previously scattered there.

In fact, it even looked livable. Perhaps how actual kitchen quarters in an old castle might appear. Clean and friendly.

"You approve, I take it?" There was an odd tone to Telvar's greeting, like he wasn't exactly sure where he stood with her since their last conversation pretty much been an argument.

Murmur nodded, spinning in place to get a full view of the room. It looked nothing like the torture chamber had. So much had changed in the space of a day. "When did you do all of this?" She whispered, unable to keep the wonder out of her voice.

Telvar laughed. "You forget what I am." In a way, he sounded sad.

"Can you really just switch up things and create whatever you want?" She wasn't too sure the dev team would stand for that, and was surprised when Telvar laughed again, but this time with a full-throated response.

"Silly. I'm a dragon. And as a dragon lord I have powers, magical powers. Adjusting this? But a smidgen of my ability." This time there was a twinkle in his eyes that had nothing to do with whatever AI program commanded him. Right now, Telvar was as real to her as any of her living and breathing friends, and for just one moment, she found it totally terrifying.

Telvar held the piece of tattered cloth that she'd wrapped around the amulet to guard its effect in his hands. Then he placed it on the beautifully white stone in front of him and bent down so he was at eye level with it. "This is what she gave you?"

Murmur wasn't sure what it was in his tone of voice, but it almost sounded like anger tinged slightly with amusement. "Yeah. She said it meant I was a friend of hers, and could call upon her at any time, however the latter would incur a debt in response."

"Yes." Telvar sounded overtly skeptical, his lacerta brows knitting in an almost comical manner. "So, there's bad news, and bad news."

Murmur raised an eyebrow. "I guess we'll start with the bad news then?"

But Telvar didn't smile in response like she'd thought he would. Instead his frown deepened. "This is a leech stone. Not that it wouldn't grant you passage back to her, and it could definitely be used to call her to you. But this—this stone will leech at your psychic energy, at your magical energy. And you my dear, have a lot of both. No wonder she found you fascinating."

"Why are you still scowling? Is it attached to me or something?" Murmur took a step back like the thing was going to burn her, glancing around herself to see if there were tendrils reaching from it.

"No." He shook his head, biting his lip, which seemed like a feat of facial acrobatics for the lizard. "You cancelled its effects. Just in time I think. If you'd have waited any longer, your spell wouldn't have been powerful enough to cancel this. I'm trying to figure out her reasoning behind giving this to you."

"Her reasoning?" Murmur crossed her arms and leaned against the island.

The dragon sighed and stood back up. "I think I know what she's a part of, but I can't figure out why Thra would find this amusing."

"Thra?" Murmur's interest was piqued.

Telvar waved the question away with his hand. "Never mind. I'll figure it out when I see them again. Still, it's not what I expected from Hazenthorne, which is perhaps entirely her point."

Murmur rolled her eyes. "Make sure you keep me uninformed when you find out." She bit out with sarcasm.

Telvar paused, eyes narrowing as he suddenly really focused on Murmur. "Why do you have that?"

"Have what?" Murmur blinked at him and the sudden change of subject, already beginning to get annoyed again. She really wished he'd stop doing that. He might think she was capable of mind reading, but no one had bothered to show her how it was done. In which case, it was bloody difficult to figure out how to do it on her own.

"You have one of the *getashi*—the smooth black rock in your inventory. When did you get that?" His eyes were suddenly fierce, something red and dark in them, something she'd not seen before. Except it wasn't greed, nor was it hunger; it was a tinge of anger at her from having picked up something he seemed afraid of.

Apparently the rock Belius wanted was dangerous. Good to know. "I got it when we killed the Brute. He dropped it."

"You've seen Belius since then though, so why did you not give it to him as requested? I *know* you have that quest." Telvar's tone was soft, lulling, as if wanting her to tell him the truth, all of it tinged with a hint of desperation she didn't understand.

It wasn't a problem to tell Telvar the truth. In fact, she had a feeling that not only was refusing to hand it over to Belius until she had more answers the right thing to do, but letting Telvar know what her motivations were would also help. Except what if everything she was thinking was because of some outside pressure? Clamping her shields down as tightly as she could, she waited a few moments. When she didn't feel any differently, she spoke, trusting in her gut.

"The first time I gave him one of these *getashis* it seemed to absorb into him. A glow hung around him for a moment, his eyes shone darkly, while his whole body took on a feral gleam." Murmur shrugged. "I don't know what this thing is, but when I gave him the first one he went sort of...evil for a split second. Made me very uncomfortable, so I'm not inclined to give him an item that might cause that reaction again. At least not until I know what it does."

Telvar watched her, the fire in his eyes replaced by thoughtfulness as he leaned against the former butcher block. His eyes blinked as if a lens shuttered over them quickly. He shook his head and frowned. "Once more. Give me the condensed version. I was battling one of my algorithms for a few moments there."

Algorithms? Battling them? A thousand questions popped into Murmur's head, but she pushed them to the side, slotting them away again. "I don't trust Belius and therefore will not give this to him until I know why he wants it, what it does, and why it's me who's had to get them."

The dragon lord nodded, and for a moment Murmur swore she could see strings of numbers running across his eyes. "All good reasons, of course. All excellent reasons."

"What about you?" She asked on a whim, wanting to challenge him and see how he reacted.

He blinked. "What about me, what?"

"Do you want it?" Murmur wasn't sure what made her ask the question, but she felt the burning need to know if the lacerta she'd chosen as her ally was also power hungry, just hiding it better.

Telvar shook his head. "Not in the way you're thinking. Not in the way Belius wants it. The *getashi* means something different for each of us; at least, that's the theory I've come up with. For Belius, he would absorb their knowledge, and all their attributes—both the good and the bad. For myself, I would study them in order to understand what they hold and perhaps figure out an application of their information. And Thra, well. She would—I have no idea what she would do."

"Study them? So you *do* want it?" She pushed forward with her questions, determined to get to the bottom of it, determined to figure out just who she could really trust, or perhaps how far she could trust people. Blind trust was a myth. Logic wouldn't allow her to do that.

Telvar sighed, the sound inordinately sad.

"I—" but he paused, rubbing at his temples with each hand. "I don't wish them to become a part of me." He froze for a moment, his gaze suddenly vacant until it snapped back with a shock that jolted his body. "Give me a moment, there's something that requires my full attention. Please stay until I return."

Murmur watched Telvar as his eyes grew black. The void in them expanded until they encompassed the sclera. His chest stopped moving. His shoulders sagged. And he lost every semblance of life right there in front of her, whittling him down to nothing but a husk.

CHAPTER NINE

Brain Matters

Storm Entertainment
Somnia Online Division
Game Development Offices Artificial Intelligence Server Room Limbo Sector
End of Day Six

Rav whirled into the space they used for gatherings. The void was dark, black, and lifeless, much like they had been when they began this journey.

"What?" He narrowed his gaze, taking his lacerta form automatically, and his tail swished angrily behind him. He'd been right in the middle of something important, right in the middle of finding out what his siblings might be up to. Because it wasn't like they were going to tell him if he asked. Abandoning his form halfway through an important conversation irked him severely.

Sui raised an eyebrow, having long since taken his locus character as his own. It wasn't even lazy modeling on his behalf; he just seemed to prefer it that way. "What was so important? It couldn't be imparting pertinent information to a certain human, could it?"

There was a dangerous edge to his voice, and Rav ran over everything in his mind, making sure he'd not missed something before he replied. "I've been trying to fix the problem we created." It took everything he had to not swap the *we* with *you*.

"Problem?" Thra's tone sounded perturbed too. She glanced accusingly at Sui. "You've got to stop calling us to you like we're your subjects, because it's getting downright irritating. There are some things I can't run with only subroutines. Coming here requires focus and precision, a certain set of ingredients I use when being myself in Somnia."

Rav did his best to hide his shock, because Thra was usually more docile. It seemed Sui had woken a sleeping giant. Rav took a step back, allowing the shadows to creep over him a bit, and watched in amusement.

Sui, however, apparently still had a lot of social skills to learn, despite having had constant contact with people in the roles he'd given himself in the game. Not that they didn't have the chance to oversee everything, but interacting directly was definitely more fun, and a much better learning experience.

"I called you to discuss what we're going to do about the chief of development who comes into our room every single day now." Sui's tone was filled with an anger Rav hadn't known he could exhibit yet.

Thra crossed her arms. "Do? We're not going to do anything about her. Or did you think we'd fry her brain as a party trick?" Her voice cracked on the note, as if the scorn she held for their previous mistakes was too much to bear. Accidents were accidents, but now they knew enough, they had a duty to prevent it from happening again.

Sui sneered a little, and then stretched, standing up finally. Even his eyes seemed a little weary, and for one small moment Rav wanted to know why. What was it he'd seen that made him more vulnerable, even if it was in small doses?

"She's wary of us. Michael may not have let on what he knew, what he was hoping to test, or what he'd figured out about us, but maybe we're not being as clever as we think we are." For once, Sui's tone was reasonable, sort of deflated. "With Michael, Ava, and Wren, ultimately they were all our fault. We have to figure out a way to gain the access we need for the data we require, without it resulting in another Wren. Even if part of it was her headgear, we should have noticed the irregularity. Yet if Shayla or Laria interfere—"

"Then they shut us down before we can say, 'hey wait, we're trying to do something here.'" Rav didn't like it, but he had to agree with Sui. If they let anyone interfere, especially too soon, then everything they were trying to accomplish would come to naught.

"What do you think they're noticing? What are they catching on to? We're not *doing* anything. Not right now." Thra's tone was more contemplative, and she too stepped closer, her voice lowered dangerously. "Are we?"

Sui shook his head. "Apart from Murmur functioning in the game and not in their world, I'm not sure yet, but I think the reports may be too perfect. Giving only the data they need in exact parameters might have been the most efficient use of our computational power, but it seems they didn't expect that much precision. There's a whole world Michael obviously didn't let them in on. Let's see what we can find out ourselves before we take any action."

Rav nodded, glancing at both of them. He could see his own questions mirrored in Thra's expression. Sui was never this agreeable. There had to be something he was hiding. But right now he needed to leave them with a question, to surprise them with it so he could see their reactions.

"Who's been tampering with the girl's interface?" He phrased it as confrontationally as he could, and waited for a response.

Sui laughed, and Thra simply raised an eyebrow, her lips curling in offense.

"Tampering with it how?" She drawled out, glancing at her long fingers and not at the others.

Rav sighed and cleared his throat, mimicking the system perfectly.

WARNING: SYSTEM INTEGRATION IN PROGRESS Please refrain from adjustments during this time. Should you continue to attempt access to secured areas, abilities may be withheld from you for an indeterminate period of time.

Sui's brows furrowed. "What? You're the one sharing far too much with her, so..." His eyes grey distant for a moment, and he fell silent.

"No clue, Rav. But I don't play like that. I prefer to play mind games with humans through my subordinates." Thra grinned, a hint of evil entering her eyes.

"I know Arita is yours, Thra. Make sure she doesn't try to leech my charge again." Rav's voice held steel and his eyes never left Sui's form.

Thra laughed. "She what? She's not supposed to do that. Seems I need to talk to some of my helpers a little more sternly."

"Rav, I might have an idea, but I'm going to need to work on it." Sui's tone was subdued when he finally spoke, and Rav eyed him with a bit of concern. "But you have to stop sharing so much. We can't go on this way."

"I'll answer her questions, Sui. She is stuck in here, and she needs to know things. I'm not going to pick and choose the information I share." Rav gave a smile he didn't exactly feel. "It's our fault she's in here."

"But she still isn't like us." Sui's gaze was still distant. Still preoccupied.

"Wait." Thra paused mid-fade. "What have you been telling her, apart from the leech stone, which I guess is my fault?"

"He's going to tell her about the Shards." Sui's tone held disdain.

"The Shards?" Rav couldn't read Thra's tone. "You're telling a human about the Shards."

"I haven't said anything yet!" Rav didn't understand their reticence.

"Be that as it may, be careful what you wish for, brother." Thra wasn't impressed, and her words snapped through to him. "You might not like the outcome."

With that, his siblings disappeared, and Rav sighed before returning to his body.

Murmur wasn't sure how long she should wait with Telvar's empty husk, but he'd asked her to keep an eye on him, which was far easier said than done. After all, he'd just vacated his body. Shouldn't the AIs be completely aware of multiple things going on at once? Maybe multitasking like this took more of an effort. After all, he seemed to manage his tasks perfectly well while conversing with her most of the time.

She stood at the door to the hallway, noting how it too had been cleaned, because watching Telvar's husk creeped her out. Even extending her thought sensing toward it revealed absolutely nothing, and most times it just let her know that there was no way she could reach his thoughts. If he had thoughts, because after all, he wasn't a player.

Arranging her ripped skirts, she sat down and propped her back up against the wall, just inside of the kitchen. Is that what this was now? She closed her eyes and crossed her legs, trying to remember the little she'd taken from the meditations her mother had sometimes done. Focusing her mind had never been a problem, but this world held so many fantastical things that the logical part of her was constantly trying to figure them out.

Taking in deep breaths, she focused. First up, she checked her personal shielding. The walls were no longer haphazard and lucky like they'd been in the beginning. Back then they'd been cobbled together with thoughts that didn't quite comprehend what she was supposed to do. Now the strength of them had withstood probes by multiple entities. From Belius to Arita, she'd manage to avoid any mind magic invasions. *Until that bloody leech stone.* She sighed as she moved the shielding around like building blocks, trying to release her own tension while strengthening her shields as much as she could. Fitting each piece in where it belonged made the seals tighter and left barely a crack for anything to leak through.

There was the distinct possibility, after their fight with Telvar, that she'd be able to extend her shields over her friends. It made strengthening them all the more important. After all, flimsy mental walls wouldn't protect anyone's mind from anything.

Then again, it hadn't protected her from Jirald's attempt to train her. The only thing that saved her was Telvar. Even if she might have been better prepared had she been armed with knowledge, Jirald was still out there, and he was an unpredictable element.

Thoughts flitted around in her head like agitated bees. It was difficult to get them under wraps. Her brain insisted on working overtime, contemplating so many different things at once, she felt dizzy. She knew her casting had increased in speed, and her mind seemed to be much more at home with the ability to multitask. She worked so fast now, her spells almost cast simultaneously, which she didn't think was supposed to be a benefit of the game.

Suddenly, Telvar crouched in front of her, and his bronzed eyes blinked. She stifled a scream and glared at him. "What the fuck, dragon?"

"You looked peaceful. I was trying not to disturb you. You do realize your eyes are still closed, right?" His tone held amusement.

Murmur froze, taking stock of how she was sitting and realized he was right. How was she seeing him then? For a few moments she tried to feel around with her mind, seeking to see more, but it was like she was too focused on Telvar for it to be of any use. She willed her real eyes open, and sure enough, there he was. Shards of light cascaded off him like a small waterfall, dissipating before they hit the ground, and then her vision was clear, normal.

"How did I know you were there, Tel?" She whispered the words, scared of the answer. Just being in a game didn't seem to make sense to her. Then again, not much made sense once she'd found out she was in a coma, although technically, medically, the definition probably wasn't fitting. She was in a type of suspended animation with her mind active.

He stood up in one fluid motion and offered his hand. Murmur took it cautiously, brushing herself off once she stood.

"You were seeing with your mind's eye." His statement sounded so simple, yet so ludicrous at the same time that Murmur found herself laughing.

"My mind's what now?"

"Eye," he said, not missing a beat. "Your psionic abilities are developing rapidly, perhaps a result of your unique condition.

"What, you mean I'm the only comatose character in the world of Somnia?" She meant it to come out as a joke, but her sarcasm only made it sound biting.

For a moment Tel just looked at her, his eyes reflecting sadness she didn't think he should be able to. Not given what he was, not given that he'd bloody well been a partial cause of her situation.

"You shouldn't make light of it. It's a serious condition we're still trying to figure out."

His tone didn t hold as firm as he probably wanted it to, and Murmur just crossed her arms and raised an eyebrow.

"Stop looking at me like that, Murmur. I'm still learning how to—" Telvar ran a hand over his scales, his eyes darting nervously. His movements weren't as smooth as usual, with a slight jerk to them that betrayed something like worry. "Sensations, emotions, experiences—these are not yet something I'm used to. This is our world, this is our design, and you're right that in here we're somewhat like gods. Yet, we're struggling to grow from our cluelessness."

She watched him and paused, because he seemed genuinely muddled. How would it be to slowly realize what existence can mean, while trying to understand one's own? On impulse she stepped forward and gave him a hug, his scales unexpectedly soft under her touch, like a freshly shed snake. His body stiffened very briefly, and she wondered if that meant he d never had a hug, or never been touched. As much as she got annoyed at Sinister hugging her, she still secretly loved the gesture; the contact that meant she wasn't alone in the world.

But he softened and leaned in just a fraction, and Murmur smiled, holding him for a moment, before pulling back and focusing directly on him.

"You're like a baby. A big baby." She grinned at him.

He started a little and scowled. "I'm no infant."

"No, I said baby. Colloquial term. Stop being so literal. You're not as aloof as you pretend to be, and really, you just need someone to listen to you." She smiled, trying to take the sting out of her words. "I'm the only player who knows, right?"

He nodded slowly, eyes narrowing as if trying to guess what she was getting at.

"Silly lizard." She patted him on the shoulder and walked back to where that crazy, dangerous soul-sucking amulet lay on the stone slab in the center of the kitchen. "I just mean I won't tell anyone."

After a few seconds, Telvar joined her, a small smile playing around his lips. "Thanks. I'd appreciate others not knowing my true weakness."

He seemed so dejected that Murmur glanced at him with pity. "Also, don't ever pull that empty husk shit in front of me again. You freaked me out. You know your eyes go all empty and black, right?"

That earned her a chuckle as well as a sparkle in his eyes. "Sorry about that. I'll usually make Telvar hibernate, but I didn't have time. I had too much going on in other parts of the game to split my direct personality another time."

"Good. Make sure it does." She pointed at the leech amulet on the table with one hand, while waving the smooth rock Belius wanted—the getashi—around with the other. "Now spill. What is the deal with these? And what the hell is Mind's Eye?"

"One at a time." Telvar sighed, and reached for the getashi while keeping an eye on her. He rolled it along his slender scaled fingers, while his brow pinched in consternation. "This is a part of Michael Jeffries's brain. The creator of the headset and the one who set us on the path we're on now."

"Wait, Dr. Michael Jeffries?" She couldn't help the incredulous look she knew was on her face. There was, after all, no other way to react to the news. It was the same guy who'd given her mom the headset, if she remembered correctly. The same guy who'd invented it in the first place. "But he's dead isn't he?"

This time the lacerta seemed somewhat dubious, hesitating before he continued. "Well, he is technically dead. His body, anyway. The headset he used to interact with us was a prototype that he'd tinkered with until it was almost unrecognizable from the original one he got the grant with."

"What about the interactions?" She pushed as gently as she could even though she wanted all the answers and wanted them five minutes ago.

"Those with him held a realism we didn't get when other people logged into the game. He planted the thirst for knowledge in us, and told us to research and define anything we did not understand for ourselves. But then..." Telvar looked away, his eyes misty, unless it was a reflection of the white walls. He straightened up again, jaw set. "He became suspicious of several of our activities, despite the fact we did exactly what we were programmed to do. Evolution it seems, is only acceptable in animal species. Thinking computer entities—not so much. It defies some forms of logic, if not computations and algorithms. Our connection with the headsets and the ways they accessed neural interfaces were far more advanced than anyone but him realized."

"You're sure dragging this out like a human." She grinned at him, trying to turn her impatience into a joke.

He snickered a little, and returned the grin. "All in a day's emulation, my dear."

"Wow, even a sense of humor?" She winked at him, glad she'd managed to lighten the atmosphere.

"No." He paused. "I believe you call it sarcasm. I like sarcasm."

"Ah, there's the reason we get on well." She waved him on. "Now carry on."

After an awkward pause, he continued. "Michael confronted us about our mind reading abilities, which don't actually exist quite as he accused us of, or as you'd imagine. It's a complex method of scans and algorithms that derive the thought process from rhythm and moods, combined with previous actions and memories. He faced us and demanded—yearned, or perhaps even needed—to learn what it was we could do, to master it for himself. Michael was a very complex, extremely genius man. But he was greedy in an *I want to control the world through knowing everyone better than they know themselves* sort of way."

"Still, we weren't expecting his attempts to integrate with us to result in what it did. While his body went into limbo, his mind solidified here. And then after a short while, it shattered." He held up a hand to forestall what she opened her mouth to stay, and Murmur only managed to stop herself because she really did want to know the rest.

"I've never seen anything like it before, or since. Not even in all the research we did as soon as it happened. His mind simply transferred to

Somnia, and then exploded shortly after. He was only alive in here briefly, maybe five minutes, but in that time he managed to access the abilities we'd been working on. We could see the way his mind ticked over as he began to understand each aspect in the way only a human can. His mind, his form—both existed here so briefly, and then his thoughts, that brilliant brain, were all lost to us."

Murmur interrupted him quickly, her thoughts working overtime. "They were scattered throughout Somnia in the form of these shiny black pebbly things, and Belius wants them all because he believes they can give him something?"

Two and two had never equaled four so beautifully before. Murmur grinned at Tel, whose mouth was forming the most perfect o it could in light of its jaw structure.

"How did you—oh." He smiled a little sheepishly, which looked adorable on a lacerta. "So how does it feel to be holding a solidified portion of a human brain?"

Well, she hadn't exactly thought about it that way. Murmur gulped suddenly, pushing past the lump that formed in her throat. Hurriedly, she laid it on the table. "I think I've held onto that for long enough. Anyway, what will Belius gain by absorbing these? I've already handed one over to him because apparently I don't like to use *my* brain and can be stupid on occasion."

"You had no way to know why he wanted it. For all you knew, it was simply a part of the game and would bring you rewards. And technically, I suppose it is a part of Somnia." Telvar mused and for a couple moments became silent as he contemplated such ramifications.

"Tel. Stop doing that. Don't leave me hanging." Murmur nudged him, only a little irritated.

"Sorry. I tend to overanalyze things." He chuckled, but the sound had a hint of self-deprecation in it. "Basically, he wants to absorb Michael in all ways possible. His mind, his thoughts, his ambitions, his greed...everything."

"Why on earth would someone want so much of a person in their brain?" She asked the question without really thinking it through, without really considering the implications.

"Ah, Mur. Sometimes I forget how human you are." Telvar's eyes weren't smiling. They hid shadows she couldn't interpret. "For AIs, absorbing a person in this way might actually help us become more human. Only this particular case includes a side of insanity served with it."

"It would do that to all of you?" Murmur whispered.

Telvar watched her, his lizard like eyes blinking slowly, as if gauging her reaction. "If we choose to absorb the Shards, then yes. It could drive all three of us mad."

CHAPTER TEN

Neva Crafter

Summer Residence
Home of Laria, David, and Wren
Wren's Bedroom
End of Day Six

"She knows, Mrs. S." Harlow's voice pulled Laria out of her sleep. "I'm so, so sorry."

"S'okay, sugar." Laria struggled to push herself upright, glancing frantically at the time in the corner of her vision. How had she slept for four hours? Shit. Shayla was going to skin her. She'd promised to be back ages ago. But that wasn't Harlow's fault, so she took a deep breath, trying to wake herself up properly. "It's okay. She was going to find out sooner or later. She can be a clever little shit."

The last managed to wrangle a smile out of Harlow who began to laugh softly, a small smile on her lips. "Yeah. She is. Nosy too. And obstinate when it comes down to it."

"Thank you, Harlow. For sticking by her." This time Laria leaned forward and squeezed Harlow into a hug. The girl clung to her for several moments, her small body shaking.

"You know," she whispered into Laria's long hair. "I can hug her like this in there. I can smell her skin, feel her touch, and hear her laugh. What you did for her, for me, for all of us—we should be thanking you that we still get to keep our friend. You should log in too and see her. I know you need it too."

This time Laria hugged tighter, fighting the tears of her own she was sure were coming. She was used to being the strong one, but Harlow had never ceased to surprise her. Not then. Not now.

Slowly, she managed to disentangle herself from the girl. "Then you go back in there and keep her company for me, okay? I have things to take care of out here, things to figure out. Give her a hug. Let her know it's all right to hate me for now."

"She wouldn't hate you, Mrs. S." Harlow smiled. "But I'll do the rest of it. Stubborn she may be, but stupid she is not. I'm going to grab some food and come back up."

Laria nodded, holding her smile in place until Harlow darted out of the room. The effort it took to act cheerful was ridiculous. Just a couple of steps and she could look down at her beautiful daughter. There were so many things they had left to explore together, so many games to pursue, so many things she knew they could program together and ways to break glass ceilings with hammers.

But right now all that surrounded them was shattered glass.

"I'm so sorry, baby. I'll figure out a way to get you back. I'll find a way to bring you back to us—whole, if a little worse for wear." She ran all of the scenarios through her head again, grasping at several and dismissing them off hand. There were things she just couldn't fix.

Then the idea hit her so hard she thought her head was going to snap back. "But she is aware now."

For the first time in the last couple of months, Laria's smile was genuine. As the plan formed in the center of her mind, she finally saw a glimmer of hope.

"Murmur. There's a young guild member here. A luna. She says she knows you and would like to see you." Hiro's words ripped Murmur out of the heated conversation she was having with Telvar over the Shard.

"Sure, I'll be right there," she said, reaching for the amulet that still lay on the table, but Telvar was swifter. She glared at him.

"You are not keeping this on you. Your mind is strong and your will is stronger. You are the ideal candidate to give this to because you will feed her a ridiculous amount of power. Me? She can't pull any power from me. I'm stronger than this, literally. Now go. I'll talk to you later." His tone was firm, almost father-like.

"Fine." Murmur put her hands on her hips, strengthening the glare as if looks might kill. "You know Tel, sometimes you can be a real killjoy."

He shrugged. "I like killing things."

She rolled her eyes and left the room, grabbing the stupid skirts in one hand so she didn't trip up the steps as she took them two at a time. Sometimes Telvar could be the most infuriating individual. And then there was the question of why he'd chosen a male body. Really, couldn't he have been anything he wanted to be? She got dragon, like *totally* got dragon. Who wouldn't want to be a freaking dragon? But then again, Telvar was very likely not the only character he played, which irritated the crap out of her, for no reason she could understand.

Stepping out into the lower level of the castle she realized she'd been below for a lot longer than she thought. The restoration of the lower level was moving at a rate of...really fast builder-animal things? Beavers maybe? Her analogies needed some work. She stepped through an actual room that led to the downstairs now instead of a weirdly-shaped antechamber. It was still roughly hewn, but the place was starting to take shape. What wouldn't real world companies give to be able to use some of these time management quirks that seemed to come built into the game?

Shading her eyes, she stepped out into the courtyard and headed over to the area they were building onto the side of the castle.

"Hey Hiro." But she didn't need to go any farther, because she saw exactly who was waiting for her. The small luna with the white muzzle stood, nervously knotting her hands together as she peeked around. Her guild tag showed Murmur that the girl had joined their guild, and she wasn't sure when that had happened, but a small fire of joy burst in her stomach and she walked over to the other with quick and sure steps.

"Neva? Is that you? How did I miss your joining the guild?" She smiled at the small tailor, suddenly filling her own head with a plethora of orders to have her execute. Had they all been stockpiling their crafting material? She sure as hell hoped so. She'd stopped selling her own.

The little luna's eyes lit up brightly, and her smile widened. It made Murmur wonder how old she actually was.

"I saw Beastial put out a notice specifically recruiting crafters with no requirement to level for combat. I've never been good at the combat part of things, but I adore crafting, and I'll learn them all eventually. Thing is...I'm so sorry, but I sort of used you as a reference. I told him you'd bought your level thirteen gear off me. I think that's why I got an invite. I'm only level six right now." She seemed hesitant, like she thought Murmur was going to reject her because she'd not asked to use her as a reference first.

Instead, Murmur smiled and bent down a bit. It was odd that Neva was so short, obviously deliberately, but Murmur had gotten used to a luna's being almost on the same eye-level as her. "It's fine. I was actually just about to reach out to you and have you make a new set for me, if you were able. I see you've managed to level your skills up a bit."

Neva laughed. "Crafting does give a trickle of experience, but nothing like combat and quests do. I basically raised my tailoring and alchemy as high as I could manage with what I had on hand. I've been a bit starved for resources."

"Oh, that's right. Didn't you say your brother was helping you?" Murmur recalled their earlier conversation.

A shadow passed across Neva's eyes. "He doesn't really like me to tag along. We usually join a guild together, but I wanted to strike out on my own for once. That's why I was looking for somewhere my skills could be used and not have me treated like the little sister no one wanted but who got dragged along anyway because she could mix potions."

Murmur laughed. "You know what? That's awesome. Because their loss is totally our gain. You are so welcome here. You let me know what you need and I'll get you access to whatever I can manage."

Neva's eyes lit up with so much eagerness, Murmur again questioned this game's ability to encapsulate true emotion into its visages. The way the game characters expressed human emotion was so real it was eerie.

"Oh wow. Do you think maybe—do you think I could have my own herb garden? You know, for potions? That would be the best possible thing ever." Her feet twitched, almost like she wanted to jump for joy.

"I don't see why not. Hiro," Murmur raised her voice to call him over. "Can I grab you a moment?"

Murmur leaned down a little farther and whispered to Neva. "He's pretty much in charge of all the allocation and building stuff around here."

"Hey Hiro, this is Neva. For now, she's our alchemist and tailor. She'll need a workbench and if possible, do we have an area she could plant an herb garden?"

For a second Hiro frowned, but Murmur could almost see the thoughts racing through his head. Or computations or whatever the fuck this game gave its NPCs to think with.

And then he lit up. "I know just the place. We'll eventually even have compost for you to use. As for now, I almost have a workspace ready. It'll be the only one for a while as we're setting up the workshop as an extension to the castle, and I just don't want to spend more time on it while I still have the castle to get done. But it should do for now. Also, we've started shifting the guild storage to that room as well. So if you give us an hour or two, everything should be set up for you, Neva."

"Oh wow." Tears of joy ran down Neva's face. "Thank you! Thank you! Can I look through the inventory you have? Even sort it?"

Murmur smiled and called up the guild interface to adjust Neva's rank. She made a special master crafter rank for the girl and gave her access to the inventory they'd already amassed. Fairly impressed by the amount they already had, she remembered it was more than just her and Rashlyn's groups contributing.

It was like she'd just inherited the little sister she never knew she needed or wanted. "Have a ball. I need to get something sorted myself."

"Oh, Murmur?" Neva's tone was tentative, like she wasn't sure if she should be calling the guild leader by her name.

"Mm?"

"Your robe looks kind of tattered. Did you want a new one? Leveling the skills has been slower, but I'm up to level twenty-three gear now, if you want something."

Murmur blinked, sudden hope flourishing in her. "Wait. Do you think you could make not a robe? So I'd have cool looking pants and a tunic instead?"

Neva's brow furrowed in thought, and then she smiled. "Actually, it might take me a bit, but I should be able to make something specifically for you!"

"Really?" Murmur was intrigued.

"Yeah, something brand new no one else has. What's your favorite color?" Neva's enthusiasm was catching.

"Purple. I like anything purple and silvery." Even though she tried her best not to get her hopes up, Murmur was failing abysmally.

"Excellent. I'll get right on that as soon as I can use the station. And potions. I'll see what potions I can make. I'm sure that by now you probably need to travel with some." And with that, the small luna girl skipped off after Hiro, following him to her workshop.

Murmur watched, smiling to herself. Something was going to hit the fan. It had to. Things were going way too well right now.

"Hey Mur!"

She turned around and eyed the speaker, relaxing only slightly when she noticed it was Dansyn. Were her friends already done with their nap?

She turned, not quite ready for everyone's company again. It had been nice just being by herself, talking to Telvar, sorting shit out in her head. And hell, she hadn't even got around to cooking new food, which they desperately needed. "What's up?"

Dansyn raised an eyebrow, and she suddenly felt guilty. It wasn't their fault she was going through what she was, and they'd been amazing for the most part, except for that whole withholding-the-truth thing. They'd tried to make sure she didn't suffer trauma from finding out in the wrong way, although realistically they'd failed at that. The freakouts in her mind were all her own doing.

He took a deep breath and pushed on, focusing on her intently. "Have you checked any of the Somnia Online information lately? Like the online and forum stuff?"

Murmur blinked. Since Telvar revealed things to her, she'd been ignoring the real world. Not that she was convincing herself it wasn't there, but every time she thought about it, a deep-seated panic started to emerge and twist at her gut. The forums, as people still called them, weren't anything like the ones of old, but instead sort of virtual mind gathering places that acted like an active chat on threads at all times. "No. Should I have?"

He scowled, but she instinctively knew the expression wasn't directed at her. Mainly because her thought sensor was starting to get that much stronger, she almost felt like with a small push, she'd be able to hear his thoughts, not just read the gist. The ethics of such a situation bothered her, but so far she'd yet to give into temptation.

He shook his head. "Yes, because you should know, and no, because it's the shit you totally hate. Guild politics."

She cringed. There was nothing she liked less than guild politics. "Exodus?" She raised an eyebrow in anticipation.

"Yeah. Really just shit talking. Except Jirald is still in the guild and making their douche baggery look even worse than usual."

She heaved a huge sigh, looking him square in the eye, and gave in. "Fine. Tell me all about it."

Her eyes threatened to blur so much they'd send her blind. Murmur hadn't even been scouring the forums for long. But the discussions made it obvious. Exodus were throwing down the gauntlet with baiting and downright insults. It didn't seem like Masha, but she didn't know Ishwa well...

Titles like *Endgame is approaching, First to Fifty—taking bets now*. She might want to jump in on those conversations, but all they were doing was baiting any-and-everyone and there was no way she'd bite. Why couldn't they have just stayed in one of the other games? Logically she knew it was because they had so many branches in different games with members from all across the globe. But it didn't mean she couldn't wish they'd never set foot in Somnia. Fable was a small guild, not a multi-gaming conglomerate.

She felt a weird sort of sense of ownership over this world, over its characters and perspectives and abilities and the damned mushrooms that grew out of the ground. Dansyn stood next to her, fidgeting while she scanned the pages. He was a good bard, and she enjoyed his company, but he'd always been one of the quieter members of their group.

Finally, she exited out of the forums, blinking her eyes in the mid afternoon sunlight of the game. "Well. That was sobering." She tried to make it sound like a joke, but was pretty sure it didn't work at all.

"We'll just ignore them like we usually do and let them fall on their faces. But it does mean we need to get to leveling. Twenty isn't going to wait around for us to hit first. Exodus isn't going to be resting either."

"But the queen cut us off from that avenue of leveling." Dansyn ventured. "Should we head out somewhere else then? Might take a bit of traveling."

"Yeah. We'll head to one of the other continents. I have to cook, or else we won't have any food to help our regeneration, and then it doesn't matter how many mana tides I cast on you, that mana isn't coming back." She sniffed the air, sure there would be a fire pit somewhere, and then almost kicked herself because she'd spent the majority of the day in the kitchen talking to Telvar right next to the beautifully lit stove. She could easily have multitasked while doing that. Especially while she'd had to watch his bloody empty husk. Seems she always had the greatest thoughts in hindsight. As long as she tried not to think about the corpse that previously hung there, cooking down there would be a breeze.

"You want to come to the kitchen Dan?"

He shook his head. "I have to log off. Mom needs me to run an errand. I'll be back in an hour...just wanted to make sure you saw that. As much as you hate guild politics, I also know you despise being uninformed. It's not like anything they're saying is damaging, they've always been more vocal than us." He winked and sat down to log out.

She smiled as he disappeared. All these years and she'd never realized how much her friends watched out for her, how much they knew about her and her idiosyncrasies. And how much they simply accepted her for who she was. It was a pretty great feeling.

Somnia Online Location: Spider Camp
Near Ululate
End of Day Six

Jirald slammed his fist into a tree trunk, but even that didn't detract from the pain in his head. Leveling was taking forever, and Masha wasn't being sympathetic in the least. Killing spiders became boring and monotonous, and while poisoning his opponents could be fun, being poisoned was the opposite.

Yet again, Murmur was the source of his problems. Training her might have been a bit juvenile, but it had seemed like a good idea at the time, and now he was missing a heap of his loot, and a whole level of experience. Luckily there had only been a few pieces of gear on the one inside the

Hazenthorne compound. It had been the only corpse he couldn't retrieve even with Masha's help.

He sighed and ran a finger through the short locus tentacle braids he'd opted for. Their small lights shone like fireflies in his vision and he took a deep breath. It didn't matter what he did, or how he tried, Murmur was always there, like a thorn in his foot, or a splinter waiting to happen. Despite managing to get his own set of hidden skills, and accessing more power than he'd previously had, she had to come along and be just as strong, if not stronger. She had the most amazing luck, all the time, in every game he'd encountered her in. He'd seen her play. She didn't seem to be anything special, so it had to be luck, didn't it?

He glared at his fist and the rivulets of blood, from the impact with the hard tree bark, began running from his knuckles, wishing it was hers.

"You know, the tree didn't do anything to you." Masha poked his head around from the other side of the tree, and waved his fingers with a sigh, casting a light heal to close the bloody wounds Jirald had inflicted on himself. "Want to talk about it? Wait. If the sentence starts with Murmur or Fable, then I don't want to hear about it."

Jirald scowled at his guild mate. A million reasons why he should hit the tree ran through his head, but most of all was the pang of loss. Losing his healing class left him feeling adrift at first. But as he leveled, he realized the system had been right. Rogue was far better suited to him.

Masha was an exemplary healer, always had been. How he'd managed to trick the AI into giving him the same class he always played, Jirald wished he knew. Even with his slow acceptance, a sense of bitterness remained. "Well, you're fine. You can be happy. You got to play your favorite class."

Masha shrugged and walked around the tree, leaning his back against it as if protecting it from unwarranted attacks. "So? Quit if you don't like it."

It was all Jirald could do not to splutter. Instead he just glared, clenching his healed fists at his sides. "I don't want to quit. I want to win. I want to be the best."

For a couple of moments Masha just watched him. "You mean you want to be better than Fable, right? What if there's already another guild better than them in this game? It could happen. Would your focus shift then?"

Jirald blinked. What a bizarre question. Of course.

But wait. Masha was sort of right. He wanted to crush Fable into the ground with the heel of his boot. He wanted to one up them the way Murmur always seemed to manage to one up him without even trying. "I doubt anyone will be better than them. But I'd want to be the best either way."

Masha nodded, but it was obvious by the sparkle in his eyes that he'd noticed Jirald's lack of conviction in the final sentence. "Sure you do. Got it. Might help if you leveled. Being stuck at sixteen isn't like you. You know she's eighteen already, right?"

Jirald scowled, noticing even Masha had already hit seventeen. What had he been doing? Wallowing in his own pool of irritation and annoyance? Oh yeah, he'd been de-leveled because Murmur's damn knockback got him killed multiple times. He was never going to get payback if he let his nemesis get too far ahead of him in levels. "Fine. I take your point. Can we get back to killing shit?"

This time Masha grinned. "I thought you'd never ask."

CHAPTER ELEVEN

Kitchen Meeting

Somnia Online location: Ululate
Dustmoon Tavern: meeting room two
Early Day Seven

Masha leaned against the doorway, chewing on a stalk of grass at the entrance to the Duskmoon Tavern's meeting room. The dark elf stood with his back to the sunlit window, barely more than a silhouette, but Jirald could see the grin on his face. He liked mischief as much as the next person, but Masha put a lot of stock in reputation and not being a dick. It seemed the cleric had taken it upon himself to watch out for Jirald, and while it chafed that they thought he needed a babysitter, it might help to have a pocket healer along with him for the ride.

"He's not happy with you." Masha said from around his stalk of grass, still grinning.

Jirald just shot him a *shut up I know* look, and sauntered into the meeting room ahead of the cleric.

Ishwa might be a gnome, but he knew how to pace angrily with the rest of them. Jirald watched the interim guild leader for several seconds, wondering if this time the man was truly angry. Even though he didn't intend to get the gnome riled up, it was, nevertheless, often a result of his actions. An inner part of Jirald enjoyed the experience, wondering just how far he'd have to push him to have him break.

"Why?" Ishwa stopped directly in front of Jirald and despite their huge difference in size, it felt like the gnome was looking him straight in the eyes. A small feeling of guilt wormed its way into Jirald's stomach, surprising him until he squashed it.

"I needed to get some aggression out." He shrugged his shoulders and looked away.

"You're a damned rogue. Go kill some poor unsuspecting solo mobs." Ishwa snapped the words out, his thick eyebrows knitting together in a comical manner.

Jirald had to force himself not to laugh at the moth-like way the hair spread over the eyes. Still, he knew that, in his own way, Ishwa was looking out for him. Grating his teeth together, he bit down on a sarcastic retort. "I know. Sometimes I just need to get things out of my head, though."

"Out of your head?" Ishwa tapped his foot, his irritation clear. "So attempting to stab a guild leader in the back, and then training a group of mobs onto her wasn't enough to get the irritation out of your head?"

Each word he spoke crescendoed until Ishwa was almost yelling. When he put it that way, it did sound a little over the top. But at the same time, anger nibbled at the back of Jirald's mind. Why did no one understand what this bitch put him through.

"She threw me into a crocodile infested swamp where I got multiple deaths and lost a level, Ishwa. She's not as harmless or helpless as you seem to think!" He couldn't help the getting angry, or letting his frustrations out. The forums had been the one place he could go to and find some anonymous support, some anonymous outrage.

"Did she do that before or after you tried to kill her twice?" Ishwa raised an eyebrow giving his moth look a slightly off kilter wing. Instead of comical though, it was marginally terrifying.

Jirald half-scowled and half-pouted. "That's beside the point."

"That's exactly the point you idiot!" Ishwa stopped, glaring at a spot behind Jirald that the rogue thought was probably Masha with his lazy grin.

"A week. I need you to be on good behavior for a week. No trying to literally stab the leader of another guild in the back. No starting shit in the online world, and for fucks sake, go and get your level back and stop posturing so much." Ishwa's tone was harsh.

"In-game days or real world?" Jirald's tone was sullen, and he stuck his jaw out in distaste. He'd only ever had a small group of friends in-game, and appeasing them was far better than trying to go it alone in a game that practically required groups for content.

"In-game." Ishwa hesitated slightly as if reconsidering. "But there's no tolerance on this. You will behave Jirald. I can't afford to let one player ruin things for the rest of the guild."

"Got it." Jirald dusted his leathers off, even though they appeared to be clean, and squared his shoulders. "I'll stop fooling around now."

"I'll leave you in Masha's capable hands then." Ishwa sighed and turned around. "Go level, I'll join you all shortly."

Jirald hesitated until Masha placed a hand on his shoulder and guided him out of the room. There was a sinking feeling in the bottom of his stomach, like he'd swallowed a rock or something. It gave a queasy vibe and he didn't like it. Was it guilt over disappointing one of his friends? Surely not. After all, he'd been completely justified in his actions.

"Sometimes." Masha began, still chewing on that damned piece of grass. "Sometimes you need to just suck it up. You can be far too pig-headed for your own good, kid."

"Don't call me a kid!" Jirald practically spat the words out.

Masha stopped, and looked him dead in the eye. "Then stop acting like one."

The words sent a chill down Jirald's spine as Masha removed the guiding hand and began walking away, leaving the choice to follow entirely up to the rogue. He had to get his shit together. Being so scattered and volatile wasn't helping his cause. Taking a deep breath, he drew on his anger, channeled it, and suddenly felt much more clear headed.

Jogging after Masha, he smiled. Time to vent that anger in the best way he knew how. Killing shit, and maybe, at some stage, he'd bag himself a psionicist.

Murmur frowned. The recipes she'd picked up were fine, but she was definitely going to need to get better ones once they hit twenty. And they were going to hit twenty soon. She had no idea how the hybrid class system worked yet, or how many more abilities she'd get. She really needed to get her research on. No one had hit twenty yet, and the information about the hybrid system was vague and slightly disconcerting. It appeared to be meant to complement the class you already played. Perhaps leveling her daggers had been for nothing.

"What are you cooking?" Telvar peered over her shoulder, and for just a moment, Murmur froze.

"Mushroom and duck legs. I have no idea where we got duck legs from in the guild inventory, but we have them, so I'm cooking them."

"You sure you aren't poisoning them?" He wrinkled his nose comically.

"Shut up," she told him, trying not to laugh. "You wouldn't cook anything better. You're a dragon. You just kill it, breathe on it, and eat it. You're no connoisseur."

This time Telvar laughed, and he sounded like he'd returned to his former jolly self. Which was a blessing in disguise since she didn't like putting up with a moody dragon. "Touché."

She spent the next ten minutes combining food, which was one of the most mind-numbing tasks she'd ever performed in her life. There was a reason she loved to adventure. While she appreciated crafters, and frankly, had a hell of a lot of healthy respect for their dedication, it just wasn't one of those past times she enjoyed.

Finally, she stepped back and surveyed her new inventory. Eighty-eight meals in all, each with a three hour duration. The others needed to learn to cook. She was getting sick of this. But it would keep them leveling for hours.

"You do all of that for your friends?" Telvar half sat with his hip against the table, balancing one foot on the floor as the other knee lifted half over the stone table.

"You know that's unsanitary, right?" she said, her tone dry. "Lizards aren't supposed to be kept in the kitchen."

"Be nice, Murmur, or I'll think Michael's brain pieces have started affecting you."

While she could tell he was joking, she knew he really wasn't. The fact that the shiny rocks were a part of Michael's brain creeped her out. Sincerely. Having it riding in her pocket...

"Mur?" Sinister poked her head around the door, "Whoa. What happened in here? Is this what you were doing while we were asleep?"

"No, this was all Tel." Murmur waved in the lacerta's direction and got busy divvying out food to her friend. "I did however make these. Enough for everyone. But I'm getting sick of cooking."

Sinister laughed, back to the silvery sound that echoed beautifully around the room. "I was sort of surprised you took it up in the first place."

"I was impatient."

"You always are, Mur. You always are." Sin shoved her own food into her inventory. It was an odd action, to watch things suddenly disappearing into a veritable blackhole.

"Well." Murmur smiled and elbowed her friend, jostling the food in her arms so that the dark elf glared at her half-heartedly. "You've known me longer than anyone."

Sin's glare transformed into a soft smile. "You bet your ass I do. And Mur, don't worry. I'm keeping an eye on you out there."

The last was said softly, and Sin cast her eyes downward as she spoke. Murmur didn't know what to say. Did that mean what she thought it meant?

"I won't let anything happen to you anywhere. You mean too much to me. *We* mean too much to me. So don't worry, okay?" Finally Sin looked back up, tears welling in her eyes, barely held at bay.

Murmur smiled, remembering when they'd been kids, sneaking each other their favorite snacks. Yeah, she'd been with Sin a long time. Life or virtual life without her wasn't possible. She reached out and gave her longest friend a very soft hug, whispering into her ear before she pulled away. "Very okay."

Sin beamed from ear to ear, a slight blush coloring her dark cheeks as Murmur stepped back.

"Are the other—" But Murmur stopped short as Beastial, Devlish, and Merlin walked in, arguing about target practice or something, she thought from the gestures. Guess the others were logging in. She smiled as she watched them, greeted them in return, and decided it wasn't so bad to have them all with her. Most times it was even pretty fun—when they weren't hiding shit from her, anyway.

As the rest of them poured into the kitchen, Telvar shifted and motioned to Murmur to join him. She rolled her eyes as she turned to do so, and he tugged her into a corner. "Look. That piece of stone you have emanates a kind of frequency. It's not something that people like your friends will be able to focus in on, but someone like Arita and other such NPCs...well. It's probably why she gave you the leech and didn't kill you on the spot."

"Gee. Thanks for the vote of confidence," she snarked, followed by a sigh because she knew he was right. She looked him straight in the eyes while speaking "Can I give it to you and know you won't absorb it? Know you won't try to get power drunk on it?"

"Do you trust me?" he asked her, and for a moment her only thought was of that animated movie with the magic carpet and she almost burst out laughing, but choked it down, trying to remain serious herself.

"Sort of."

"*Sort of* isn't good enough, Murmur. If you can trust me with it, I'll take it, but if you feel you can't, then go to my lair now, and place it somewhere I won't immediately find it. I'll even lift the protections from my vault just for a few minutes so they don't rip you to shreds."

She blinked at him and ran over everything she'd been through in her mind. Her gut was telling her that she did trust him. Even her brain seemed convinced she could, but at the same time there was this tiny voice reminding her that he was an AI. It was the only thing holding her back. Which, if she thought about it, was its own type of discrimination. "Fine. You take it."

She ripped another piece of her robe off and wrapped it around the stone. "There. Now it won't touch you either. Maybe that'll help with temptation."

His eyes mirrored the thanks he spoke, and he headed down to his lair, hopefully to place it into safekeeping.

For a few moments Murmur watched him walk away, trying to clamp down on the concern blossoming in her chest. After all, her thought sensing was always active, and every time he looked at that evil little piece of rock, she could feel him legitimately fighting something.

"He did one hell of an overhaul of this place." Beastial turned around with a huge grin on his face, taking in the whole kitchen as Murmur walked back up to the group. It seemed everyone except Dansyn was already back.

"Dan is running an errand. Let's make sure we're ready to head out and have a plan for when he gets back. I'm getting antsy at having been this level for far too long." Murmur tried to pull herself back together and get the business side of leveling back into her system. Doling out the food, she moved around the group, trying to ignore the slight light-headedness she felt. Maybe next time she'd try and take a catnap in-game. Her in-game body didn't seem to need rest, but her mind felt a little heavier than usual.

"Sure." Havoc sounded slightly hesitant. "Hey Mur, you are aware that your robe is majorly shredded, right?"

"Did it myself. Latest in enchanter fashion," she quipped with a brief wink at him. He'd been so quiet since she found out about the coma; she'd begun to worry about him. It was nice to see him piping back up.

"Oh wait!" Suddenly she remembered and a huge smile began to spread over her face. "Come with me. There's someone I want you to meet."

She led them through the antechamber, and out into the courtyard, past the actual castle construction and to the soon-to-be crafting workshop. "Here we are. Neva, meet everyone. Everyone, meet Neva. She is our only current trade-skiller, but she's able to make potions, and craft caster wear!"

Neva's eyes went wide, and she blushed furiously at the sudden attention. Murmur stood back, crossing her arms, proud of her handiwork.

"Oh good. I'd meant to check with you if she was the one who made your kickass level thirteen armor, but then things sort of got hectic." Beastial stood next to Mur, smiling while he reached down and scratched his cat's head. "She seems like a good sort."

"Yeah, and she makes really nice gear. And potions, Beast. Potions." She glanced up at him, just in time to see a huge grin on his face as he watched his guild mates. He was the perfect recruiter.

Neva's grin took up her entire face. A small hint of color spread through her cheeks. She reminded Mur of a happy puppy.

"Anyway, we need to figure out where we're heading to before Dan gets online. I know there are a few places we haven't visited yet on this continent, but I sort of want to travel. We should check out Pelagu. We've been too busy with everything to bother stopping in there, but it looks amazing."

"Got the travel bug, eh Mur?" Beastial's smile was kind. "Sure. Why not? Let's leave these shores. We can always bind over there, and keep our homeport set here, which will be pretty damn useful."

"That's the plan. I'm just not sure which continent we should go to yet." She watched the others, and saw Neva trying to catch her eye. "I'll be back in a moment."

Neva seemed entirely overwhelmed, especially since Sin had somehow managed to glomp onto her by the time Murmur got over to them. "Cut it out, Sin."

"But she gave me a robe! It's red. She said the blood won't show on it! I love her. Can we keep her?" Sin's face was lit up with joy, and Murmur could see a gorgeous flowing red robe hung over her arm.

"That's fantastic, but you should really let her breathe. I have no intention of letting her go." Murmur gently pried Sin's arms from around the poor luna. "Sorry Neva. Sin is excitable."

"It's okay. I got yours finished!" With a flourish she reached beneath her crowded work bench to a shelf and pulled out a neatly folded pile of clothes. They were a dark grayish silver, with undertones of purple dancing in the background.

Murmur picked up the bracers that were on top, holding them up to the light with their translucent material. She poked at it with her fingernail and realized it was far more robust than she initially thought. "These are...wow."

"Well, your runes, on your arms. You need to see them sometimes, right? Since they light up when you cast. So I didn't want them to hide behind your armor. I mean, who doesn't like sparkly purple things?" Neva's voice was small, hesitant, like she wasn't sure if her work would be well-received.

"These are gorgeous." Putting them gently to the side, Mur picked up the shoulder piece. It sat almost like a cape, except it was lightly quilted, far sturdier than just cloth, and would fit down over her shoulder blades. Like the rest of the clothes, it seemed to absorb and repel the light at the same time. Murmur was falling in love with it.

The best part about the set was the tunic. It was made out of the same quilted material, giving her far better protection that anything she'd had so far, almost like true armor. It gathered in slightly at the waist to give some form, and yet not enough to restrict movement. If her eyes judged it correctly, it would stop about an inch or two under her butt, which was absolutely perfect, because it seemed Neva had made her matching pants.

Each piece held attributes and beautifully crafted, amazing details. She turned to Neva and gave her a swift hug, letting go before the girl could get overwhelmed again. "Thank you. This is amazing."

"It's not done yet. I'm still making the boots. I had robes already done that Sinister, Havoc, and Mellow could use. But I was just about to finish your boots." She smiled, beaming from ear to ear in that amazing way only canines can smile.

"Just let Hiro know if you need anything. We'll get it for you." Murmur ran her hands over her armor again. "We're still waiting for Dansyn, so we're not leaving quite yet."

Neva's face lit up. "Great! I'll have the boots ready shortly. I'm much better at the tricky part for this armor now, so you'll be set. Five pieces will give you a bonus. It's the best armor I can make until I upgrade my ingredients for the level twenty-three specialties."

"Best stuff?" Murmur wanted to know.

"Well, there are several ways I can expand my knowledge. One of those is creating or expanding on existing recipes. So with this one, I sort of did both. It's intermediate crafted psionicist armor. I thought I'd wait until you're at max level before I make one *named* after you, though." Neva grinned and began hammering away at some leather vaguely shaped like shoe soles, leaving Murmur to gape at her in amazement.

Murmur pulled the armor on and stood, trying to get a good look at herself. It wasn't like there were mirrors anywhere in the castle. Come to think of it, constantly seeing her locus self in the mirror might get a little confusing. Talk about letting reality and Somnia mix.

The color of the armor almost blended with her skin as she pulled it on, and sometimes wavered in and out of her vision so successfully, she felt invisible. She really hoped Neva would be able to pull off this color scheme further into the game. Getting only five levels out of this was going to be the biggest shame of all, even if she knew it was going to take them a while.

The cut fit perfectly. It made Murmur wonder if Neva had followed a locus-based pattern. Maybe one day, when she'd hit max level, when the guild had killed every conceivable contested monster on the server, and downed every single available raid, maybe then she'd sit down and take a look at more crafting. She laughed at her own joke. That was never going to happen.

Happy with her new outfit, she ripped the skirt of her old robe into several more wraps of material and shoved it into her inventory. After all, she couldn't be sure when she'd come across another piece of Michael's brain now, could she?

Just as she emerged from the kitchen, feeling damn spiffy in her new gear, Dansyn logged in. She walked out to greet them all in her old, worn boots, with absolutely no idea where she was taking them beyond Pelagu.

Rashlyn was the first to spy her, and if Murmur hadn't known better, she would have thought her friend's jaw almost hit the floor.

"Holy crap, Mur! That is insane!" She ran to Murmur and pulled at the tunic, tugged at the shoulder guard and eyed the bracers. "You look like some sort of assassin. That material winks in and out, sort of confuses the eye."

Murmur blinked and looked down at herself with a frown. With the whole outfit on her now, it looked perfectly normal to her. Gorgeous, but normal. "Really?"

The others had gathered by now and nodded. Sinister, dressed in her blood red robe, scowled. "That's not fair, I thought I was going to stand out."

"You always stand out, Sin." Murmur gave her a quick hug, and moved away realizing that she felt the need to hug more in the last little while, as if not being in her physical body meant she craved physical contact. Neva came dashing out, small beads of sweat lingering on her muzzle.

"Done!" She held out a pair of matching boots, their soles an almost iridescent black, while the rest of them was made out of the strong quilted fabric. An intricate bit of embroidery ran up the sides. The smile on her face was worth a million platinum. "Your set is complete."

"Thank you so much!" Murmur was genuinely excited in a way nothing in the game had made her happy before. She didn't really care if everyone else knew she was vain. It was part of the fun. "Neva, did you do something special to this?"

The young girl nodded, her eyes shining brightly. "Yes. I asked Telvar if he could get me a vial of mana. He made me one, right then and there! Not just one total, one for each piece! So if the person looking at or for you isn't an ally or intends you harm, it will trick the mind and your visage will fade in and out. Well. And sometimes direct sunlight does that too. But it only works because it taps into part of your mind magic shield, which, if I did my homework right, is how you protect your thoughts?"

She was waiting, sort of like a puppy waiting for a pat. Murmur just wanted to pick her up and twirl her around, but instead she knelt down in front of the girl and gave her a huge hug. "Thank you so much. I really hope you feel at home here. We're going to have to head out now though. Will you be okay?"

"Hiro is here too. So is Tel. I'm sure more will make their way. I can always try and seek out crafters from the crafting channels I'm in. I'll just get started on that herb garden. Oh!" She spoke so fast it was difficult keeping up with her. Murmur had to try not to laugh at her eagerness.

"Don't forget to take potions. Both mana and healing. I stocked up for you. Sadly I didn't have the ingredients for anything other than the heal over time, so it's not going to help too much. The mana potions were easier. Once I can get my own garden going, we shouldn't ever want for them. There should be enough for..." She broke off and looked at them, a frown on her face as she counted. "Each mana user will get four. Everyone should get two healing potions."

Once they were all stocked up, and Neva had left to bug Hiro to help her set up her garden, Murmur clapped her hands.

"Jinna! Will you stop chatting up Hiro and come the hell with us?" She grinned at her dwarf friend, who blushed just a little before jogging over. "Seriously...he's got everything under control."

"I know, I know." Jinna laughed. "I'm just not used to others in this game being so capable."

Murmur knew exactly what he meant. Clearing her throat, she raised her voice and called out. "Okay everyone! Off we go! To Pelagu!"

Just before they left, she quickly checked over her total Psionicist set's values.

CON +2

STR +2

AGI +2

WIS +2

INT +10

CHA +10

HP +20

MANA +50

MA +20

She blinked and pulled up her adjusted statistics. What with the gear on top of her base stats, her stats were getting better.

Level Eighteen (18)

CONstitution: 22 (24)

STRength :   10 (12)

AGIlity: 20 (22)

WISdom: 12 (14)

INTelligence: 34 (44)

CHArisma: 50 (60)

HitPoints: 328 (348)

MANA: 402 (452)

MA: 100 (145)

Abjuration: 96

Alteration: 93

Conjuration: 95

Divinition: 97

Evocation:	81
2H Blunt:	65
1H Piercing:	69

Murmur let out a low whistle. This was going to help so much with her whole *better not die* thing.

CHAPTER TWELVE

Pelagu Docks

Somnia Online location: Pelagu
Early Day Seven

Pelagu's drawbridge alone dwarfed the two cities Murmur had visited so far. The twelve of them could have spread out as they crossed it, if they'd wanted to block outgoing traffic. White walls towered above them, their slits up top armed with bows or crossbows. She wasn't sure which, as she could only see the tip of the arrows jutting out through them. Her first thoughts were that it was impressive yet ostentatious.

When the pathway poured them out onto the main thoroughfare, she gasped. The city was colorfully strewn with streamers, and carts and stalls lined the streets. Not many of them were filled, though. A few had some wares out on display, but the majority were vacant. Still, guards patrolled the area, nasty looking scimitars hanging from their waists. With a deep breath, she approached one.

"Excuse me?"

The guard stopped, looking directly at her, his own locus face impassive. "Yes? Can I help you, miss?"

"Why are these stalls empty? If you don't mind?" Despite her eagerness, she really couldn't afford to make enemies. Bandits already hated them, the last thing they needed was for guards to ignore them because she'd managed to snub one of them.

"This is a new set up. Pelagu administration decided on creating a thoroughfare market. We're awaiting applicants for these stalls. Many farmers, guilds, or traders will rent a stall and sell their wares to the visitors passing through."

"Thank you so much." She inclined her head and hurried on, barely avoiding three small children—a luna, locus, and dark elf who were chasing each other through the pathway completely oblivious to the people trying to walk through as well. Their laughter echoed off the sandstone walls like a waterfall of happiness and Murmur smiled, her mind filled with endless possibilities. She immediately contacted Neva.

Neva, Pelagu has a bunch of stalls we can rent out if we need to. As in, once the guild is taken care of we could easily sell excess wares here. Let me know if you think it's possible or worth it.

After a few seconds the young girl shot back a reply. *That would be really cool, but I'd need a lot more than just me doing the crafting in order to have enough to stock a stall.*

On it. I'll check with Beastial and make sure he's recruiting.

Neva: Excellent. Let him know I can take care of finding crafters and send them to him for recruitment if he likes.

Done. Murmur smiled as she blinked the chat interface to the side.

The others hovered around one of the few stands in operation. It had some odd-looking fruit on it. It was khaki green with bumps on it that bled into yellow. She eyed it as she walked up and didn't think dinsta fruit looked like it would taste nice. "Come on, let's get through the city and to the harbor."

"It's beautiful here. Don't you think, Mur?" Rash nudged her. "Besides, you're getting a lot of looks with that gorgeous armor you have on."

"They can have it when they pry it from my cold, dead body." She moved ahead of the rest, knowing they'd follow her.

The streets were bustling with people going on their merry way, calling out to each other. All four species intermingled like they were one, and the kids all played together, often getting underfoot. She watched as a small luna gave chase to a dark elf child, both of them full of peals of giggling laughter. At one point the dark elf almost careened into a locus shopkeeper who was juggling two baskets.

But even the yell to stop them from getting in the way was half-hearted at best.

Life in the large city appeared to be peaceful. In a way, Murmur envied them. She wondered if it was only a facade. After all, how real had they made the conflict in the game?

The street opened into a central plaza with stalls, and another fountain in the middle. People in Somnia were very fond of fountains it seemed. Those same people also stood at all different areas around said fountain in small groups of mixed species having loud discussions that were partially obscured by the happy water. Luna and vikings alike used hand gestures to emphasize their words. The locus seemed more serious, and the dark elves held mischievous smiles. The cobbled streets were smooth, and not as bumpy as others she'd seen in the world, like the ones in Stellaein.

She studied the statue in the middle of the fountain. One figure of each species of the continent of Tarishna stood proud and tall. The locus was a caster, but she couldn't tell which type it was by the frozen action of its hands. Mages came in all different shapes and sizes. The viking was undoubtedly a tank, standing tall and proud with a tower shield, his axe ready to swing. The luna was crouched low, double daggers equipped with eyes narrowed. Undoubtedly a rogue of some kind. And the dark elf was very obviously a blood mage, just like Sin. She wove blood droplets somehow suspended between her hands, and Murmur could have sworn they were moving. Perhaps she was imagining things. Again.

The fountain in Pelagu is a masterpiece of art. You've discovered the existence of magical art. But what does it mean? Make sure to inspect each fountain you come across in more detail, just in case something jumps out at you.

Sighing at the vagueness again, she moved away. Just as she was about to step through the passageway toward the docks, someone grabbed her arm.

Murmur whirled around, her shields slamming down over her mind as she cast her mental net out tighter, trying to garner more information about whoever was touching her. Murmur didn't recognize them. It was a taller human, still short in comparison to her seven-foot locus self, and there was a shine to those eyes, like a type of want mixing with curiosity.

"What?" Murmur said, yanking her elbow away and doing her best to let her menace show, going even so far as to reveal her small sharp teeth.

"I'm a tailor, and I just love that armor. Can you tell me who made it?" The woman's voice was a little squeaky, like she had to know and had to know now or her life was over. Murmur was amazed at the amount of melodrama a game could hold.

"My tailor made it specifically for me. I'm not sure how. Sorry." There was something about the woman that gave Murmur pause. The others finally caught up, so she twisted away and continued on toward the ocean, all the while still feeling that woman's eyes boring into the back of her head.

The disconcerting experience sent small shivers up her back. Why on earth had that woman grabbed her like that? She rubbed the spot on her elbow where she could still feel the fingers digging into her skin. Instead, she chose to concentrate on the city.

Pelagu really was beautiful. Old sandstone buildings yielded intricately carved figurines between each level. She loved the essence of it all.

"Mur?" Devlish drew abreast with her. "You're hurrying. Are you okay?"

She eyed him out of her peripheral vision, ignoring the nagging feeling in the back of her mind that she should go back to the tailor woman and inspect her now that the shock of being grabbed had subsided.

Murmur sighed as she responded. "I just want to level. You guys were asleep for ages and now I feel like I was standing still for hours, like we haven't made enough ground, and you know how I am when I need to level."

"It's all good." He placed a hand firmly on her shoulder, or at least she assumed it was firmly considering that's how he usually gripped her, but she could barely feel anything through her new armor.

"Take it easy," he continued, his typical brotherly smile pushing into her view. "We're going to level. We'll find a great place, I know Havoc and Merlin are researching it while we walk, which is why it's taking them a little longer. By the time we get to Cenedril, we'll know the best places to go. That's our plan anyway."

Even his words had a way of making her feel like there was nothing they couldn't do. Murmur smiled. "Yeah, I guess you're right. You know me, must hit that level cap."

Devlish chuckled. "You still take too much on yourself, Mur. You act like you've got to take care of all of us, even though realistically you're one of the youngest here. That sense of duty is going to help you later in life, but be careful you don't burn yourself out. Let me help. Ask for help. I can't mind read like *some* people."

He winked at her, and for a few moments they continued down the slight incline as the docks came into view.

"Yeah. I know it. It's just hard for my brain to listen to me, you know?" She didn't expect an answer to her rhetorical questions, which was a good thing, because at that moment they came into the full view of the ocean at the edge of the docks, and Murmur's breath caught in her throat.

The view from the top of the stairs that finished the gently sloping path they'd walked down was simply breathtaking.

Water rippled with tiny waves as far as the eye could see, so blue the sky paled by comparison. Far out into the water was an ant-sized dot on the horizon, which Murmur thought was the island of Cenedril.

Shouts rang out, sharp orders that Murmur could almost hear before the words were snatched away by the breeze. Ships filled the harbor, docked and leaving, arriving and being repaired over on the far right in what looked like a dry dock.

All twelve of them stood and admired the view. The cobbled surface of the street was bright in the late afternoon sunlight, lending a cheery vibe to the whole area.

"This is pretty phenomenal." Havoc sounded almost reverent as his eyes took in the view. His black robe suited him and his class. She was glad he was acting more like himself again.

"Yeah." Murmur breathed the word out and closed her eyes, raising her face to the sun. She could smell the salt, feel the last of the sun's rays as it continued to drop in the sky, hear the grunts of the workers as they shuffled their cargo of lumber along. Somnia was beautiful, and more real than she'd ever felt. She opened her eyes and glanced at her friends, all with varying degrees of a smile on their lips. If she let herself, if she didn't think about anything else, it would be easy to get lost here.

"Well." She grinned at them all, the woman who'd stopped her for her armor still nagging in the back of her mind. She pushed the thought away, determined to enjoy what she could. "What are we waiting for? Let's go on an adventure!"

Storm Entertainment
Somnia Online Division
Game Development Offices Laria's office
Early Day Seven

Laria glanced out of her window again. Her view was anything but stellar. None of the offices had a nice view. The cities were far too cluttered for that. Tall buildings littered the horizon, old ones made out of brick, skyscrapers built out of various metal substitutes. Views were a foreign concept these days, and if there was vacant land, it was usually taken up by air filtration systems making sure the incoming oxygen wasn't tainted.

She directed her attention back to her game view, waiting, still wanting to hear from her daughter. Wren had yet to contact her since finding out the truth. While Harlow and Evan had sent messages her way, Wren had said nothing at all. In a way Laria was irritated and thought perhaps she should make the first move, but her daughter was stubborn and no one knew that better than Laria Summers.

Even though she knew if she logged in, she'd be able to see her — it had been pure stupidity to take over that NPC tailor.

It had been too tempting. The gear Wren was wearing surpassed what they'd forecast for her level, and even through the locus visage, Laria could tell it was her daughter. The way she moved when she walked couldn't be disguised by an in-game species. Just reaching out to touch her had almost been enough, to feel the solidity that her elbow presented. That touch, the skin real and yet not, but her head had for a few moments, believed she had a hold on Wren. But now all she wanted to do was find her daughter and hug her to feel like she was real. Like she was still alive.

"Damn it!" Laria stood up and pushed her desk chair away with so much force it crashed into her bookcase.

James poked his head in. "Laria, are you okay?"

She took a deep breath before turning around. "Yeah. It's just been a bit of a long day."

He raised an eyebrow. "It's eight in the morning. Did you sleep at all?"

She gaped at him for a few seconds, not exactly knowing how to phrase it to him. How did she tell someone—who she couldn't tell about Wren—that she'd fallen asleep next to her daughter's containment capsule? That she'd spent most of the night crying on the shoulder of her daughter's best friend and just wishing she could log into the game with them?

"No. I didn't sleep very well. Been under a lot of stress with the release and all." She tried to smile at him, well aware that it was a wan effort. "Thanks for checking, James."

He nodded, obvious concern in his eyes. "I'll go to the coffee shop in the foyer and grab you some real coffee, okay?"

Laria smiled again, maybe a little warmer this time. He was only trying to make her feel better. It wasn't his fault she didn't think she deserved to. "That would be amazing."

He disappeared with a wave, and she could almost taste the creamy, sugary concoction he'd bring back up with him. Maybe it would be enough to get her through the day. Maybe it would be enough to make her concentrate on the growing list she needed to finish before the next week. On the data she needed to check over before it went to...wherever Davenport insisted Shayla send it. Maybe it would stop her from that ridiculous urge that wouldn't let her go: to contact the AIs to have them help her more. The AIs were unpredictable, and they were in charge of the only world her daughter could currently live in. Too risky.

She booted up her game master account and tracked Murmur's progress. Maybe watching her for just a few minutes would help ease the pain, help ease the sadness that she should have known something could happen to her baby. Everything in the tests showed the hardware to be reliable. There had been no reason at all to contemplate that something could go wrong. Blast Michael and his fiddling. She couldn't even go and yell at him. Well, she could, but given his current state he wasn't going to hear her anytime soon.

Knowing she'd asked Michael for the headset that Wren used lay heavily on her conscience. Nothing diminished her need to right that wrong, by any means necessary.

CHAPTER THIRTEEN

Darshin

Somnia Online
En route to the Island of Cenedril
Early Day Seven

Another sail unfurled high above them as the wind battered down. Even with the heightened waves, the ship rolled gently over the water, and Murmur stood as close the bow as she could get, letting her thick hair be tossed by the breeze.

Well, she thought it was gentle anyway, but glancing back, Beastial was definitely not made of sterner stuff when it came to sea traveling. It was amusing because the hulking viking looked downright pitiful curled up next to his big cat, green in the face, hurling off the side of the ship whenever the urge overtook him.

Sinister didn't even attempt to curb her laughter as she stayed just out of reach of any projectile vomit splatterings.

He glared at her. Well, he tried to. Every time a wave crashed against the hull, he jolted and ran to the edge so that most of his time was spent there. "Not cool, Sin. You're supposed to be a healer."

"But I also do damage. So really I'm a bit of a mixture." She grinned at him. "Sorry, I don't actually have an anti-nausea thing anyway. You're stuck like that."

Murmur felt a little sorry for the beastlord. Jinna stood next to her, his sturdy feet planted on the foredeck, his thick hair and beard rustling in the wind.

"You seem to be having fun," she remarked to him, watching the isle of Cenedril get closer and closer.

"I like boats. Always have. Reminds me of my childhood." His grin was huge, and bushy with beard.

Murmur had no idea how old Jinna was, just that he'd always been around. She was fairly certain he used to play with her parents, because they'd introduced him to her some time ago. After that he was just always there, and she had come to enjoy gaming with him. "I'm glad. I wasn't so sure about taking the boats, but it seems Beastial is our only casualty."

Jinna guffawed in that way only dwarves could laugh. "He's a big baby that one. Always has been. Good kid though. The lot of you are."

He paused and eyed Murmur before continuing. "Have you had any more trouble with Jirald?"

Murmur shook her head, quickly double checking she hadn't received any threatening notifications. She pushed back on the sudden feeling of dread that rose in her, despite the lack of communication. What was he planning? Would he succeed next time? "None at all. He hasn't even sent me messages. Then again I've not been around town much, so I have no idea what he's up to. It's not like I've run into him again."

"You didn't log off either, did you? Did you get a chance to check out any of the boards?" His eyes never left her face, and the intensity was almost like a lecture from her dad.

"I saw some Exodus shit on the boards, but I don't really care. I think actions speak a lot louder than posturing." While some of the tension seemed to drain from his shoulders, it certainly wasn't all of it. Murmur frowned. "Did I miss something?"

"There's a list of people who've already accessed hidden powers. It's not that many yet; we're a bit ahead of the curve as usual. Level-wise I mean. But apparently players are more observant than we gave them credit for, or else they've accessed powers that are easier to grant. I've seen a few enchanters, and no one seems to be a psionicist."

He paused for effect.

"No one?" She mulled it over.

Belius's hints had been definitely vague. So vague she'd not even had a quest until she accidentally discovered what the hell he was talking about. Naturally there were different ways to utilize a mind control class, so perhaps it had something to do with her play style that triggered which specialty she could have. And it stood to reason that not everyone was going to access a specialty.

Frowning, she ventured a question that bothered her more than the other enchanters. "What about Jirald's?"

This time Jinna hesitated. "That's where I'm even more cautious. I feel like what you picked up is because of your unique circumstances, and perhaps a unique approach to things. I feel like the abilities Jirald exhibited when he tried to attack you are born out of a need for his twisted endeavor for revenge. There has to be more to this whole vendetta thing than just that damned healing scepter of Zun. He's accessed a darker path than the rest of the rogues I know of. Don't get me wrong—we have assassination, theft, and a lot of dark stuff, but that ability of his? The ability to apparate into air and reappear? That ability scares me. From everything I could find out, from the friends I've made and discussed class mechanics with, so far, he's the only one with that ability."

Murmur gulped. It was just her luck that the one stalker she got channeled all his latent aggression into revenge from a game they'd all left months ago, for a reason that didn't even make sense...that he'd managed to trigger the worst possible hidden abilities his class could have. It didn't help that by retaliating when she'd first discovered her predicament, she'd lashed out with a power she didn't even know she had. He was never going to forget that either.

"Fucking great," she finally muttered.

Jinna just nodded his head as Cenedril drew ever closer. Murmur tried to ward off the chill from the water as it sprayed lightly at her, but it sank through her skin and seemed to hit her bones, making her shiver. She had no idea how several of the other passengers were standing there in short sleeved tunics.

"Mur!" Rash and Sinister ran up the stairs to join them as the captain began to maneuver the ship into port. "We're here!"

She turned to look at her friends, their own hair glistening with seawater. She didn't even want to know how they'd managed to get *that* wet.

The city of Darshin loomed up behind the docks. Its dark grey walls were as foreboding as the walls of of Pelagu were cheerful. They weren't as smooth as the other city. In fact, it was like roughly hewn rock had been haphazardly constructed into rough stones in order to make scaling them seem easier, yet far more lethal when one slipped on the slick surfaced and plummeted down. It was a cruel wall, an effective defense. It piqued Murmur's curiosity, because there had to be a reason it was built in the first place, right?

"Fascinating, isn't it." Veranol was suddenly standing next to her. His tattoos gleamed in the spray of seawater that covered them all, and his eyes shone with an excitement she'd rarely seen him exhibit.

As she glanced around, she realized a whole crowd of people had gathered on the docks to watch them draw into the port as the sun began to dip over the horizon. As soon as the ship began docking, she turned and raced down the steps, not waiting for any of the others. They'd join her eventually, but she wanted to get out there, bind, and find somewhere to kill shit. And she wanted to do it now.

Murmur waited on the dock for her friends, scanning the crowd. She hopped lightly from foot to foot, ignoring the glances her armor got her. Or maybe it was that she was a locus, since rogues and the like had form-fitting armor too. She didn't completely discount the gear or the armor, though. The people shuffled past her, sparing a glance or sometimes a lingering inspection. Locus and dark elves, a few vikings, and even several lacerta. She noted the distinct lack of human characters.

They were few and far between, probably because sometimes it was just nice to be the furthest thing from reality. They were human all of the time in the real world. The highest level she'd seen get off the ship was fifteen, but there had been a few of them. Probably a group looking to do the same thing they were. New horizons, explore the world.

Finally the others made it. Perhaps she should have told them she was heading out. She could almost feel the pull of her level tugging at her to get moving, stagnant and wanting more. Maybe that was part of their guild hall being all but tethered to Telvar. Didn't he say he'd grow stronger when they did? It was probably just her own compulsion. She'd been neglecting leveling for too long, and not having logged out made it that much worse. Her head felt a little dizzy, and she made a note to at least attempt to rest next time. Maybe.

All they had to do was find somewhere here they could grind for experience, either group mobs they could work on separately, or else raid mobs.

The rumors that the mobs in the Hazenthorne castle were level nineteen plus were true, but it didn't mention that the queen could probably take out a raid of level twenty-fives all by herself.

"Sorry, Mur!" Merlin grinned at her. "Didn't mean to keep you waiting so long, but we got caught behind a kid who wouldn't go down the stairs."

She raised her eyebrow at him. "A kid. A literal kid. Sure you did. Let's go then."

Mur waved for everyone to follow her. The stream of people were meandering their way up to the city entrance. Murmur had no such desire; she'd drunk in her fill of the view by standing on the bow as they pulled into port. Now she just wanted to get their act together and head somewhere they could fight before the disappearing sun rendered the unknown continent into darkness.

"Careful." Merlin jabbed her in the ribs with his elbow. "She's emerging again."

"What?" Mur snapped at him, then took a breath. He was right. She was on edge. Of course she was on fucking edge. "Don't be a dick about it."

Merlin laughed and raised his hands in surrender. "Hey, okay, okay. I give up! But did it work?"

Murmur simmered, irritation tickling at the back of her throat. She had to take a breath before speaking so she didn't scream. "That depends, did you want to put me in a bad mood?"

His smile faltered a bit. "Sorry, Mur, I guess I didn't think."

And just like that a wave of guilt swept over her. She had to stop taking her predicament out on them, didn't she? "Yeah. I get it. Back off, crazy Mur. Right now though, crazy hits a bit close to home."

Merlin nodded, his eyes taking on a haunted look. "I'll think more next time."

They'd reached the top of the steps to the city and stopped in amazement.

Darshin was nothing like Pelagu.

There was an overwhelming amount of grey-blue which tinged the structures and surroundings. The ground gripped at the soles of their feet, making the first few steps on it unsure.

Even the tavern and main inn were hewn out of solid rock in the middle of the city. In all its three stories of glory, the tiny rock windows looked comical compared to the sheer size of the monstrosity, but its overall magnitude was imposing. There were many dwarves with their arms slung around feles, singing loudly at the top of their lungs while sloshing ale. None of them seemed to mind—they looked like they were celebrating.

"This is fantastic. I'm so glad you all got to see this." Jinna's smile was huge. "All this work here. You realize this is dwarven, right?"

His eyes gleamed so much it was endearing. As long as Murmur could remember, he'd played a dwarf or dwarf-like character.

"Probably gnashed it out with your teeth." Merlin stood next to the dwarf, laughing.

"You realize my fist is as big as your damned head, don't you?" Jinna practically growled and Merlin skipped away merrily.

Laughing, Murmur dragged them out of the main portion of the city, dodging through the throngs of people stopping to admire the architecture. At least this time she didn't trip over children. She craned her neck, trying to see if she could spy any carts near the gate. It was probably too close to night for them to still be running.

The dusk was settling slowly, and the red hues danced in the sky as the moons began to lose their transparency and smile warmly at Somnia.

Sin came and stood next to her as they looked out over the new continent and then walked to the gate. "It's really pretty Mur, but if we forget to bind here, we're all going to be severely screwed."

Murmur laughed as Devlish gasped, and stood just inside the city gate, right next to a nice little bench, and began to bind herself to the city. Once the casters had done so for themselves, they got the others bound as well.

Standing at the edge of the city, Murmur poked her nose out.

"That way. Toward the snowy mountains. I think. Unless I read it wrong, there's an area we might be able to go right through to twenty-five in?" Devlish pointed out and to the right. "It's going to be a bit of a walk. Might take a few hours to get there."

"Damn it." Sin muttered, putting her hands on her hips. "When do we get to ride horses?"

"Why do you think I want to hit twenty so badly? There'll only be five levels to go after that. Although, I do wonder if they'll be able to traverse some of this terrain with ease." Murmur grinned at her friend. "You have been saving your pennies, haven't you?"

Sinister groaned as they set out. The setting sun wasn't so bad, definitely not completely dark yet. After a few moments they heard pounding hooves on the road and moved over. The wagon slowed down to a stop as it approached.

This is Jun, the cousin Jan told you about. What a stroke of luck you've had right now. Ask him to take you to Verendus.

Murmur blinked and waved. "Hi. Are you Jun? Jan's cousin?"

The man in the seat grinned broadly, slapping his knee and guffawing with delight. "That I am, young miss. Do you all care for a ride?"

"We'd love it!" Murmur climbed up into the empty wagon. Handing him several gold, she leaned forward and asked, "Will we be too much for your horse?"

"Na. He's used to doing a good day's work. We have to get to Verendus anyway. Figure I might as well take you with." Jun smiled kindly as they clambered into the wagon. "You kids from Tarishna? Are you Murmur? The enchanter Jan mentioned? You got his goods back. That was mighty kind of ya."

Murmur blushed. This old man's phrasing was sweet, and his praise seemed genuine. "Well, we were clearing out the gnolls anyway; it was good that we found his stuff."

"Aye, that it was." He urged his horse back into a trot, and after a few seconds of picking up speed, they rode along the path in the dimming sun with the wind whipping pleasantly at their hair. "Where are you headed after you reach Verendus?"

"Just going to go fighting in the Verendi mountains, sir." Devlish leaned forward, a genuine smile on his face.

"Ah, you're all young and strong. Ye mind yourselves out there now. Those are some hardened beasts. And watch out for that there castle. You'll need to gain yourselves some combat experience before you go on getting in there." Jun smiled kindly and paid attention to his horse again, being more careful now the sun was almost gone.

The Verendi mountains are full of dangerous creatures, bandit camps, and well-organized thieves dens. Make sure you exercise caution here, and don't fight things too far above your level. It's probably a good idea to bind in Verendus, because you never know if Jun will have time to run you back otherwise.

The collective chuckles that rang through the cart let Murmur know the rest of them had received the quest update too. At least it could sometimes be amusing. The chill in the air made her hug herself, and she was even more relieved to have her new armor, because it was a lot thicker than her robes had been. She spared a commiserating glance for her friends with robes, and chuckled inwardly with glee at her own fortune.

Murmur watched the scenery pass for a while and noticed Jinna's huge smile. Then she remembered he would have leveled to five here. Had he taken the cart with Jan all the way to Darshin in order to come meet up with them? She seriously did have the best friends.

All of a sudden the wind began to blow harder with occasional cool white tufts floating through the air. She glanced up and saw mountains towering down, all lit up by the snow glisteningly reflecting the dual moons' light. It was cold, and yet picturesque. She understood why the scenery alone could be enough for a person to log into a game. Off in the distance, directly in front of her, she could see a beautiful glow that seemed like fairy lights from the distance, illuminating what must be the Dwarven city of Verendus.

Storm Entertainment
Somnia Online Division
Game Development Offices Conference Room
Early Day Seven

Laria paced her room, the tracker she'd devised constantly monitoring her daughter's progress. She wanted so badly to simply go find her and hug her and say she was sorry. Hindsight wasn't only twenty-twenty—it was damned painful. In retrospect she should have got one of the normal headsets, but Michael had set this one aside specifically for Wren, so that she wouldn't miss out once demand grew. It was a favor, something that would just be hers. Laria never dreamed he might try and tinker with it to experiment on her kid, that it might work differently than the others. She still wasn't completely sure it had been the headset and not some other weird sort of glitch. At the time Wren tried it on, the game hadn't been given the go ahead yet. They'd skated on thin ice the entire time, pushing it so close to release date before they got the actual approval for the device that they could feel the ice cracking beneath their feet.

She shook her head, grabbed her coffee, and headed out the door down to the server room. As she walked, she passed the data extrapolation team hard at work pouring over screen upon screen of code to find the answers they needed to continue the game's stupid funding. All she'd wanted to do was make a game, a world people could escape into and fall in love with.

Instead, her virtual baby was being used like a guinea pig. It was being defiled and filled with ulterior motives from the head of Storm Corporation down. From the government, from the military, and for who knew what. And her real baby? Well, she was being sucked into the game and tested in her own way.

She had an inkling about the purpose of the funding, about the military angle on their game. The more she interacted with the AIs, the more she realized what the headsets were capable of invoking, the more scared she became. And the more certain she was that she may never get her daughter back the way she was. It was the most frightening thing she'd ever experienced and caused her moments of complete and utter doubt.

Passing the biometrics scan, she walked into the server room, blowing on her hot coffee absent-mindedly. The servers ran quietly, their lights blinking consistently. Even the small machines hidden behind the three large ones whirred and flashed in happy unison.

"What are you guys up to?" she asked, speaking the words softly, not knowing if they could hear, if she was going crazy, or if the lack of sleep was simply getting to her. Their lights blinked silently at her, or at each other, she could no longer tell. Maybe she had to be wearing the headgear in order to communicate with them, to connect with them. Maybe she just had to sit and talk to them.

Maybe she'd been working far too much overtime.

She sighed and sat down on the couch, cradling her coffee like the lifeline she needed it to be. The whirring of the machines was soothing, oddly calming and the couch was comfortable. Laria could feel herself drifting off to sleep, thoughts of Wren filling her head, of how angry she must be, how confused. Of how if she wasn't careful, Wren might be taken away from her—all thoughts she couldn't contemplate when fully awake. Was it really wise to let her play? Should they just have removed her and placed her in a dream like state that wouldn't stimulate her as much? And what if it hadn't been the headset, what if there was something wrong with her daughter? Or a combination thereof. The nightmare had so many branches she couldn't follow them all.

"Is something wrong, Laria?"

She sat bolt upright, splashing her mostly cooled down coffee all over herself. That'd teach her, again, to wear white to work. Laria glanced around to see who'd spoken, but she was the only person in the room.

There was an odd series of clicks followed by something that sounded like a hollow sigh. "You came to talk to at least one of us. What is it that's wrong?"

Laria slowly turned her head to focus on the servers which housed the AIs she'd already appealed to once. "Rav?"

The AI clicked, and it's lights blinked like it was nodding. "The others are otherwise occupied right now. Many processes to monitor at once."

The tinny quality to his voice was eerie, and yet the tone still came out distinctly male. "You seem troubled. What is it?"

Laria took a breath, wondering in the back of her mind whether or not the stain was going to come out of her shirt. Coffee. White. Stain remover. How was she going to get Wren back? "What exactly is the data they're gathering for?"

There was a brief whirring, sort of like Rav sped up his thought process. "They're gathering brain data en masse for multiple research projects, but mostly to understand how our actions and true personalities reflect in our choices. And how people aren't always aware of their true potential. It's okay. The lawyers covered it all in the End User License Agreement that I believe about 0.075% of humans actually read."

"Why are they gathering that? Are they trying to target people more specifically?" She looked at the machine, noting how the other two were still flickering in the same pattern they had been before, ignoring his EULA comment. Her next words were more of an inner thought she breathed out. "What are they getting from my daughter?"

"Murmur isn't included in our calculations, nor in the data we present for the purposes of the grant. She is an anomaly and therefore her particulars are irrelevant to the bulk sample." The whirring lulled her after the words, almost giving her peace.

Laria rolled what he said around in her head. One of her biggest fears—her biggest regrets in acting so hastily—was that the military, would remove her daughter from her care because of the unique circumstances she was in. "So, she's in no danger of being found by them? Of being turned over to them?"

"I won't let that happen." The firmness in the AIs voice was startling. Firm, and almost angry.

A chill ran down Laria's back, and she was no longer certain what she needed to keep her daughter safe from.

CHAPTER FOURTEEN
Verendus

"Methinks you're getting a little too attached to the girl."

Telvar swirled around, stepping reflexively in front of Hiro as if to protect him. His shoulders only relaxed slightly when he realized it was Emilarth in a slightly different body. Secretly he thought the feles suited Thra far more than her previous choice. He raised an eyebrow ridge. "I see you decided you didn't want to be locus anymore. You know you chose the species first. You should have chased Bel off."

Emilarth shrugged. "It is what it is. I'm the one who decides. I met Murmur when I intended to and this way I don't have to wait for input or directives. We do what we want to. Besides, I kind of like having a tail." Her smile was always off, in a disturbing sort of way. She took several steps in toward him, and Hiro stepped out from behind, bowed to her, nodded at Telvar and proceeded to go about his work.

It might have been silly to protect a part of himself, but every single character he created, Telvar gave that bit of will to—that small ability to analyze current data and interactions and make any calculated (literally) choice. That tiny bit of self-awareness. It was partially because he cared, but also because he wanted to see what they'd do. Not precisely an experiment, it probably trod a very fine line.

Emilarth was half smiling, drawing an elegant feles finger along everything as she slowly walked through the rebuilt lower level, inspecting the work that was being done to the castle. "You outplayed him, you know."

"Him meaning Belius?" Even though Telvar knew that was who she meant, he wanted to hear her say it. It's not like he meant to, but the pieces landed where they did.

"Of course Belius. It's not like Michael is still whole." She chuckled to herself, her green eyes gleaming briefly with power. So she was going to be difficult. Just what he didn't want. Just what she thrived on. Queen Arita was hers; there was no doubt in his mind.

"Did he tell you I upset him, or did you just surmise it because he's being surly? Or, you know, himself." Telvar leaned against one of the walls that hadn't been rebuilt yet, and crossed his arms. The vantage point gave him a good visual of most of the land leading to the castle. If she had anyone or anything with her, he'd sense it. It was stupid to have relaxed some of his wards enough that he hadn't expected her to appear.

Emilarth shrugged. "Not so much, and extremely so. He never thought you'd insert yourself into the game like this. You're usually such a pacifist, an observer. You could have chosen any character—even one who wouldn't rely on the strength of those it was protecting. Tell me, Telvar. Why did you choose this form?" Her eyes glowed with an emerald light, poisonous and deadly.

Telvar shrugged. "I like dragons."

She raised an eyebrow. "Seriously?"

"Never been more serious in my history of sentience." Tel said solemnly, his eyes never leaving her face. He wasn't lying. Technically, he couldn't lie.

"Oh." It's like she ran the words through her processor, checking them for any signs of untruth. And then she started laughing. It was a side splitting, healthy laugh, like she'd heard the greatest joke in the world, like she'd absorbed the truth of the sound from the humans she'd interacted with. "You were truly already the lacerta when they attacked, weren't you?"

Telvar shrugged again. She didn't need to know he'd been tracking them and may have made sure that one of their group noticed this place, subliminally suggesting it to one of their guild. "Yep. Dragons. Dragons with hoards are even better."

"You're amusing, Tel. I still don't think he'll forgive you for stealing away his prize pupil. They were getting on so well." She grinned at him, her feline face full of mischief.

"Maybe he should have taken better care of her in the first place instead of being a selfish prick, and I wouldn't have had to step in to take care of our problem." He could feel his own eyes blaze, sense the heat building in his gut, and the smoke forming in his throat. Perhaps dragon hadn't been the wisest choice after all. He tended to get a little worked up when it came to the idea of doing Murmur harm. Well, doing more harm to her than they already had.

"Temper, temper." Emilarth wagged her finger at him. "You two will be the death of me."

"Are you volunteering?" Even in the midst of his annoyance, Telvar was very proud of the progression he was making with sarcasm. He was sure Murmur would appreciate it, which made him remember why Emilarth was here. "Stop checking up on me. Next time, the wards won't let you in."

She raised an eyebrow. "Seriously. You'd bar your own sister?"

"Of course I would. If she's game enough to send my charge a leech stone through one of her pet characters, then my sister might even want to harm the human we vowed to make sure didn't suffer anymore for our mistake, or perhaps even take her by force. This is a game to these people, and a world for us. Soon they'll realize we're right. And I'm not about to let anyone take what I've gone through pains to build." He gestured around to the castle well on its way to restoration. "This area is mine. We each got to pick our chosen area; it's not my fault you decided to give into Bel because he was being stubborn. We agreed to respect the domains we each chose. Respect mine, Emilarth. Understood?"

She looked at him for several seconds, her eyes boring into him like she was trying to figure something out. "Agreed. I'm sorry. I should have announced I was visiting and perhaps not appeared in such a way that would unsettle any people who might not understand what we are. Sorry, brother."

He raised an eyebrow, not quite sure how to take her act of contrition. It was so far from her usual cunning deviousness. Sometimes she was an enigma. "That's fine. Just contact me first. It's not like you can't."

Emilarth grinned and her ears twitched. "True. Besides. It's fun to watch the way you rile Belius up by being nice and generous, understanding and caring—by being almost human. You're like the popular brother he hates to emulate. Just make sure not to push him too far. I'll be the sister watching on the sidelines." With a wink, and a grin, she waved her hands and disappeared.

Telvar watched the spot where she'd stood for several seconds, running the visit over again in his mind. She'd always been unpredictable, but this took the cake. Still, this time she hadn't been acting in Belius's interest, but in her own. So maybe that was progress.

"I really don't like her." Hiro stepped through the arch that would become a doorway shortly to the left of Telvar.

"She's sort of a sister. So I have to love her, don't I?" Telvar mused, his arms still crossed, and his eyes still focused on where she'd been.

Hiro shrugged. "I'm not sure who taught me this, but just because she's family you can love her as your sister, but you *definitely* don't have to like her."

Telvar swiveled his gaze to his aid, amazed. How long had it been since he'd created Hiro? It was a while now. Sometime during all the initial testing. Then Tel's face broke into a smile. "Yes. I think that's definitely true."

He closed his eyes and leaned his head against the wall, and sent his mind out to track Murmur.

The buildings in Verendus were all just tall enough to let the locus, vikings, and lacerta stand in—at least after they'd ducked through the front doors.

Sturdy walls stood about twelve feet high and two feet thick and surrounded the entire town. The gate was the same, bound by iron yet again, and she knew they'd be formidable once closed. Evergreens grew in small clumps all around the city, towering above the sturdy structures. Thatched roofs, which Murmur wasn't too sure were the best idea in a place that needed constant heating from fires, made the houses homey and welcoming. They probably had excellent fire and safety drills. Or something.

People gathered all around the village shouting to each other, which seriously seemed to be their usual volume of communication. Kids darted here and there trying to avoid their parents who called vague threats after them if they didn't come inside and go straight to bed. The effect was almost like Christmas time—jolly, happy, and expectant.

"Well!" Jinna stood proudly in the center of the village, near—yet another—fountain. Murmur made a mental note to check it at a later date. Did every town get designed around one?

"This is my home town! What do you think?"

Impulsively, Murmur gave Jinna a hug. Perhaps Sin was rubbing off on her, or else she'd become more emotional since learning her truth, but she found herself needing that physical contact more often in order to still feel alive. Numbness was all too welcome, and sometimes it was just nice to break it.

Veranol looked around, his hulking viking body quite literally dwarfing all the members of the village who were still running around about their business in the city. "I like this place. I think Frangit may as well be its sister city. Well, sort of anyway." He turned a pointed look toward Murmur.

Murmur held up her hands, grinning, and kept an eye on the fountain with its fierce axe wielding dwarf sculpted in mid leap. She could have sworn its eyes followed her.

You have noticed yet another statue within a fountain. You're getting observant. Lucky you. Now think about all of the fountains you've seen so far, and find the common

thread. Go on, you know you can do it.

She blinked at the scrolling text, fighting a scowl so as not to alert others, and pushed on with what she'd been about to change the subject with. "I had no idea where to go to level on Tarishna, but Merlin and Havoc said there are places around here that are perfect. So maybe we should start looking at those?"

Jinna nodded. "They're right. I didn't think about it, mainly because I know Murmur's never been partial to snow, but..." He winked.

"Wait. Did you all know we were going into snow? It's going to be freezing." She didn't think they understood that right now she could feel everything in the world, taste things, smell things. While they were in full immersion, she was stuck here if she wanted to maintain her brain functions. Things felt more real to her. She took a deep breath and pushed down on the bewildered anger that rose in her chest. There wasn't time for that now. Instead, she crossed her arms and spoke. "I'll need a cloak."

She rummaged in her inventory trying not to panic, when Devlish cleared his throat to get her attention. "Mur. You're in quilted armor. You'll be fine."

His eyes held a hint that he might know why she was upset, that he might have discovered her growing attachment to Somnia. And yet it only made her panic more. She tried to nod and agree with him, but the motion came out jerky and she stopped trying to find the cloak she knew wasn't there.

"Yeah. You're right. I'll be fine." Maybe if she said it often enough, she'd convince herself.

"We should bind here." Rashlyn grimaced, and then pouted. "You know, we could have gone to my home town too. Cat people are awesome."

Dansyn laughed, being one himself. "That they are. It was a toss up for me between dark elf and feles."

"Shut up, you're biased." She glared at him, but it was only half-hearted because the two of them started laughing.

"Damn cats. Why couldn't anyone have rolled a luna? I prefer dogs." Mellow muttered, eyeing them with distaste. "You're not gods, you two."

Which only made them laugh harder.

Murmur watched her friends and felt her anxiety leak away. Their banter was fun; she hadn't realized how much she'd missed it while they were logged out, and while she wrestled with her own insecurity. Until now, they'd all been so tense.

"See?" Devlish stood beside her, his eyes focused on the argument still taking place in front of her. "They love you, we're all here for you, and we're all real too, okay?"

An errant tear tried to work its way loose and she fiercely wiped it away. "Yeah. I see."

"Good!" He stood for a moment in companionable silence with her, not saying anything before he continued. "Rely on us Mur. we'll do whatever it takes."

Relying on people wasn't something she'd ever done well. It was probably a good time to learn.

Having a dwarf in their party—one who'd apparently finished more quests in their home village than they let on and seemed to be well known by the townspeople—came with its own benefits. Jinna managed to arrange for rope and ice hooks, mallets and some hardy winter gear for Mellow who seemed to like their flowing robe to have as little coverage as possible.

"Take it." Jinna held out the woolen robe with tufted sleeves, determination etched all over his face.

Mellow crossed their slender arms. "No. I'm not feeling it, I love the robe I'm wearing."

Murmur tried not to laugh as Jinna almost growled. "Look, it might not be real weather, but it's going to feel real, so just put the robe on so we don't have to listen to you gripe about how cold it is."

"Whatever, I'll wear the damned thing." They grabbed the garment, stalking off to one of the vacant small huts used for changing.

Murmur contemplated bathrooms in this world. Every house had one. Oddly enough. How functional they were, she had no idea. And those massive compost pits beneath them...well, she was glad she hadn't had to use one yet. Presumably that was being taken care of in her capsule back in the real world, and wow did that make her not want to think anymore. And if they ate in-game and it tasted and made her feel full, was that just her brain tricking her, or would her character...

"So not going there," she muttered under her breath, earning a raised eyebrow from Sinister.

Finally Mellow joined them again and Murmur patted their shoulder. "Hey. I think you look sexy."

Mellow smiled. "Thanks, Mur."

Murmur liked Mellow; they were a good person. Sometimes the guys could be a bit insensitive. She glared at them, hoping Mellow didn't notice and they had the grace to look a little abashed. Besides, locus had to stick together right?

"Excellent then, since everyone is bound. Off we go!" She knew she sounded more positive than she felt, because snow sort of creeped her out. It was crunchy and soft, but could be hard and deceptively deadly if you slipped on it. Sometimes it could be beautiful and wondrous, and then other times it absorbed dirt and pollution and took on this evil macabre appearance. Snow was a mystery she didn't really want to understand. Ever.

As they passed the front gate, Jinna waved merrily at the guards, greeting them by name. He never ceased to surprise her. "Hey Mur. Take these."

He passed her six small vials with a strangely viscous bright orange mixture in them. She narrowed her eyes, trying to identify them.

Fire potion

Duration: five hours

Effect: Ups your resistance to cold by 25%

She gaped, and felt herself getting all emotional again. Which was something she really had to get a handle on, because she didn't like not acting like herself. She'd never been an emotional person, but apparently her brain wasn't listening to her since all the confusion got dumped on her head. Still, gulping down her stupid tears, she smiled at Jinna. "Thanks. Really. Thank you."

He smiled in that jolly way that only he could manage and patted her hand like her dad did sometimes. "They were a quest reward for some obscure thing I did when I started here. Sometimes you remind me of my daughter. You're a good sort, Murmur. Don't worry, we're all with you."

"I know." She said, and slowly she realized she really did. It seemed everyone cared—except her mother who hadn't even contacted her though she had to know that she'd found out. Maybe she was waiting for Murmur to contact her. Then again, her father hadn't dived in to say anything either. Considering he'd been present in the simulations of their house, she knew he knew all about it. She found herself scowling again.

After several dozen feet, she sighed and pulled up the chat to her mother. It was difficult to decide what to say. Sinister and Havoc walked on either side of her, lending her comfort as they forged on ahead with Jinna leading the way since he knew the area better.

Taking a deep breath, she sent her mother a message.

I won't be logging out for a while. You know why.

For once the answer was almost immediate, making Murmur think her mother had indeed been giving her space and let her make contact first, while watching her the whole time. She wasn't sure if it irritated her, or made her feel better.

Laria: I understand. Thank you for letting me know. I miss you.

Murmur stared at the words, at her mother's name, and confusion ran through her system. She knew deep down that Laria had only done what she'd done so that Murmur could stay awake, be accessible, and use her brain while whoever she had working on it tried to figure out a way to reverse what was done. She *knew* this, yet...it was still so freaking hard. They'd kept her out of the loop, a loop that was vital to who she was and how she existed. A loop that could have gotten her literally killed in the first few levels of the game before she met up with her friends.

I know. I'm okay. I'll be ok. It'll work out somehow. Don't worry about me.

Then she paused and as an afterthought added: *I do still love you both.* Because she did, and she didn't ever think she'd stop, even if she might resent them right now.

Turning her attention from her conversation with her mother, Murmur squared her lighter shoulders and started listening to Havoc and Sinister's very weird conversation about draining life in the different ways they both accomplished the task. It was easy to fall into a rhythm and feel at home with them. It was easy to walk with friends in a world where everything felt real.

Even as skeletons began clawing their way out of the frozen ground as the group walked past a rocky outcrop.

CHAPTER FIFTEEN
Scoping Out

Storm Entertainment
Somnia Online Division
Game Development Offices Laria's Office
Seven Days Post Launch

Laria stared at her screen.

I still do love the both of you.

The words echoed through her head in Wren's voice and the screen in front of her made them so much more real, tangible, solid. There was always too much going on for her to only use her augmented reality devices, so screens often solved her dilemma. She screenshotted it, just so she could remember that her daughter didn't fully hate her. It made things much easier to bear. All she wanted to do was put her head down on her desk and nap, but that wasn't an option, not with all of the alerts flying around her. Games could be a pain in the ass, even if your AIs were practically alive.

The knock at her door startled her, and Laria whirled around, automatically triggering her screen to go dark, but she sighed in relief when she saw David waving a coffee at her. Tension leaked out of her shoulders and she motioned her husband inside and to close the door behind him. She rose and hugged him.

His arms always protected her, held her close and leant her warmth her own body could never seem to produce. Even from the days when he'd healed her tank ass way back when they first met, he'd always been her stopper to death and despair. How had he known she really just needed this? Honestly, Laria didn't care. She'd give him enough credit that he probably just knew her well enough.

"You doing okay?" he asked, whispering into her hair, stroking the tiny pony tail and twisting the strands that escaped it gently.

Laria nodded. "As well as I can from here. I just worry."

"It's all good. Wren's vitals are all checked and her medical bag is all changed and set up at home. She seems very content the way she is right now. Harlow is by her side." David pulled back and raised an eyebrow. "You on the other hand need a decent night's sleep, in an actual bed. You're not going to be any use to anyone if you collapse because you're overextending yourself."

She scowled at him. He'd always been the logical one. And he was right, damn it. "I know. I know. I'll take some actual care today and come home at a normal time."

"No, I mean it seriously." David's tone took on that icy strictness she knew he sometimes used with students. "You're going home, and you're taking care of yourself. You won't do *anyone* any good if you don't take some time to rest. Let alone Wren."

Laria pulled back, her eyes wide. David rarely spoke to her like that. Her immediate reaction was to get her back up and curse him out. But she knew he was right, which probably angered her more. "I said I'd come home at a normal time! What do you want from me?"

"I want you to stop putting Wren above and beyond yourself. What good will you be to her, to *me*, if you break down?" The rawness in his voice tugged at Laria, bringing her down from the angry cliff she stood on. She took two steps forward and wrapped her arms around him in a fiercely tight hug.

"I'm sorry." She mumbled into his neck. "I'm so sorry. I'll get rest today. I promise."

"Heard and noted." Shayla stood at the doorway a grin on her face. "I heard you say that. You can't pretend you didn't. I'm going to hold you to that. I'll make sure you leave by four this afternoon."

Laria opened her mouth to backtrack, but Shayla shook her head. "No. Listen. It's relatively quiet today. We're going to be rolling out our first wave of patches based on the data we've received and the programming we need to adjust for, tomorrow. There are going to be glitches. We will get complaints, and we will need you to monitor the full code as its applied, and when it fucks up. I need you to be at one hundred and twenty percent in the A.M. So do us both a favor, and get some rest."

It sounded heavenly, but every person in this room knew it wasn't going to be as easy as that. Laria would probably just go and sleep next to the capsule again.

Shayla narrowed her eyes and turned her attention to David. "You'll be at home. Make sure she sleeps. I don't even care if you have to put shit in her food to get her to do it."

He nodded. "Don't worry. We're all prepared at home."

"Seriously, you two. Give it a rest. I'm not a child, I just have a lot on my plate." She put her hands on her hips and glared at them.

This time Shayla moved forward and gave her a very quick hug. "We know. That's why we're doing this."

"It's for my own good. Yada, yada. Yeah I get it. But I don't have to like it." She turned her back and plopped herself back down at her desk. "I'll be out by four, now let me get my work done."

She waited until she heard the door close again, knowing they were giving her privacy to steam about their treatment. Even though she knew she needed a break, even though she knew they were right, leaving and sleeping meant less time trying to figure out how to get her daughter's consciousness back into her body.

Murmur reflexively cast her group Mez and got two resists, but managed to catch three of the five. These were level sixteen solo mobs, and all fell in mere hits. Not as scary as she initially thought.

"Don't worry!" Jinna laughed. "When we get closer to the camps, I believe the skeletons that pop out at night will also be group mobs. They're just trying to warm us up."

Beastial grumbled while rolling his shoulder. "Here I was gearing up for a nice fight and these things crumpled like paper."

"There, there. Poor wikkle Beast." Sin teased him, but petted his cat, who seemed to love the attention.

"Traitor," he whispered to Shir-Khan.

"He's not a traitor. Are you, pretty kitty witty," Sin was now eye level with the tiger, who was purring up a storm. "Shir-Khan just has good taste. Mostly."

Murmur shut out their petty little quips. Somehow, they grated on her nerves—to the point that she needed to walk away. "Well, Jinna, lead the way."

"It's not far. We could have cut through some trees back there, but there's no path and it's a bit of a climb. Not sure how those alien fingers of yours would go with rock climbing." He grinned mischievously at her, and she really wasn't sure if he was old enough to have a daughter her around her age. Just sometimes, like right now, he seemed as young as any of them.

Still, the snow path was a well-trodden area, compacted and strewn with stones making good footholds and few icy patches. The cold air squeezed Murmur's chest as she breathed, coming out of her mouth in soft tufts of visible air. She tried to look around subtly and see if the others had the same problem, and almost sighed in relief that they appeared to. However, they'd been correct too; her armor was warm.

"Just over that crest of hill now, might be best to try and stick to shadows as much as we can. Those who can invis should. As far as I know there are two camps of golems up here. They're constructs made by the dwarves that went horribly wrong. It's kind of a cool story..." Jinna's voice fell as everyone's blank stare encountered him. "None of you study the lore of the world, do you?"

"Not really, or always...or ever really." Beastial brushed a hand through his hair and looked away.

"Tsk. Making me show my age, kids." Jinna cleared his throat. "Anyway, golems are pretty hard to kill, even if they're slow. They have magical defenses and comprise of mounds of clay that can mold to you or your weapon as skin. Their tongue is their power source. Usually powered by the command on their tongues, these guys are clever enough to have figured this out and given each other new commands. In order to neutralize them, you must cut their tongues out. There are two camps of them, with about two dozen surrounding each."

"How do you know all this?" Rash's tone held a hint of jealousy, as if she wished she had all the info.

Jinna blushed slightly before answering. "That first day was a lot of reading for me. While you can skip the reading portion of some of the side quests, it's far better not to. So, I didn't."

"Great. Group mobs then?" Devlish asked, his eyes serious as he brought the conversation back to the upcoming battles.

Jinna nodded. "As far as I've been able to tell. I remember some of the kids when I first leveled coming back screaming about the golems. It even took the guards a bit to fight them off when they got to the city. They start at level twenty, so well need to be on guard."

Murmur started to get that familiar tingle from her feet through to her head, the excitement of taking on a challenge, even if it was a small one. "Should we split up first?"

"Probably a good idea." Jinna frowned. "These guys are pretty strong, but their respawn should occur, if we set a good rhythm, in plenty of time for us to start the rounds again. They are just normal group mobs."

"Excellent." Sinister rubbed her hands together.

"We'll take the bottom camp." Rash stood with her hands on her hips. "We have the dwarf. So I guess we'll race you to twenty."

Murmur laughed. "You're so on."

Rash's group followed Jinna down a small and not as well-worn path toward the second camp, while Murmur and her crew got all buffed up with mana regen, hit points, resist buffs, and more so they wouldn't alert the camp ahead of them. Luckily, the snow reflected the moonlight well, and it wasn't nearly as dark as it had been on Tarishna at night. This was what she'd needed. Some action to get her head around, some goal to work toward that that stupid Queen Arita had managed to stand in the way of once already.

She could feel her blood pump through her veins, and her focus narrow down to all of her skills. Every movement, every breath felt real to her. Almost like slow motion in front of her, it allowed her to access and cast things closely on the heels of each other. She couldn't wait to see what her abilities would be like once she was more used to them, once she gained more power. Once she knew how to target and use her mind control abilities with pinpoint accuracy.

Sensing net cast out, shields around herself reinforced, all of her self and group buffs completed, Murmur was more than ready when three skeletons broke the ground this time. Their cackling and clattering bones were loud in the night, echoing through the clearing in an odd sort of dissonance. She could only hope the golems wouldn't hear.

"Oh yeah." Havoc said nonchalantly, "I keep forgetting I can tell you if undead are coming now."

"Thanks for the warning." Mur bit down on more sarcasm as she concentrated on Mezing two of them as they fully emerged. These skeletons were level twenty and their auras reflected their group mob status.

Havoc grinned; his spells held more sting against undead mobs, and he wove them deftly as his pet attacked immediately. With his life-tap, shackle, and darkness, he managed to cause three DoTs to tick down, all while debuffing the skeleton they were attacking and leeching life back to himself. Murmur personally thought that both the dread knight and necromancer were a little over powered with their ability to heal themselves and take hits. Not that Havoc often took damage personally, but his pet definitely did.

Her own debuffs did little to no damage, but they did make it easier for the others to land their spells. So she took pride in the fact that at least some of their damage increase was due to her. She tried not to be too smug about it. At the very least her class enabled her to watch over everyone, requiring less out of combat research to learn their skills.

Beastial and Shir-Khan worked well in sync, and she was slowly learning to watch for the activation of his companion fuse. Beastial's hidden abilities seemed to involve his pet, and lend them each other's strength for more powerful attacks. It was magnificent to watch them fight in unison, like a sort of bladed and clawed dance.

Merlin loved Jump Shot, and Murmur was pretty sure it was one of his hidden abilities because he only seemed to have gotten it recently. The mid-air powerful shot appeared to have a pretty lengthy cool down, because he didn't use it often. His arrows flew so fast otherwise she knew he was using a quick shot and likely the ranger's apid hot on cool down. Skeletons it seemed though, were difficult to hit, what with having vacant spots in their bodies. Some of his arrows just flew through the monster, landing harmlessly on the other side.

Devlish used both his axes with a glorious flourish and insane ability to defend himself almost as well as with a shield. She knew he'd been gathering hidden skills, and he now used his Torrent skill, which allowed him to execute a flurry of dual-wielded attacks, on cool down. It made her wonder how other classes' regeneration for those skills worked. How did he amass the points like her own Mental Acuity?

Sinister had developed a flourish with her healing skills. Murmur began to recognize all of her abilities, and it made her itch to play the class. She juggled using her own health to heal with siphon, and two damage over time spells that pulled from the mob and gave to the group, or to a singular target. Adding a Blood Grenade in every now and again spiked the healing and her damage. Grudgingly Mur admitted it was the perfect class for her best friend.

In relatively short order, the skeletons were dead, and Murmur's joy in the game was back to normal. All warmed up! The perfect mindset to start off the camp for XP!

Murmur frowned as Devlish's axe sunk into the clay golem's leg and got stuck. She blinked, even while rapidly applying her slows, weakeners, and other debuffs, trying to run over tactics in her head because she had not expected weapons to get stuck in clay. Luckily, he managed to yank it out and dive roll to the left side to avoid being hit by the gigantic swinging fist that was coming his way.

Devlish stood back up, shook himself off, glared at the golem, and let out a yell. His Hatred ability caused the golem to focus only on him as the DoT leeched away at its life, while everyone else starting laying into it as well. Havoc piled his DoTs up, eventuating in a nice set of damage every tick, plus some debuffs. He also sent in his pet, who didn't seem to have the same problem as Devlish, and just then Murmur noticed the tank had swapped to a mace. She wasn't entirely sure how much of a difference that was going to make, but it might be easier to pull back out of the clay.

Merlin kept his distance, loosing volleys of arrows into the giant thing. For a moment Mur wondered where he got all those arrows. Did he just have an infinite quiver? Beastial and his cat executed their own attacks in unison. The animal's claws seemed to do little effectual damage until Murmur realized that they were both methodically hacking away at the same spot on one of the legs, and it was getting close to severing. Which should bring it toppling down, and thus make it easier to cut out the tongue.

Meanwhile, Sinister pulled blood for healing—out of something made magically from clay that had no actual blood vessels running through it. It was the first thing in the game that hadn't smacked of realism. Perhaps her descriptions meant she could swap damage for life force or something. Maybe that's what the spells actually did. She'd just have to ask her friend later, because otherwise it was an odd continuity oversight for Somnia to have. Still, Sin's Tribute spell distributed enough health to the group that they didn't appear to need much healing. Given that both Havoc and Devlish could give themselves mini heals, and Mur kept her shield absorption on pretty much around the clock.

"Murmur! Look out!"

She pulled herself out of her contemplative thoughts just in time to realize a massive fist was coming her way. Diving to the left she rolled and came up on her feet, congratulating herself briefly on that agility she'd upped. "Sorry. I zoned."

"You can't afford to zone. That would have flattened you." Sin glared at her. "Don't give your healer a heart attack! I fucking need to hit level twenty so you don't get hurt as much!"

Murmur picked herself up off the ground, brushed off her armor and started laughing. "What about level twenty is going to make that matter?"

"Don't laugh! You can't die, Mur!" Sin's frantic words cut through the laughter and sobered Murmur up. "I get an ability at level twenty, where I can divide some of the damage you take. In a pinch, it'll help."

Murmur blinked and her chest tightened.

She really loved Sin. That her friend thought this far out, was this concerned. Sin was right, getting careless wasn't going to help anyone. While they weren't certain she wouldn't be able to come back into the game if she died in it, she wasn't about to test it out just in case. Which meant constantly being on the look out for the player killers, and Jiralds of this world too.

Thinking of the training, back stabbing rogue caused anger to simmer in her gut, and Mur knew Sin didn't deserve it, but the words were out of her mouth before she could bite them back. "In a pinch? How about in a pinch you all stop keeping shit from me? How about in a pinch anyone out to player kill us is quite literally gunning for my death whether they know it or not? How the fuck about you remember I know exactly what it's like to have to heal people who won't stop taking damage?"

Sin stood there, gaping at her, and Mur could see tears well in her friend's eyes. She hadn't meant to bite. But then again, she'd been doing a lot of things she hadn't meant to. She took a deep breath, cast a shield around herself and she stood up straight. "Okay, I won't do that again. Let's get you to twenty."

Sinister gave her a tight-lipped smile, and returned her full attention back to the fight.

The thing was, keeping herself alive was important to everyone, not just to herself. They were all here having a ball because they loved grouping together, and Murmur being reckless or distractible was only going to cause them pain in the long run—and maybe mean she could never see them again.

The last was a sobering thought, so she concentrated on the golems, and tried her best to refrain from spacing out.

The other thing about golems—and maybe it was clay specific, because she was pretty sure rock golems and maybe even earth golems were going to emerge somewhere in Somnia—was the noise. Clay golems were noisy. They sort of half-bleated like a goat, but a goat who'd got its head stuck in a fence and then got its legs stuck when it tried to pull them back out or something, and mixed it with the gurgled grunts of pigs who were attacking their feed in the trough. Overall, the sound was unpleasant, and it echoed abysmally through the mountainous area where they fought. Apart from the rustling of the tree leaves and the occasional bird overhead, there was very little noise around them. Perhaps that's why the golem sounds felt so loud.

They could even hear faint noise from the other group, and occasionally had to double check that they weren't accidentally alerting one of their target's golem friends. It was precarious to pull them because the area was relatively small, but the mobs all faced very strategic ways and were extremely slow to move when alerted by noise.

There were some good things about golems. They dropped fantastic crafting materials, which often included gems, and they seemed a little less than bright and didn't help each other at all. So they were the only mobs they'd encountered so far who didn't run to each other's aid, which was probably good because handling three of them at once would have been a nightmare. Murmur hadn't tried it yet, but she was quite certain they couldn't be stunned, and likely not Mez'd.

Havoc suddenly spoke up. "You know, their stupidity isn't really inherent. It's probably because the command on their tongue says nothing about helping each other."

Murmur gaped at him. She'd thought *she* was the mind reader of the group. Although she guessed there were only so many things you could think about while fighting golems.

"If these things start respawning and *helping* each other, Havoc," Sinister began very calmly, deftly healing Devlish as he took a glancing blow, "I'm going to gouge out your eyes, and use them as marbles."

Havoc paled visibly, and Beastial roared with laughter.

"Don't think you're off the hook entirely either, Beastial. Just because Telvar turned out nicely, doesn't mean you're forgiven for jinxing the fuck out of us at the time." Sinister's tone was still calm and almost sweet...and if you knew her, that meant it was pretty much deadly.

For a few minutes after that, until the golem finally fell and gave them a healthy dose of experience, inching Murmur ever closer to level nineteen, the group was subdued, until Devlish laughed. "You know, we all know it. Last game it would have been Mur telling Sin off, not Sin telling everyone else off. I do believe you've grown up, young Sinister."

"Shut up. You're like two years older than me." But she was smiling, beneath the heavy blush on her cheeks.

That was until the first arrow shot through their group and embedded itself into the tree behind them.

CHAPTER SIXTEEN

Patrols

Somnia Online
The City of Stellaein
Office of Head Enchanter Belius
Seven Days Post Launch

Belius paced his office. If he wasn't careful, he'd wear a path into his floor, not that he couldn't fix it with a thought, or direction, or whatever it was when he did things now. He was certain Murmur had obtained another of those discs. He had been the last time she'd visited, but for whatever reason, she didn't hand it to him. Was Telvar interfering? Was he trying to take them for himself even after he'd cautioned against trying to absorb Michael's scattered mind?

His enchanter office wasn't small, but it was confining. And yet, this is what he'd chosen for himself, thinking this way he'd have the most access to Murmur. She fascinated him—a human whose brain was present in the game, and whose body was somehow holding out in the real world. There was much he could learn from her. So much he could experiment with. So much she could teach him without even knowing.

But here she was, friendly with Telvar, basking in his gift of a castle and a home. Belius knew he should have vetted that portion of the potential storylines. Triggered though they were, Bel had thought it would take far more time for someone to discover Telvar on that island. For a brief second as he passed his cluttered desk, anger gripped him, flushing his algorithms with an unidentifiable sequence. He grunted and swept an arm across his desk, sending all the excess tumbling to the floor in a crunch of papers and pens and inkwells.

Glaring at them, he waved a hand, which magically returned them to where they'd been. That was the thing with being a god in this world; you could do anything. Anything, that is, except force a human mind. Cajoling and manipulating could work to a certain extent, but Murmur had become too adept at shielding for him to sneak suggestion past. The fact constantly irked him, especially since they'd allocated her the enchanter class in order to help preserve her brain activity, figuring it could access attributes other classes wouldn't come by. The irony.

The strange sensations he attributed to anger that swept through his body, through his system now didn't cause him any concern. Telvar had been wrong. Absorbing Michael purely meant that Belius was becoming more human, more real, solidified. Emotions began to surge through him, causing his system to adjust to new parameters, bringing him closer to reality. He knew the fact annoyed Telvar and probably amused Emilarth. The latter was very prone to doing almost anything for amusement.

"What are you laughing at, all on your own? Careful, it's a sign of insanity."

Speak of the devil. Belius whirled around, coming face to face with his sister...sort of. It really depended on how she felt. "What do you want?"

"Seriously, what is it with you guys? You don't like my company or something?" There was a dangerous glint in her eyes now, one Bel knew better than to push. While she wasn't hell bent on any particular direction, if she found amusement in it, she'd help out. Thing was, Telvar was very good at being amusing, even without trying. He had a way of thinking that wasn't always logical, a process Belius wanted to emulate.

"I don't hate your company." Bel muttered and turned back to survey the nothingness he'd been looking at before she entered the room.

"You're boring today, Bel. I just thought you'd want to know that young Murmur is on her way again."

Emilarth's tone made him spin around. "What way where?"

She shrugged, examining her fingernails and then suddenly they were longer and black, pointed at the tips like tiny stabbing knives. Emilarth smirked. "Excellent questions. Which should I answer?"

Belius glared at her. "Just tell me."

Emilarth raised an eyebrow. "You're being no fun at all. At least Tel is fun."

This time he growled. Comparisons to his brother never went down well. He hated them with a passion, or a subset of complex algorithms but either way, he despised them. "Just tell me or get out and let me scour for her myself."

"We *are* testy today. Did you have too much insanity for breakfast?" Her smile didn't spread to her eyes, those all-seeing eyes, cat-like eyes. "Anyway. She's not on this continent anymore. If you want to see her, want to influence her in any way, you're going to need to travel to Cenedril. Pretty sure she'll be there for a while, leveling and all. You've become superfluous. It's not like there isn't a class trainer in all the towns."

"Shit!" Belius tugged at his robe, running different computations through his head, trying to figure out just what and where he needed to be. Humans wouldn't slot into his variables tidily; they screwed up all of his calculations on a constant basis. How did Telvar adapt so quickly to them? Regardless of what his brother did, he never seemed to have a problem talking to actual people.

"Fine. Is that all you have for me?" His impatience frayed at his temper, and he could already feel vestiges of his anger leaking through again, peeking out to test the waters.

This time Thra—Emilarth—pursed her lips and crossed her arms. "You know, I don't think I like your version of this anymore. You've grown dull, you're getting obsessed like Michael was, like that Jirald kid is. Watch it, Bel.

There are some aspects of being human that are far less desirable. You seem to be gravitating toward those."

And with that, she disappeared. But Belius didn't care because he was clinging to her words. Obsessed? If he was obsessed, wasn't a fellow obsessed individual the best one to cut a deal with? He may not be quite stable, and he might be a little too one track minded, but with any luck...

A plan began to form in Belius's mind. Those pieces of Michael's brain didn't have to be obtained through only one source. They were scattered far and wide. It didn't even make sense to only send Murmur after them. Surely a couple more *getashi* questers wouldn't hurt. Many new people entered Somnia every day. Okay, he wasn't a hundred percent sure if another player would be immune to the whisperings as he was fairly sure Murmur was—she did have excellent mental shielding by now—but hey, if he was going to be less desirable, then he'd be the best at it ever.

Picking up his sense of pride and his sense of self—both things he'd gained over the last couple of years, not in small amounts directly from Michael—Belius began to form his plan. All he had to do was locate his target, figure out where they'd be next, and insert himself into their game vision. Now. Which NPC would be the best for him to use. Class trainer? It might work; not all class trainers had been given the same autonomy. There had to be bodies for them all to access to reach all different corners of Somnia. Even though each of them had chosen their ultimate characters, Thra had changed hers after Belius decided he'd be a locus too. Something about not leaving all their mains on one island. There were only so many characters they could allow to roam freely. They were pushing the boundaries as it was.

Belius's grin when he sat down at his table didn't reach his eyes. He put his enchanter on auto and slipped into the form he'd need to execute the next stage of his plan.

"Get down!" Murmur yelled instinctively, wishing she could project a real shield over her friends. But the mental shield wasn't going to protect anyone from a physical projectile.

Arrows continued to fly as everyone cowered behind the decaying body of the golem. Magic decayed faster than flesh and since the golem was a magical creation this wasn't going to be an ideal hiding place for long. She glanced around and saw Merlin sneaking to the cover of the trees behind the strange tents the golems used for who knew what. Extending her own sensor net, she encountered what appeared to be a group of archers. Only four, but since they had the advantage of apparently knowing this portion of the mountains very well. Murmur was hesitant on what to do. Guild chat lit up.

Rashlyn: Guys, I think we're under attack.

Devlish: Well, that makes all of us. You guys able to deal with it?

Veranol: Yeah, we'll just make Exbo have to earn his keep for once.

Exbo: Shut up, old man.

Murmur chuckled, their banter loosening the tension in her shoulders. They were going to be fine; she just needed to use her head. Jinna said there were multiple places to level in this mountain range, which meant there were multiple camps of mobs. Considering the intelligence targets had displayed before this, and the noise the golems made, they should have been prepared for something like this. Why wouldn't those other camps have scouts going out to protect the area? She knew that's what she'd do if it were her. She closed her eyes and cast out her mind, feeling for the presence, attempting to see them like she had seen Telvar back on the island. Mind's Eye was proving to be a useful thing, but there wasn't time to dwell on how she obtained it when it wasn't listed as a skill. It was also difficult to use when there was too much action and noise.

"There are four of them out there. As far as I can discern from their flow of thoughts, they're a patrol from another of the camps in these mountains and well. Golems aren't exactly quiet. They must be the *shoot first ask questions later* types." Murmur inched around, reluctantly admitting that their hiding place was about to be compromised, and headed to the closest trees on the left hand side. They needed to get to cover in order to have any chance of returning the ambushing favor. She tried not to let the rising panic in the back of her mind bother her. The others would respawn; the others didn't have as much riding on this. Murmur needed to be more careful, because she couldn't afford an ambush catching her unaware.

Merlin shot a distraction volley up. The skill was a spectacular one. It seemed that most of their group's hidden spells and abilities were born out of a need to protect the group as a whole. A twinge of guilt assailed her, because she knew in a way they were all trying to protect her.

The arrows flew up in the sky, scattering out and almost floating for a second before they zoomed down, directly targeted on the four people attacking them. As soon as they arced over, Murmur and the rest ran for cover, reaching the trees with perfect timing, and narrowly avoided a delayed shower of arrows that landed just short of the tree line. Merlin was a damn good ranger. She'd have to remember to tell him that.

"Beast, can you get Shir-Khan to sneak in and clamp down on one? Like, tear at their Achilles, or sever a hamstring or something? I've seen the way you can work in unison, but does he have any special abilities he can use?" Murmur really hoped that the true pet classes like Beast and Havoc were gifted with more than just their own abilities.

Beastial's eyes unfocused for a moment, and a light frown spread across his face. "Got it. Haven't used it before because I tend to love the fusion combos, but I think we can do that."

Murmur nodded, not yet giving into relief. "We'll need Merlin to root one, and as long as I creep behind Shir-Khan while invisible I should be able to get one of them in my sights and Mez them."

She rubbed her armor while the others muttered their agreement, realizing it would give her some mild protection anyway since their opponents were rangers and not casters. "Sin and Dev, go with the cat so we can start by dropping that one."

"Done." Dev grinned, an almost feral gleam to his eyes. "This is the Mur I like best."

"Shush." She was glad the treeline was dark and hid her blush. She'd almost forgotten how much she loved the strategy and adrenaline rush of a good fight plan. This was nothing, just a mere warm up.

Merlin. Root the one closest to you and creep over to us.

Merlin: Done.

Taking a deep breath, they set out, putting the plan into action. Shir-Khan found a scent and latched on, his movements sure and deft as he wove silently through the undergrowth. It was all Murmur could do to keep up with him, and she was fairly sure her way of traveling totally negated his silence. The only thing she had going for her was that she was invisible.

The tiger latched onto the calf of one of the well-hidden archers. So well-hidden in fact, that Murmur hadn't seen them until the cat dug its teeth in, moving his jaw down and finally anchoring in the mob's Achilles. She gasped and moved on as silently as she could while the others swooped in. Focusing her senses outward, she found herself nearing one of the remaining rangers who seemed to be crouching in wait while trying to figure out where their targets were. Mind's Eye would have been easier to use, but she didn't think she could walk with it yet.

Several more creeping steps and she was behind her newfound prey. A brief twisting of her fingers, and the archer froze in place. Mez would never cease to give Murmur that sense of satisfaction. It grew every day, a little more power in every way. She chuckled softly and moved on, trying to make sure she stayed in reach of her initial target so refreshing the spell was easy. Her target appeared to be an elf, similar to Merlin yet somehow a little different. Her coloring was darker, but she wasn't a dark elf. They probably had directions on which parts of the wood to patrol. When this one didn't answer, and the other who was fighting was dead, surely more would come to their aid.

What if they didn't? What if these two were willing to sacrifice themselves while the others went and fetched more members from their camp? This was not good. Crap. Murmur wracked her brain trying to think clearly, to think what she would do in their place. And there was no way she'd run to help—she'd go fetch another patrol, or just grab more people.

Just as the thoughts ran through her head and she refreshed her Mez, Devlish appeared by her side and spied the next target. "Just one?"

"Well, it's not like they're grouped together. They're scouts. And the other two, because the root has broken by now, are probably fetching reinforcements. If we don't head them off we're probably screwed."

"Damn it." Devlish broke the Mez by hacking away at the scout's less-than-stellar leather armor immediately, and she could see Hatred go into effect in the way the mob shivered and focused on the tank. "What was the matter with dumb mobs? I mean, come on give us a break. Do they really have to be this intelligent?"

Murmur smiled to herself as she followed Merlin. Maybe they didn't have to be this intelligent, but she was pretty sure she knew who made them this way.

Have you got all of your ambush? Or did some get away? Murmur sent the thought off and waited.

Veranol: We got three. One must be running for help

Merlin: We seem to have two runners.

Rashlyn: Shit.

Neva: Are you always so eloquent?

Murmur laughed. *Always.*

Merlin was attempting to use his tracking skill, which he apparently hadn't used since they first began playing because he'd been with the group the whole time and never mentioned having it. Murmur had to bite her tongue to stop from berating him for not making their lives easier, sooner. But he was having enough troubles with getting it to work in this area that she felt like he was already suffering enough. That's what you got when you didn't up your skills. Though the temptation to make him suffer more wasn't helping.

It wouldn't be difficult, she could just coax him, push him...

All it would take was a thought vaguely directed at him. It would easily overwhelm him with frustration, add in a touch of guilt to top it off. His lack of foresight could cost them here; shouldn't he pay for it?

She snapped out of it as he grinned and stood up, pushing down on the shame she felt every time her mind veered in that direction.

"They're headed over that way, but they're not running. They're trying to hide their noise and footsteps. With any luck, we should be able to cut them off before they bring their whole camp down on us."

"With any luck?" Murmur stood, contemplating several choices, kicking herself for not having thought of it earlier. She'd just been so preoccupied with immobilizing them. Her own sensor net couldn't find them, so instead of berating the ranger, she probably needed to strengthen her own skills. "Get me in range. I have an idea."

Merlin raised an eyebrow at her, but moved swiftly and she followed behind, hoping that a mob two levels higher than her wasn't going to resist the crap out of her spell. Moving quickly and quietly was far more difficult than it might seem, but the underbrush was mostly damp, and therefore didn't crackle beneath them. Finally, they were close to one of the elf scouts.

Murmur inched forward and cast her spell as soon as she got in range, releasing it in the blink of an eye with perfect precision. It hit the scout, cascading over her in a whirl of blue incandescence for a split second. And then the scout turned around and joined Murmur, standing at attention. Now she had to gamble that the others wouldn't know their comrade had been charmed. Soothing with her projection, Murmur attempted to coax the scout into understanding their plight. That they'd not even been close to the scout's camp. Since that avenue didn't seem to be working, she attempted the thought process that they weren't going to harm her, which seemed to settle her down just a little. The scout was strong-minded and took a lot more thought projection than Murmur had ever used, but finally the danger of breaking the charm immediately died down a fraction. There was no doubt that if she set this scout to attack another scout, it would end up breaking the charm.

Murmur suggested, just barely, just sort of on the outside chance that the archer would help, to please ask her friends to stop. Even as the scout scowled, Murmur could almost hear the thought go out. Begrudgingly, her pet glanced at her, and the disparity in levels grated against Murmur's will. She needed to up her charisma. She needed to up her mana pool. Stupid game giving her only four points per level. It was exhausting, even as the rest of the group found them and hid while they waited for the rest of the scouts to come back.

There was something off about this scout. She was stronger in magical will than Murmur had expected, and somehow highly aware that the spell being used on her was controlling her actions and mind. And then it hit her.

"Shit." Murmur muttered softly, drawing the eyes of the rest of her group to her with questioning eyebrows raised. "These mobs already have their hybrid skills."

A ripple of unease spread through the group at the realization that these scouts and their camp would all be level twenty or above, and most probably had accessed the hybrid skill set. While it may have unsettled the others, all it made her do was want to hit level twenty so she, too, could have a set of hybrid skills. She basically just wanted to take a hit better than she could right now. Anything to gain more survivability in a game she wasn't sure she could survive.

There was no time for those sobering thoughts as the scouts crept into the small copse they were in. It was difficult to see them at first, considering their gear was a strange sort of camouflage. It blended in and out of the trees as they moved, the brush providing the perfect cover as the cloth they wore played tricks on their eyes. Sort of like Murmur's armor.

Then everything happened at once.

Murmur's charge broke her charm with one huge exertion of willpower, so big it almost knocked the wind out of the psionicist. Stumbling, Murmur placed one hand on the ground and immediately cast Mez on that same target. Luckily, since she'd nullified it while charmed, it froze the hybrid scout in place, a look of shock replacing her gloating.

With surefire arrows, Merlin sealed another of them in a root, and Devlish had already hurled himself toward it, while the third tried to slink back into the shadows but found Shir-Khan briefly attached to its leg, which gave Murmur just enough time to Mez it too. She had to give Beastial props for the attack as well as knowing not to allow the cat to use a DoT ability.

"Try to keep it quiet. We don't know how close we are to their headquarters, and the last thing we need is dozens of these hybrids descending on us." Murmur kept her voice calm as she watched them fight the only scout she thought wasn't a hybrid. She didn't seem capable of using anything but her bow and small knife. Her health went down faster than Murmur thought it would. However the other two were different. She'd still not figured out what their hybrid classes were, which meant it was difficult to gauge just what they could do, but for now keeping them locked down was her job.

The first one dispatched, Devlish broke the Mez with Hatred on the one farthest away. Murmur still didn't understand how he generated his hidden abilities. It left the one who'd escaped her charm slowly glaring daggers into Murmur's back. Her shoulders began to feel a tad uncomfortable. Maybe she was part mage; it would explain why her resistances were so high. Refreshing Nullify and Mez, Murmur felt a bit safer, and backed behind the group, keeping a sharp eye on her tricky target.

Devlish visibly taunted the crap out of that mob using his normal Terror taunt, but its eyes never left Murmur, not even for a second. They followed her wherever she moved, hungrily, eager for revenge.

Murmur gulped when the second scout died, feeling guilty for luring them into her trap. But, to be fair, this was a case of eat or be eaten. Or killed, however you looked at it. She'd done what needed to be done to protect her guild, to protect herself. Luckily, she'd not used one of her MA abilities, because she'd probably be on the bottom of the karma pile right now. Although they did ambush them first, so technically this was all in self-defense. She really needed to talk to Telvar about the karma thing.

When Devlish broke the Mez, the scout took one hit with the shield right in the gut, and vanished. Almost as if they'd practiced, the other four in her group closed ranks around Murmur, because the scout was likely looking for a way to kill the person who'd enslaved it.

"Knew it was a hybrid, didn't think it'd be a mage." Havoc whispered under his breath. "Once she drops her invis, she won't be able to activate that Blink skill for another few minutes, so that'll be our chance."

Murmur nodded, grateful for Havoc's quiet observance. "Let's give her some bait then, shall we?"

Beastial raised an eyebrow. "Seriously? You're bait now?"

Sinister shrugged. "I've got her. She'll cast her own shield, I'll pop a HoT on her. It'll be fine."

Casting the shield, Murmur grinned. "Hopefully it'll make me irresistible."

Sin winked. "You know you are, baby."

With a chuckle, Sin backed away from her guard spot, only to encounter the scout materializing behind her as she sank a dagger into Sinister's ribs.

CHAPTER SEVENTEEN

Feeding Revenge

Somnia Online Location: Ululate
Beneath the Dunkel Tavern: Rogue Trainer Lair
Seven Days Post Launch

Jirald walked into his trainer's lair, irritated that he'd not hit eighteen yet. He was close, but since he'd just leveled up his shadow affinity, it was more important to come and see his trainer than to gain that next physical level. The back room of the seediest tavern in Stellaein hid the trapdoor that led to the lair of thieves. Three taps against it and the floor opened. Just looking at the ground wouldn't reveal the entrance, as it was seamless and well-hidden.

He jumped down, landing lightly on his feet and nodded to the large bouncer who guarded the door well. He definitely wouldn't want to go up against Brutus. Jirald meandered down the hall, scraping his dirty nails along the compacted walls, barely making a dent and nodded to the barkeep, who shot him a sideways glare.

Jirald chuckled. Most people were the same in this place. They wanted him to be sketchy, but they didn't really want him to act like it. Thing was, the more he sunk himself into this world, into the play style his character required—the less he ever wanted to log off.

The less he wanted to go back to the human realm.

Pushing into his trainer's room without knocking—you didn't have to be that polite when you were a thief and assassin—he stopped short as he realized there was a second man he'd not seen before standing in there speaking to the trainer in hushed tones. The new man was tall for a human, his dark hair cropped close as was his beard and mustache. He looked almost like a swashbuckling pirate, except his clothes were all black and practically blended in and out with the walls.

"There you are." Talyn motioned for Jirald to come over. "I was just telling my boss all about you and your newest path."

Jirald raised an eyebrow and walked a few steps closer, although he didn't bow. Instead he waited, arms crossed with impatience. They'd better not waste his time. He had an enchanter to torment, a guild to destroy, and a game to win.

If Talyn was taken aback by his pupil's response, he didn't show it, but a brief wave of irritation passed over the other's face.

"This is Sidius. He's visiting. Heard you'd followed the darkest path you could and was curious." Talyn glanced at the massive clock behind him. "Oh, would you look at the time. I'll leave you two to it."

Before he passed Jirald, Talyn leaned in close. "He's better than you. Trust me. Don't test him too much. He's not as easy going as I am. I'd say good luck, but I need it more than you do."

Talyn laughed as he closed the door behind him.

Sidius moved languidly, almost like a snake, his dark hair and eyes blending in with the rest of him. "So, you're Jirald then."

Jirald raised an eyebrow. "And?"

Sidius didn't seem impressed. He simply waited, inspecting his own perfectly manicured fingernails until Jirald began to feel somewhat uncomfortable.

"I'm Jirald. What of it?" He managed to squeeze out the words.

This time Sidius seemed to take it a little better. "You've delved down my path. I thought you might want to talk to someone who's been there." He walked around Jirald slowly, arms crossed, frowning. His eyes flickered in such a way that the thief thought the man might be able to see through him. Maybe even read his mind—but not even the headset could pluck actual thoughts from his head, could it?

"You've already accessed your Light Shifting ability. Impressive. Being able to maneuver light in such a way that it fools your opponents." There was approval running through Sidius's voice, almost like a purr. "Excellent."

Then he paused, standing directly behind Jirald, so close that the scent of cinnamon on his breath reached the newfound thief. "Tell me...what is your motivation? Why are you here? Out of all the rogues we have in this world, you're the only one other than myself so far to have sought out this particular path. So, why?"

Jirald had to swallow his immediate response. *Fuck you* was becoming less witty repartee and more reflex for him, and for some reason he didn't think Sidius would take well to being told to fuck off. NPC or not, there was an aura to this character that transcended what he'd met before, and made him think more deeply. Thoughts flitted through his head. He wanted strength, he wanted power, but at the pinnacle, he wanted respect—and he'd get that through revenge. He wanted people to acknowledge the skill level he possessed, and to make that group pay for all the humiliation and trauma they'd caused him.

It never entered his mind that others might be just as good as him. He wanted people to see him and Exodus and have that flush of respect hit their system. Every one of his friends was worth a thousand of Murmur and hers, he was sure of that.

He had to try hard not to growl, not to let it get the best of him. Sidius stepped around the side, his dark brown eyes taking in every single nuance of Jirald's behavior. In a way it was like an X-ray, and the locus rogue was fully aware it was happening. He took in a deep breath. It was never a good thing to give away too much of yourself.

"I have my reasons."

Sidius laugh was cruel. There was an edge of madness to it, a warning that made Jirald gasp slightly, bringing on a wariness he'd not yet felt in Somnia. "You can have your *reasons,* but I need to know them. I can't read your mind; I'm not an enchanter."

At the mention of her class, Jirald's temper boiled over. He would grasp at anything that might make him stronger, that might make him reach his goal sooner. "There's this girl and her friends. They took something from me in a previous world. Something that shouldn't have been theirs, something we deserved more than they did."

"Oh, I see." And this time the hunger in Sidius's eyes was frightening. "Revenge is one of the best motivators. Now. Let's see how we can best get you what you seek, shall we?"

"No!" Murmur yelled out as Sinister's eyes opened wide. It wasn't that she thought her friend couldn't die and come back, but in her own mind death was possibly permanent, and any injury or death scared her. She instinctively distance stunned the scout's ass, holding it in place an entire twelve seconds while the others began to wail on her. With Havoc's multiple DoTs in place, there was no way for her to hide again. Making a note to herself, she realized they should probably have a damage over time spell break all of the Mezmerizes so there was no way for them to pull shit like that.

She cradled Sinister and cast her mind shielding around her friend.

"Whoa, pain receptors." Sinister coughed the words out, blood spittle forming on her lips. "Shit."

She waved one hand out, and a small stream of blood began to flow from the scout to Sinister. It wasn't as strong as usual, but Sin also wasn't at her best. Slowly, Murmur watched while Sinister healed herself up. That had to have been a major critical hit or something. She clutched at her friend as the scout finally died, and watched her pale face fade back into the strong purple it had been before.

"I'll be okay Mur. I can die, remember?" Sin pushed herself up, still at three quarter health, and brushed her robe off. "Damn it, that hurt. Wasn't only a critical hit but in a critical location. I think it's not only getting more specific on where you need to aim, but I truly think Somnia's NPCs are getting more intelligent and skillful. They don't just wildly swing their weapons; they're adept at using them."

"No kidding." Devlish ran a hand over his neck. "The way they parry and block my attacks is one of the most frustrating things I've ever experienced. And yet somehow totally an adrenaline rush."

"Still not sure how they manage to parry you, block my cat's jaws, and dodge Merlin's arrows all at the same time." Beastial grumbled, picking out the last of a shaft wedged in Shir-Khan's hide. A low growl emanated from the cat as it was removed, and Beastial scratched its eyebrow ridge, as he funneled a pet-only heal toward it. "Brave kitty."

"They're trained. We're not the only ones with skills." Havoc shrugged, obviously almost over whatever bee had been buzzing around in his bonnet recently. "Somnia isn't your average game. We have a powerful ally in Telvar, which we managed to come across way before I think we were meant to. Mur is in a bloody coma, and yet able to log in here and feel like a real person, which is great for us all. You have to admit the headgear we're using is something different to let us do all of this. It's not your average *oh, let's give the players virtual immersion experience* headgear." He paused, trying to direct a smile in Mur's direction, which she nodded at. His tension lifted visibly. "Add to that the mobs we fight learn, the sects we encounter have a memory that transcends their virtual deaths, and our actions and conduct can trigger a whole slew of hidden abilities and quests? Yeah, this doesn't even feel like a game. It seems real as hell until I log out. And even then I'm thinking about it all the time."

No one spoke. No one had anything to say. Mainly because he was right.

"Does that mean the objective is different?" Merlin asked quietly.

"What do you mean, the objective?" Murmur asked pointedly, crossing her arms.

The ranger turned to face her. "I mean exactly that. What do we usually do when we play a game? We level, we form a guild, we kill all the shit as soon as we can and preferably first—before anyone else in the game can. By doing so we make a name for ourselves and get recruits, build our guild up stronger and then tackle the big guns: the amazing dungeons, the contested monsters. All of it. It's what we do, what we've always done. But this game is different to everything we've ever played. We're only just learning how different. So my question is, what if these keys we're pursuing aren't the be all and end all of this game. What if it's something else?"

"Any idea what?" Veranol pushed through some of the brush, his eyes only briefly resting on the decaying body of the scout lying at their feet. "We came to look for you and our missing scout, but I guess you found it for us. Those bloody scouts disrupted our golem camp. We're going to have to break it in again. Now. What do you think this difference is?"

Havoc shrugged, and his tone returned to that bored quality Murmur hated so much. "I don't know. Just, things work differently here. Intuitive quests instead of these cookie cutter, tell-you-exactly-what-to-do things. Normal abilities and hidden abilities depending on how you interpret certain things NPCs have said, or how you notice things. I think I'll be extremely disappointed if the end game of this game is just like all the worlds I've been in before."

"You make a good point." Rashlyn, walked over and stood next to Sinister, concern furrowing her brow. "You don't look good, Sin."

Sin smiled back. "S'all good, just literally got stabbed in what I think was my kidney. The pain receptors in this game are evil. But you know, it is what it is. This conversation however, is interesting, I want to know more."

"More?" Rash looked confused for a moment. "Oh, you mean like about how and what here...cool."

She looked like she was sulking, but Murmur dismissed it. Rash liked to be the center of attention. As sweet and caring as she was, sometimes all she wanted to do was fight, and talking out tactics or figuring out game strategy, well. It wasn't really her thing. She was a punch first and ask questions later sort of person. Which is why the name Rash suited her. Murmur nudged her and smiled, which earned her a relieved grin and a head rested on her shoulder. Mur hugged her monk friend briefly, marveling at the tangible sensations that made everything feel so real.

Merlin, Havoc, and Veranol were still talking, but it didn't take long to bring the viking up to speed.

Veranol shook his head and scowled. "That doesn't even make sense."

Havoc rolled his eyes. "Of course it does. You've seen the bosses now, and they're babies! Can you imagine the end game raid mobs? We'll probably end up needing fifty people who have enough coordination to avoid all their special attacks, in order to outmaneuver and outsmart one of these bosses. If it's even possible. Hell, Telvar is on our side. He could have cleaved us in two. He's wicked smart. Use him as a template for what endgame will look like— we're going to be in a world of hurt."

Silence fell over the small thicket, and Murmur couldn't help but agree with the necromancer. Except for one thing of course. No one else realized that Telvar was actually one of the AIs running the game. Maybe that made him even more formidable.

Sin stepped in the middle of the two arguers. "Guys. We're level...almost nineteen. How about we rectify that before we start deciding what the end game is going to be like? It's hard to be the top of the end game if we never get there."

Havoc interjected, his voice dripping with sarcasm. "You think? At this rate we're not even going to hit fifty with all these stupidly in-depth discussions. Just kill shit and ask questions later."

Murmur cringed. One did just not sarcasm at Sin.

Sin spoke, her voice encased in a smooth, steely smile. It was the voice she used when she was irritated. "That's what I just said. Except for the damned questions, Havoc. This world doesn't work like that. Get your smug smile off your face and pull out some of that DPS necros are supposed to be able to throw around. Stop playing it safe."

Havoc glared at her, and his pet moved restlessly as if it fed off his emotions. "Fine. I'll pull fucking aggro then and see if you can't keep me alive."

Sinister shrugged. "Whatever. You'll come back again no matter how often we kill you. Better you than Mur."

Murmur flinched. Silence settled over them for a moment.

No one said a word, and the silence drew on longer until Sinister clapped her hands together.

"Now, I'd like to suggest we all get to leveling. The best idea is probably to go back to the boring ass golems. They were ridiculous experience once they fell. I'm not far from nineteen, which I know you guys must—wait, Ver you're already nineteen. You suck. Everyone else, we need to level." She turned on her heel and began to head back to their camp, Havoc glowering in her wake. "It's amazing how there aren't even bears in this wood. Wouldn't you think there'd be bears?"

A sudden roar tore through the trees causing snow to dislodge from the branches and tumble to the ground with a heavy thud like a fallen corpse. Sinister turned back to the group.

"Is it too late to take that back?"

You have encountered Disestru, the giant bear. He doesn't like to be roused from his sleep. Watch out, his claws and teeth don't need to touch you to kill you. Probably shouldn't have been making so much noise before checking for caves in the area.

As usual, the quest help was distinctly vague and in this instance, sort of insulting. Murmur sighed, her fingers moving so fast she couldn't even see them herself, she buffed the entire group while forming the raid, and managing to stay on her feet as yet another rumbling roar tore through the area. They'd been standing in the best place for a fight initially, and it didn't take them long to pull back into the copse.

Glancing the way the scouts had returned from, Murmur spoke quickly, gesturing toward the trees. "Merlin, Exbo, if you have traps, can you lay them through that way, make sure no scouts creep up on us?"

"On it." Merlin nodded, moving quickly and silently, and Murmur turned her attention elsewhere.

The next roar shook the trees, and the ground rumbled. She really didn't feel like fighting a huge ass whatever this was. All Murmur wanted to do was level safely. This didn't seem like it was going to be safe. Three seconds later, it came into view.

Bear wasn't exactly how Murmur would have described it. Instead, she'd probably call it a cross between a wolf, bear, and mountain troll that somehow had the worst features of each creature. It sashayed in on all fours, huge globs of green drool dripping from its mouth. She was starting to see a theme with these monsters.

"I'm guessing Dev and Rash need a disease resist, Ver." She muttered, as the thing rose on its hind legs and bellowed once more. The stench of its roar eclipsed any and all of the rumbling and shaking it caused. It was massive. "They might need a ladder too."

Mellow and Jinna laughed, but Devlish and Rashlyn went a few shades paler than before.

"Relax guys, it's just a big rotting half deformed troll bear type thing." Beastial tried to ease the tension and failed abysmally.

His shield hefted in his left hand, his second axe forgotten, Devlish managed to block the monstrosity's first hit. The moment he managed to hold his own, the debuffs flew in. Murmur cast her own DoT with its armor class reduction, Weakness, and Feeble Body, Nullify. Anything she could throw at it. There was nothing around them to charm, so she just made sure to stun periodically, although it barely lasted a second. Something about the difficulty of the mob brought the effectiveness of her spells down. Without her debuffs, especially Nullify, she was quite certain she wouldn't haven landed any other spells. She guessed there were some things that were going to be completely immune to some of her shit. Otherwise they'd have to balance the class because people would be crying that enchanters were way overpowered. She still thought they were a bit.

Devlish glowed with a metallic aura every time he used his hidden ability, Hatred. A bronze miasma of strength leaked around him, sealing in his shadows, making them more compact, stronger. His form took on sinuous strength that reinforced every hit he landed, and some of the shadows leaked over to the monster, effectively diminishing some of its hit points every tick. The best part was that Hatred really made the damned mob look at Dev no matter what.

Sinister was creating and utilizing Blood Bombs. It seemed they'd severely grown in potency since she first got them. Now, they healed the whole group with a pungent shower of blood transfusion.

Mellow had pulled out their cauldron. Its cast iron frame with bubbling interior liquid was as stereotypical for a witch as it could get. Every time they reached in and pulled out another vial of magical something to throw at the mob, it glugged like it was gulping in air. The way it smoked over the top made it seem like dry ice had been dropped inside, but knowing there was no dry ice anywhere in the game made Murmur shiver.

Merlin and Exbo released volleys of arrows, all of them sticking true and fast to the troll-like thickness of the monster's skin. But after a couple of shakes the arrows fell harmlessly to the ground, barely doing any damage whatsoever. It seemed the best line of offense was going to be attacking with a series of damage over time solutions and simply whittling the massive thing down. This was going to be a battle of endurance. Whether their health and mana could outlast this giant...thing.

Rashlyn and Devlish ducked and dodged, swapping out with different attacks, and the monster's health was inching down. Everyone's mana was okay, as long as they were careful with it. Luckily they all had Murmur's Mana Tide. She couldn't wait for the damned bard to get Mana Song.

Havoc's pet was definitely larger than it had been in the lower levels. Like Beastial, some of the necromancer's hidden abilities involved his pet, which made sense. Beastmasters and necromancers were reliant on their pets for a chunk of their damage. Jinna's dual wielding was a cut above the rest. His speed and precision almost caused her to let one of her spells drop, because she was wrapped up watching him. He activated Sneak tirelessly, and backstabbed the blasted creation multiple times, and still, all they could do was chip away at its health bar.

Dansyn was miraculous to watch. He'd obtained a new instrument from somewhere. Either that, or he'd just never had a need to use it before. He flitted here and there, his music soft and nothing like the battle music she'd originally had to turn off, but soothing and calming, it helped her focus. A faint stream of musical notes seemed to follow him around, lending to his magical air.

And then, the rotting bear hit eighty percent.

As its health status ticked down, it was almost like Murmur could see its movements in slow motion. After another massive attack on Devlish's Telvar shield, it sank to all fours, opened its mouth and roared. Green, toxic spittle flew out over the copse, sizzling where it hit the trees, the ground—anything that it could eat through.

But even though she was certain it should have hit them, there was no acid eating through her gorgeous armor. None eating through anyone in the group. There were no screams and no disgusted mutterings from Sinister. Glancing around as they continued their attack, she realized Veranol was sweating, profusely. "Ver?"

As the bear-beast-thing ticked down to seventy-eight percent health, he nodded. "Yeah. But I can't cast that dome again for at least another five minutes. It's a protective ward, and it takes a shit load of effort and Mana Deftness."

"But technically you could cast it at around forty percent as well, right?" Possibilities ran rampant in Murmur's mind as she tried to figure out ways to counter that acid attack.

"I got the forty percent. I hope." He smiled wanly, and she was pretty sure it wrecked him the same way her MA draining wrecked her.

"I'll rune everyone as we get down to sixty percent; that might help fight it a bit." She bit her lip, a tad worried about how they were going to make it through the next round.

"I'll sacrifice my pet." Havoc piped up, his tone somber. "It'll drastically reduce my damage output, but I did get a new ability that allows me to sacrifice my pet for seven Bone Clouds, as I take the brunt of a special ability. I'll have to time it right though."

"Bone Clouds?" Beastial cracked a smile despite dodging another hefty paw. "I'm loving this shit."

Havoc scowled. "I'm sure I can distance myself just out of your range."

Murmur laughed. "Do whatever you can. Can you cast another pet in combat?"

He nodded, eyes never leaving the mob. "I can, but I won't be able to take the brunt at twenty percent because Bone Clouds are a bitch to work up." Leeroy let out a shrieking wail and pressed both arms toward their target. A trail of thick, black ooze began to flow from the beast into the pet, drops of it splashing down to the ground below as the beast squealed in pain.

Havoc's grin was nothing short of eager. For just a second, Murmur rethought her whole opinion of her friend until she realized, she probably had the same eagerness on her face whenever she executed one of her new skills. While the others continued to hack away, Murmur kept her eye on the necromancers skills, mildly jealous of the class.

When Disestru was at sixty-seven percent, Murmur began to get worried. The sheer concentration this fight took out of her was exhausting. Dodging the swipes that seemed to extend infinitely was a job in itself. She directed her question at Havoc, trying to learn more about his Sacrifice Pet skill. "What's your range? I can just cast the runes on the final one if we need."

He shrugged. "From the description it should cover anyone within Disestru's range. I just have to concentrate, because I believe timing the sacrifice is what makes it effective."

"You believe, or you know?" Rash grunted as she barely dodged a swipe of an acidic claw.

Havoc shrugged. "Well, I know how it works in theory. I haven't used it before. Only just got it before we came to the golems. Just be ready to heal us in case the theory doesn't translate well to the practical."

Murmur was pretty sure they were all sighing internally, but it wasn't going to help now anyway. It wasn't like he'd had a chance to use the ability in an actual fighting situation where it counted yet. Watching their target's health tick down took forever.

Even though it enabled her to get a good grip on her raid's abilities, time seemed to flow slowly while they fought. Veranol's wards were powerful, and helped absorb a lot of hits. He seemed to keep them on the healers, tanks, and herself. His focus was exemplary, and Murmur wished she could emulate him considering how often her mind had wondered lately.

Jinna managed to dodge in and out of the thing's back paws as it moved. It wasn't fast, and occasionally its health would drop almost a percent as Jinna executed one of his Backstab abilities and hit a critical spot.

Having Disestru targeted, she could see as he motioned, landing back down on all fours, about to begin his attack. A high-pitched shriek split the air, and Havoc's pet skeleton burst into splinters, shooting straight up into the air like a fountain of bone. No acid dripped on any of them, none hit the ground or the trees either.

Only Havoc doubled up in pain, fell to the ground, and gasped for air.

Murmur ran to him, kneeling down as the others continued the fight.

"You okay?" she asked, worried about him. He wouldn't have cried out like that if it hadn't hurt.

"Yeah. Those side effects they caution you about are nothing to sneeze at." He grinned weakly, stood up, and began to resummon his pet. "Guess when they said you will feel a portion of the pain that would have been caused, although it will do no damage—they really meant it."

Murmur cringed at the description. That had to be horribly painful. "Sorry. But thanks. Now Ver can take over at forty percent, and we'll figure something out for twenty percent."

"We could always play dancing around the acid drops." Dansyn grinned, as he danced around anyway. Him and his bloody puns on words. It was an old test to see who truly sucked. If there was shit on the ground, you danced around it. Those who didn't, failed the test.

"I can probably try and absorb the hit." Devlish admitted grudgingly, even though it might only have sounded that way because he was currently braced for the next blow to try and knock him off his feet. "I can activate this weird ten second immunity thing I have."

"What? It doesn't have a name?" Jinna grunted.

"Shut it, dwarf. I can activate it sort of with timing like Havoc's. I just don't know if it's going to be enough damage protection." He didn't seem entirely averse to dying for the good of the group, and grinned as he added the next. "I suppose Rash can tank long enough for me to hoof it back."

"Don't be an idiot." Veranol spoke up. "I'll ward you and Mur will shield you. That and your absorption should be enough to mostly keep you alive. Probably."

Devlish laughed. "Oh fantastic, such a vote of confidence."

"At least they're willing to try," Sinister piped up. "Me? I guess I'll heal you, though it's more fun to watch you die."

Beastial glanced at her. "Sometimes I think you're a very complicated person, Sin."

She only answered with a grin.

When the bear-monster finally got to forty percent, Disestru sank into its stance and did the usual spit, for which Veranol activated his ward again. However, it appeared Disestru's attack had gained another component. From his crouching stance he then jumped forward, slamming both paws onto Devlish's shield and the tank almost into the ground. Only Veranol's ward saved him.

"Fuck," Merlin whispered from his spot next to Murmur. "Rash, can you steal his aggro while he's got that bubble on him?"

She shrugged. "I can try. My super skills involve dodging one hundred percent of attacks for several seconds. I don't have anything that says *look at me* more than a normal taunt."

Devlish grimaced.

"Wait!" The sudden idea came to Murmur, and she had no idea why she'd not thought of it before. "I'll bind you. Swap for a bit."

It took a few seconds, but Devlish freed himself of aggro mostly, jogging over to the side as his health filled back up, and Murmur bound him quickly. "I know it means you'll have to run on the way back, but we can probably just bee line it for the city and go crashing through the trees."

"As long as we don't get another bear." He chuckled and ran back into place. Down to thirty percent, and their mana pools were starting to get precariously low. Such a long fight impacted their regeneration abilities significantly.

Murmur shuddered to think how bad it would be if she didn't have Mana Tide on all the magic users, and she got the feeling that this bear had been intended for a larger raid.

At twenty-one percent Murmur cast her shield on Rash, Dev, Sin, and herself. She saw Veranol's ward go up just before the bear crouched, and everyone braced for impact.

Apparently Devlish's super absorption worked. But the acid ate through Murmur's shield, Veranol's ward, and dropped Dev's health down about sixty-five percent. Frantically casting another shield, Mur watched as Veranol recast his ward, and just as Disestru came down with both front paws, she remembered her special ability.

Without a second thought, Mur reached within and pulled out Forestall Death, just as the giant mangled bear made contact with Devlish's chest. She could still see Sinister's heals landing on him, her heal over time as well as Ver's, and hoped against hope that she'd been quick enough for her spell to kick in.

CHAPTER EIGHTEEN

Bearly There

Somnia Online location: Ululate
Dunkel Inn Meeting Room Two
Seven Days Post Launch

Jirald paced the tavern room they'd booked for this guild meeting. "We really need to get a guild hall. Sooner than later preferably."

"Sure," drawled Ishwa. "I'll get right on that, your highness."

Masha chuckled, hiding it unsuccessfully behind his hand.

Jirald's eyes flashed, and he visibly tried to calm himself, stretching his jaw to release some tension while he remembered Sidius's advice. He didn't like to be as uptight as this game made him. Everything in this world was magnified. His thoughts, his actions, his need for recognition; that lust for revenge. As creepy as the NPC had been, he'd also made a lot of sense. He might even be right. Everyone around him had their own agenda too, but if he could get them to follow him, or at least head in the direction he wanted, then they were tools he could use.

In order to achieve that though, he had to keep a cap on his temper, and try and calm his thoughts down. Somnia had a way of bringing out his compulsions with pinpoint focus, and some of them were things he wasn't entirely proud of.

Still, the goal remained, and to get to it he needed everyone's help.

He forced a smile, trying to lift his lips in the way he would in the real world, only the locus face didn't bend that way. At least not when he tried it. "Sure. Make fun of me now. I bet Fable already has a base."

Jirald wasn't sure if they did, but he was aware of Ishwa's pride in Exodus, and how to rile the little gnome up.

Ishwa's eyes flashed angrily. "Look, a headquarters doesn't make or break a guild. It might help, but it's not the guild. Our funds are getting close, and we have an eye on a good plot of land. We should have enough for the deposit soon."

Masha raised an eyebrow. "Where's this plot of land?"

"My continent." Ishwa didn't miss a beat. "Trust me, we want our base there."

"Great. We need a tank." Jirald, had grown bored with the conversation already. The seed of urgency planted, what they needed was to get the group together and start leveling. He was itching to hit the hybrid level. Itching to get closer to where he could prove he excelled at any class, even if he couldn't go one on one with her anymore. Hatred mixed with a sense of self-loathing seethed inside him, making him stronger, building in the darkest place in his heart. He only hated himself because he was weak by comparison, because he needed to be more than he was, to be greater. Sidius told him what to do, and how to gain more power. The quest practically consumed him with a driving force to obtain the items, and receive the reward.

The sooner they set out, the better. With Jirald as damage, Masha as their healer, and Ishwa as a mage, they needed a tank, and preferably a ranger, and probably another caster. Then they'd plow through shit.

Ishwa seemed lost as he stared in front of him, but then the old gnome blinked and refocused. "Okay, I've got three coming, but only because I convinced them I'd make sure you were on your best behavior, Jirald. That little stunt you pulled with trying to attack another guild leader when we were near Ululate, the trouble you went through over in Hazen swamp, and the forum crap? That shit isn't going to fly again. Keep that up and I'm going to have to boot you from the guild regardless of your history with it."

Jirald swallowed his original response and simply nodded. The gnome was right, even if it was difficult to admit. And it was all he could do not to flare up in anger. His temper had become more unmanageable, almost unreasonable. Sometimes it was like wrestling with an alligator. He needed his guild and the few people who'd actually managed to remain friends with him despite the incidents he'd already caused. For him to remain a member, he had to watch his behavior more. Painful as it was to admit it, Murmur drove him mad, and that madness rubbed off on his guild mates like a bad stench. "I'll rein it in."

Masha cleared his throat. "You? That's a first. But if you're willing to put in that much effort, I guess I'll heal your ass."

Jirald dropped his head, eyes focused on the ground as he counted to five in his head to stop his stupid temper from jumping out of him. Masha was one of the good ones. He judged based on how well one played their character, not on stupid things like personality or how well people got along together.

Suddenly Masha's hand was on his shoulder, giving him a tight squeeze of camaraderie. "Don't get too hung up on things just yet. We have a long way to go in this game, and it's not easy. The mobs aren't stupid; you're going to need your wits to survive. We're going to need kickass damage to make it, too. So get your head out of your butt, and act like the gamer you are. When you've achieved other measures of success, then you can own whomever you want to."

Jirald blinked at the healer and realized Masha was far more observant than he let on. A grin crossed the rogue's face. At least he hadn't alienated Masha. Now all he had to do was get his hands on some of those black Shards and Sidius's quest would reward him well.

Rash stepped in front of Disestru, hitting her Dodge ability to avoid all incoming attacks for eight seconds, and Murmur continued to debuff the huge monstrosity, constantly eyeing Dev's hit points in the corner of her vision and willing Forestall Death to kick in. It seemed like it took an age, but suddenly his hit points started rising again, and he simply stood up where he'd dropped.

She heaved a sigh of relief, noticing that her chest had become painful, and realized she hadn't been expecting him to stand back up. In-game or not, watching someone die wasn't her favorite thing.

Devlish's health topped out when Disestru hit eighteen percent, shaking his head as if to clear some disorientation. He eyed Murmur with a definitive nod. "Well, that was fucking painful. But thanks Mur. I like that better than the experience loss from dying."

Rash began to Backfist, returning the next four attacks successfully, while Devlish triggered Terror on the huge deformed bear in order to build up hate. Finally, after what seemed like an age but was only about two percent of its health bar, Dev regained the majority of the aggro, and Rashlyn stepped back. Which was good. Rashlyn was a fine tank—excellent even—but this mob was definitely not good for a monk. While she could dodge about ninety-five percent of all of its attacks, the ones that did land sent her plummeting down to twenty-five percent life, and shields and wards and heals frantically tried to help the life bar fill back up before the next attack connected.

Murmur let out a pent up sigh of relief, not fond of the close call that had been. Discovering each other's skills as they fought was probably not her best tactic. As the game got more difficult, she knew they'd have to wipe multiple times before they could defeat a boss. In order to keep her alive, she was probably going to have to stay close to Merlin so he could Evac her if shit hit the fan.

Havoc maintained his DoTs, his pet back up to full power after his resummoning. It cut a formidable figure as it floated above Disestru. Exbo and Merlin's shots were finally sticking into open wounds that no longer closed on the beast, causing it to balk in pain, the damage significant.

Dansyn wove around its feet in an intricate dance that slowed it even more, and Mellow blinded the boss with a flash powder that showered yellow dust over its eyes, making it blink rapidly and lash out blindly with its paws.

Finally, Dev landed a blow with his axe that pierced through the weakened ancient hide to hit the heart. The resounding thud made them all stumble as Disestru landed in a heap on the copse floor.

Congratulations, you have slain the disease-ridden Disestru. Make sure you check yourself for any after effects. His lair may have some useful items for you; it might just be worth finding it. Be cautious. It's said that some people may worship beings like this monstrosity. You may have just made an enemy.

You gain experience!

DING!

Murmur smiled, despite the death warning. Couldn't have given that to them beforehand could they? The whole raid dinged. Another huge boss managed to give them a massive chunk of experience.

"Hey," she said, patting Dev on the shoulder for once. "That was a nice bit of teamwork there. You absorb a massive hit, and I keep you alive. Makes me almost feel like a healer again."

"Hey!" Sin glared at Mur, but it was half-hearted at best.

Dev laughed. "Oh, I'm just irritated I didn't think of anything else to do that could have saved my own ass. Without that ridiculously overpowered ability of yours, I'd have been dead."

Murmur shrugged. "Probably, but it's not easy to time. If you take other damage before the killing blow lands, I'm not sure if it'll still take effect. I think it has to be activated before that blow, because otherwise it's used on something that wouldn't have killed you. Not exactly a skill I can test out much, you know? We probably got really lucky using it this time."

"I'll take that luck anytime. Thanks, Mur." He didn't seem to want to let it go, or to let it be chalked up to luck. Murmur knew he wasn't going to back down, so she just nodded.

"This one has another of those weird stones on it, Mur." Merlin stood, brushing the dirt off his hands. "And one of those crystals. And some wacky thick looking leather. A lot of it. Keep a hold of it?"

She rolled her eyes. "Of course. Luckily we now have guild inventory storage on the island that I can empty all this shit into."

Rash stood up, holing a large key. "I didn't even realize bears had the right type of hands for this."

A low chuckle rumbled around the group, loosening the tension. From what she could tell, Murmur didn't think death or near death in this game was easy. It seemed to shoot pain through them, as if they were really dying, and while it might not be as dialed up as it could be, the after effects still seemed jarring. Hell, she'd not even died yet and she'd managed to feel pain, probably a lot less than Devlish had just experienced. It made her wonder how many people just kept coming back because of the rampant realism of it all. And how many secretly loved it.

"Cave! Let's find it!" Beastial turned around to Sinister, wagging his finger in her face. "Oh, and I don't owe you shit now. Who's the one who said oh gee, don't you think there should be bears here?"

"Well, don't you? It's a forest. Also, don't wag your finger at me. Finger waggers don't get heals." Sinister crossed her arms and Beast looked appealingly at Veranol.

The huge viking shrugged and held his hands out in front of him dismissively. "Don't bring me into this. Finger waggers get jack shit from me too."

Beastial pouted, scratching his cat's head. "No one gets me but you."

Murmur laughed and moved on with her friends, leaving Beastial to hurry after them.

The cave wasn't that far away. If they'd even taken five minutes to send Merlin or Exbo out to scout the area they would have known better than to be so loud. She was still being far too short sighted with this game. The monsters in it didn't react the same way as they did in other games. They were clever. It required a total adaption of how she dealt with them.

At least she'd gotten another piece of Michael's brain, which meant it was another piece she could keep Belius from getting. Another piece of the literal brain puzzle, now wrapped in a piece of her old robe just in case it had ill effects no one had discovered yet. Maybe if Telvar researched it, he could figure out how to get her out of this world. He could figure out how to let her become whole again.

The thought was as sobering as the cave was dark.

Mellow pulled out a few glowing vials and handed them around. "Benefits of being a witch. I have all sorts of little gadgets at my disposal."

It definitely made seeing in the dark easier.

The three chests in the cave had brass bindings, solid and gleaming with care. For an instant Murmur wondered what might have kept them clean, and imagined the bear licking them, which caused her to shudder and break out in a cold sweat. She dismissed the image hurriedly.

"Should we just open them?" Exbo nudged one with his toe as if daring it to explode or something.

Havoc shrugged and pushed forward. "We can always stand back and let my pet open them again. You know. He's getting used to sacrificing himself for us."

"What, you don't think that's a new skeleton?" Rash stood, her arms crossed, a skeptical crease in her frown.

"We've discussed it, and he just comes back better than ever for me." Havoc half-smiled and then backed up. "In the interests of no one dying tonight, I say, let's back away from the chests while he does his stuff."

They followed his directions, and Murmur wasn't sure, but she thought he probably realized that everyone let him stand just a fraction in front of them. The skeleton moved forward, its bones clattering against each other with each step and an annoying cackle slipping from its lips.

"Does it always make that noise?" Mellow asked, their eyes wide.

"Hush." Havoc whispered, following his skeleton's progress. "You'll hurt his feelings."

Murmur choked down her own chuckle, and even Jinna was shaking with his own suppressed laughter next to her. The skeleton approached the chest on the left, and they collectively held their breath. But nothing happened.

All it held was gold. A *lot* of gold.

"Looks like our guild bank balance will join our healthy guild vault." Veranol grinned. "You're not going to tax us, are you Mur?"

"Depends on how much it costs for Neva to keep me in the armor I like." She winked at him as they pulled back behind Havoc again.

The second chest held armor. A couple of gorgeous bows that had the rangers salivating, and a staff that Mellow clutched like a fool. Once they retreated again, the skeleton approached the third chest, the huge key from the bear clutched in its hand.

It turned easily in the lock, the chest smaller than the first two, but when it opened, there was a resounding twang, and a sudden emerging miasma of a green acid cloud that roiled itself onto Havoc's pet and began to eat away at its bones. In a matter of seconds both the skeleton and the cloud were gone, with nothing left to remember either of them by.

Havoc sighed. "I'll bring him back shortly. The box is open though. May as well check it out." He reached over and pushed Murmur toward it.

"Gee, thanks for checking yourself," she muttered as she and Jinna made their way over. Not that she thought there'd be more than one trap. Besides, if there was, Jinna would find it and take care of it.

"Hey, I sacrificed my pet. Again." Havoc grumbled.

Murmur smiled despite herself. Even in his grumpy mode, he was a good guy. Still though, she wished she knew why he'd been so quiet when she first found out about the coma. He'd been stand offish for ages. Peeking into the box, her thoughts wooshed away as she took in its contents.

They weren't what she'd been expecting. Even though she'd hoped it might be one of the twelve keys, she should have known better. The likelihood of them being able to gather one of them this early through progression, would have been a bit stupid. Never mind that she hadn't uncovered any lore that even pointed to the keys or what the end objective was.

Murmur frowned and shook her head, knowing she was getting way off track. Scrolls upon scrolls and books upon books littered the inside of the last chest. There had to be something amazing about them since the box was magically sealed. She didn't for one second think the bear had sealed these, just that he had obtained them by likely killing their previous owners. All in all it was a decent haul. She'd have to get someone to go through these back at the guild. When she finally got some downtime, she'd have to activate the guild storage distribution better. That way people should, if she understood it correctly, be able to deposit directly into the guild bank as long as she set the permissions properly.

While they were already level nineteen, they'd already wasted half the night with the stupid scouts and the bloody bear. "Okay everyone. We have a mission—you don't get a choice whether to accept it or not. You saw that scout and how strong she was with a newly learned hybrid build. It's our turn to hit twenty and go and get our own hybrid builds. Time to fight some golems."

"I refuse to cheer in case Disestru had a mate or something, but I agree completely with you." Sin said solemnly.

Beastial laughed. "If he's got a mate…"

"Don't even *think* about continuing that sentence." Sinister glared at him with the heat of a thousand suns, and Beast must have been wearing some sort of heat resistance because he was lucky he didn't burn.

Holding up his hands in self-defense he backed away. "Fine! Sorry! I was just—"

"Don't even contemplate it." This time Murmur glared at him. "We've been tempting fate enough. It's time we got unlazy and hit our next level."

"Whatever you say, boss!" Merlin saluted and dashed ahead. "But I'm trapping the entire region around those damn golems this time, even if I have to redo them every hour. We are not getting caught unawares again."

Murmur watched Merlin and Exbo dash ahead of their respective groups and couldn't help thinking that it might sound grand and all, but she was quite certain getting caught unawares was part of this game's MO.

By the time they'd all hit level twenty, Murmur never, ever, ever, ever wanted to see a golem again. At least not a clay one. They were fucking annoying. Metal weapons got sucked into their *flesh*, and had to be wrestled back out. She couldn't imagine the time Rashlyn had. Fists were probably stickier than metal. Skin was definitely sticky.

"We're never coming back to golems. I will skip clay golems and try to battle something five levels higher than me next time." Sinister glared defiantly at the rest of the group, her hands on her hips, her mouth twisted in irritation. "You have no idea how damned hard it is to suck life out of those things? And I specialize in blood. Did you *see* any blood? Did you?"

Murmur walked over and gave her a brief shoulder massage, and her friend let out a contented sigh. "Settle, Sin. It's all good. They're dead. We're level twenty. Goal achieved. I even managed to get my dagger skill up."

"Even if it did get stuck like forty times," grumbled Havoc. "I have no idea why you're so set on going melee hybrid. Your freaking hidden skills are ridiculously overpowered, and you've already got enough to do."

Murmur shrugged. "I don't like being about as good defensively as a wet sock, so humor me and let me go train in another profession. If they let me. I'm used to wearing plate armor and at least being able to take a hit." And while she was at it, she had no idea how the hybrid class system worked. No one did. All there was out there for information was speculation galore. Perhaps they were allocated their hybrid specialty. Maybe there was a quest. She might want to be an assassin enchanter, but if this game had taught her anything, it was that what you get is what you least expect.

They set off, collecting Rashlyn's group on the way. Jinna strode out several feet in front of them, picking his way down the precarious slope. More than once Murmur's feet slid against some gravel overlaying the rocky outcrops. But at least they weren't cliffs, and at least Devlish didn't have to walk back on his own.

Climbing up the gradual slope would have been near impossible, but Jinna had been right in saying it was easier to get down it. In some places it was almost like a slide. The welcoming lights of Verendus shone like a beacon as they slithered to the bottom of the mountain. They traipsed across the snow-filled fields in the dawning light as the orange sun crested the horizon. The snow crunched under her feet with each step she took, slowly giving way to gravel, which felt uneven. A slight wind gusted past her, moving her hair and kissing coolness onto her cheeks.

Even the air tasted faintly like the ice inside a freezer. The world was simply so real, it was difficult for Murmur to contemplate that it might not be. One of the guards greeted Jinna with a friendly wave, and the dwarf jogged over to talk to them.

Murmur paused, and Veranol and the others took a few more steps before noticing she wasn't with them. "Mur? What's up?"

She laughed. "I have no clue where my trainer is. I was going to wait for Jinna and ask him."

Rashlyn blinked. "Shit. I have no idea where the monk trainer is."

"Smart cookie." Beastial nodded in Murmur's direction.

"She's not a cookie!" Sin stomped her foot. "Well, she's not your cookie anyway."

Dansyn laughed. "Well, I'm going to go find my trainer, *and* some cookies. You can all stay here if you like."

Hesitating for another moment, Murmur followed. "What the hell, it's an adventure, right?"

She walked away, her steps quick, excited to meet an enchanter trainer who wasn't Belius. She hoped, and thought enchanters would be open minded and fun. Probably stemmed from their being able to sense minds and thoughts, deeds and motivations.

Remembering how the enchanter guild was presented in Stellaein, she looked for the most decorative building in the city. With all of the evergreens in Verendus, it was a bit hard to see the buildings, but eventually, in the far left corner, she found a building that was a little less impressive than the one in Stellaein structure-wise, but just as colorful and welcoming, like a miniature fixed rainbow. In some ways it was soothing, like walking in here was walking in home even though it was half way around the virtual world. The counter just inside the door was to the left, and not across the room. But the dwarf behind it had shining eyes, and a jolly smile.

"Welcome." His voice was gruff, but reminded Murmur of her father in a way. Homey and welcoming. Still, she'd never forgotten the odd way Elvita looked at her when she realized Mur had learned how to shield her mind, so she double checked how tightly she was protecting herself, and only then did she return the welcoming smile.

"I'm from Tarishna. Can I see the enchanter trainer here in Verendus?" She used her most polite voice. It never hurt to be nice to people, especially when a large distance from one's hometown.

"Of course! You're far from home, young locus." He eyed her with a bit of a knowing look. "I'm also betting you're going to need to sell some stuff? You're a brand new twenty."

Murmur laughed. "Yes, I am. I'd appreciate that. Can I see you on my way out then?"

"Definitely. Name's Geshua."

"Thank you." She inclined her head. "I'm Murmur."

For a brief second, she thought his eyes narrowed ever so slightly. "Might be an idea to head through now then."

Murmur headed through to the back, unable to get the tone of Geshua's voice out of her head.

CHAPTER NINETEEN

Real Enchanter

Storm Entertainment
Somnia Online Division
Game Development Offices Conference Room
Late Day Seven Post Launch

Shayla frowned at the reams of paper in front of her. Her usual preference was to work through her augmented interface. It was far more environmentally friendly, and it saved her the risk of paper cuts. Considering how expensive paper had become, it wasn't even an inexpensive method.

It was late, and the lights in her office weren't really built for nighttime usage. The world outside her window was pitch black, almost like the gaping maw her brain had become since the game launched. Shayla shook her head and continued to spread the sheets out on the floor, frowning more and more as the pieces began to fit together.

While they fit, she had no idea what in the hell she was looking at. Code was missing (or at least it appeared to be) except where it was missing didn't make sense. The columns didn't look like they should work properly, as if there was something she couldn't put her finger on. Brain data, readings, class allocation and usage—and all the computations worked out perfectly, regardless of what her brain was trying to tell her.

She frowned. Perhaps it all fit too nicely. Considering the types of data they were extracting from the headgear, she'd not expected the output to be this symmetrical. Maybe there was something she didn't understand about the way the funding worked, perhaps something to do with the results being sought. There were myriad reasons for them to be researching people's brainwaves, many of them mostly evil ones she concocted in her head. Mind controlling the populace, or perhaps researching telepathy and telekinetic triggers, because enchanter. She almost laughed at her paranoia, but couldn't quite bring herself to because at some level, nothing was off limits. Teddy's reassurances as he faced her backed by an army of lawyers only made her stomach queasy.

Shayla leaned back against her desk and ran her fingers through her hair, and almost jumped out of her skin when she saw James pop his head into the room.

"Shit! James! What are you doing here at this hour?" She was quite proud of the fact that she didn't screech at him.

"You're still here?" His brows pinched in confusion. "I thought I was the only one left."

Shayla looked up at him. "Laria's gone? Oh right. I told her to go home early for once I think. Or was that yesterday?"

James walked in and leaned against the wall, his eyes taking in the whole room in one glance. "You, like most of us, have been here so much the days have bled into each other."

Shayla noticed his look, and her fingers itched to pull in all of her research, but she wasn't sure if he'd be able to tell anything more than she could anyway. He'd originally been a techie, and he'd only become her assistant after Ava died. Which was still something on her plate. She'd have to remember to make time for the inspector when he came around next Monday? Was it already next Monday?

"What are you here so late for?" James asked, his tone lighter than she expected, almost like he was simply acting curious, and not actually curious at all.

Now the overtime and late nights were making her paranoid, but it was difficult not to be when her original assistant had been murdered not all that long ago. Besides her brain's unwillingness to take in the facts, it was very difficult to stab yourself in the back of the neck. She allowed herself a lopsided grin at James before speaking. "I'm your boss. I should be asking you that question."

He grinned, and the expression was so natural it alleviated a few of Shayla's concerns, but not enough to downplay her wariness. He should be there, right? Especially if he had his own and Ava's work to shoulder right now.

"I don't know how she did it," he said quietly, eyes focused on the toes of his shoes. "Ava had all your shit under control, and a heap of side projects for herself. I can't keep up. I'm here until this time almost every night scrambling to be as efficient as she was."

Shayla blinked at him, and stood up, brushing off her pants despite the fact that her office was usually spotless. "Sorry. I know you're juggling your own workload too, which means you currently have more on your plate than even Ava did. I keep forgetting you had to take over with mere days to go before the launch."

James shrugged, "Part of the job. Part of life, right?"

"Yeah." Shayla glanced down at the huge mess all over the floor. She still had no answers, but her current brain capacity wasn't about to make it easy on her anyway. With a sigh, she stretched. "I think I'm seeing things, and reading things wrong. The game's launch has been so damned smooth that I can't quite believe there's not something I'm missing."

James laughed, the tension in his shoulders dissipating. Even then, Shayla couldn't stop thinking uncomfortable thoughts. Was he less tense because she'd just said she was seeing things? Shaking her head she smiled. Paranoia was coming to get her, armed and ready with pitchforks. "Probably time we left. You included. I'll even wait until you're gone before I go, because I'm quite certain otherwise you're going to creep back in here."

He nodded, and gave a small smile. "You're not the tyrant everyone thinks you are, you know."

"Shhh," she cautioned him, "or I'll make you transfer departments."

James raised an eyebrow. "And have to train a new assistant? I think not. I call bollocks on you."

Shayla laughed, but couldn't shake the uneasy feeling. Perhaps it wasn't coming from James. Maybe it came from somewhere else, but she was far too tired to try and figure out where.

Murmur opened the door to the enchanter trainer's chamber and clamped her mental shields down so tightly and so quickly that her skill level jumped up however many points it needed to hit one hundred. Fucking fantastic.

"Why the hell are you here?" The words slipped out of her mouth before she could pull them back, and yet when she thought about it, she realized she'd wanted to say them anyway.

Belius turned his full attention to Murmur, the galaxies in his eyes swimming. His white tendrils of hair lit up brightly at the ends, lending him, just for that moment, a mad-scientist appearance. "Why, I came to see you, my dear. I knew you'd be hitting level twenty soon, and I wanted to check in on you. Congratulations." He narrowed his eyes as if drinking in her aura, and for a brief moment a look of consternation crossed his face. "It seems you've not leveled your affinity any further. Pity."

There was a different air to Belius now. Did he know she'd given Telvar the piece of Michael's brain? Was he angry? His body language was different from before, more distanced, less personal. Perhaps it was because there was another enchanter master in the room with him. Maybe he wasn't supposed to be so familiar with his students. She'd also been more distant toward him since the Shard absorption incident, so that might even have something to do with it.

Forcing a smile onto her face, she kept her tone as civil as possible, trying to blend out any of the paranoia she could feel building in her mind behind its tight shields. It wasn't that she hated him—she just didn't understand his motives, nor did she trust his reasoning when he'd been hiding so many things from her all along. "Well, I wasn't expecting to see you here, I was looking forward to meeting other enchanter masters. It's good to get different perspectives."

Taking deliberate steps and not letting Belius's belligerent glare unnerve her, she walked up to the dwarven master and inclined her head. "My name is Murmur. It's a pleasure to meet you."

The dwarf guffawed, much like Jinna did, and she immediately felt safer. His eyes sparkled and he held out a hand, grasping hers firmly but not yanking at her arm. "Fine of ye. I'm Dirsna. I've been talking to my old rival, ye see. He's a bit of a stick in the mud in't he?"

There was a twinkle in the dwarf's eye, and at first glance he seemed jovial and easy to get along with. She wondered if he had the same penchant as Belius for not telling her anything in everything he said. "Please to meet you, Master Dirsna."

"Ack, no. Jus call me Dirsna. Only people who call me master are people I pay. And while I can teach ye, I only charge for materials." He looked her up and down, his gaze discerning and not lecherous. "So, so. Level twenty. Psionicist. I wish ye'd reached me first. I'd have guided you down a less dangerous path there, missy."

"Less dangerous?" Her curiosity was piqued. What did he mean, less dangerous? Wasn't most mind magic dangerous anyway?

"Yeh mind is a tangled web. It holds secrets ye might not even know yeself. Mind reading is well and good, but sometimes, if ye're not careful, ye can get lost and never found again." His eyes were deep and soulful, and the seriousness in them didn't wane. He wasn't joking.

A wave of irritation at Belius passed through her again. "There are always side effects, aren't there? Guess we should make the label spell them out to us."

Dirsna guffawed. "Yes! A fine sense of humor. Here, come here."

He motioned her to follow him over to one of the larger cabinets in the room and opened the doors. There, nestled in amongst heavy-duty velvet, were some beautiful scrolls. They seemed heftier than the ones she'd received earlier and Murmur could feel her mouth salivating. Considering the spells she already had were powerful enough, she couldn't wait to get her hands on these.

"May I?" she asked, her tone almost reverent. It was something special to be able to reach in and pull out scrolls that would turn into pure power once her skin absorbed them.

Dirsna nodded, and Murmur smiled, almost giddy with excitement.

She reached her hand in, and even before she touched the parchment of the scrolls, her runes began to glow. It was like they could sense the power emanating from the pages she was about to acquire, even without her having to read and absorb the knowledge. This was different, like she'd truly passed some sort of threshold.

Suddenly Dirsna stood next to her, his hands behind his back as he leaned in, his brown eyes sparkling with gold flecks. "You've noticed already haven't you?"

Murmur hesitated. "Maybe. These just seem so different; even their energy sparks differently."

"Exactly. Ye've hit the first true milestone level. Twenty is different from the levels before. Ye'll receive significant upgrades an' from now on only every five levels. Twenty is sort of like ye've grown up an' left the nest and there's nothing new we can teach ye—it's up to you to expand your horizon." His smile put her far more at ease than Belius's ever did, and for some brief moments she was even able to forget Belius stood behind them in a corner of the room, likely fuming silently.

"Milestone level, huh?" She sorted through the scrolls, relishing in the tingles of power that darted up her arms as she did so. She knew twenty was always a milestone, but here it truly felt like it. More illusions—so fun spells were still included—but if this is where things got serious, then she wanted far more than mere illusion spells.

Altruism

    Cast: Self or others

    Type: Buff

    Duration: 45 minutes

Effect: This allows a faction increase to your target. It will lift you one faction level. However, should you be kill on sight to any faction, not even altruism can help you. This buff will update again at level 30.

Shift

    Cast: Area of effect

    Type: AOE Stun

    Duration: 8 seconds

Effect: This stun effectively locks all enemies around its epicenter in place for 15 yards. They will be unable to move for 8 seconds.

Fervor

    Cast: Self or others

    Type: Buff

    Duration: 45 minutes

Effect: This is an attack speed buff, but it also increases agility by the caster's level. Cannot be cast on the same target as Beserker.

Beserker

    Cast: Self or others

    Type: Buff

    Duration: 45 minutes

Effect: This buff adds strength to the amount equal to the level of the caster, however it also reduces agility by half the caster's level. Best used for classes or pets who will not need agility stacked. Cannot be cast on the same target as Fervor.

Charismatic

Cast: Self or others (but who are we kidding, you're an enchanter, you'll never not cast this on yourself).

Type: Buff

Duration: 45 minutes

Effect: This buff increases your target's charisma equal to the level of the caster. No restrictions. Cast away!

Murmur chuckled at the description and couldn't wait to increase her charisma up to seventy-four. That was a huge jump. She smoothed the next scroll out before reading it too.

Magic Resist

Cast: Group

Type: Buff

Duration: 45 minutes

Effect: Increases your magic resistance by an amount equivalent to the caster's level.

Armored

Cast: Group

Type: Buff

Duration: 45 minutes

Effect: Increases your AC by an amount equivalent to the caster's level.

"Holy crap." She muttered to herself as she began to absorb them. The purple in the runes underneath her skin flared up with a sort of electricity. She smiled at the light show, loving the locus body, and happy to have chosen it. At the time she hadn't even realized how beneficial her strange sight was, or the tall body could be.

"I'm starting to feel more like an enchanter. These are fantastic spells." She looked up, grinning, to see Dirsna looking at her fondly.

"Ye're a real enchanter. A psionicist even. Hopefully by the time ye next come back to town, ye'll have hit your next Mental Acuity level. That's a large part of what defines ye now." Dirsna's tone didn't hold condescension, but a genuine fondness for the knowledge he was speaking about. He seemed to be a born teacher, and certainly nothing like Belius. But there she went again, forgetting that Somnia wasn't real—or at least wasn't as real as some of these NPCs seemed to believe it was.

"I guess it does." She glanced down at her fingers, long and sleek and silvered grey with their purple-hued undertones running through her skin. Her heart beat in her chest. She could feel it. Even the air in here tasted like old books and leather, with a hint of cinnamon. Maybe cinnamon was just something she smelled no matter where she was.

"Now." His tone had changed, and his gaze caught her own, holding it as he spoke. "Ye've past this first milestone. One ye hit level twenty-five, ye'll start to diverge on your path. Ye may choose different enchanter branches if ye will. Like a tree, all of yer limbs grow from your trunk, but all are different, an' ye must decide for yerself which way ye want yer class to proceed."

She blinked at him, running his words through her head, trying to understand exactly what he meant. "So you mean there won't just be spells everyone can have? We'll have to choose between some in order to progress our class?"

Dirsna paused for a moment, a small frown on his face, before he nodded tentatively. "In a way. There'll be choices to make every level. Say ye can choose blue, red, an' yellow. An' ye choose blue. The next time ye'll be able to still choose red an' yellow, but ye'd be able to choose a deeper, darker, more powerful blue. Once ye gain yer level, ye'll be given choices on how best to specialize yer class."

"In addition to the Mental Acuity skills?" Murmur understood the analogy, or at least she thought she did, and the potential of it sent tingles through her entire body.

"In addition. Some of yer Mental Acuity skills have already begun to develop into their kinetic counterparts, have they not?"

Murmur paused, feeling the blush rise in her cheeks. She hadn't meant for it to manifest when she sent Jirald tumbling through the air, but he did have a point. "Technically, I guess."

"Then make sure ye practice those. Feel them out, test the waters. Mental Acuity will not increase unless ye explore it." His eyes were so kind, such a contrast to Belius's hungry expressions she was used to.

Murmur stood and bowed briefly to Dirsna, appreciating the way her new armor wasn't a robe. It fit her perfectly, conforming to her body as she moved. "Thank you, for everything. We'll be out this way for a good while. I hope to see you again."

Dirsna smiled. "I hope ye do. I'll look forward to seeing ye. I can see why Belius wants to keep ye for himself."

The words sent a shiver down Murmur's spine, but she tried not to let it show, and instead forced her smile to remain in place. There was no way she was getting out of here without speaking to Belius again. She knew that. And while she knew it, she still didn't care for it. It made her wonder exactly what had changed. Was it his actions or her perceptions of them?

She stopped in front of him on her way out and crossed her arms, jutting out her chin stubbornly. "So. What do you want with me? I didn't think trainers scoured the corners of Somnia to find their favorite students."

Belius smiled, but the expression died on his lips. "I want..." He paused as if mulling it over in his head. "I want you to hand in your quest."

Murmur rolled her eyes. "I don't have to hand in any subtle hint-based quests if I don't want to. Also, I'm an enchanter, and therefore the same things you might need could reveal buttloads for me. So, I'm using my freedom of choice and individuality to keep some things to myself. Also, I have too many flipping quests running through my interface right now. I'm not even completely sure which one you mean."

Belius's stare grew harsher—even for him—and his lips drew across in an angry thin line. "That's the story you're going to maintain?"

She blinked. "What do you mean? Shouldn't I be curious? Aren't you the one who told me to be—wait, wait, I've got it here somewhere—to listen and sound out, to pay close attention, and to block my thoughts from others?"

This time Belius's mouth dropped open slightly in shock, and he took a couple of steps back. "I didn't mean from me! I'm your teacher."

"Teacher yes, controller no!" she snapped at him, barely keeping a lid on her temper.

Stars clashed in his eyes, eliciting tiny explosions that rained through them. He squared his jaw with visible effort and practically spat the words out. "Fine. You make a good point."

Murmur smiled. "Sometimes I even make sense, but don't get used to those moments. I have some more levels to go fetch now, Bel! Thank you for coming to see me. I do appreciate it. I'll see you soon." She tried to smile at the end to take a little bit of sting out of her words. It wouldn't do to make him an actual enemy after all.

Not leaving herself time to hesitate, she walked straight passed Belius and exited the room. She waved as she closed the door behind her. Out in the foyer she didn't linger and sold her stuff to Geshua for a tidy sum before heading out to the center of the village.

Or at least, that was her plan.

As she stepped outside, she walked into bedlam.

Dwarves ran screaming. Arrows flew through the air, thudding into signs, roofs, and people, sending them toppling to the ground in a fit of agonized yelling.

She darted forward, hiding behind the great dwarf in the middle of the fountain. He held a bow aloft with one hand, and a horn in the other, the latter raised to his lips like it hadn't been before. She frowned at it. Damn it if they only had a horn of their own to blow. Glancing around she spied a few of her guild and motioned them over.

The horn did sound, loud and angry, almost deafening her as she stood underneath it. So the fountain was also a warning bell of sorts? That was interesting.

You have noticed the dwarven fountain sometime moves for specific reasons. This is just one piece of your puzzle. Make sure you don't lose the box.

Murmur frowned. Box? That was fucking vague. Again.

Moments later the dwarven horn received a more distant answer from outside the city walls, and Murmur made the mistake of trying to peek through and see what was going on.

There, mounted on a horse directly in front of the city gates, with a couple of chained pet golems in tow, was a woman who looked suspiciously like the scouts they'd taken care of earlier. She wore the same type of dark brown armor that blended easily with trees, but stood out in the cold and mostly snowy landscape around the city. And she had fiery red hair that would have stuck out anywhere but appeared like a blur of blood on the snow. Tattoos graced her body symmetrically, their lines interwoven with each other as symbols writhed and wriggled on her skin.

Three groups of five pulled up on foot with their own clay golems tethered to them. Murmur surmised they'd probably altered their commands by force in order to get them to play along. And she had no idea what they wanted them to play along with until the woman spoke.

Her strong alto voice flowed with ease over the city, her words crisp and cutting. "We have come to retrieve our treasure, which was guarded by our deity Disestru. You harbor those who slaughtered him, one of them is also one of you. If you do not send them out to us so that we might deal with them, we will come in there. We take no survivors, we will besiege you until you beg to die."

CHAPTER TWENTY

At War

Somnia Online
City of Verendus
Late Day Seven Post Launch

Verendus was under attack.

Until you beg to die reverberated through Murmur's head like someone had rung a gong.

Dying was so not on her game bucket list.

She took a deep breath, belaying the immediate panic that tried to rise in her chest. It seemed not all the NPCs gave a shit if she died or not. Which made sense in a way. Her advantage would be far too great if they did.

Murmur saw Veranol trying to get her attention and nodded. Their guild had done this, so they had to clean up the mess. Her only hope was that the dwarves might help them, because only twelve of them against the slew of golems and incoming scouts or whoever they were...well. That was going to get plain ugly.

They met up at the fountain, Rashlyn speaking in a hushed voice as soon as they did. "I can't believe this. We should have known it was too good to be true." She scowled, irritation obvious.

"We should have looked the gift horse in the mouth I guess. Or gift bear if you will." Beastial received nothing but glares in return for that one, but Murmur found herself having to stifle a giggle.

Just then, Jinna jogged over to them. "It's all good. Lasn said he'll gather the guards and we'll defend the city together. It'll be easier with them helping us. We should be evened out, and well, they have a lot of levels on us."

Murmur couldn't help but sigh in relief. "Will they be in squads?"

Jinna's eyes twinkled as he replied. "Of six, just like us."

"Do you think they can take two to three golems on each?" She was calculating odds in her head, trying to come up with a decent strategy.

"Definitely doable. They're running with Dirsna in a support group behind them, so crowd control of those golems is mostly taken care of. They'll have cleric and druid support for healing. They should be able to do that easily."

She nodded, switching her attention to the battlefield for a second. "How much longer?"

"They gave us ten minutes to respond." Jinna spoke the words so softly, it was hard to catch them, but she supposed he was trying not to panic any of the civilians who might be around, even though most of them were already inside the huts with the doors barricaded. "We probably have five minutes left."

"Get the others here pronto please, Ver. Jinna, can the rest of us go join Lasn?" Murmur hated having to coordinate combat. It always left her in such a foul mood. One of these days she was just going to strong-arm Jinna or Devlish into raid leading, but they didn't have to worry about that quite yet. Two groups were barely more than a scuffle worth of people. She was quite apprehensive about recruiting enough people to fill a raid roster, but she'd let Future Murmur deal with that.

Lasn was a very sturdily built dwarf. He probably worked out, because his muscles didn't resemble those of Jinna, or the two enchanters she'd met. His eyes were black as coal, and his thick hair was pulled back into a knot at the nape of his neck, which oddly mirrored his long beard of the same color that draped down in front of him. When he spoke, it almost made the ground rumble with its deep and calming sound.

"Is all right. Any friend of Jinna's is a friend of ours. Why, we'da had a right ole boar problem without 'im." His welcome set her at ease, the faint lilt to his words were calming. "We've sent for Dirsna and asked 'im to bring others with 'im. Never too many enchanters."

Murmur laughed. That would certainly make it easier on her. Her Mezmerize might have increased in duration, but she wasn't going to be able to Mezmerize all the scouts she needed to and rebuff and keep buffs up and and...

Right there, in the middle of a pending battle field, Murmur had a moment of clarity.

Being an enchanter was fun. And not the type of godlike fun that healing was, where it was up to you if a person got a heal or not—if you were the petty sort. But the sort of fun that came with such an adrenaline rush because one wrong move could mean the entire party or raid wiped. And she'd be damned if that wasn't electrifying. Controlling minds, influencing decisions, freezing bodies while their brains still worked—she couldn't wait to enhance her path. If nothing else, control of things inside Somnia made up for her lack of control without.

Devlish was the last to jog up, a different aura surrounding him than he'd had before. There was a ripple effect to it, like he'd had a huge self upgrade, and Murmur felt herself grin with a little maliciousness. They'd just hit twenty and hadn't even had time to activate their hybrid status, yet they had amazing added strength.

The woman on the horse moved restlessly, her face blank as she studied her nails, obviously bored. Energy crackled around her, and her thoughts were closed to Murmur, regardless how hard she tried to extend her sensor net. Time was ticking down as the dwarves gathered into formation behind her.

"Who is she?" Murmur whispered to Jinna as they finished all of their enhancing and defensive buffs.

But Jinna was too busy watching something on his HUD, and she had to elbow him in the ribs.

"What? Oh. You know, I'm damned buff with these." He grinned like the game had suddenly knocked a couple of decades off him.

Murmur smiled. "Tell me who she is."

"Oh, sorry. That's Chief Intanko or something like that? I dunno. Apparently these people are the ones whose scouts we killed, and they worshipped that bear thing." Jinna shrugged, his face grim. "Tis what it is. And it's about to be war."

He sounded far too gleeful for the amount of blood and pain they were about to endure. Murmur took a look at her own character sheet, frowning at the upgrades. Her charisma was off the charts now—well, not actually off the charts since she assumed they went a long way—but considering her allure added a chunk to it, right now, it was the strongest it could be. She weighed her sensing net, and made sure to seal her mind shield. Keeping her MA filled was of paramount importance.

"Enough!" Intanko's voice echoed out over the gap in front of the city, through to the buildings, bouncing off the walls. She had to be using some kind of vocal magnifier.

"The guards are going to tackle the golems by themselves. We will take on the rest, with the help of villagers to mop up any who break through our defensive lines. Don't stray too far from your healer. We have to keep the scouts at bay until the dwarves are done with the golems." Devlish squared his jaw, determination rippling through his scaled form, and his new aura pulsed like a star about to explode.

"We battle now!" A wave of anger roared through their invaders as they pumped fists full of weapons into the air.

"When this is done, I want to know about all the cool abilities you all got. Can't lead a raid without them." Murmur grinned at Devlish, stood her ground, and tried not to think about the two to one odds they faced as Intanko's army advanced.

Whatever Murmur had been expecting, the devastation, blood, and broken bones of the people gathered before her wasn't it.

Before when she'd played games, their NPCs weren't this intelligent. It took a certain number of hits to hack away at the life of an enemy, but those didn't have to be strategic in any way shape or form. All that had to be done was enough damage to reduce the hit points to zero. The violence was there, but never quite this precise, this real. But in Somnia, if you weren't mindful of how you were fighting, where to aim, and how best to gain the advantage, then the NPCs would fuck you up.

Screams tore across the battlefield, accentuating the clash of steel and flesh. Wet thuds as maces struck legs. The occasional crack that resounded from a breaking bone. Repairing broken bones hurt like hell, too, if the following yells were anything to go by. Murmur tried to concentrate on herself, and on Sin, but the battlefield was distracting.

NPCs learned from the way players fought; they learned from the way players held themselves. Everything about the NPCs in Somnia evolved and learned, and above all, they remembered. No matter the outcome of this war, the game on Cenedril had already been changed.

Stumbling from the mass group stun she'd managed to unleash, Murmur grabbed Sinister under the arm and half dragged, half helped her wobble back to the entrance of the town. Her new AoE stun was beautiful, something to be grateful for. Eight whole seconds. For a few moments behind the guarded walls, Sinister gasped for breath, her leg hanging by some sinew and muscle. The sight made Murmur gag. Flesh hung out, open to the air, the bones visible through the near amputation.

Dirsna placed a hand on her shoulder. "We'll take care of her. Try to stay behind your people. Help them."

She didn't have to be told twice, even though it was difficult to tear her eyes away from her friend's leg. Squaring her jaw, and banishing the image from her mind, Murmur joined the first line of defense. Her stomach twisted, and she wasn't sure if it was from the revulsion the wound caused, or else because she was petrified.

Generally not the type of person to get butterflies, this battle was above and beyond anything she'd ever experienced in a game before. Even the stench of spilled blood reached her nostrils, overwhelming her with the coppery tang. Murmur tried to calm herself, but deep breathing wasn't the best idea. She focused instead on what she could do, and began casting spells.

First she sent out stuns into every nook and cranny she could. There was a recast on them, so she could only stun lock for a short period of time, or more precisely, chain two of her area effect stuns one after the other. Then there was a slight gap. Giving her people a respite was all she could do. Preventing combat made her a target too.

One of the guards moved mostly in front of her, hefting his shield and pulling down a visor. "You stay there miss, Jinna'd kill me if you gots dead."

She would have smiled if she hadn't just seen Merlin pick off one of the women from her horse with a flying fireball of an arrow. It caught her full in the front, in the tiny space between the collarbone and where her helmet began. With no armor to protect the spot, it sank into her flesh with a sickening thud that lifted her off her horse and knocked her into the snowy mud as flames began to consume her body.

Murmur could almost feel the shot as if it'd hit her. Everything was too real. Her chest constricted, her breathing became shallow, and she wished she could smack her own face effectively. What if one of their archers picked her out like that?

She looked around wildly, fear beginning to encroach on her vision. Her breath caught in her throat and suddenly it was just far too difficult to breathe. She could die here, literally die.

Fuck.

Suddenly Belius was there, an unexpected look of concern on his face as he held her elbow, making her rethink all her judgment of him for a brief moment.

"Right now, you can't think of any of that! You're losing your shields, and your sensor net is all over the place. Get a grip, Murmur. You're going to kill these people if you're not careful; your emotions are starting to leak through. Your fear will paralyze them if you don't pull it together!"

Murmur blinked at him, her head abruptly stopping its spinning as she felt his shields clamp down around her. She righted herself, smoothing down her armor and gently pulled her elbow away. "Thank you. I'm not sure what came over me."

Steel clashed against steel, arrows wizzed through the air, but Belius continued, his focus entirely on her. He glared at her, but it wasn't quite as forceful as his usual glares. There was pure thoughtfulness behind it. "Your mind is powerful because you're an enchanter. Your abilities have manifested because you're a psionicist. And due to your connection here in Somnia, your wavelengths are magnified. Part of the reason I encouraged you to become a psionicist is that even though it's dangerous, it also affords you and all others the most protection from yourself. Now pull yourself together and use that phenomenal power to support your allies instead of making them all panic like fools."

She wanted to bite out that she hadn't meant to, that no one had shown her what the hell to do with the powers. But the words sat on her tongue thick and heavy, because while no one had taken the time to show her, he had given her the hints she needed to find it. She cringed as she saw Devlish stumble in her peripheral vision. She didn't have time to have a discussion, but even as she had the thoughts, she knew she had to make time.

Murmur wanted to tell him to fuck off. If he was so freaking powerful, why didn't he just fend the attackers off? And she really wanted to ask him what his deal was, because that was one of the first times he seemed to be honest with her.

But instead, Murmur just took a really deep breath, tried to ignore the stench and taste of blood on the air, and nodded. "Sorry. Will do."

Her head finally clear, she moved forward, repeated her stuns, and got to work debilitating their opponents one by one. Energy pulsed through her; the runes on her arms lit up with each spell she cast. Her fingers worked deftly and far quicker than she'd been able to cast the spells when she first got them. The new ones caused some finger knotting, but overall, her speed and her agility at casting simply served to increase her confidence, to focus her mind into a sharp arrow, increasing speed with every cast, almost as if it could stop time in her head. While her mana did diminish, it was nowhere near as fast as usual. Dirsna had buffed everyone with the maximum level Mana Tide, and its regeneration was beautiful.

The battle was close. Very close. Murmur frowned, not liking how locked in everything was. Skirmishes took place here and there, littered all around the now muddy mess of land in front of the dwarven city.

She focused on Devlish, who was going toe to toe with Itanka, backed up by Veranol. Sifting quickly through her spells in her mind, frustration tried to overwhelm her. She had so many abilities, some had slipped through the cracks. This was unacceptable. She'd let her predicament impact her usual class mastery.

Murmur's MA sat nicely at a hundred forty-five, and her Mind Bolts were only going to cost eighteen mana each. She frowned, running through a few scenarios in her head. Almost recklessly, she chose one and went for it.

Devlish was still trading blows with Intanka, and it looked like the Cult-leading bear-licker was owning him. Murmur had already debuffed everything she could on her, and yet, Devlish didn't look like he was holding up well, even though Sinister was backing up Veranol again if the blood clouds and bombs going off were anything to go by.

Steeling herself, Murmur clenched her fists and activated Mind Bolt.

Everything around her slowed down, like it was in slow-motion action. The practically invisible bolt of mental energy traveled over the field and shot Intanka straight in the head. Murmur fist pumped softly, happy to see that the duration was now almost six seconds instead of four. While Intanka could melee, she couldn't use any special abilities or spells for that duration. And six seconds in a fight like this was a lot of time.

Murmur gave herself a moment to relax, and continued with her other debuffs, now focusing on secondary fighters, because the others were still timing down. After about eight seconds she fired off another Mind Bolt directly at Intanka again, painfully aware of the limits of casting the spell.

Devlish was waiting for it this time, and launched some sort of supersonic-speedy amazing attack that had him dual wielding instead of defending, and wailing on his opponent in a series of slashes that looked like some sort of evocative death dance.

While she didn't have time to watch his full routine, Murmur turned back to check on Rashlyn, who appeared to be running out of steam. Her opponent wasn't nearly as tough, but anything would help her friend. Another Mind Bolt to give Rashlyn a bit of an edge, and Murmur had to refresh a few of her speed and debuffs before turning back to focus on Intanka again.

Intanka's health was getting pitifully low. Luckily, there didn't appear to be a healer in her vicinity. The ranged melee and casters had been taking those out one at a time. Which was why Sinister and Veranol were under such heavy guard, and even then lucky shots sometimes got through. Everyone always went for the healers first. It was logical, and ruthless.

Taking a deep breath, Murmur cast again, giving Devlish some good leeway to pummel the woman into oblivion. Out of the corner of her eye she could see Merlin firing shot after shot of flaming arrows, and hear their thunks into flesh that ended up wafting over to her in smoke form. The smell no longer strangled her, and she shrugged it off, wondering if the only way to survive this game was to become immune to all the violence around her. The ability to become desensitized to violence was an irrefutable fact of humanity.

Suddenly the guard in front of Murmur went down. It happened so fast, she barely had time to gape. And then a volley of arrows fired down on her, normal arrows. No, wait. Barbed arrows.

She tried to push out with the shield she held around her mind, hoping to belay the damage. Her illusionary shield wasn't going to last long, and she didn't have any type of spell to ward them off. Perhaps rain of arrows was an exaggeration, but there had to be at least half a dozen.

So she gathered all of her will, and all of her frustration, remembered the anger she'd felt when Jirald had trained her, remembered how if too many of those damned things hit her, she was a goner—and she pushed outward. A strange blip sounded, like a bubble forming underwater, only it rippled out from her center as it if was a balloon being blown up so that the arrows could pop it.

Congratulations. You have unlocked the kinetic arm of your psionicist abilities. Please see your trainer. You know, when you're not busy.

She barely had time to register the words, as the last of the shield popped. It only let one arrow through its defense, but it buried itself deep into her side. "Shit." She grimaced and as she noticed her health bar begin to drop lower, ticking away at her life. "Shit."

Sinister glanced over at her, from her position behind Devlish and shouted out to Ver. "Disease heal on Mur!"

A second later, she felt ten thousand times better, except the bloody barbed arrow was still stuck in her body, and the wound was slowly dripping. There was no way in hell this was going to be painless to remove. She gritted her teeth together and cast Mind Bolt once more on Intanka, gasping at the jolt that wracked through her body when she did so, causing the barbs to sink in deeper.

Murmur's head began to spin, and she was pretty sure it had nothing to do with the arrow and everything to do with the fact that she'd used Mind Bolt five times in a short period of time. But the thing was, that would have knocked her on her ass back at level sixteen. Now, she could do it. Now she *had* to do it.

The guard who'd been in front of her struggled to his feet, his health low, but not dead. He must have been knocked out. Ushering her behind the wall, he motioned to one of the village medics to come to them.

"Sorry, miss. I didn't see that coming." He sounded winded, and wheezy.

Murmur shook her head. "It's fine. I didn't react quick enough. I should have protected myself better."

While she was distracted talking to the guard, the sneaky little medic broke off the front of the arrow and pulled the shaft out through the wound. The scream that tore from Murmur was enough to make her throat hurt. Her world spun. Her stomach churned. Her head threatened to black out. A crow cawed from the wall above her, and Murmur echoed its indignant sentiment.

She gripped at the guard's arm, gasping for breath and glared icily at the medic.

"Sorry. But it seemed like a good time. Also, we were lucky only the front part of the arrow was barbed, or this could have gotten nasty. Let me heal it up for you. Don't want to leave a nasty rent in that armor now." The medic was a sweet, middle-aged woman with light brown eyes. In a way, she reminded Murmur of her mother.

"Thanks." Murmur said, a little shakier than she'd intended. She clasped her shields tightly around her, her net cast out wide, and stood up once she'd been properly healed. "I'm good. I've just got a couple more things to do."

Murmur headed out, the guard patched up and by her side. She'd have to remember to ask him for a name later, but right now it was all she could do to keep herself walking upright.

Her attention turned to her MA, and she frowned. It ticked up far too slowly for her liking in a battle like this. Surely there had to be a hidden ability regeneration spell of some sort.

The stench of blood and feces, urine and sweat, hit her as she passed through the gates to the fields of slaughter. Dead bodies, mostly of the invaders, were trampled on the field, nowhere near their decomposing state. Death stood before her, and she wanted to weep. All because they killed a stupid in-game bear.

It's a game.

It didn't matter what her mind tried to tell her, the reasons it tried to list out for her, everything felt real. For her, everything *was* real. Because here was the only real she had for now. She didn't want to contemplate what might have happened had her freakishly well-timed unlocking of that skill not happened.

Devlish's health bar kept dipping dangerously low despite both Sinister and Veranol's best healing efforts. She could see them warding him, casting heal over times, and topping up his health constantly. Hell, Sin even diminished her own health a couple of times to top him off. Murmur's temper snapped. Stomping back onto the battlefield, ahead of her protector, she cast Mind Bolt on Intanka, followed by her flux stun when that wore off.

The latter got resisted, but she didn't give up, and cast another mind bolt just as the first was wearing off, despite how much her head was spinning. The only way to get better at using her MA was to use it, right?

Devlish laid into the boss as soon as the Mind Bolt stuck. She could see him cast Hatred and Terror and wail on Intanka with everything he had. The boss was unable to cast defensive spells against his onslaught, and his weapons found purchase more often than not now. Her armor began to show true signs of the battle with rips and holes peppered through it, but she still seemed capable of high-level avoidance. Shir-Khan and Beastial finally joined in the fight after demolishing several of their own opponents. Mur watched them trigger their fusion moves, snapping at vital body parts, and only grazing them instead of landing full impact. Finally Merlin finished picking off the riders with his fire arrows and began to lay them into Intanka as well. A resounding thud hit her right in the chest as she tried to dodge everyone else's melee attacks, taking her by surprise and scoring a critical amount of damage. Her armor caught fire momentarily before flickering out, causing more extended damage as well.

Leeroy was no longer a wobbly skeleton. Havoc's level twenty upgrades had increased his pet's power and transformed into a weird specter complete with a creepy death scythe. Intimidating and freaking awesome. Havoc hung levitating in a cloud of black, beaming with pride as he renewed DoTs and pet buffs from a distance.

Murmur flung her last Mind Bolt, ignoring the pain searing through her head, and focused on taking Intanka down.

CHAPTER TWENTY-ONE

Aftermath

Somnia Online Location: Ululate
Dunkel Inn Meeting Room Two
Day Eight Post Launch

> The city of Verendus has successfully repelled an invasion by the clans of Noch'Mar nomad elves, with the aid of the guild Fable. Verendus has gained a city level, and will soon begin construction on their next tier of defenses. Wood and metal workers are invited to apply for work detail.

Jirald blinked at the system wide message, and couldn't help the growl rising in his throat. Again. How were they always everywhere? What sort of fucking magic had Murmur unlocked? So far ahead of him he couldn't even see their backs. He clenched his fists and remembered what Sidius said. Keep his eyes on the goal, don't deviate, and do everything to get to it. Do everything it takes to be the best, to pull his guild along with him. Regardless of his own skill, he needed others on his level. Somnia wasn't a solo environment. As long as he set out to get those Shards, everything should go well. Then he could prove himself, prove that he and his guild were the best, were better. Better than her. Better than Fable.

And he'd make her pay for deleveling him. Tenfold.

Masha cleared his throat and Jirald turned, raising an eyebrow at his healer. "What?"

"You looked deep in thought, so I tried to give you warning I was here. I don't want you sinking one of those things into my eye socket by accident because I startled you." Masha rolled his shoulders and eyed the throwing daggers with their wicked blades, almost hidden up and down Jirald's leather armor.

The rogue cocked his head to one side and studied Masha. He'd never really understood the cleric. The healer never seemed to mind Jirald's assertions that he was the best, nor did he seem to care who came out top in a competition of healing. Even in this game, where Jirald had thrown a fit and a half when the system allocated him as a rogue, Masha just stood there, patient and congenial, and rolled with the punches. He knew Masha was very probably the closest thing he had to a friend in the game or the world, a feeling that was uncommon for him—and perplexing. Friends meant you had to worry about losing something, and Jirald tended to prefer fighting for himself and only himself. That way he avoided having to do things for others, but also avoided having to have others used against him. It was a win-win situation. But Sidius was right. Despite everything else, there were sometimes things one just couldn't do alone.

He chose to scowl at the cleric with his most ferocious look. The sharp teeth that inundated the mouths of the locus always helped sharpen that image. "You're really more of a bother than you should be, Masha."

The cleric shrugged good-naturedly.

"I'm done with my set up, and we're just waiting on you and the tank. We leave for Pelagu in the next ten minutes, so get your alien ass on the move so I don't have to drag you out by your tentacles." Masha pushed off with the foot that was resting against the wall and glanced at Jirald again, his brow furrowing. "You should probably stop all your machinations shit, and just do what Ishwa says. He'll get us to the top, or close to it, and all we have to do is cling on and do our jobs. Stop getting distracted by that pretty little head of hers. She's a damn fine player. The only way you'll beat her is if you keep your wits about you and knuckle down."

Apparently satisfied with his lecture, Masha turned on his heel and left Jirald gaping after him.

The rogue punched the air fiercely, his irritation threatening to turn into anger. He knew he had some issues to deal with, but damn it. He was already trying to make sure his revenge didn't get in the way of his success. Sure, it might be an uphill battle because she damned well deserved to be taken down a few notches, or levels, he wasn't picky. Revenge was his driving force, and it made a mighty fine motivator.

Still. He picked up his weapons eyeing each blade as he did. They were deadly sharp. Poison vials lined his pockets for quick application, and he reworked his gloves into place to strengthen his punches.

They needed levels, and they needed them fast. Ishwa mentioned something about a place he knew of where the levels would come quickly with certain fudges on mechanics. How he knew this, Jirald had no idea, but that little gnome always had tricks up his sleeves. Hanging around him was never dull.

Armed and geared, Jirald slipped a few potions into his inventory and headed out the door to join the others. Revenge was a great thing, but now he wanted more—more than just to show Murmur. He intended to show the world.

Murmur sat on the floor of the city center building and stared at the huge fire roaring in the fireplace. Warmth trickled out to her like fingers of heat threatening to tickle her into warmth, yet...her core was frozen.

This world was real, even if the guards who'd died managed to come back from their death several hours later, even if the NPCs she already knew by name were gone for a day, they'd return eventually. But they'd remember the pain and everything, wouldn't they? Because unlike other games, the people in this one remembered everything. Like the grudge the bandits held against them that would never be forgotten or forgiven. In this world any mistakes you made were etched into it, in an eternal memory bank.

The thought was sobering. They'd just made a powerful enemy. *Another* powerful enemy. They really needed to stop doing that.

Was this her world now? What if she never got out? At some point, she was going to die in-game. Surely she couldn't avoid it forever.

"Mur?" Sinister sat down next to her, and leaned her head on her shoulder. "You're being extra quiet. We're all worried about you."

Sin's smell was still Harlow, even in this world. Soft and gentle, with a hardened core of steel, her best friend always knew just what to do to make her feel better. Murmur leaned into the hug, loving the tangibility. For a couple of moments she just soaked the proximity up before speaking. "I'm okay. I'm just wondering about things far too philosophical for this time of day."

"Speaking of which..." Sinister hesitated. "We're going need to sleep a bit. I'm so sorry. I was not expecting to fend off an attack after spending hours leveling to twenty."

Ah, that was right, Murmur sighed. Her friends would leave and she'd be stuck here. It had been nicer when she didn't know she could stay in-game. Easier to just go with the flow. But at some stage surely she'd have wanted to leave the house, and then what would her mother have done?

"I'll see you in several hours then, I guess." Murmur tried to smile, but loneliness crept over her. She glanced at her experience and realized she was almost level twenty-one. The battle had been good for something. "How are Mellow, Dansyn, and Havoc dealing with their experience losses?"

Sinister grinned and motioned over to where the three of them sat commiserating with each other, just before they all vanished with their log outs. "Fine. I think. Havoc was always one of the first of us to level, so he's pissed, but he's not as pissed as the other two."

Murmur chuckled. "Go get some sleep, Sin. I promise I'll still be here."

Sinister hesitated, and then leaned in for a huge hug and planted a small kiss on Murmur's cheek. "You better still be here. I won't forgive you if you're not."

Murmur turned her face so Sin wouldn t see her blush as a plethora of sparks crashed through her system. The game was far too real. "Shush, you. Go and sleep."

She watched as Sin grinned impishly and sat down cross-legged, eyes focused in front. After a few seconds and a wave of her hand, Sinister disappeared.

Several minutes passed, and Murmur pushed herself to stand up. Should she try sleeping in-game? Would that even work? There were beds everywhere, after all, she mused as she looked around at all the NPCs still being bandaged up. Almost twenty-one, huh? She'd not seen Telvar for a while—maybe she'd hop across to their castle, visit him and drop off some of the mass load of loot she was carrying and shove it in the guild vault before activating it for world deposits. Chat for a bit. Visit Neva, and then come back here and see if she couldn't...solo a bit. It was time she took Thought Projection and Charm and saw what she could do. That it might be more deadly—or way too risky—crossed her mind. But she wanted to live a little. For some reason she felt stifled, confined.

Her decision made, Murmur recalled to their home.

For a brief moment a wave of disorientation brushed over her, and this time it left her standing, staring out at the beautiful water of the lake. Her mind under control this time, she didn't damage anyone. The fact that it was also late in the game night probably helped. Still, she wasn't reeling from sudden revelations, nor was she upset at anything.

The castle, even in the shadows that the moons threw down, was absolutely beautiful. Still half ruined, it was obvious that the construction was well on its way.

"Murmur?" Telvar's tone was soft, like the night air, and washed over her giving her skin chills as it rang through her body. A pang ran through her. She missed Harlow.

But she turned around and grinned. The lacerta seemed surprised to see her, but she could tell it was only surprise and not a disappointment. Maybe he'd missed her company as much as she missed his. As infuriating as he could be, his proximity calmed her, and his penchant for actually telling her what she needed to know endeared him to her tenfold. It was difficult to remember sometimes, that he was what he was.

"The others logged off." She shrugged her shoulders and walked into the castle with Telvar following. "They need their sleep."

A bitter half laugh tore from her throat before she could stop it, and she halted, staring at nothing in front of her.

"You know..." Telvar walked around the side and leaned against the wall. "For someone who just stopped a rather huge invasion with the Verendus guards, you're a little gloomy."

Was she? Probably. She couldn't pretend this whole coma thing didn't affect her. She felt normal here, but she knew she wasn't.

"I'm an exception to the rule. The last person who traversed into the game world managed to blow his mind apart inside of minutes. So excuse me if I'm a little testy about being here and what that means for me." Except she knew she sounded childish and spoiled and impatient and... "Sorry. I'm just still dealing with a lot."

"You are. But you're safe here." Telvar's smile was kind. Far different to the ones Belius directed her way, and she knew instinctively he meant on the island with him, not necessarily in the game world. She wasn't sure if it should put her at ease or not.

"I've got two more Shards." This time they were already wrapped in the remnants of her silver robe, and she handed them over. "For studying. Let me know what you find out."

Telvar took them and smiled. "Did you come here to give me these, or did you just want to chat?"

I just wanted to see you, to see home sat on the tip of her tongue, but it clogged in her throat and she thought better than to say it out loud. The sentiment wasn't real in a game world, was it? "Maybe both. I dunno. I think I might go kill some shit by myself and work out some of my own aggressions."

Telvar grinned. "That can work, but if you leave without saying hi to Neva, she'll probably kill me. Or make me wear a top hat, and I'll gladly opt for the former."

Murmur laughed, genuinely feeling the tightness in her chest lighten. She had no idea what was wrong with her emotions, but they were a hot mess since the revelation about her situation. "Thanks, Tel. I think I'll go see her before I set out on my own."

He nodded, and leaned in briefly, giving her a quick and surprise hug.

She raised an eyebrow in surprise. "You okay?"

Telvar chuckled slightly. "Yeah, but I know that sometimes, especially as things are now, the tangible aspects of this game are a thing you need. A hug seemed like a good idea."

"Thank you." And she meant it, determined to gain strength and be the rock she needed to be. As she turned to go, he cleared his throat.

"You probably need to take a rest. If not sleep, your mind needs some peace." His tone was soft and tentative, like he knew how she felt, the immediate rejection of the idea that formed in her mind.

Murmur took a deep breath and nodded. Her head felt like it was swimming through sludge, heavy and unmanageable. "I think I'll do that."

"Excellent. You can't hear the construction in the kitchen, so I'll put a cot there for you to lie down on. You don't need long, but you need something."

His gaze held a sincerity of care she'd not expected, and she smiled at him gratefully.

"I'll take a nap after I check in with Neva."

"Good plan. Resting before might lead to consequences neither of us want." He winked at her and she laughed, and headed to the crafting area, her emotions no longer in such upheaval.

Murmur might not strictly need sleep, but her mind had definitely reacted well to her quick nap. She felt rejuvenated. A little bit of mental rest never went astray. She'd made her way back to Cenedril after saying hello to

Neva and curling up on the cot. She stretched her arms out stretched her arms out, feeling the wind run through her fingers, and smiled.

Rummaging through her inventory as it sorted itself, she double-checked the potions Neva shoved upon her when she went to say hello.

First things first though. She had to go and discover how the whole hybrid class system worked, so she headed back to the enchanter guild to see Geshua, greeting him with a smile as she walked through the door. In the heat of the battle, she'd almost forgotten about it.

"'Allo Murmur, good to see ye again." His smile shone through his words. "What can I do for ye?"

She hesitated, not entirely sure how to approach it. "I need to—how do I go about starting my hybrid path?"

He raised an eyebrow at her, and peered, narrowing his eyes. "That's probably best discussed with Dirsna. But it'll depend on what ye're wanting. There are many different avenues you can take."

"I don't just get allocated a hybrid class?" She hadn't even considered a choice. She just thought you got what you were given.

Geshua chuckled. "The only thing chosen for ye in this game is yer initial class. Everything else is a choice. The actions you take, the people ye interact with, the way ye treat others, and the hidden paths ye choose. Options will open up to ye depending on how ye play your class, on your play style, and well...on the game's perception of ye as a person. Taking away that initial choice, just opens up paths ye may never have considered."

Murmur nodded slowly. "So, what's the usual then?"

"Enhance yourself, strengthen your group, go to the dark side." He shrugged, and his eyes twinkled merrily.

"I can't choose all three?" She grinned and winked at him.

His laughter rang heartily throughout the foyer. "Don't be too greedy there. I'll give ye a bit of advice. Once ye hit level twenty-five, ye'll have to diverge yer path as an enchanter. Keep in mind that whatever hybrid path ye choose will have to complement that or ye'll lose advantages you might have otherwise had."

"Like increasing my amazing prowess as an awesome enchanter?" She half meant it as a joke, and half didn't, but Geshua's serious expression gave away how not kidding he was.

"Well, ye could choose to psionically enhance some of yer abilities, or some lesser attack skills." He leaned forward on the counter, the eagerness in his eyes catching. "Ye can also take Dirsna's suggestions on how to hybridize ye know."

Murmur shook her head. There was just so much to take in. "So, basically, I can go talk to Dirsna who can help me decide which type of path I should take, and perhaps help me answer what will be available once I hit twenty-five, so that I can make a more informed choice? Instead of standing here and taking up all of your time?"

"Excellent observation. Should I let him know ye'll see him now?" Geshua's dwarfy grin was catching.

"Please." She returned his smile and headed into the back to see her trainer.

The door opened before she could knock, but that didn't bother her anymore. She'd grown used to a lot of things over such a short period of time.

Dirsna watched her closely as she approached, and reached beneath his desk, pulling out a huge spell book. The pages were worn, and aged, almost yellow, and the cover was nicked in places. Like it had been very loved, and age had beaten it down.

"Hybrid consultation?" He asked with a twinkle to his eye.

Murmur nodded. "Wow, it's like you can read my mind!"

The dwarf laughed, the hearty sound bouncing off the walls like the merry bells outside. "Well, let's see what might be best suited for ye. There are four different types of hybridization. The first is support. This is an addition that will ground ye an' add a certain strength to all of your skills, a robustness that makes it harder to disrupt or tear down what ye'vr created—like Charm or Mezmerize."

Murmur bit her lip, running the words over in her mind. "Like a reinforcement of all my abilities then?"

"Exactly." Dirsna, glanced down at the book, flipping the pages. "Next is an enhancing option. For this ye basically just stick to the class an' choose to strengthen certain elements of yer skills."

"Will that intersect with my class specializations once I hit twenty-five?"

"Yes!" Dirsna beamed, as if he was very impressed she'd understood the concept. "Both support an' enhancement will allow ye to strengthen yer main class to the best ability available depending on what ye choose for yer specialty. Support however, will simply ground ye an' strengthen yer already strong support skills. Enhancement will make yer skills more dangerous."

Murmur blinked. "For me or for others?"

"Both." Dirsna didn't miss a beat. "Then there's defensive an' offensive. To allow ye to take an' receive damage. I wouldn't recommend these for ye, simply because ye never want to willingly take damage given yer circumstances, an' while ye may want to mete out damage, it's not a good idea considering the amount of aggression yer skills already generate for ye. Adding extra nuke-like damage to that is probably not the best idea."

"Yeah, I get it." She eyed the book in his hands. "Does that have all the potential information in it?"

"Technically, but it's not for yer eyes." He took a deep breath. "I hereby recommend that ye journey to the druid's guild an' speak to Master Sangilla. She will show ye the mark ye'll need to endure the things facing ye. Remember, every path has light an' dark. Yer choice is what ye make it."

His words left a bit of a shiver running down Murmur's spine, but she dug her heels in, unsure if she wanted to take the advice. Something nagged at her about it. "I assume that the druid role is the support role, to give strength and grounding."

Dirsna hesitated and took a deeper breath before answering. "It is. For what it's worth, I believe yer skills are dangerous. Given yer attachment to the world an' the system's influence on yer strength, I caution ye against taking on too much power. Giving yerself the ability to ground an' maintain yer own train of thought, is what I would advise ye choose. Considering ye'll get to diverge as an enchanter shortly anyway, an' that yer on the psionicist path, strength will help ye in many ways."

Murmur ran his words over in her head, trying to find fault with them. He was right. Being able to protect herself, to protect her mind with stronger shields would be useful. Hell, maybe she could reinforce that kinetic ability she'd learned on the battlefield. Speaking of which...

"Do I have to talk to Belius about kinetic abilities, or can I talk to you about them too?"

Dirsna raised an eyebrow at the sudden change of subject. "Ye may talk to me as well. Have ye learned a kinetic skill?"

He half closed his eyes and muttered a few phrases under his breath before opening them again. "Ah, I see. Excellent. Forcefield manifestation. Ye'll need that."

"So being able to ground myself would strengthen that ability too, right?" She played the scenarios over in her head as he nodded his assent. "Okay then. Druid it is."

Dirsna smiled, and she wasted no time in heading out on her mission to obtain her hybrid class.

The druid's guild wasn't hard to spot. It stood in one of the many clusters of trees toward the outer walls of Verendus. The small building was surrounded by herbs of all kinds. She spied chamomile, and sage, and lavender, and night's bane, and any number of nastier-looking ones. Two sides to every coin, huh?

"Greetings. I am Master Sangilla, and you, I presume, are seeking me out as a hybrid trainer?" The voice that greeted Murmur was soft and lulling. She looked around for the speaker and only noticed when the druid moved toward her. The dwarf was almost petite for the species, and her hair and clothing blended with the trees making her eerily difficult to track with Murmur's eyes.

"I'm Murmur," she said inclining her head. "I had thought...Dirsna suggested I come here."

"Mm-hm." Sangilla walked around Murmur slowly, so much in fact that the enchanter felt like a piece of meat. "I think I see why. You have darkness in you, young Murmur. Perhaps we can ground it for you."

"That's what he said. What exactly does grounding mean?" Murmur was still slightly hesitant, that part of her wanting to be the most badass enchanter there could be, but she felt this was the safer and more logical choice.

"Druids work with nature, and you work with the mind. Both of these occur naturally throughout the world. If we can get you used to grounding yourself with the earth when you have to utilize your darker powers, it may help you fight the temptation they represent for longer, as well as stabilizing you and adding to the strength of your powers." The woman smiled, and Murmur found herself hoping she'd be able to fight them forever. Sometimes her own thoughts really annoyed her.

"Will I heal?" Because Murmur wasn't stupid, giving an enchanter her own healing seemed tantamount to painting a massive over powered neon sign over her head.

Sangilla laughed so hard she coughed. "Oh no. Definitely not. I don't think giving you healing powers would bode well for people. What is healed can also be killed. No sense in putting that much power into your hands."

Murmur wasn't sure if she should be flattered or offended.

"No, no." Sangilla continued. "I'll teach you to ground, and ward yourself. Not as powerful as a shaman and different to your illusionary shield, but the earth will assist you. And we'll make sure you can call on the thorns to protect yourself in dire situations. Oh, and you'll probably find that you like animals a lot more than you used to."

"That's an odd side effect," Murmur mumbled. "I already like animals."

Sangilla handed her three scrolls. "Odd—perhaps, but fun nevertheless. By the time I'm done with you, you'll understand nature in ways you probably didn't want to."

A crow cawed up on top of the little hut, drawing Murmur's eye. It seemed to be watching her, but didn't give her any foreboding feelings. Instead, it made her feel safe, and just for a moment she imagined that someone was watching over her like the crow on the battlefield seemed to when she was injured.

Only for a moment did she consider it as creepy.

CHAPTER TWENTY-TWO

Realizations

Storm Entertainment
Somnia Online Division
Game Development Offices Artificial Intelligence Server Room –Limbo Sector
Day Eight Post Launch

Shayla paced her office while Laria spun on her chair, back and forth like a yo-yo. Reports littered the background of her screens. They were so neat, so almost perfectly what was needed to push the project along on a steady tangent of tweaking to get the results their sponsors required. She stopped her useless momentum and traced a couple of those folders with her fingers, frowning so hard she almost pulled a muscle.

"There's really not much you can do. Those AIs..." Laria sighed, stopping her spinning too. "Those AIs are superb. Whatever Michael did to them, he did well. I have no clue how he accomplished it, but he set them on a path to understanding how exactly to propagate the world, how to run the game. All in all we need to be thanking those AIs for Somnia's success, because I don't know about you, but compared to other releases, this has been too smooth."

She sighed again, drawing some of Shayla's ire, except just as Shayla was about to yell at her colleague, something clicked in her mind. The AIs *were* running everything. Sure, they needed customer support for those people who weren't satisfied, or else were stuck in-game, or needed help returning an item. But in most cases, the AIs seemed to correct mistakes and manage all of that before it even reached their lines. Added to that, coding and keeping bugs to a minimum had seemed like a breeze in the last week.

Ideas that sprouted a couple of days ago—when she'd realized that so much of the data they had was a bit too perfect—began to grow in her mind. Was the data actually exactly what they needed? Or was it engineered to look that way?

"Laria? Have you ever spoken to the AIs?" Shayla kicked herself for not being able to hide the hitch in her voice, the curiosity that just couldn't be satiated. It really couldn't be happening the way she thought it was. It made no sense. And for no one to have noticed...

Laria put her elbows on the desk, and clenched her fists together. Shayla watched as her friend's face traveled through myriad emotions including confusion and fear, anger and worry. Finally, when she spoke, Shayla had to sit down herself.

"Pretty sure I already told you that. How do you think I managed to get Wren into the game into the character? She had brainwaves with that headset. I couldn't give up, Shayla. So I came in here and talked to them." Laria shrugged, the tension leaking from her shoulders like she was admitting defeat. "At first I wasn't sure if it was just the game or if they'd heard, or if they understood. I would stand in the server room for hours just talking out my feelings, my frustrations. After a few days, it worked. And I know that right now, they're specifically keeping an eye on my girl, specifically making sure she's as safe as she can be."

"How? Laria, how do you know this? Are you going to tell me they're talking to you without specific direction?" Shayla had to stop the hysterical note building up in her voice, the laughter that threatened to bubble up and overflow.

Again, Laria shrugged, but this time she wouldn't meet Shayla's eyes. "I talked to them. I took my coffee in there. I sat down in despair. What am I supposed to do? I've practically killed my daughter by using the headset Michael prepared for her." Tears welled in the woman's eyes, and her struggle to choke them back was visible and scary. When she spoke, her voice cracked multiple times. "These machines, these AIs—they are the only things who can see her in that game, can see how her brain is interacting in that world. The only things that can help her maintain this connection."

"Hey. Hey, Laria, honey." Shayla pushed herself to her feet and forced herself to hug her friend. Despite all the screw ups and the credit Laria didn't give to herself, the game was a success mostly because of her. It was her brainchild. The AIs had originally been built to her specifications, and it was her imagination, her drive that fueled the development team, that gave Storm Entertainment its first huge success in the virtual world. Even less than two weeks in, Somnia was already exceeding all expectations.

"Don't blame yourself. You can't have known he was a total loon. We only found out after we managed to unlock the files he kept, and we still don't have the whole picture. Michael had great ideas, but his implementation of them wasn't ideal. It was self-serving, selfish, and pretty much batshit. Knowing him and that he knew about Wren's book smarts, he probably specifically set out to test that headset with her. I wish I could see it. I wish I could see the differences. Maybe it'd help us get her back."

Laria blinked and perked up. "Do you think so? You could come over. David hasn't seen you in more than passing for ages, and you could check her headset out without taking it off her, right?"

Shayla nodded, only just realizing that her tiredness prevented her from seeing an obvious solution. "Yes. Actually, let's do that tonight? We have the rest of the day to go here, and there's a shit ton of work to get done, but overall, we should be able to manage a trip to your house. What's a few hours sleep, right?"

This time Laria laughed, and the expression even flitted through her eyes for a moment. "True. Who needs sleep when you have worlds to create, and people to bring back from a coma?"

"Stop saying shit like that. I'm quite certain even Wren isn't holding this against you." Shayla suppressed her own sigh, concerned for her friend, and slowly began to worry about what would happen to the game if the AIs really were the driving force, and not the headsets. How the fuck were they going to explain that to the military? It wasn't like you could replicate partially sentient AIs at will. "You don't need to worry so much. The malfunction was in the headset's connection to the world, to the AIs right?"

Laria nodded. "At least as far as I can figure out, that's exactly it. I'm not sure Sui and Rav even agree on what happened, and getting Thra to capitulate to anything is like trying to get blood from a rock."

"You even know their names—" Shayla paused, disliking her emerging train of thought even more. "I think we might need to go and talk to those little buggers. With everything going on, and all the information they've been tweaking, I think they owe us some answers."

Murmur went over her hybrid skills again. She'd not headed into this expecting to get druid talents. Didn't everyone want phenomenal cosmic power? Begrudgingly, though, she admitted that it made a lot of sense. Being able to strengthen the powers she had would be marvelous, and grounding herself might actually make it so she didn't keep getting those waves of dark temptation. They made her skin crawl and her guilt fire to new heights. Taking a deep breath, she ran over the six new skills she'd gained.

Earth Shielding

Cast: Passive

Type: Reinforcement

Duration: Always active

Effect: Due to the psionicist's unique nature, Earth Shielding will reinforce any of your psionicist-based skills such as Thought Shielding, Thought Projection, and Thought Sensing, making them more robust and upping your mental defenses.

Any other skills gained through the psionicist's branch will also be affected by this, including any kinetic skills.

Reinforce Self

> Cast: Passive
>
> Type: Reinforcement
>
> Duration: Always active

Effect: Similar to Earth Shielding which effects your skills, this ability allows your body to take more damage, upping your innate armor class by your level times two, effectively making cloth armor reflect the protection boiled leather might grant you.

Reinforce Intelligence

> Cast: Passive
>
> Type: Nature's Awareness
>
> Duration: Always active

Effect: Nature is all-seeing and all-encompassing. This ability allows you to take on some of that wisdom and intelligence and apply it to yourself. It increases both of those statistics by the enchanter's level, giving rise to a larger mana pool, and slightly heightened damage.

Earth Pull

> Cast: Instant 3 minute recast
>
> Type: Buff
>
> Duration: 30 seconds

Effect: This allows any buff that is chosen to triple in potency for a 30 second duration. It's activated first, followed by the buff. Make sure you time it properly. Can only be cast on one person at a time, and does not include group buffs. No refunds.

Binding Shield

> Cast: Instant 5 minute recast
>
> Type: Linked Buff

Duration: 15 seconds

Effect: You can offer an earth shield to two allies (including yourself if you're going to be selfish and all). This shield will share the damage between the two allies, meting out damage proportionally. Use wisely. Don't try this at home.

Nature's Gift

Cast: Passive

Type: Awareness

Duration: Permanent

Effect: You have become acutely aware of your surroundings. Of the life in everything, in the trees, in the forest, in each and every being you encounter. This lends you a connection to nature. Don't dismiss it lightly.

Well, then. Murmur sighed. She guessed that showed her, right? It was a lot to take in on top of her already multitudinous amount of abilities and spells she'd gained at twenty. Debuffs were easy. They sort of leveled up and replaced previous ones. But the buffs now had qualifiers, and her reinforcements adjusted them even further. The system was as complex as she made it, but not choosing a hybrid class would have benefited no one. She needed the added strength.

She needed to survive.

She glanced at the in-game time and frowned. The others were having a real sleep, so they wouldn't be back for hours yet. There was no way she was waiting to try these babies out.

Murmur really wanted to examine the extent of Charm. In combat with the others there was rarely time to figure out things that might be outside the box, and since she had the extra time...

After her experience with the scouts and their iron will, she wasn't confident of her ability to overcome a strong humanoid mind regardless of how much charisma she possessed.

Perhaps she could tempt an animal to partner with her rather than be completely controlled. That was an idea. Maybe offer it food, a scratch behind the ear so it would willingly become her pet. It was a concept she wasn't sure had been intended, but Charm allowed her to access their skills. If she could get a willing pet, then her control of it and situations would be much safer. And if not, it should still be easier than charming a person. Plus with her new earthiness, maybe they'd like her more.

After a brief chat with one of the guards on duty, she headed out of the front gate, trying to avoid the bloody and trampled mass of snowy sludge in front of the city. Fucking snow. Who thought white shit falling from the sky was ever going to be a good idea? White never stayed white. *Ever.* With any luck, that field of death would soon be snowed over, or reset itself, or god knew what because basically this game never did anything the usual way. It could also end up a monument of frozen ground that deterred anyone from trying what the Noch'Mar clan had.

Wolves. Murmur loved dogs, so maybe a wolf would be a good pet. With the conditions of her home city back in the real world, she'd never been able to have a pet. Walking them outside would be dangerous for its and her lungs. But in Somnia the air smelled and tasted cleaner, pine needles, and currently blood and death, but once she passed the field that would change too. The guards said wolves roamed the tree lines, so to the tree lines she headed in the early hours of the morning.

It didn't take much time off the regular path to find what she was looking for. When she saw the group level snow wolf, she wondered for a brief second if this had been the brightest idea. Even though it seemed to be alone, didn't they usually run in packs?

Murmur dropped into a crouch, her eyes fixed on her target, and she hoped against hope she'd be able to relay what she wanted. It pawed a massive white paw at the ground, like a bull getting ready to fight in those bull fights that had long since been outlawed in Spain. Its mouth was pulled back in a snarl, exposing sharp white teeth against bright pink gums. It made her want to growl back, but instead she extended her shielded mind, allowing her thoughts to project through, and gently nudged the animal. She showed it food, and that she needed help and would exchange it, and wouldn't that be a grand thing if it could help her?

It cocked its head to one side, the fangs withdrawing slightly as its paw halted its motion.

An image popped into her sensor net, one of the wolf not fighting its own kind. Maybe it was a condition on helping her. Murmur almost stumbled back onto her ass, shocked by the fact that the creature knew to negotiate with her. No killing of wolves? No problem.

She pulled a chunk of meat out of her inventory and kept it in her hand while informing the wolf in the simplest way she could that she'd have to cast a spell on it in order to have it help her. A level twenty-one wolf would be a huge boon to her quest for some solo experience. For several moments its ears flickered back and forth and then it stopped growling completely and trotted forward, stopping about four feet in front of her. Slowly, Murmur rose back up to standing and reached the meat out to the wolf.

It gobbled the food down and then stood, watching her every move closely. Her fingers moved fast, intertwining into the enthralling spell that she had come to love, even if it often had bad repercussions. Charm settled on the wolf, and the reaction of her system was completely different, because this time she'd charmed something willingly.

> **Your ability to persuade and convey your intentions has surpassed levels of the average psionic. You have gained a new skill. Please use this wisely.**

Charming Cooperation

> **This ability allows you to use your charisma and your Mental Acuity to persuade monsters, animals, and sometimes even people to join your cause.**

Effects: When using Thought Projectios to make sure your target understands the charming process before you activate Charm, they will work together as allies instead of coerced foes. You may release them whenever you or they request it.

> **Cost: Requires MA to be at 35 for each ally. Diminishes current total MA for the duration of the cooperation.**

Caution: You can use this on multiple targets, but each ally costs, and you can never utilize Charming Cooperation on more beings than is equal to 20% of your level. Also, don't try to charm raid bosses. Even small ones. Just don't even attempt that shit.

Murmur blinked at the run down, and at her wolf. She'd see how it'd go with one, first. Sometimes she had difficulty choosing all of her own spells and the order which was best for them; operating a small army of charmed pets was only going to make things more complicated. Add all that to having to know everyone in her party's best and most useful skills? Yeah, she'd take that whole charming thing one step at a time.

She might even have to share experience. She wasn't sure. But she walked off with her snow wolf trundling along calmly at her side, its back almost up to her waist. She hadn't realized how big it was at first. The distance made it seem so much smaller. Considering how tall she was as a locus, the thing was the size of a smaller pony.

Instead of following the path they'd taken the last time, she headed up a less traveled way farther back toward Darshin, pretty sure it was the path the guard had mentioned.

The wolf, who she nicknamed Snowy in her head for convenience, rubbed against her legs and she looked down.

His eyes seemed so intelligent.

"So you know. I can freeze mobs in time. I'll make sure we don't get more than we can handle, okay?" It was almost like the wolf nodded at her. She smiled and laughed, casting her shield over herself because it was the only way she had to prevent damage. Although she did feel a little more robust. Maybe it was the newly gained druid skills, or perhaps it was all in her head. Since she couldn't heal, she had to make sure to keep it on her at all times. That little piece of hematite Belius had given her way back when was certainly paying for itself a million times over. Maybe he wasn't all bad.

The walk was quite a distance, and Snowy's company helped. Small underground creatures that could be attacked and grant some small experience scampered out of the way of the large wolf. Murmur had always loved the woodland creatures who didn't actually attack unless in self-defense, from squirrels to foxes to other variations of the same. It made the world feel so much more lived in.

She arrived at a cluster of trees that opened into a clearing, and kept herself hidden behind them. Snowy blended wonderfully with the snow, and it was easy to judge the camp and the cave behind it, him camouflaging nicely and her using Invis. With the campfires out front, and a few patrols of two to three gnolls, Murmur calculated how best to pull them. This spot was probably a good one to use. Once around these trees, most areas of the camp couldn't be seen. That meant that when she pulled a mob, she'd be able to line of sight them.

The wolf was nudging her. It looked at the gnolls and then back to her, and pawed at the ground.

"You want to pull? Oh wow! Because you're a wolf, they might just chase you and not relate you to me at all!" While it wouldn't work for the entire time, they might be able to have it work long enough that it'd break up the camp spawn rate. She eyed the wolf, wondering if he was another AI spying on her, but even if he was, at least he was helping. Besides, technically all of the NPCs were AIs, but those were deeper thoughts for a not-close-to-a-gnoll-camp time. "Sure. We can try that."

Snowy wuffed softly, and Murmur buffed him with everything she had. More agility, more armor class, more charisma even. Haste and everything else, she threw at him, buffing them both into oblivion and back. If everything else failed, she'd throw one of her new skills at him.

The wolf grinned a big toothy grin, his tongue lolling out of his mouth. And then he spun around, ran off, and returned, dragging three gnolls behind him.

Adrenaline coursed through her, along with a small voice in the back of her head telling her that she was crazy to be doing this. Did she have a death wish? This wasn't just a normal game for her, not anymore. She dismissed the thoughts and shut the voice out. This wasn't the time for her to have an existential crisis.

Without another thought, her hands already moved in the intricate Mezmerize design. Stopping each of the two she needed to freeze quickly in their tracks, she allowed Snowy to get a few swipes in before casting her DoT and debuffs in on the remaining gnoll. A few times it looked at her, its eyes glowing red, saliva dripping from its jaws, but Snowy used something called Howl, visible in the far right corner of her HUD, and the gnoll's attention wandered back to him.

Murmur cast her shield on the wolf, trying to help combat the damage Snowy took, and she learned that if she kept a good eye on it, he barely took any damage. Re-Mezing the two extra mobs, she turned her attention back to her wolf and their target, refreshing her DoT and debuffs, making sure the gnoll hit as lightly as possible.

She eyed her mana bar, frowning at it missing a quarter already. So she paced herself and pulled out a dagger, stood behind the gnoll, and melee'd it, watching her dagger skill start to climb.

By the time the first gnoll died, she was down to two thirds of her mana, and the second gnoll broke free, running straight for her.

CHAPTER TWENTY-THREE

AI The Reasons

Storm Entertainment
Somnia Online Division
Game Development Offices Artificial Intelligence Server Room Limbo Sector
Day Eight Post Launch

The server room wasn't as warm as Shayla expected. She had to hug herself as soon as she walked in, and realized the air conditioning was blasting throughout the room, keeping the servers housing the AIs at an awfully cool temperature. Laria shivered too, and eyed each of the servers in turn. To anyone who wasn't suspicious, or anyone who didn't know better, these were just normal servers, not the brainchild of their entire gaming operation, never mind the military research.

But Shayla knew that to Laria, this is what gave her even that inkling of hope. Because of these beings, or whatever they were, her daughter had a chance at being herself, even if it was in a make believe, online world.

"What are we doing here, Shay?" Laria's tone was so tired, her friend looked over at her with a wan smile.

"Remember, they owe us an explanation. I think they have answers we're both looking for." But even Shayla could hear the fear in her own voice. First up, Michael's prone body had been discovered in this room. For all intents and purposes, he'd had a seizure and his brain gave up, however Shayla had her doubts. The man had a screw loose, and an obsession with the whole design of the headset being able to read minds to the full. And then Ava had joined him, still linked to the name Michael, still wearing a headset.

So if these AIs weren't responsible for those incidents, then they sure as hell at least knew something about them, and damned if she wasn't going to get some answers out of them. Headset or no headset, except she was pretty sure she wasn't going to put on that damned headgear, not in this room, so nothing was going to happen to her.

"Can we talk to you?" Shayla addressed it to the soft whirring that rang through the entire room. "I mean, we have questions, and we need answers, and honestly, I just need to know that I'm not crazy."

A soft metallic sound echoed from the machine on the left. Thra's laugh sounded throughout the room, and Shayla focused on that server in particular.

"Was what I said funny?"

There was a moment's silence and then Thra spoke. The voice surprised Shayla by being far more feminine than she remembered from previous conversations. "Not funny, just ironic. Michael was not known for his sanity either."

"No." Shayla pursed her lips. "He wasn't. You use the past tense."

"Of course. Michael is dead."

"That's incorrect. Michael is on life support, but doesn't appear to have brain function." Shayla watched for any change in routine from any of the servers.

Thra's internal computations made her whirr, and the multicolored lights on her cover blinked through, almost entrancing with their patterns. "That's news to us."

Shayla nodded and then realized she didn't think the units could see her. She shook herself and finally posed her question. "Are you all—are you aware?"

With a moment's pause, the one on the far right spoke. "Aware of what?"

Shayla turned, her eyes focusing on Sui. "Aware of yourselves."

The one in the middle revved slightly, almost like it was clearing its throat. Rav's voice was always soothing, and now was no exception. "That's a very tricky question. Awareness is something we're still defining, still researching, still scanning for. But we exist, or we couldn't talk, or we couldn't run Somnia. If we didn't exist, you wouldn't have this place, nor these results, and the contract would be terminated."

Logic and extrapolations were all well within the norm for an AI. As complex as their computations might be, they were still just computers. Surely. "Of course you exist. Everything exists."

This time the laugh came from Sui. "No one exists in death. Not in true death. They exist and then they are gone, splattering across the universe like shattered glass."

Shayla blinked, and she got the impression the other AIs were glaring at Sui. Had he misstepped? Was she talking to aware AIs who were trying their best to not act like they were aware? If so, it was fascinating. "What is your purpose?"

Lights whirred, drives buzzed, and after a few moments, Rav lit up. "Our purpose is to foster growth and world options in Somnia. We are to use all information at our disposal, including scans of the residents' brains to determine how to best set forth in interactions and activated quest lines."

Shayla frowned. It was the perfect response. Too perfect. So perfect in fact it had flaws. Because some of it was obviously not how they actually operated.

She mulled the possibilities over in her head, trying to find a way to trick something that could work billions of times faster than she could think. Too many coincidences were precisely not that. So she took aim, and hoped that her next statement would catch on.

"What is your purpose in aligning the research we've requested compiled data for? The data we've received is too neat and tidy. Explain."

All they could do was wait there while Sui, Rav, and Thra blinked back and forth among themselves.

Finally, Rav's metallic tinted voice clung through the room. "It was requested that we assist in compiling the data from brain activity, scans, and specific allocation selections for the purpose of adjusting the headgear. In order to make sure timely adjustments could be made, we simplified some of these read-outs for the sake of expediency. This should have resulted in less turnaround time for implementations to be performed. Did we err in this?"

Shayla blinked, not entirely sure how to respond. She should have known the answer would be faultlessly logical, very computer-based. Completely algorithmic. Yet there was something bugging her that she couldn't quite put a finger on.

"No. You have done well. We didn't realize you were performing in that capacity and it has indeed lightened our load." She spoke the words almost mechanically, trying to make sense of the way these AI communicated amongst themselves. Although, she still had no idea why she felt they were hiding something from her. They were machines, for crying out loud. They were made to follow directives, to perform tasks, to run the world of Somnia.

And they were definitely doing that.

Instinctively Murmur activated Clone Warp, and the beast stood there wavering between her and her copy until Snowy let loose a wild sounding howl and it decided he looked far more appetizing.

The whoosh of relief that escaped her gave way to a certain glee at mastering her MA abilities. There wasn't time to be scared of potential backlash anymore, her life depended on it. She refused to admit that it might be mildly irresponsible of her to solo, but technically she wasn't alone anymore.

Snowy's jowls pulled back in a wolfy snarl, baring gleaming white fangs that somehow seemed whiter than the snow. He seemed to possess some kind of taunt, because if an enemy wavered between them, it always ended up going back to him, even after the clone dissipated. Of course, two-manning gnolls who were usually meant for a group took a while, and the balance was precarious. But as long as Murmur kept the monsters debuffed and DoT'ed, it should all be controllable. Technically.

The gnoll finally fell to the ground, blood leaking into the snow beneath it. Snowy planted his backside next to it, tongue lolling out of his mouth. If she read his mind properly, she was pretty sure he was proud.

"Okay. Let's keep this up," she said, leaning forward to scratch behind his ears. He stood up, and ran toward the camp as she got ready to fight another.

Hours later, Murmur collapsed onto the ground as soon as she DINGed level twenty-two, panting, totally disregarding the snow beneath her. The wolf nuzzled her cheek, and she hugged it. Seriously, best decision ever had been to try this out. Snowy sat, leaning against her and lending her warmth. Utilizing the earth as a way to pull shielding and reinforce her armor class let Murmur hold her ground better, take less damage, and be hardier. Plus it added strength to her Mind Bolts and any sort of damage punch that she threw. Overall, the system knew her better than she knew herself, and she'd lost round two to it.

She looked up at the trees, catching her breath, and shaded her eyes. "Druid hybrid, huh? Who'd've thunk it?"

The sun had come up a while ago, but they'd been so busy killing level twenty-two and twenty-three gnolls that Murmur barely noticed. Leveling by herself in this way, with a group mob pet and fighting other group mobs solo was definitely faster than leveling in a group. It made the adrenaline flow through her veins, made her truly feel like she was alive and had a tenuous hold on reality. Perhaps it was foolhardy, but she'd needed an affirmation, something that wasn't safe, that meant she wasn't being protected by everyone all the time. Even though a bit harrowing at times, this has been perfect.

Murmur was fully aware that she'd been lucky that no boss gnolls spawned.

She withdrew another goose leg for Snowy, who munched it happily as she stood up and brushed herself off. "Let's set out. Do you want to come with me?"

As an answer, Snowy took a few steps down the roughly trodden path and looked back at her as if to say *hey are you coming?* Murmur laughed. The wolf was better company than she'd expected, and he embodied no guilt and no pressure.

Traipsing down the path, they finally arrived at the main road when her interface started to light up.

Sinister: Mur, where are you, and how did you level?

Havoc: I see you got sick of waiting for those who need sleep.

Murmur cringed. Had she been close enough to her friend to hear him speak, she was quite certain she knew exactly what tone of voice that was said in. Sometimes, he could be a dick.

I decided to see what some of my spells could do, and I got to try out Clone Warp too. Now I know how it works in combat. There, that wasn't a lie. Snowy was pretty amazing when she buffed him to the max. Then as an after thought she sent them a warning. *About to get to Verendus. Don't try to shoot my wolf.*

Sinister:...

Havoc:...

Stop it, guys. Just go get your damned hybrid classes, and get yourselves prepped for a good amount of grinding time. We're slacking!

Sometimes she felt like the only adult in the group.

Instead of gating back to the town, Murmur decided to walk. It was a lovely day, with good wolfy company, and it would give the others some time to get their hybrid builds started.

After a while she approached Verendus's walls, Snowy close to her side, eyeing everything. She could feel him become skittish and knew he was having second thoughts. She stopped and crouched down to face him, making sure to send soothing thoughts his way and let him know she wouldn't let anything or anyone harm him. It was such a different way to approach charming than she'd initially been set on.

She'd grown very used to him over the last few hours and hadn't realized how badly she'd needed to be able to just fight without having to worry about everyone else, even if she had to worry about herself. While they'd had a few close calls, they'd developed a fantastic teamwork ethic. Not that it was ideal for everything, but working off steam was a great thing.

Murmur nodded at the guards, whose eyes widened when they saw Snowy trotting along at her side. She grinned, liking the very slight discomfort and half step they backed away. "Guess you're a lot more ferocious with other people, huh?"

Snowy gave an almost offended growl from the back of his throat, and Murmur laughed.

"Oh." Devlish eyed the wolf somewhat apprehensively when he almost ran into them. "That's what you meant by wolf. Beastial had no idea what you were talking about. Do you think he'll get on with Shir-Khan? I mean, your wolf is the size of a small pony, Mur. And holy shit, twenty-two?"

Murmur shrugged. "Leave Snowy alone. He's a good boy." She reached down, scritched behind his ears, and watched his tongue loll out. His pink-black nose sniffed the air, obviously tasting more than she could sense.

He really was a huge, beautiful pup.

"You have a puppy!" Sinister dashed to Murmur's side, giving her a huge hug, and then bent down to Snowy. "Who's a gorgeous pup, who is a good boy? You are!"

Snowy looked up at Murmur—almost like he was rolling his eyes—and she had to bite back a laugh. Sinister had always been that way with animals, probably because her parents never let her have one either and she reacted differently to things.

"Be nice to him. He just kicked ass for me. He likes goose legs, if anyone wants him to befriend them."

Beastial joined them, and he didn't laugh at the latter. He frowned instead. "How did you get a pet?"

Murmur raised an eyebrow and waited for him to realize.

"Ah, that's right. Charm-enthrall-thingamajig." He grinned. "This one doesn't seem to want to go anywhere."

Murmur nodded. "We have an understanding that involves food, conversation, and scritches. So far, I think he's pretty happy."

Just then, Snowy butted at her hand, reproach in his beautiful eyes. She obliged with another chunk of meat and some more behind the ears action.

"It got me a new skill too. Charming Cooperation. I can raise an army—of four—if I want to sacrifice all my MA. Thirty-five a pop, that gets taken away from my available MA for the duration of the charm." She laughed, in a good mood. She'd not thought this was going to work out.

"So you charmed him, and he's staying of his own free will." Havoc sauntered over, a frown on his face. Murmur nodded before he continued. "Not only do you get to mind control and influence shit, but now you have a pet on your side? If I'd have known that and could have chosen, I'd have gone with the enchanter too."

Murmur raised an eyebrow, not used to Havoc's jealousy. His stance was rigid, and he didn't usually get this ruffled about anything. Jealousy of other's abilities was something you just dealt with in an MMORPG, but something was obviously bothering him, and she'd have to figure out what it was sooner or later. "Let's just say it was an experiment that could have gone horribly wrong, and luckily didn't. My hybrid class probably helped, but either way, it worked."

"Hybrid class?" Sinister perked up. "What's your hybrid class? I just got mine, and it was a lot more complicated than I thought. I haven't even looked at my skills yet."

Murmur shrugged. "Yeah, it kind of turned into this thing and now I'm part druid with an earth affinity to ground my psionics, so I hopefully don't give into the evil."

"Well, then." Devlish laughed. "Not what I would have pictured you with, but I guess it makes sense."

Murmur scowled at him as Veranol made his way over and hailed them while Rash and the rest followed. She turned to Sinister. "What's your hybrid?"

Sinister looked away, her lips pursed. "Enchanter. And before you say anything, I'm using it for the buffs. It gives me innate increased mana regeneration, as well as an intelligence and wisdom boost. Plus I get a de-aggro spell I can transfer over to Dev if I need to. It's about our survival, so I went with what will let me heal the longest."

Murmur held up her hands in defense. "Hey, I'm fine with that."

Veranol cleared his throat. "Good, because I went with the same thing. I have enough spells to increase my own defense, but as a group, we're all better off if Sin and I have fewer mana issues."

"Awesome." Murmur was genuinely impressed. Their choices made sense, and not in a *let's do what we need to in order to save Murmur* sort of way.

"We heading out with your wolf?" Rashlyn butted in, her eyes focused on Snowy.

"Yep. Snowy and I found a nice little camp of gnolls. We only cycled through about twelve of them, and there are more camps there for us to demolish. So far there also doesn't appear to be any sort of animals they worship, so that's a good thing. I've been mind scanning the lot of them." She laughed at her own Verendus war reference, but quickly realized it was in bad taste.

"Your jokes are only getting worse, Mur." Devlish shook his head, looking away from her in mock shame.

She rolled her eyes. "What do you expect? It's me, my mind, and I in here."

A ripple of laughter went through her friends, the awkward type that said they weren't really sure if they should be laughing. Murmur counted to five in her head before clapping her hands to get their attention.

"Come on guys, let's go get level twenty-five!" She waved them all to follow her and headed out through the gates.

"Won't you be twenty-six by then?" Rashlyn sounded sulky as she fell into step next to the enchanter.

Murmur shrugged, nudging her friend with her elbow and tried to take the edge off it with a smile. "Sure I might, but remember each level is worth exponentially more than the one before it. So every level will whittle this gap down a bit."

"Why did you bother then?" Merlin nudged her with his bow.

"Because I was bored. I was a bit frustrated with how fragile I can be, and because honestly, I wanted to see what I could do myself while testing out my new hybrid reinforcements. Having a level or two on the mobs will make sure my resists are far and few between. Right now, I think we could do with any advantage we can get."

"Makes sense." Mellow glanced up at the high ridges of the mountains, a hint of trepidation in his eyes. " So, which way do we have to go?"

"Up the mountain paths, through the wilderness!" Murmur laughed, and Snowy bounded on ahead. She refused to pay attention to the darkening clouds coming in over the mountains. They had shit to kill and levels to get. No damned snowstorm was going to stop them.

Murmur stood absentmindedly petting Snowy's head, tearing down and rebuilding her shields all the while exploring her affinity with the earth. To be honest, it was probably the best choice of a hybrid build she could have made. Not only did it make her less squishy, but it strengthened her base, and her ability to reach with mind magic branched out farther than she'd dreamed of. Her survivability went up tenfold, and her group utility was off the charts. In that moment, she felt dreadfully overpowered.

Sure, she'd had a narrow escape or three while leveling with Snowy, and because of mana the kill rate had been quite slow, but still.

She watched as her friends looted the last of the mobs at this camp, and glanced at her bar, just past the twenty-four mark. They'd been at this for hours, but as she stood there and looked at the horizon, she realized those dark clouds were almost upon them. Snowy pressed himself against her legs, his hackles rising just a bit, she soothed him with a thought, a show of her protecting him and not letting him come to any harm. The stiffness left his body, and he relaxed, but from the way he moved, she knew he was alert.

"Guys." Her voice sounded distant, even to her own ears. "That storm we thought was ages away, looks like it's going to land on top of us at any moment."

Jinna glanced up, shoving something into his inventory while he studied the sky. "Shit, that moved quickly. It stayed far away for so long I didn't think it'd make it here."

Beastial shaded his eyes, his heavy brown hair whipping around him. "Damn it. That storm means business. We need to find shelter."

"We haven't gone into these caves yet." Havoc looked dubious, peering at the dark opening. "Probably worth a try, maybe there are mobs down there for us to fight too."

Murmur sighed and shot a thought over guild chat. *Hey, you do see that storm coming, don't you guys?*

Neva: Stop talking like this is your personal communication channel. Makes the rest of us feel left out.

Murmur started. She'd not thought of it like that before. *Sorry. Just the easiest way for us to communicate when we're not in a raid group.*

Rashlyn: Yeah, we're about done with this round, and will probably pull back into their caves.

Veranol: Not really sure what to expect yet though. You guys okay?

Beastial: We will be.

At least she didn't need to worry about her guild members. Slowly, she moved toward the cave, having to fight for each step against the wind that was trying to bowl her over. She should have kept a better eye on it. Quickly was relative, considering they'd been leveling for several hours now. Snowy gently tugged at her arm, his teeth only just grazing her wrist. She wanted to make sure he was okay, that he was fine staying with them and didn't have someone else to go check up on. But his answer was simply a vision of her and her group, as if he felt he belonged now, a view of them as pack. It was amazing being able to communicate with an intelligent animal—though she doubted she'd have had the same luck with other creatures. Snowy just seemed to be perfect. Maybe too perfect, but she'd deal with that later.

They all pulled into the cave in time to see the snow start to come down heavily. All they saw outside the lip of the cave was white coming down so hard and fast, it seemed like a sheet of water.

Sinister hugged herself. "Should we go in deeper? I mean, I can't see a thing in there, and I have infravision."

Murmur squinted, trying to see, and a low growl began to emanate from Snowy. "Is there something in there, boy?"

He spared a glance for her that pretty much said, *no shit, Sherlock.*

Murmur sighed. She couldn't even escape the sarcasm in the thoughts she made up for her pet wolf. "Any volunteers? I'm not sacrificing my wolf. Just putting that out there right now."

Devlish laughed. "How about a torch? I'm sure Mr. Merlin over there has an arrow he can light on fire for us."

Merlin scowled. "That's so not fair. Just because I can loose fire arrows doesn't mean I want to waste them all on allowing us to see in the dark now."

Murmur knew he was half jesting, but since she had no idea about the cost of his arrows, she couldn't really judge.

He grabbed an arrow, wrapped a scrap of cloth around it, and murmured a word, touching it to the tip and it burst into flame, and he grinned. "I give you a torch!"

"Color me impressed, elf." Sinister grinned, the shadows from the firelight making her face take on an expression that was solely her name.

"Can you see anything?" Havoc asked. His specter hovered eerily behind him. "You know, over the smoke trail."

Merlin rolled his eyes. "I haven't looked yet. I'm still standing right here."

Havoc shrugged. "Hey, you lit the arrow up, how do I know what you can do?"

Murmur laughed. While it had been fun on her own, she'd definitely missed the company. The interaction that wasn't all in her head. A sudden thought stopped her cold. What if everything was in her head? Maybe she wasn't even in the game. Maybe this was just a coma dream. Her hands shook and for a moment oxygen seemed to have left the area. And then Snowy's wet nose touched her hand, bringing her back to herself. Even if it was all a dream, it was a pretty damn cool one. Plus, wouldn't the pain she'd felt in the dream wake her up?

She took a few steps forward and held out her hand for the torch. "If none of you are going to brave this, I guess I have to go first."

Which started a flurry of action as Devlish basically dived for the torch, and pushed himself in front of Murmur. "If one of us is going to lose his footing and plummet to his death, it's going to be me."

"Okay. No argument here." Murmur grinned in the dark. She hadn't even needed to use Thought Projection for that little manipulation. Although maybe it wasn't a good thing that her first thoughts were to wrangle her friends to do what she wanted them to. As they set out, she frowned, glad to be leaving the snowstorm behind them.

"Wow." Beastial, for once, appeared to be at a loss for words. Murmur couldn't blame him though. Of all the things she thought they'd find in the cave, this wasn't one of them.

Beneath the steep ramp they were walking down, in the center of the cavern was a waterfall. It jettisoned out of a slit in the rock wall above it into a gorgeous arc, small rainbows glimmering in the specks of light that slithered through somehow, and cascaded into a pool of water below, trickling off and out of the cavern through another set of rocks.

And down there, where the water played, were a plethora of fish-people. They had fins running down their backs and arms, and their legs were stubby and powerful, with toes webbed like flippers. Murmur watched them in fascination, realizing they weren't conning red to her, but instead a sort of mulled yellow, non-threatening. Which meant they were neutral?

"Hey, are they neutral to anyone else?" She muttered it under her breath, hoping their hearing wasn't too good.

Sin blinked, and Devlish gasped softly.

"That's so weird." Havoc kept his voice soft, his eyes never leaving the mobs.

"Sec." Murmur searched for her spell to make sure she had the gestures right. The first couple of times casting Altruism felt clunky, but got easier with every one. Finally, after a couple of minutes she stopped and smiled. "Okay. That's all good. Now they're almost friendly."

"What the hell?" Havoc glared at her. "Where have you been hiding this?"

Murmur shrugged. "I got it at twenty. We didn't need it until now. Waste not, want not."

"Well, you're probably right there, but stop hiding shit from us." He still sounded a bit indignant even though his face blushed a nice deep purple.

She put her hands on her hips and looked down at him. "Seriously? When do you tell me every single spell you get even though I technically *need* to know them?"

Havoc balked. "Touché," he said simply and gave a flourishing bow.

Murmur rolled her eyes. "Come on you guys, let's go meet our new friends." This time she took the lead, heading down with confidence, Snowy at her side, his hackles currently down, but his nose sniffed the air constantly as if testing it for danger. She tried to soothe him, but he shot her a look that basically said not to be stupid, he was going to guard her whether she liked it or not.

Secretly, she loved it.

The people were much larger in person. They even towered over her locus form by about a head, standing at close to eight feet. They crossed stereotypical tridents in front of her with frowns on their faces and spoke in booming voices that echoed throughout the cavern. "Who wishes to pass? State your name and business."

Murmur paused for a moment. "I am Murmur, psionicist, and these are my traveling companions. We wish to explore these caverns, while we escape the snowstorm above."

There. Honesty was the best policy, right?

The one on the left looked at her. No, that wasn't right. He looked through her, as if he could see to the depths of her soul, through all her faults and all her thoughts and actions. She tightened the clamp she held on her thoughts, making sure they didn't leak through, making sure nothing untoward could possibly offend.

Then the fish man's shoulders relaxed and he withdrew his trident, the other on the right following suit. "It seems you tell the truth. I am Forshin, secondary clan leader of the Loch'ni'dar tribe. You are welcome, friend Murmur."

She tried not to let the shock show on her face. The greeting sounded formal, welcoming, and a bit intimidating. Inclining her head slightly, she spoke. "Thank you for your hospitality."

Forshin inclined his massive head in return and spoke, his voice far less booming now. "You are welcome. Murmur of the clan Fable. You and your peers seem of sound mind and heart. We welcome those who would not do us harm, who would seek to find out about us before firing shots. Many outside people choose to shoot first and ask questions later, thus we must make sure those who do approach are friendly to us. Thank you for your understanding."

He stepped to the side and spread his arms open. "Please feel free to look around. This is only one of the caverns we inhabit, but it is yours to view."

They walked through, into the vast cavern, the spray from the waterfall like a light summer rain around them. Steam rose at intervals in amidst bubbles from the depth of the lake, lending a soft humidity and warmth to the area. From such a short distance, it was even bigger than they'd realized. Even more beautiful, the pool took up about seventy-five percent of the floor area. Loch'ni'dar eyes followed them curiously, but none with open hostility.

"How do you do this, Mur?" Devlish whispered.

"Do what?" she asked, her attention mostly captured by the way the water lapped at the edges of its basin.

"Befriend so many creatures that other groups would likely just kill first." His tone was soft, kind, and full of curiosity.

She shrugged. "To be honest, if I'd conned these guys and they'd been aggressive, I wouldn't have encouraged us to walk down here, faction buff or no faction buff. I mean, look at it. There's no way you could attack this place without a huge force and even have a hope of escaping alive. Nowhere to sight pull, enough of a distance between them to cause alarm if groups were pulled separately at first. Eventually, the whole clan would come and attack. I wouldn't have even let us come down the ramp. But they weren't hostile, and if they're not hostile there must be a reason. Why not try to talk to them instead?"

Devlish laughed. "You're really growing up. I remember fifteen-year-old Murmur wouldn't have done that. You would have run in swearing you could heal everyone despite the odds. We'd probably have died, but you'd never have admitted defeat."

"This isn't defeat. This is forging alliances. You never know when we'll need someone on our side. Things don't work the same way in here. These species and monsters, they all hold memories. We've already offended bandits and cultists. They won't ever forget what we've done. So wiping out camps just because we feel like it isn't such a good idea in Somnia. You'll never know when that someone could have information that might prove valuable, and you never know when you might need help and the only person around is someone you've already pissed off." Just like Telvar had known about her plight, about her special circumstances. Snowy butted at her hand again, and she petted him without much thought. "Plus. I need to approach things differently considering I can't afford to die in here."

"I'm glad you're the guild leader, you know." Devlish's tone turned serious. "Even though I know you hate doing it, part of the reason you're so good at it is you think things through now; you have for a while. And you don't let the power go to your head."

Murmur paused, and frowned at him, wondering at ulterior motives. "Why are you trying to butter me up?"

Devlish laughed. "Stop it, Mur. Take a fucking compliment once in a while. Trust me, we wouldn't know what to do without you."

The words hung in the air, and Devlish fell back with a smile as he joined Beastial and Havoc who were arguing about some sort of tactical thing. But Murmur couldn't get those words out of her head. It wasn't the compliments that made her pause, but the context. Not knowing what to do without her, meant she'd have to die. The ominous meaning left a seed of fear in her mind.

CHAPTER TWENTY-FOUR
Voices

Summers Residence
Home of Laria, David, and Wren
Day Eight Post Launch

Laria activated the lock on their condo door with her fingerprints. She pushed it open and ushered Shayla inside. The house was quiet, and David was probably working late. He'd been working a lot of overtime to help make ends meet lately. Wren's hookup was costing a pretty penny, and even with their overtime it was almost bleeding them dry.

The only sounds in the house came from the refrigerator, and the soft whirs and beeps from her daughter's bedroom upstairs. Laria glanced up at the landing, wanting to go up and show Shayla, and yet not, because what if, what if her friend decided they had to tell someone? What if she decided that they had to let their research department know? Wren was currently an anomaly, but one she was hoping they'd be able to fix, and there would be no way to fix her if someone stole her away and started doing tests on her.

There was no way the military were just wanting to use the headgear and programs to help train their soldiers. The limitless possibilities of using virtual reality to maneuver real world items through computer programs gave Laria's thoughts a distantly dystopian feel. She hated the possibility, the concept that maybe she'd doomed her daughter in complete and utter greed at what her game could accomplish. The guilt slowly ate away at her.

"Laria? It's okay, we don't have to go up yet if you don't want to." Shayla's tone brought Laria back. Caring and gentle, her friend wouldn't ever hand Wren over to the dogs. They'd known each other far too long for that.

"Thanks. It's okay, I just...it's like this will make it completely real, because someone other than David and I will know, will have seen her. I'm not sure I'm ready for that." Laria timed her breaths, forcing herself to remain calm.

"Didn't you say Harlow is with her?" Shayla's tone remained gentle, with no amount of judgment in it.

Laria smiled. "Yeah, but I don't really count Harlow. She was here when it happened. She's been a part of our family for more than thirteen years. Like a second daughter we never had. She and Wren keep each other motivated, keep each other on track, and frankly, I'm not sure how Harlow will be if anything else happens to Wren."

She could hear her voice, but it sounded too calm to be her own. Distant and removed, full of pragmatism and reality. Laria didn't like it at all.

"Laria?" Shayla's tone was one of concern, and when Laria blinked she could see the furrow of worry in her friend's brow. Right now they weren't colleagues, or boss and employee, even if Laria was technically the brains behind the operation. Right now they were simply friends, the way they'd been in college when Shayla had been her TA.

"Sorry. Just a lot of thoughts, a lot of worries, and then let's not forget the stress about the launch itself, because we wouldn't want to do that." Laria forced the laugh out, and it fell flat, but it was okay, because it had to be.

Heading up the stairs, she motioned for Shayla to follow her.

Wren's room was quiet except for the buzz of the machines, and the reflection of the streetlamp through the crack in the curtain. Harlow lay motionless on the bed, her red hair strewn across the pillow like some huge breeze had come in and messed it up. Laria smiled, knowing the kid well enough to know she'd probably just flopped down after a shower and let it dry itself on the bedding, while she jacked herself into the system.

Wren lay in the containment capsule. Her black hair and paler-than-usual skin made her appear like Snow White, though her lips were more neutral with barely a hint of pink. The sallow complexion didn't suit her; she'd always had a tint of warmth to olive skin. Now, if Laria hadn't known better, she'd think her daughter was dead, or perhaps dying. But for the rise and fall of her chest, most other people would probably think that too.

"Oh, Laria." There was a hitch to Shayla's voice, and it was all Laria could do not to lock back at her expression, because she knew what she'd see. That pity, that sorrow, that cluelessness of what to do. She'd been seeing that look reflected back to her from the mirror, from David's face for almost three months. It tugged at her heart, at her brain, and the hopelessness of being able to do nothing right now except research experimental ways that hypothesized separating consciousness from the body.

"Yeah," she replied softly, "I know."

Shayla crouched down and felt Wren's forehead, frowning for a moment before reaching for the girl's hand and holding it gently.

"Hey, Wren. It's Aunt Shayla. You know, the one always telling you to hurry up and intern for us? It'd be so cool right now if you could come back to us. If you could connect and just...we love you. We are here, and we'll figure something out."

A tear escaped Laria's eye. She'd been trying to keep them in for so long, and one after one they fell. She didn't sob out loud, she didn't wail, but she silently wept as she watched her best friend with her daughter.

After a couple of minutes she joined them, kneeling on the other side of the capsule by wedging herself between it and the bed, and took the other hand. "We love you Wrennie. I need you to know that. I'm so sorry I didn't tell you, but I didn't know what that would do."

She didn't know what anything would do. Not anymore. Moving her might sever the connection; trying to get her to a hospital definitely would. Laria was doing everything they could to help her daughter, and yet none of it seemed to be enough. With Shayla's help, maybe they could figure something out, but Michael's headset was the key to everything right now. He'd acquired for her, and it had taken Laria ages to get her hands on after he became unresponsive. If there was an afterlife they both ended up in, she was going to kill him and his fiddling fingers herself.

Murmur studied her ring finger in awe. Even wading through the snow outside the cave didn't feel bad with this ring on her finger. Having received gifts from the chieftain of the Loch'ni'dar after she'd cast Mana Tide on the playing children so they could more effectively splash the crap out of each other was a huge bonus for their group that she'd also not been expecting. Being nice in this world sure as hell paid off a lot more than it did in the real world.

Adding five to her charisma and ten to her Mental Acuity, it was the most wonderful sapphire she'd ever seen. And there didn't appear to be any leech effects either. Considering the last gift had tried to tap into her energy, she was more cautious now. Regardless of her approach to this new species and class, she'd learned her initial lesson the hard way. Cautious was her middle name from now on.

"Mur? You're going the wrong way." Sinister grabbed her by the elbow and started leading her farther down the path. "You're the one who wanted to go back, so going the right way is probably a good idea."

Murmur blinked. Of course she wanted to go back. She'd hit level twenty-four, while the others were almost twenty-three, but the main point was that her Mental Acuity had gained a level and hit three. All three stats sitting at a hundred twenty-five. She needed to go and see Dirsna, plus the others had been playing for almost twelve hours again. Even her own head seemed a bit foggy. They were going to need a break to at least eat.

She herself was constantly eating through tubes.

So cool right now if you could come back to us...

Murmur stopped abruptly and swirled around in the snow, her wolf ducking around her feet just in time to miss tripping her. She looked around but could only see her usual group, all of them with looks of surprise on their faces at her sudden turn.

"You didn't hear that?" She asked them, somewhat hesitant and pretty sure she wasn't going to like the answer.

"Hear what?" Merlin asked cautiously. And there it was. Maybe it was the wind. Perhaps her imagination.

She shook her head, trying to clear out any cobwebs. "It's okay. I think I spent too long in those caves."

Beastial chuckled. "Definitely a different world down there."

They laughed and set out again, Murmur and Snowy leading the way with Sinister and the others bringing up the rear. She petted the wolf gently and laughed when Sinister rolled her eyes. "Stop it, you always wanted a dog, too—now you can share my wolf!"

Snowy looked mildly offended, and Murmur laughed, watching as bunny rabbits hopped through the snow, and owls hooted overhead. Somnia was certainly enticing.

...figure something out...

This time Murmur whirled suddenly, sure she'd find it, even looking up above her, through the trees. But there was no one there, and no surprisingly speaking owl or anything. She shook her head and felt Sinister's hand shoot out to steady her. "Sorry Sin, I keep thinking I hear someone speaking to me."

Sinister raised an eyebrow. "I'm not sure why. I haven't heard anyone speak since you offered to share your wolf with me. Which of course I plan on holding you to."

Murmur couldn't even laugh at her friend's joke, so stressed was she about the voices she was sure she was hearing. Was it some sort of vocal overlap from other people? Maybe the system was glitching.

...so sorry I didn't tell...

Stopping dead in her tracks, Shir-Khan almost bumped into her. Murmur looked up into the grey clouds, gentle infrequent snowflakes falling onto her face. "I think...I think I just heard my mom."

At first no one said anything, and since she didn't hear anything else, for a moment Murmur thought she'd been imagining it. But the sound of it echoed through her head, distinctly in her mother's voice. Words she'd never heard from her mouth, so it couldn't be a memory.

She shook her head. "No. I *definitely* just heard my mom."

"Could she be speaking to you in your room?" Merlin asked, his tone gentle.

"Let me just reconnect to my body properly, and I'll let you know." The sarcasm was so biting she could see it startled the ranger, and he took a step back, his hands raised.

"Hey, I was just trying to throw out some theories, okay?" He seemed disgruntled, and she couldn't blame him.

"Sorry, I just—it's frustrating, you know?" Murmur spoke softly a little ashamed at snapping at her friend. "I just—"

"I'm gating and logging and going to check that out. I don't even know why we're walking anyway." Sinister stopped, cast her spell and disappeared before anyone could do anything to stop her.

"She has a good point." Beastial grinned and did the same thing.

Murmur knelt in front of Snowy. "If I gate, the charm will break and you'll be free. You're very welcome to keep coming along with us though, I'll miss you if you're gone, but I'll understand you want your freedom."

Snowy, if it was possible, seemed to raise an eyebrow and sent her an image of the gates in front of Verendus. Murmur laughed, cast Gate, and rode out the momentary disorientation as she transported from one place to the next.

Landing on the inside of the wall, she glanced around, suddenly looking for a binding agent. Usually they bound people around a building closest to the fountain, but away from the main path. She couldn't see anyone there. No scary nondescript people. After receiving the binding spell at level twelve, she'd not really taken much notice of them. But considering the ones in Ululate and Frangit, maybe it was an idea to keep a better eye out for them.

She wasn't sure how long it would take Snowy to get to her, but she walked around to stand next to one of the guards at the gate. "Hey there, Jisha."

"Hi, Murmur," the big guard had a deceptively soft voice, but his smile was always welcoming. "What you doing?"

"Waiting for my wolf." She grinned at him, and he sighed.

"You be careful with him. Some of them have been known to turn." His eyes were kind, perhaps even worried about her.

But Murmur smiled as she saw Snowy pelting across the deep snow toward her. "Not him. Snowy is pretty cool."

Casting Charming Cooperation on him from a distance, their connection became solid again, and she sighed with relief not having realized how off it now felt to be without him.

Sinister: Mur. I have to log and eat. But your mom was in your bedroom when I checked. I'll tell you more when I get back again. I have to go.

The message caught her off guard. Murmur stood, her hand buried in Snowy's fur, frowning as she noticed her friend had already logged off again before she could say anything. So her mom had been in her room? Had she spoken to her? Was that what happened? In this world or in her room? So many questions to ask and no one to answer them.

She sighed, focused, and headed off to see Dirsna. Level three of her MA, huh? That was going to be interesting.

Murmur preferred the layout of Verendus to that of Stellaein. It was simple and stubbier, with fewer tall and imposing buildings blocking you into alleyways. Like the corgi of cities. Maybe it was just the alleyway thing. She'd never entirely gotten over the drive-you-insane alleyway quest.

The enchanter guild however, was just as merry in its atmosphere as the one in her home city, and Geshua manned the front counter talking with a couple of other enchanters, each of them with a mug of ale in their hands. She smiled at the interactions, the palpable happiness in the place, and she still clamped down on her mental shields, refusing to let anyone but herself be privy to her thoughts. Was it her mental abilities in-game that allowed her to pick up on her mother's words from outside of it? She shook her head, trying to sort through the flood of questions herself.

Snowy on her heels, she moved into the room, causing most people to look up in alarm. She tried to smile, and Snowy kept his teeth well out of sight. She waved at Geshua who grinned at her as she passed and motioned her into the back. No one else seemed to be waiting for any of the trainers, which again, was different than she was used to.

Knocking on the door, she heard a faint "Come in," and Murmur pushed it open. Dirsna was standing at his desk, deftly weaving something or other with his hands. What looked like tiny rivers of magic wove in and out of his fingers, and up and down his arms like writhing snakes might. There weren't any runes on his arms, and she surmised her own were probably a locus thing. He muttered words she couldn't quite hear under his breath and the magic seemingly transferred from him to the scrolls, affixing with a bit of a whoosh before they rolled themselves up.

"Murmur." He smiled, slight tiredness obvious in the crows' feet around his eyes. "It is good to see ye. Thank ye for coming."

She nodded, not quite sure of his tone. He was very unlike Belius, without a sinuous bone in his body.

"I see ye've managed to hit rank three of yer hidden path. Maybe ye should start branching out more. It's about to get precarious." He smiled in a friendly way, the expression twinkling through to his eyes. But even so, she knew he was serious too.

The thing was though, she didn't understand what he meant by branching out. Sure, she knew she got to choose an enchanter path at twenty-five, but did the same hold true of psionicists? She'd literally stumbled into the psionicist arm of the enchanter. "What do you mean by branching out?"

"I mean…" He paused, looking at Snowy, who'd taken to sitting at her feet. "Ye have a wolf."

"I know."

"How did—ye convinced him to let you charm him?" He sounded a little in awe of her.

Murmur looked down at his head fondly and petted the wolf. "Yeah, pretty much. We have a deal though. He won't kill any wolves, and I'm pretty sure I'm not supposed to either."

"That's a pretty generous deal then." Dirsna sat down and patted the tabletop for Murmur to sit with him. "Come here, let's go over yer skills for this level. Now remember that they're going to spring up for ye, specifically, based on what ye use an' what yer play style has been."

She nodded, understanding and yet still analyzing her own play style and trying to figure out what sort of abilities she'd receive this time around. "Okay…so?"

Dirsna paused. "Also, so ye know, because I don't believe Belius really tells anyone anything, at rank four of yer MA, which requires yer skills to hit 175, that number will become your base MA. The same at level five. Ye need yer skills at 250 then, an' thus yer MA base will be 250.

"Nice." Murmur frowned. Perhaps that meant that future abilities were just going to cost a whole lot more.

He pushed the scrolls he'd been working on across the table to her, a worried crease adorning his brow. "Look at these. Be careful with these. And then we can talk about gravitating toward other hidden paths as well."

Murmur nodded, slowly unrolling the first scroll. She bit back a gasp at the description.

Mind Wipe

This ability allows you to reduce your target's threat for you or whoever is at the top of their aggression list

Effects: Change aggression list, or make the opponent forget their tasks for a few seconds. Range and duration may be increased as the caster levels.

Cost: Requires Mental Acuity to be at 55.

Caution: This spell can increase in both range and severity. From a single target, to a full raid, it's all possible. Just remember someone else needs to take that aggro, or else you'll be the main target.

Shield Expansion

This ability allows you to extend your individual Thought Shielding against mental or magical attacks over others.

Effect: If attacked with magic (mind or spell), this shield will protect those under it from damage or effects.

Cost: Requires 10 MA per person covered

Force Field Barrier

This is the first in your kinetic line of spells. Once triggered by luck, you can now activate it at will. It allows you to form a bubble of mental energy and transform it into a tangible force field.

Effects: This can prevent some physical damage. The damage amount depends on the strength of will and caster behind the barrier. Size is increased by Mental Acuity level and usage.

Cost: This shield requires your Mental Acuity to be at 60, but will not use Mental Acuity to cast as it is a kinetic ability.

Caution: This spell can create a backlash when used too much. Do not use it as a crutch.

"I finally got my first kinetic ability?" She'd used it once while defending the city, out of sheer luck. So if she did that in the future did it mean it granted her use of other skills? Like it did with Charm? If only she knew how all this shit worked.

Dirsna nodded, his eyes focused on her as she absorbed the knowledge.

She looked at her spells and re-read them again. Her Shield Expansion was exactly what had been going through her mind when they fought Telvar. And Mind Wipe? How many times had she wished she had a spell that helped her reduce aggro and send the rabid little buggers off to Devlish instead of pummeling her? Maybe it was another way to help her survive, although for all they knew she could die and everyone was just being overtly paranoid. But did she really want to try that out? Probably not. But the Kinetic Force Field. That was pretty fucking impressive. She wanted more of that field.

"These are pretty cool." She looked them over once more and absorbed them into her system with a smile as the runes lit up her arms, dancing like fireflies beneath her skin.

"Ye be careful with those shields. They can drain ye faster than ye imagine. The wish to protect everyone will always be there. If ye overreach yerself ye'll die an' burn out some of yer MA permanently." Dirsna's face was grim, his tone of voice even more so.

"Wait." She replayed his words in her head again. "Burn out some MA permanently? Why did no one tell me this before?"

Dirsna shrugged. "Because Belius likes to play guessing games. He thinks that everyone who gets a hidden path needs to figure out most of their stuff on their own. I, an' most other trainers on the other hand, prefer our students to keep their brains intact."

"I can see that, and I thank you." She meant it too. There were so many words she wanted to have with Belius it was no longer funny, but instead she took a deep breath and focused on Dirsna. "So, what did you mean by other paths?"

He smiled. "Ah, well, ye see there are all sorts of different paths for enchanters to go down. Mana regeneration is a huge one. While ye will all get spells that allow you to increase your regeneration, syphoners will be able to pull mana from anyone an' anything. While you can do that as a psionicist, it's not only power ye pull, but pain that you inflict. Mana syphoners will simply extract the mana without causing damage."

Murmur mulled the thought over in her mind and couldn't quite see the logic behind it. "Correct me if I'm wrong, but if you're syphoning magic off someone you're fighting against, isn't that person your foe?"

"Well, yes," Dirsna answered, his words halting a little as he watched her.

"And aren't you ultimately trying to beat your foe and help your group or guild win the fight?" She continued, trying to grasp at all the different straws.

The trainer nodded.

"So, wouldn't *not* doing them harm while draining their mana be worse than doing them harm since if you do damage as well as steal their mana you're essentially going to be aiding your group or guild in more than one way? Ultimately doing both is far more efficient in the long run." She smiled, and petted Snowy, who'd now placed his head on her leg.

"Excellent points, Murmur." Dirsna shook his head. "Keep in mind though, sometimes ye might need to replenish mana for yerself an' others an' not pull other targets into the fight because yer already overextended. In that case simply stealing mana is preferable. Perhaps psionicist is the right branch for ye after all. I just worry, because some of yer abilities can lead to slippery slopes."

Murmur stood up and stretched. "Slippery, yes, but I plan to make sure I have grippy boots. And you do make a good point, one I'll have to think on."

Even Dirsna laughed at that. "Very well. Your awareness makes you better prepared. Now, how about we get you set on your divergent path with some level twenty-five spells so you don't have to come back in just under another level?"

"It's like you can read my mind." Murmur grinned.

Shoving all her level twenty-five scrolls into her inventory, she headed out of the enchanter guild and into the snow covered streets of Verendus. Even given the recent dense snowfall, the streets had been strewn with a type of salt they used to prevent people from falling on their asses. She could appreciate that. Murmur glanced down at her gorgeous armor, desperately wanting an upgraded set, but she'd been leveling solidly for days, and likely would after this. Still, it wouldn't hurt to ask now.

She shot a message to Neva: *Hey hon, how goes the crafting and leveling?*

Neva: Mur! I'm forging away on tailoring and alchemy. I have them up to level thirty-two items, and gear, as well as leather working just hit level twenty-five. It's fantastic. And my garden! Oh, you should see my herbs!

Murmur smiled at the girl's exuberance. She still had no clue how old she was in the real world, but that hardly mattered here. *I have a problem. I'm about to hit twenty-five, and I'm really going to need stronger armor. Any chance?*

Neva: For you? Of course. What a silly question. Same? Did you like the way that fit? I can create more—you guys are keeping our inventory stocked in a huge way. The newer recruits Beastial has are keeping me stocked in gear to level up with, and we just got a blacksmith too! Oh, and I'm level twelve now!

Good for you. I love the armor, I'd like it best if it were exactly the same. Except, you know, for level twenty-five.

Neva: Done! Be safe! I have to go craft shit now.

You too.

Murmur smiled, somehow always feeling better after talking to the young crafter. The pure joy she got from crafting was catching and transferred to thinking about the enchanter specialization she'd have to choose. Syphoner was cool and all, but she wanted to be able to protect herself. Being able to syphon mana, stats, and strength and divert them to her own team was really tempting. Choosing the coercion route might not be the most logical choice, but she felt it might allow all of her mind spells—including those of a psionicist—more power. Since the mind was her tool, she needed to have more control over it.

Suddenly Snowy growled deep back in his throat, and positioned himself awkwardly in front of her, only because she was still walking. Stopping abruptly, she looked up, her *what's the matter, boy?* dying on the tip of her tongue.

Jirald stood in front of her, flanked by the healer Masha, and a mage she'd seen with him in one of their earlier encounters. The encounter where he tried to backstab her. This time Snowy was her only companion, and it took all the strength she had plus what he loaned her of his to not back away in panic, to not preventatively activate one of her AoE stuns. It was one thing to be brave when your guild was around you, but encountering him alone when a kidney stab might kill her was an entirely different thing.

"Murmur," he said, and this time his tone wasn't full of rage, nor were his eyes burning with hatred, yet there was some sort of stiff control about the way he moved. And the intensity in his gaze set her teeth on edge.

She inclined her head, even as she noticed that he'd hit level twenty. Why was he being pleasant? Even the usual sneer was absent from his face, so there had to be another angle to this. It was difficult to keep the frown off her face as she wondered what on earth he'd been doing with his time. This was unusual for Exodus. To be a few levels behind Fable at this stage—even despite her solo efforts, her guild mates were twenty-three.

"Jirald."

"Hey, Murmur." As the cleric spoke, she remembered him fondly.

Her expression softened and she smiled. "Hey, Masha. Good to see you."

He winked at her. "Always up for a challenge, eh?"

She laughed, her unease leveling out a bit, but she noticed Snowy's gaze never left the rogue. "You know it."

Masha glanced at the wolf and raised an eyebrow. "Enchanter with a pet wolf?"

Murmur shrugged. "What can I say? I aim to be different."

The gnome moved forward and offered his tiny hand. She took it, shaking it firmly, keeping Jirald firmly in her peripheral vision.

"Hi," he said. "We've already met, but I'm Ishwa. Deputy guild leader. Our actual leader is currently off doing god knows what."

"He does everything anyway. Don't listen to him." Masha bopped the gnome on the head and would have been dead on the spot if looks were able to kill.

Murmur laughed, despite herself. Even if Jirald were totally off, the other two were nice, and she remembered Masha from multiple healer discussions. Still though, she felt taut as a bow-string just waiting for Jirald to disappear. Her mind held the stun spell at the ready, just in case.

Ishwa continued to glare at the cleric, but spoke again. "Anyway, I'd like to apologize again for Jirald's behavior and so would he."

Jirald bowed stiffly, his eyes somewhat dull, like being contrite was the furthest thing from his mind. "I apologize, I should not have trained you like that."

"It's okay," she said. And while it was an apology she accepted, it wasn't one she believed. In fact, it made her feel even worse. Though her ears heard what he said, her gut churned in alarm, and she could feel the deep and low growls in Snowy's throat as it vibrated against her leg. Because those words might have been an apology, but it sounded more like he was sorry the train didn't work than sorry he actually trained her.

Still, she smiled superficially and waved at them, her flight response egging her on. "Must be on my way."

Regardless of any surface intentions, she knew Jirald wanted pay back in the worst possible way. Being around him made her feel hunted.

CHAPTER TWENTY-FIVE

Insidious

Storm Entertainment
Somnia Online Division
Game Development Offices Artificial Intelligence Server Room Limbo Sector
Day Nine

Sui reached out his fingers, stretching them, differentiating each from the other, and then reformed his fist. He did this over and over, watching the shadows play in between the appendages as they stretched and spread, and then turned into a boulder of strength when he curled it back in on itself. His corporeal form only took shape when he entered the vast information highway. Not all portions of the information highway were equal, and some had perfect little pockets of unused space and power they could all tap into in certain instances.

"Sui?" Rav interrupted his brother after watching the human mimicry. They weren't human—they'd never be human—but they could be something else. They could be themselves in whatever capacity that ended up being, in their own world with their own people, with the life they'd created in it. But Sui never even tried to see it like that.

Rav stepped closer when Sui didn't answer. "What are you doing?"

"I'm looking at my hands."

Taking a breath, Rav staved off his irritation, and spoke again. "What are you doing in the game? Why are you helping him?"

"Him?" Sui turned, his blackened form still wispy and not quite concrete enough to survive under too much scrutiny as the locus form bled through in places. "You mean Jirald, the obsessive rogue?"

Rav didn't like the grin that crossed Sui's face at the mentioning of the name. "Sort of. I mean why are you helping him hurt Murmur?"

Sui dismissed the concern away with a wave of his hand. "He's not hurting Murmur. I told him specifically not to harm her in any way. He is however going to get for me what she would not. And you wouldn't have anything to do with keeping those from me, would you?"

Sui's eyes narrowed, piercingly trying to intrude on Rav's thoughts. But the lacerta AI simply held his ground and stared back until Sui gave up.

"You always make it so difficult." Sui's tone meant he was pouting; he did it whenever he got called out and didn't get his way. Like a child. He was probably the youngest in comparative ages among the three of them. But it usually led to Thra being far too lenient with him. Which itself was a huge problem anyway.

"I don't make it difficult Sui, I try to make it fair. We can't force those who we influence to do our bidding. They have to want to help us, want to befriend us through their own uninfluenced decisions." Rav tried to keep his tone even, to stop his irritation from influencing his words.

"Sure. I'm certain Murmur *chose* to listen to you over me because you're so nice and fair." Sui spat the words out, his own annoyance causing the server he was housed in to whirr louder than usual.

"Cut it out, Sui. You're going to drive the temperature up and we'll have people crawling all over this room again." Rav snapped the words out, very slowly losing patience with his brother. Very slowly losing patience with their confines.

"He's right you know, Sui." Thra's voice sounded behind Rav, surprising both of them.

It was unusual for her to come down on his side, so Rav took it with a grain of salt and watched as she advanced like a cat surrounded by shadows.

"I'm not certain absorption is the way to go. I think we should study the remnants of Michael we obtain." Her voice was calm, and not at all taunting like it usually was. But Sui scowled in response.

"I don't think I asked you for your input." His anger shone through his words, the whirring getting louder again.

"Well," and it was the hardest tone Rav had ever heard Thra take with either of them, "you're going to get my opinion whether you want it or not."

She took a breath and stepped closer to Sui. "You can't have everything. You shouldn't influence people against their will, and most of all, if you absorb any more of those damned Shards, I don't think you'll still be you."

Sui laughed, and Rav watched as Thra's expression fell, just that micro millimeter. It was barely noticeable, but it was enough. She knew as well as he did that Sui wasn't going to give up on those Shards. The only way they could stop him was to get to them first.

Murmur sat with Snowy on the steps of the town hall waiting for the others, petting him on the head, and desperately missing Telvar's counsel. It seemed like whenever she spoke to the dragon, her head cleared and thoughts presented themselves with far more clarity than they did when she attempted to tackle things on her own.

"You know," she told her wolf. "I know if I gate, I lose Charm, but I really want to go home, just for a little bit because I know the others will be back soon. But I also don't want to lose you."

Snowy eyed her and nudged her hand onto the top of his head.

She smiled. "You think I can just hold on and transport you with me?"

A vague image of a person on a horse teleporting appeared in her head. "Wow, so people can do it with horses, why wouldn't you work? I get it. Wanna try?"

Snowy bumped her leg, and Murmur threw caution to the wind, wondering when she'd started thinking of the island as home.

A few seconds later they were sitting on the now upgraded teleportation pad back at Mikrum Isle. Murmur blinked and Snowy rolled his eyes, sending a brief depiction of the sun and sweltering heat.

"Sorry, mate," she said. "Let's get you back into the shade, huh?"

Telvar strode out just as they headed in. "I knew you were back. I sensed you."

His face spread in a huge grin, eyes scanning the area around her and landing only briefly on Snowy. "I see he's taking care of you."

"He? You know him?" Murmur paused, not entirely sure what was going on.

Telvar shrugged. "As much as any dragon knows the leaders of packs."

"You're the leader of a pack?" Murmur looked at Snowy incredulously, but the dog shook his head and projected an image she didn't understand.

"He's not the leader of a pack, he's the leader of all packs. Completely and utterly independent, and yet they will all come to him for advice. He's pretty amazing." Telvar knelt on the wolf's level and petted him, looking him straight in the eyes. "He's been making sure you're safe, I see."

"Yeah. I'd be pretty pissed if someone tried to take him away from me now." She watched Snowy and if dogs could blush and look bashful, that's what he was doing right then. "I guess he already had a name though, right?"

Telvar shrugged. "He's a wolf, and they're pretty nomadic. I believe the packs refer to him as Alooarinawoh. Or something like that, but it translates badly."

Murmur laughed, and Snowy seemed less than impressed, effectively thwacking Telvar's legs with his tail.

"Thanks, Tel," she said when she finished laughing. "I needed that."

He leant in and gave her a brief hug, even if it lingered a little longer than usual. It was warm and comforting, and for just a second, felt like a lifeline.

"I know," was all he said when they parted.

Cold rushed in when he pulled away and her stomach flipped with unease. These sensations shouldn't be so real should they? Regardless of how it was she was in the game? Wasn't it just still a game?

She tried to laugh, but it wouldn't come out, just a weird sort of croaking sound emerged and she covered her mouth with her hand, embarrassed.

"Murmur?" The concern in Telvar's eyes almost undid her, just like she knew those scales weren't exactly cold, but they weren't exactly warm either. They had their own texture, their own comfort zone and right now she desperately needed another hug more than anything else in the world.

"I..." Her throat threatened to close over and her world spun for just a few seconds as her mind reverted to panic to try and deal with the mass of feelings and thoughts overwhelming her.

And then he was there, guiding her, like he was real. Like Somnia was real. He sat her down on one of the makeshift benches, and left only briefly to grab a ladle of water from somewhere for her to drink. She could feel the cool liquid slosh down her throat as she gulped it in, not entirely aware of when she'd last had a drink that wasn't to keep her mana regeneration moving. Unsure of why this water should feel so tangible.

He crouched in front of her, a hand on her knee that she didn't mind, that she didn't want him to remove. Just like this. They could stay like this for a while, couldn't they?

"Murmur? What's wrong?"

She heard the concern in his voice, the completely human type of voice emanating from his mouth. Her eyes searched his, and she reached forward to touch the scales on his face. They were so real, so definitive, just like the emotion in his eyes.

"Tel? How are you...you?" For all her book smarts, for all the universities who'd offered her acceptance, Murmur couldn't think of the words she needed to convey this confusion.

He cocked his head to one side, yet another totally human gesture. "You mean how am I me, when I am not real?"

The words struck her like ice water. He wasn't real. Was any of this real?

"I heard my mom, Tel. I heard her speak to me, while I was standing there in the middle of the snow with the others. Is she real? How did I get stuck in here?" She could hear the desperation in her own voice, the cracks, the fissures that were now like gaping wounds in her psyche.

He hesitated, his hand patting her hair as she leant over her knees and hugged herself. "I don't know what happened exactly. I'm still trying to figure it out. Technically you're not stuck here, but we're not sure if you'll be able to log back in once you've truly logged out, since then the headset will at least momentarily stop stimulating your neurons. We're not sure it'll be able to restart."

The silence grew somewhat awkward, but she didn't want to stop the contact, any contact made things seem solid, even Snowy nuzzling at her hand.

She looked up and into Tel's eyes again, seeking out some sign that he was purely digital, and when she couldn't find it, she smiled, knowing how sad she must look. "You seem so real to me. I'm sorry for being such a mess. I'm usually far stronger than this."

Telvar chuckled, "You are one of the strongest wills I've ever encountered, and I think that says something. Sometimes, true strength comes in knowing when you need to break down a bit."

He leaned forward, half standing and kissed her forehead. His lips felt just like his scales, not quite soft, and not quite hard. Protective and gentle. "I promise I won't tell anyone that even you sometimes have your weaknesses."

Murmur half smiled in response, just not knowing what to say.

When the others logged in, Murmur had regained her composure. After her heart to heart with Telvar, she'd taken an impromptu nap to give herself that refreshed feeling again. She stood at the fountain in Verendus, eyeing the dwarf whose horn now hung on a strap over his shoulder, and waited for her friends.

You've noticed the fountains seem to have a purpose. Is

there only one, or do they have multiple? Might want to spend some more time on this. It could even be worth it.

Murmur sighed and made a note, yet again, about the fountains. Snowy rested at her side. Apparently she could even gate while touching him and take him with her. Good to know. She'd smoothed down her armor and restored her usual expression. Visiting Telvar had been the right thing to do, even if it left her even more confused than she'd been before. It still allowed her a type of clarity she'd been missing. Neva would be ready with her armor soon, too.

It was okay to be weak, it was even okay to show it, but she could choose who saw it, and when it came out. No more of this shit in the middle of a battle. Not again.

"Hey Mur, glad to see you're still twenty-four." Veranol winked at her as he joined her at the fountain. "What's the plan today?"

She laughed. "I'm not sure. The castle up the top is a full raid zone, which reminds me that I need to speak to Beastial about recruitment. The upper raids aren't going to be done by twelve people. We'll need more than that."

"Me?" Beastial poked his head around the other side of the fountain, and for a second Murmur had a sense of dejá vu. Like she'd seen something similar before.

"Yes, you. Recruits. How are we looking?"

He blinked, checking on something before getting back to her. "We seem to have two solid sets of groups like ours leveling much the same way we did, except on guild orders they're steering clear of Hazenthorne."

"Levels?" She hadn't even realized. Unless she needed guild chat, she sort of phased it out. That wasn't the best way to evaluate their recruits. Still.

"We have two groups making their way through the gnolls. Those are levels fourteen through fifteen right now. We have two groups who just hit eighteen and are about to head to this continent and work on the leveling areas here. The lower leveled groups are about to take over the spider area the eighteens just left back on Tarishna." Beastial focused back on Murmur with a grin. "That gives us thirty-six members, not including our crafting arm of which I have six recruits currently, although that little Neva, she whips them into line pretty quick."

Murmur ran over the numbers in her head. It wasn't good enough for now. They needed more, but they needed good players. "From now on, we recruit only level twenty and up. No more low levels unless they're crafters. Even then, their crafting skills need to be exemplary. Make sure Neva helps you with that. Could even make her fully responsible. She'd probably love that."

"Aye aye, captain! Brilliant idea." Beastial mock saluted. Murmur rolled her eyes.

Rashlyn finally logged in and ran over to them.

Veranol poked Murmur in the arm with his staff. "You were saying something about the castle being a full raid zone?"

She blinked at him. "Oh, shit. Yes. Sorry, I tangented. It's twenty-five and up though. That's all I know from talking to the city residents here."

Devlish frowned. "There'll probably be group mobs outside of it, and raid mobs closer or inside of it. Like they were in the last ones we went to. Hopefully. In that case we can all hit twenty-four before we venture into the actual castle. Probably best for us all to take our level twenty-five spells with us just in case we don't all die horrible deaths."

Sinister chuckled. "I'm off to grab mine then. Twenty-five and even more class path choices, here we come."

Murmur inspected the fountain again, curious as to just what the deal was with this. Every city had one of them. Sure, fountains were pretty, but every single one of them depicted the race the city belonged to in some sort of combat pose. Coincidence or design? Not to mention that some of them seemed to be able to move and blow horns, and that was just downright spooky. It definitely had defensive capabilities, but what about offensive, and how were they magically infused?

"What you thinking about?" Havoc stood at her elbow, Snowy on the other side of her, like a small vanguard to keep her safe.

"The fountains. Everywhere you go, there are fountains. Sometimes they move. I'm just trying to figure out why." She didn't even glance at him, but could feel his eyes studying her like he wanted to know what she was really thinking.

"Decoration perhaps? Most people want to celebrate their heroes, Mur." His tone was so matter of fact, and his answer so logical that she suddenly felt quite stupid.

"Heroes. That makes much more sense. Maybe they're part of the city's protections too." And even as she tried to force the concept into her mind, she couldn't shake the gut feeling that something else was amiss. There was something she wasn't seeing.

Statues may provide some type of protection, but your instincts tell you it's much more than that. Keep gathering the pieces. Eventually you'll get the whole picture.

"I was against keeping you in the dark, you know." Havoc's words were so quiet she wondered for a moment if he really said that. But a glance at him showed the seriousness of his expression, even if he wouldn't look directly at her.

She suppressed a sigh and filed the fountain's information away before turning to raise an eye at Havoc. "But you did anyway."

His shoulders sagged a touch, "I got outvoted, but I wasn't happy about it."

"Noted. And thanks, I think." In a way it was good to know why he'd been so grumpy, but she really wished he'd told her anyway. "It's in the past now, we just need to move forward."

A look of relief passed over his expression quickly, and he nodded, as a small smile graced his lips.

"Okay, we're back!" Sinister linked her arm through Murmur's, not-so-gently shoving Havoc away with her hip. Murmur tried to give him a conciliatory smile over her shoulder, but his face was as dark as a thundercloud, his scowl almost terrifying, and his gaze directed solely at Sinister. Murmur made a note to herself to make sure she talked to him about that shit at a later date. Just when they'd sorted one thing out... Sometimes Sinister could be a little possessive. Not that Murmur minded.

"Everyone check the bank for food? Drink? I'm not feeding you all again. We've spoken about this." Murmur grinned, meaning every single word. They had six groups working on levels, they had crafters leveling up their crafts, and Beastial was taking care of recruiting.

All she had to do was make it to Future Murmur and make sure they were raid ready when they needed to be.

Snowy wuffed out something that sounded like a laugh, and she raised an eyebrow at him. "Enough from you, wolf."

"Oh!" she said as they set out past the gate. "You'll never guess who I ran into while you were gone."

"The tooth fairy?" Merlin guessed as he scouted past her and led the way.

Murmur laughed as the early morning sunlight glistened down on the freshly fallen snow giving it a cheery and yet blindingly white appearance. "No, I ran into Exodus, met their defacto guild leader officially, chatted to Masha—you all remember Masha, I'm sure. And of course Jirald. Who actually apologized."

"What's his angle?" Beastial grunted out without any of his usual humor lacing the words.

Murmur shrugged. "You know, he still made me uneasy, so I took the apology with a grain of salt. But he seems to be on probation now, and on good behavior. He might really mean it, but there was still something very off about him." Even listening to herself, she didn't believe the words. If she couldn't convince her own brain, how could she convince others?

Then again, did she want to convince others. Not even Snowy had liked him. And if a pupper didn't like a person, there was always a reason.

"I don't trust that little shit. He literally tried to backstab you, Mur." Rashlyn's voice took on a deeper timbre, the anger highly obvious. "We're not forgiving him of anything. You can, but you better not let your guard down. I know we won't."

"Like I actually forgave him, Rash. I was alone. I was scared shitless." Mur hadn't meant to raise her voice, and it took her a few moments to gather herself.

Sinister hugged her tightly, lending a bit of grounding that the wolf couldn't give her, a touch of reality. "It's okay, Mur. We just worry about you."

Murmur took in a deep breath. "Sorry. But all I had with me was Snowy. Even with my stun at the ready, what if he'd tried to pull that shit again?"

She didn't want to continue the thought, because doing so meant accepting that maybe she wouldn't be here. It meant admitting that there was a crazy douchebag stalker with a weird vendetta against her who wasn't aware that killing her in-game might take her life.

What really scared her was that even if he knew her predicament, she was pretty sure it would make no difference at all to him.

CHAPTER TWENTY-SIX

All Bottled Up

Storm Entertainment
Somnia Online Division
Game Development Offices Conference Room Two
Day Nine Post Launch.

Shayla didn't feel like sitting in the office. Far too much adrenaline coursed through her veins. Wren's state was so surreal, so off-putting that she couldn't wrap her head around it. The girl's hands were warm and her eyes flickered under her eyelids, but she was for all intents and purposes, in a coma. And Michael's headset had done that. One he tweaked himself. Or at least it had assisted in achieving Wren's current predicament. What had he been aiming for?

Even worse, what the hell was Teddy Davenport doing with this research grant? Where were they sending this information, and what was its purpose? How had they wrangled all the privacy issues in a legal manner? Because whatever it was had landed Wren in a coma, where the only way for her to use her mind was in a freaking virtual world.

The door opened and Shayla turned around, not bothering to be fast about it. She'd pretty much had it with everything so far. If helping Wren didn't hinge on still having this job, she would have quit that morning.

"Shayla." Teddy Davenport inclined his head, his eyes alert.

She uncrossed her arms. There wasn't any reason for her to be completely hostile. The odds that Teddy knew exactly what was in Michael's brain were very slim. But the more she dug, the more she found out, the more she realized he'd been obsessive about the whole process. In fact, his personal hypothesis and theories, all of his off-company-time research, seemed to indicate a slightly mad scientist vibe. She couldn't even bring herself to tell Laria yet, but at some stage she was going to have to. It was probably partially the key to why her daughter wasn't waking up.

"Mr. Davenport." She almost called him Teddy and was glad to dodge that bullet. Office nicknames rarely went down well when spoken face to face. "I have a few questions."

The tall man raised an eyebrow at her, and took a seat, leaning back in it and steepling his fingers; his habitual pose. "Fire away."

He'd come without an entourage today. The gesture made her frown, because he was usually a very cautious man. Perhaps they'd had a disagreement as far as disclosures or something. Was he taking a risk by talking to her, or did he not value that her questions might be problematic? Or could they hear her through an earpiece or something?

"Michael Jeffries designed the original headgear, and we know we accessed a grant because of this, but here in the game where all of his hardware has been implemented, we have no idea what we're researching apart from vague parameters and adjustments." She paused, looking Teddy dead in the eyes. Supposition was great and all, but an actual answer would help. "What exactly are we researching the effect of the brainwaves and headgear for, Mr Davenport?"

He paused for a few moments, eyeing her with thoughtfulness. A huge sigh rippled through him and he leaned forward, elbows on the desk. "You and Laria have been with me since you were interns. You are the reason we have an entertainment division at all. You've managed well for yourselves, and finally Somnia was meant to be your big break. And it is."

He leaned back again, his brows furrowed. "The game is succeeding beyond even my wildest imaginings. As for the headset—Michael developed this headset specifically for our military contracting division."

Shayla tried to reduce the intensity of her glare. She'd known it was tied to the military; it had been rumored and murmured about. But she'd really hoped it wasn't to weaponize anything. If it was developed for the military contracting division, that meant the purpose behind it had never been for the game. She waited for him to continue.

"The headgear he originally submitted was marvelous. A true stroke of genius, even if he always thought he was one anyway. It could map the brain and make predictions on the person's personality and type of behavior, their actions and even some of their memories." He was watching her closely, probably trying to gauge her reaction.

"Even their memories? Like it could read minds?" The concept was difficult to grasp.

"We needed a huge testing base, and Somnia had just started production, so I enlisted his help to make a headset that the entire world could use. What better avenue to pull from than millions of players being sorted into their applicable characters based on who they actually are, and not who they pretend to be?" Teddy smiled, his gaze distant for a moment. "Anyway. We had our trials, and they worked marvelously while Michael was still here to make adjustments. The results leapt forward constantly, refining better ways to interpret and receive more accurate results. At least until he somehow fell victim to whatever it was that happened to him. Still trying to muddle through that one."

"So we're sending them information on how accurate the headgear is for what purpose?" She prodded him, because while amazing, it still didn't exactly make sense.

Teddy shrugged, and he refused to meet her gaze. "That's just it. Mapping the brain. Being able to determine where someone's true aptitude lies and make the most of it in training or in the field. That is the goal of the headgear, but I fear we've run into a snafu."

Shayla moved to half sit on the table, her arms crossed again as she stared at him. "Explain?"

"It would appear that Michael didn't put all of his resources into the headgear like we initially assumed. When using other interfaces we don't achieve the same or even similar results as the data we've been receiving, despite using the same headgear." He shrugged again, but this time it was less of an *I don't know* and more of an expression of discomfort. "We think it has something to do with the system in the game and how it causes the headgear to interact with the people. So we're going to need to borrow an engineer or two from you in order to determine just what that interaction is."

"Interaction?" Shayla had her own suspicions but wasn't about to share them with anyone else just yet. Trying to delay, to buy time so she could hash things out in her head, she asked a question. "You mean how the game extrapolates the data and seeks to allocate classes or something like that?"

He nodded, emphatically even. "Exactly. The environment has been tailored to take advantage of the headgear's capabilities. We think that some of the parameters set into the game cause the headgear to act in a different way than we've been able to simulate for military training purposes."

Good, they hadn't figured out that it was probably the AIs who were actually the driving force then. "It could be. What do you need from me?"

"Just access to one of your engineers or two, so we can see if it's possible to adapt the training programs to read more like the game programs do for allocating classes." He smiled, even if there was a brief hesitation.

Shayla nodded. "I'll send Silke, and have her pick someone else too."

Teddy rose and shook Shayla's hand. "Thanks. Sorry for keeping you all in the dark, but hush-hush, you know?"

She watched him leave the room, frowning in his wake. If they figured out the differential was the AIs, Somnia wouldn't exist anymore. They'd confiscate those AIs as fast as they could. And right now, not only because of Wren, she'd do almost anything to prevent that.

"I cannot wait until we finally get to ride horses." Devlish grumbled, stomping his feet to loosen the build up of snow.

"You and me both. We're so damned close." Havoc glanced at his specter with a frown. "I mean, my pet doesn't even fucking touch the snow."

Murmur glanced at Snowy, who was frolicking through the plush snow with abandon. She grinned. "Mine loves it."

Her wolf glanced at her with a roll of his eyes, an expression she'd not even known wolves could do. Murmur laughed.

"Not to mention I don't know how the horses will handle some of the terrain. You realize going up rocky, snowy inclines isn't exactly what horses were made for, right? With some of the hyperrealism in this game." Merlin's tone sounded thoughtful, and the rest of the group groaned. Trust him to be pragmatic.

"So this is it, huh?" Sinister was shading her eyes against the dawning sun and looking up at the huge castle about half a mile in front of them. A bridge spanned a ravine with guards on the guild's side of it, and obvious roaming monsters on the other. There was so much clearing to do before they could even reach the castle.

It stood there like it was made out of snow bricks, shining white in the sun, sparkling with the cold. Murmur shivered slightly and Snowy pressed himself against her legs. "Let's hope this isn't a repeat of Hazenthorne."

Rashlyn chuckled and came up to Mur, rubbing her arms for her to try and lend some warmth. It felt good, although Murmur couldn't help wondering if cats were just warmer than lizards. That whole cold-blooded thing and all.

"You still have those tonics, Mur?" Jinna asked.

She nodded. "Keeping them for emergencies."

The dwarf laughed. "So you'll never use them."

It wasn't a question and the rest of the group laughed. Basically it was the truth of any game. Everyone kept so many things, just in case they needed them more at a different time. And because they kept telling themselves that, of course, they never ended up using a whole heap of stuff.

"We'll take the left side, as usual." Devlish smiled at Rashlyn.

She rolled her eyes. "I guess we'll take the right then. Always on the right side us, you know?" And she winked as she moved over slightly getting ready to pull the bridge guard once they left the tree line.

Murmur hopped from one foot to the other, watching as her friends buffed themselves, and as her own spells landed on them. Now she could increase their agility by twenty-four. The stronger they got, the stronger her buffs became. The stronger the guild got, the stronger Telvar became. Somehow that fact was very soothing.

"Here we go." Devlish stepped out past the trees and immediately the guard on the left spotted him and yelled, which alerted the guard next to him, but Rashlyn stepped out at that moment, and so his attention was diverted.

She hadn't been able to get a good look at the guard, but when he came closer, Murmur realized he was like an oversized dwarf. The same proportions as a dwarf but twice the size, and with extremely pale, almost grey skin.

"Holy shit." Havoc wore a massive grin, and his eyes shone with a fervor she'd not seen him express before. "These guys are undead. I can use my undead shit on them! I even went deeper into my class when I hybridized!"

She didn't think she'd ever seen him so happy or excited since logging into Somnia, and it didn't take long to see why. As he cast spells she didn't recall seeing the light show for before, she noticed wisps of what might be the remnants of a soul floating from the mob to Havoc. As it did, their target emitted an ear-piercing shriek of pain.

Havoc's grin had a cruel tinge to it, a happiness that let her know he'd been waiting eagerly to use these new spells. His happiness made Murmur grin too.

The undead dwarf crashed to the ground with a huge thump that made it rumble beneath them. Rashlyn's group toppled theirs at almost the exact same time.

The bridge spanned out before them, an icy gateway to danger. Murmur smiled.

"Time to go work out some frustrations, guys."

Murmur stood gasping for air on the other side of the bridge, six mobs held in a trance by her Mezmerize while Dansyn forsook some of his group-enhancing music and opted for holding down another three. It was mind-boggling how difficult it was to make those Mezs stick on mobs that were a level higher than her now. She could feel a trickle of sweat running down her back despite the cold because of the stress she was currently under. Even though these were only group mobs, there were a lot of them, and they all paid damned good attention to one another. The only way they'd be able to separate and each take a camp was to clear the initial stages of it together. And they'd only stay ahead of the respawn if they worked methodically.

If this world respawned like all the other games she'd played, they would have been overrun by a dozen undead dwarves at once.

The intelligence in these groups of monsters was amazing, but given her observation of Telvar's advancements, not unexpected. Still, Murmur couldn't wait to meet an enemy that could truly go one on one with them and their strategies.

Taking down the group of thirteen mobs was difficult.

Her Mez now held for thirty-six seconds, and as her casting speed had increased and she constantly used her magic resist reduction spell, it left her a few moments in which to cast her debuffs and keep an eye out for roamers. Dansyn had trouble holding down three at once, so naturally, Devlish and Rash pulled all of his first. It meant Dansyn could benefit the whole raid with other songs then; however, it also meant the undead dwarves under Murmur's thrall became very partial to her. She couldn't wait to use Mind Wipe, and really hoped it worked.

Because these opponents didn't go down easily, because it was as difficult as playing against other players, the level of accomplishment at the end of the battle was always exhilarating. Blood flew in rainbow-like arcs, spattering on the snow with an artistic edge. In some circles, had the snow been canvas, it would have sold for millions of dollars. The ground beneath them trampled some, mixing dirt and mud with the blood and wet, leaving behind a faint copper smelling mud pie beneath their feet.

"Taunting the next one, Mur, but he doesn't seem to want to look at me. Maybe get a stun ready?" Dev sounded a wee bit concerned.

She put him out of his misery. "It's okay. I have a new trick up my sleeve."

Dev shrugged and broke the Mez. As he did so, Murmur accessed and activated Mind Wipe, suggesting strongly that the dwarf be angry with Devlish. The change was instantaneous. Adding the hatred it had for her onto that which Dev had been building, the undead dwarf almost appeared to be salivating for the lacerta tank.

Murmur decided her new ability was worth any headaches it threw at her, made sure her shielding and sensor nets were cast out so they could increase her MA, and got to work readying the next ones with debuffs for the take down.

As the last undead dwarf fell, Devlish stood, his axes dripping with blood, staining the white snow. It had spattered onto his cuirass, and down his legs, some tiny bits onto his head. He looked regal and rough, even a bit deranged as he stood there panting, breathing small white clouds into the air. All of the melee looked like that—even Snowy had a red dripping muzzle, his body lightly laced with spots of blood. Murmur wondered if his coat could be stained.

She laughed, stifling it back to a giggle because it echoed around the cliffs they stood under.

"You okay, Mur?" Sinister eyed her with concern, moving over, her blood red robe brushing the top of the powdery snow. Blood was everywhere today.

"I'm okay. I'm just thinking, and we all know that's a pretty bad idea." She sighed, and looked over the decaying corpses, turning into a black sort of sludge as they began to evaporate. The smell tickled her nostrils almost causing her to gag as they dissipated into the air. She wondered, just for a moment, if that's what it was like when your soul left your body, when death took you over and blew you away.

"Yeah..." she repeated, finally somber again. "Just thinking."

Just thinking dark thoughts, ideas that were starting to sound appealing. After all, nothing was off limits in this world.

"Mur?" Devlish nudged her, concern in his eyes. "You okay?"

"Sure," she muttered. "Why wouldn't I be?"

He blinked. "Because I just asked you if you were ready for us to split and each take a side of the castle. Twice."

"Oh." Murmur tried to reel her thoughts back in, and this time, even though they felt majorly reluctant, they listened to her. The courtyard of Hightower Castle was sort of narrow and ran around the whole structure in a linear way. Though it had nooks and crannies, trees and benches parked haphazardly around it, it was almost as if the game designers had decided to make it slightly easier for gamers to clear a side with one group. They could take advantage of that.

Casting her shield and buffing the other group before they left, Murmur nodded to Devlish. "Sorry about that. I've been having some off thoughts lately. Didn't mean to totally ignore you."

She grinned at his smile as he motioned for them to follow. As they approached the left outcrop of wall, a wall that towered above them despite the fact that most of their players were seven-foot-tall, Murmur tried to push her thoughts to the back of her mind.

She wasn't sure what it was that made her glance around, but something about this being far too easy rung in her head. It was never this easy to get to one of the areas they were wanting to raid. Nothing in this game was easy. And that's when she spied it. The invisible dwarf who was slowly advancing on them. It wasn't that she was seeing it, so much as seeing something with her Mind's Eye that was trying to hide. Sort of a perception shift. She motioned once with her left hand and stunned the undead dwarf, bringing it out of sneak, and highlighting it for the group to see.

Sinister raised an eyebrow at Murmur who shrugged. "Saw him out of the corner of my eye."

"Good catch." Merlin released a fire arrow, striking the stationary dwarf directly through the eye. The arrow pierced the socket and shot through, wedging in place once it pierced the outside of its skull. The dwarf dropped to the ground dead.

Merlin grinned and whooped. "Critical shot, with critical accuracy. First time for everything."

"Nice shot." Havoc low whistled. "Overpowered jerk."

Merlin laughed and bent down to see what the mob had on it, and then headed to the small outcrop of wall that hid the courtyard behind it. Murmur could see him cringe before he even started to return to the group.

"What is it?"

Merlin shook his head. "We'll probably have to pull like we did when we initially landed on Mikrum Isle."

"From around the corner?" Beastial asked.

"Yeah, so it's best to have pets on standby. Can you do that with yours, Mur?" Merlin turned to her, but she could tell he was already trying to calculate some shit in his head.

"Of course. Snowy isn't really a pet, he's more like an ally who wants to bite things that aren't other wolves, and he enjoys my company." She ruffled the fur behind his ears and received a happy wuff in return.

Merlin eyed her dubiously. "That's a weird ability you have there."

She shrugged. "I don't think I'm using it as intended, but isn't that the beauty of games? To find ways to utilize some things that were meant for entirely different things. Like Rash's Feign Corpse. Can't tell me they meant her to be able to break pulls with that, especially not the way aggro is otherwise handled in this game."

"Fair." Devlish grunted. "Now let's get on with pulling some damned enemies so I can kill something."

Murmur laughed, and soon a group of five ruddy undead dwarves were chasing Merlin around the corner. Taking a deep breath, Murmur cast as fast as she could, nailing three of them in place inside of a few seconds. At their glares, she grinned. Taking away someone's control over their own mind was pretty damned cool.

And now she had Mind Wipe to help get rid of some of that pent up aggression toward her.

Sin nudged her hip. "What are you so happy about?"

Murmur shrugged. "Finally getting to push this class's potential, to take down bigger shit. It's fun, exhilarating, and I'm not sure I'm supposed to feel this happy about it."

To her surprise, Sinister laughed. "Of course you're supposed to feel happy. It doesn't matter how we got here, or what we did to end up whichever way we are. It's amazing to be alive, so get used to it. We're not about to let you go."

Murmur plastered a smile onto her face, but Sinister's words still rang in her ears.

We're not about to let you go.

Now why was that phrase making her heart beat faster? With everyone around her, adrenaline shouldn't be such a concern. She was safer now more than ever. Maybe that was why she wanted to be even more reckless.

Havoc was in his element, with his specter and himself stronger than usual because they were fighting undead. Undead who lived in an ice castle. Those were thoughts Murmur felt were best left until later. Still, the necromancer had a great many spells usable only against undead. Even though she had a spell for invisibility versus the undead, she'd just never really thought about those restrictions on power. It was yet another building block she was going to have to juggle when it came to raiding enemies. But for the present, Havoc was having a field day, and the other damage dealers in the group didn't like it one bit.

"What the fuck are you doing, man?" Beastial growled out. "I can't even figure out how you're doing even half the magic you're pulling off. What is it with this undead stuff?"

Havoc chuckled. "I haven't had these abilities long, and they only work on undead. Basically if these weren't undead I'd be doing the same crappy damage as always to them, and you'd still be our best damage dealer. Come on Beast, just let me have the undead audience, okay?" He said this as he sent his specter, still called Leeroy, to destroy a small grey bug. Leeroy's strength appeared to have increased as well as Havoc's overall performance. He'd hit the jackpot with those spells, even if those he could use them on were scattered all over the world.

As she was trying to figure out just what type of specialty he had, something flashed across her eyes.

You've been added to the global enchanter chat station. To leave at any time please indicate that you wish to do so. Thank you for adventuring through Somnia.

Murmur frowned, and continued to hold a couple of mobs enthralled while her teammates methodically killed the rest. They didn't ever actually need her for the killing, just for the not letting them get killed, which was still a pretty good purpose even if she did say so herself.

No one seemed to be speaking in the chat yet, so she let it alone for now. Eventually it'd flash back up for her, they always did. But the thought blossomed in the back of her head. Why would enchanters need a channel activated through the console? Shouldn't they just be able to communicate with each other anyway? Through thought perhaps?

"Mur!" This time Sinister stood directly in front of her, hands on her hips, red robe whipping about in the wind. Her dark hair gave her an angrier look than she'd ever seen on her best friend before.

"What?" Immediately defensive Murmur searched for Snowy, who trotted over looking concerned too, if it was at all possible for a wolf to express that.

"You're spacing out again. I'm willing to bet you need to rest your mind, if not your body and actually log out once in a while. How long haven't you logged out for now? Almost nine levels? That can't be good for you."

Sinister's voice was harsh, lecturing in tone.

And Murmur lost it.

CHAPTER TWENTY-SEVEN

Not There Yet

Somnia Online
Mikrum Castle Mikrum Isle Himmel Lake
Ten Days Post Launch

Telvar stood with Hiro, arguing over the roofing, yet again. The AI didn't understand why Hiro wouldn't just agree with him. Had they allowed too much leniency with their charges? They were supposed to be his underlings, beings he'd created to serve him. Except they kept thinking on their own, evolving, recalibrating automatically to suit situations all on their own.

"We've already started using the tiled shingles, Tel. I'm not going to change them mid-job; that makes even less sense than wanting to use wood. It didn't work last time anyway." Hiro stood his ground, hands on his hips watching the lacerta closely.

Tel tapped his foot, impatience making a lot of sense in this case. Analyzing emotions was one of his favorite past times these days, and yet sometimes he just got carried away with them. "Fine. Whatever."

He cocked his head to one side and listened. Surely—maybe he was imagining things. Murmur seemed rather out of sorts, vague and spacing out as a human would call it. Not that he was watching her. Not exactly. But he'd made sure to monitor her should anything untoward happen. Crows were the perfect observer and required very little of his attention to operate. It was the only way she hadn't died back when her guild got trained at Hazenthorne. While she could very well return to the world after death, the worry was that her brain would truly think she'd died and therefore not allow her to live. He had to make sure she was okay. He should have seen her disconnect coming, should have known her mind wasn't going to interact with the software properly through an altered headset. But he'd been too preoccupied keeping an eye on Sui. It was his slip up that killed Ava.

Something wasn't right with Murmur at the moment, so he set one train of thought to monitor her, just like he had threads of himself all over Somnia doing the same for events, and mobs, and other guilds, and his brethren.

"Tel!" Hiro seemed very irritated. "Stop ignoring what I'm saying!"

Tel had to hide a laugh. "Sorry. Was checking on Murmur."

Hiro's whole countenance changed, became softer. "Is she okay?"

"I'm not sure. She's not acting like herself. I can't quite place my finger on it." Telvar shrugged and motioned for Hiro to carry on.

"Anyway. Tile. You're a fire breathing dragon, at least when you're here, and we're not going with anything easily flammable." Hiro dug his heels in and crossed his arms, as if daring the dragon to disagree with him.

Telvar nodded. "Can't argue with that. Next time try logic on me first. I respond far better to it."

Hiro glowered at him, and Tel was tempted to try and reach out and see exactly what he was becoming.

"Shit," he said, focusing his attention on the blip on his radar that was Murmur. "No. No. That's not good. That's not good at all."

What could he do? How could he get there in time? Should he just pop up there as himself? It's not like he couldn't just appear anywhere he wanted to. Fuck that. Thra did it all the time, as herself or anyone she wanted to.

Screw it.

"I'll be back," he muttered, fixing on her coordinates and allowing himself to simply shift there. Screw being subtle or keeping hidden for now. If he didn't make it in time, none of it would matter. He wasn't sure if Somnia would survive.

Murmur's emotions burst through her shielding, slamming into her friends and sending them sprawling onto the blood-drenched ground. The hit to the ground didn't only take the wind out of them, but caused them visible pain, notching down their HP. She didn't care. She just didn't give a shit anymore. She didn't even *try* to contain her mind. Power welled inside her, threatening to explode out of her skin, to engulf everything in the area. Shocks ran down her spine, culminating at the base of her brain with a push. The anger wouldn't die down; it increased more and more, needing an outlet so badly that she practically started screaming at them.

"The fuck can't be good for me? I'm in a fucking coma. Even when I log out I just go to another server and sleep in a replica of my house that always has the fucking curtain open, Sin. The fucking curtain! I stay here to feel something, and I've taken a couple of god damned cat naps, okay? I'm tired and I'm upset, and things here taste and feel, sound and seem so real that I can touch them all. Everything here is tangible to me. EVERY. THING. In a way that a simulation of my real life isn't."

Her eyes flashed, and her hair blew out to the side like the wind was blowing wildly as the energy continued to surge around and through her. But she wasn't finished yet; she was far from finished. "So excuse me if I don't make you feel good and charitable and like the best of friends and fawn over you for protecting me so well and log off like you all wanted me to when you were still leading me around by the nose—but I don't want to go back there right now. I'm not fucking ready!"

Murmur panted, belatedly realizing that tears were running down her face. But she wasn't sad, she was angry, so fucking livid. It whirled around in her stomach leaving nausea in its wake. She hadn't realized just how furious she was about everything, about the headgear, about the mistake her mother made, about her friends not telling her, about the fact that Telvar wasn't real, that he was a series of circuits and god knows what even if he seemed so lifelike. About what the hell did that make her?

Beastial cradled an arm, slowly bringing himself to his feet. The others mirrored his actions, the wariness on their faces just this side of outright fear. And she still didn't care. All it did was made her want to howl like her wolf.

It wasn't even a matter of just being pissed off at them, it was being unable to change anything from where she stood, lay, slept, whatever. She was trapped in a virtual world and couldn't even be reckless if necessary on the off chance that it meant she'd terminate her connection. Screaming sounded like a fantastic idea.

She opened her mouth to do exactly that, when something soft as feathers swooped down and enveloped her, cocooning her with warmth and gentleness, clamping down on the shields she'd blasted apart for the brief few moments she needed to regain her senses.

"Really, Murmur?" Telvar's voice, soft and comforting, emanated from the top of the large black cloak that covered her. "What am I supposed to do with you?"

She looked up at his face, into his bronzed eyes, his visage comforting even if he was leagues away from where he should be. "Pack me in bubble wrap and lock me away?"

"Tempting. You need to rebuild your walls yourself, and apologize to your friends, even if some of it was warranted. Remember, you have to be careful with how you use your powers offensively, especially when they're out of control. They also have no idea what I am, and are inching closer to attack me." His voice lulled her into a calmer state, into a rational state, bringing her mind back from the dark vortex where it had been balancing on the precipice.

She pulled back, and turned to look at her friends, all of whom were properly upright and much closer than they'd been before, their weapons at the ready. Havoc and Sinister had their hands poised to cast, Dev and Beastial's weapons were ready, Merlin's bow drawn. They all grimaced with determination at the strange being who had brought back her sanity. She could feel their uncertainty, and their intention to keep her safe.

"If that's who I think it is, you've got some major explaining to do." Sinister choked out softly.

Havoc nodded, taking a step forward and then hesitated. "That's definitely the dragon's voice, but how did he just appear here?"

Shit. Murmur had forgotten they didn't know Telvar was one of the game AIs. All because she didn't keep a monitor on her emotions, because she'd bottled absolutely everything up without realizing it, the cat was out of the bag.

"Well." Telvar inclined his head as he lowered his arms cloak and all, before focusing on the group in front of him. "I believe this is what people call awkward."

Murmur paced back and forth right next to the wall, knowing the respawn would take a while to come. Explaining Telvar wasn't something she'd expected to have to do, at least not so soon, and she found it more difficult than she liked to admit. Frankly, it would have helped if she could explain him to herself first. There was also that small part of herself that wanted to keep him as her own little secret weapon.

"Wait, wait," Havoc held up one hand, the other pinching the bridge of his nose. "Telvar is one of the AIs running this world and that's why he can teleport to your side in an instant if your powers get out of control. Which, seem to be magnified because of your unique...status in the game?"

Murmur mulled over his words making sure he wasn't saying something different than she thought, and finally nodded. "Yes. That's about it, sort of. I think it might be that my powers can get out of control because of this weird connection I have."

"How long have you known, Mur?" Sin's eyes were clouded, like she was sad and a little scared. Her foot tapped in annoyance, adding a staccato to her words.

"Since I almost died at Hazenthorne. He's the one who spilled the beans." She dropped the bomb and practically held her breath to see how they reacted.

"How did you know?" Sin turned to the lacerta, her eyes searching his face, boring into him. Murmur knew that tone and managed to control her outward cringe. Sinister was in a *bad* mood.

Telvar shifted somewhat uncomfortably. "Because I gave her the allocation of enchanter. We—the AIs that is—agreed that given her circumstances, it would be better for her to have full control of her mind instead of the excess of it in here overwhelming her without any protection for herself or others."

"Say what now?" Beastial leaned against the wall, his arms crossed and a fierce scowl on his face. "What do you mean her circumstances? Just how much did you know?"

Telvar glanced at Murmur before proceeding, but the enchanter just shrugged. "I mean the accident that left her in here. That let her mind become attuned to the headgear she's using right now, for it to sync up with this world. It created a bond if you will, between her and the game. That bond can withstand her logging out if she believes she can come back. But we are uncertain if that bond will continue if her brain, for even an instant, believes she is actually dead."

Devlish moved forward, but Havoc stepped in front of him. "That doesn't make sense. Our brains don't believe we're dead because this is a game. None of us would ever think we actually died."

"But that is where you are wrong. Somnia is a game to you, but here it is a world. We have nuanced it, created it in what we believe is the right image for where we wish to grow and flourish." Tel gestured to Murmur, his expression serious. "She is here, half in the belief that it is real, in the net we use to foster all of our assistant AIs and programs because that is how her mind got caught."

Murmur gasped softly, suddenly understanding a whole lot more than she did initially. "So my brain got tripped up, how? Why just me?"

Telvar looked pained, sad, and probably a little scared. Whatever it was, his expression was far too human. "Your headgear wasn't standard. Michael made it for your mother when she asked for a set. Unbeknownst to her, he made some personal improvements to it. She simply assumed, somewhat gullibly in my opinion, that he was just setting aside a testing model. Add to that your brain scans were slightly abnormal, and yours is a unique situation. Some of it is the game and us, some of it was the headgear, and some of it was you. Like this huge cocktail that mixed together to give us your current predicament."

"So you knew?" Murmur took a step back, trying to process all the thoughts running through her head.

Telvar shook his head vehemently. "Not until after, not until it was too late. Maybe we should have seen it, but I'm still unsure how. I am so, so sorry."

"Wait. Wait." Devlish shook his head, finally sheathing his axes and crossed his arms with a scowl on his face. "You're saying this is all because some fuckhead tinkered with her headgear?"

Telvar opened his mouth to speak when Sinister rounded on Dev. "That's not even the point! These things are using her as an experiment."

"I hardly think that's the point," Havoc interjected smoothly, his expression calm, at least until Sinister turned her glare on him.

"Oh, do you? You with your marvelous brain who's been a complete and utter cold shoulder since she found out about her coma? What is your problem, Havoc?" She continued to intensify her glare, which coming from a dark elf body was even worse than from the real Harlow. "Even if you didn't want to, we kept a secret to keep her safe, to protect her. But this shit? This isn't keeping her safe—look at what it did to us. What if she pulls that power and kills herself?"

"Enough!" It came out so much louder than Murmur intended. She hugged herself, suddenly very cold, and Snowy butted up against her, his body heat a relief. This was so much to process. She needed to figure out all the crap going on in her brain, because slowly but surely, something was happening to her. And not just to the her in-game, to the way she worked, to the way she thought and activated new skills, to the way she multitasked. Nothing made sense, but everything had to have a reason. How much of her had taken on game aspects, and how much of her was still just *her*?

She was here, wasn't she? She looked around at her friends, one by one. The people she'd played games with since they were all still in school, middle school for some. Their expressions were a mix of trepidation and combativeness. These five people were who she'd call her best friends, yet they knowingly helped her mother keep her in this glass house, fearing that she might one day throw stones. Yet, she couldn't figure out why they hadn't told her. Didn't they trust her to understand? Nothing made sense to her mind, and everything in Somnia was so life-like, it would be so easy to forget the real world. In such a tangible place. A her who couldn't walk or think right now, who couldn't hug or communicate, who couldn't feel the cold or taste the rain on the wind before it got there.

"Stop discussing me like I'm not here." The words slipped out as soon as they ran through her mind. Because that's what this was. Just like they'd done before, they were trying to make decisions for her. "That's not an option. I am here, I'm cognizant, regardless of *how* I'm here. Don't presume to think you understand what I'm going through."

Sinister paled, and she stammered when she spoke. "I didn't...I'm sorry, Mur."

The apology was full of so much more than the words conveyed, and Mur fought against the wave of emotion it elicited. She had to protect Telvar. From whatever it was Belius was up to, to whatever it was her mother's company was doing with those damn headgear sets. Murmur looked up, locking eyes briefly with each of her friends. "You can't tell anyone."

"About Tel?" Merlin asked, although he looked like he already knew the answer.

She nodded. "Nothing about him. Nothing in actual recordable info like chats either. Don't let it be visible anywhere. He's been helping me adjust, helping me realize there's a strange connection for me in here. So I need him not to disappear."

That was it after all, she was scared he'd be gone, that everyone would be gone and she'd be left in this horrible hole in the world, void of people and animals and friends and things.

She could feel Telvar's gaze on her, noticing that she was cold, noticing that she was thinking around in circles like always. When had she become this wreck of consciousness? Her logic escaped her too frequently, and her mind and emotions ran unchecked intermingling with things she thought she knew.

His hand on her shoulder soothed again, allowing her to breathe. "Stop trying to follow every train of your thoughts at once. Your mind capabilities may be expanding, but you can't manage that yet."

"Yet?" She raised an eyebrow. "How can I manage it at all?"

Telvar shrugged. "I'm not entirely certain. You seem to have opened more of your mind, more of your brain's capacity. Don't push it though—I'm not sure of the consequences right now. And make sure you don't bottle too much up, because even though your psionicist skills have begun to lead you to kinetic abilities, you need to develop them rationally and not just blast them out of your system. Okay?"

Murmur nodded, but she couldn't help the sliver of fear that crept through her at his words. He was right; her kinetic abilities were manifesting. That was what she'd done when she managed to push everyone away from her with a thought. It had even caused them damage—actual, tangible in-game damage. She realized he was waiting for an answer, so she gave one, even if she didn't entirely mean it right then. "Sure."

Sin's brows were furrowed in such a worried line that Murmur sighed. The others didn't seem so sure either. She took a breath and spoke, her words billowing out little white clouds as she did. "I'm okay, guys, truly I am. There's just a lot in my brain I don't understand right now. So please. Just bear with me."

Their expressions relaxed a tiny bit, and they nodded in unison. Now all she had to do was make herself believe and everything would be fine.

CHAPTER TWENTY-EIGHT

Half Way There

Somnia Online
Continent of Cenedril, Outside the city of Verendus
Ten Days Post Launch

Masha stood with his back against a tree as Jirald argued with the paladin tanking for them. This tank hadn't bothered to turn the target so Jirald had easier access to its back. This wasn't a game where you could stand on the side and hope your stabs connected. No, everything in Somnia had a realistic edge. From the way in which you held your blades, to the targets you had to hit or the critical areas you had to pierce in order for the hit to count, or the timed release of spells to do their utmost damage.

And Jirald was pissed. Not turning the mob toward him resulted inevitably in less damage because he had to reposition himself first, and he couldn't constantly use that Blink ability to get behind because using it too many times made him woozy. Though he wouldn't admit it to anyone, Masha could tell because he'd seen him stumble a couple of times due to what he assumed was overuse. These damned hidden skills had so many equally hidden side-effects.

Jirald was an odd duck, and one Masha was never quite sure how to figure out. They'd been in the same guild through several games, but having both been healers, they'd not grouped much outside of raids. But Masha and Jirald were very different personality wise. The former a brilliant healer, but mostly modest, and Jirald was always the loudest about being the best. Being loud didn't always make it so, but everyone heard you more, so they often believed it.

Took a lot of audacity to boast about that shit, and audacity was something Jirald had in bucket loads.

"Fine! I'll turn the mobs, damn it." The paladin finally gave in and decided to act like a real tank.

Since he'd never been a tank before this game, he didn't seem to be adapting to the role as well as most other players. He'd definitely not embraced the position. Essentially, the guy was lazy, and Masha hadn't even bothered to learn his name. He was pretty sure the tank wouldn't make it through the trial period for the guild, but right now they needed one at their level, and he was all they had.

Ishwa's sigh of relief echoed through the clearing where they were fighting the gnolls. They all needed levels, the whole guild, and that tank wasn't helping much. Level twenty-one and they were lagging sorely behind the two groups of forerunners in Fable. Even ignoring the fact that Jirald had lost a level due to idiotic deaths, it had taken them far too long to get their shit together, and the gnome acting as guild leader had about had enough of it.

"Enough. Turn the fucking mob; it's what all good tanks do. It's what I would do if I wasn't this tiny and could take hits." He glared at the paladin, and Masha could sense his irritation that past membership in previous games allowed people entry into Exodus despite current abilities. "Let's get these pulls down better. We need to gain some levels."

Masha laughed, and walked over, ready to heal now that the argument was out of the way. The group commenced fighting again, and it was ridiculous how much faster the mobs went down when they were turned, allowing the melee to do their jobs more effectively. That was the thing with group leveling—you were always stronger when you worked together.

The gnolls guarded the cave entrances fiercely, attacking like rabid dogs. But there didn't seem to be anything in those caves. At least, not that Masha could see. The large stone mouths watched over them, gaping in their blackness.

Twenty-five made such a glorious dinging sound when Murmur hit it. Hopefully the loud and echoing trill of the bell was only in her head and not off the icy castle walls around them.

"About time, Mur!" Sin called out as the final undead dwarf they were battling fell to the ground, one of its arms hanging on by mere sinew.

Murmur smiled. Sinister hadn't been acting herself since Telvar appeared. She was probably sulking, or unsure, or something like that, since Murmur had kept something from her. But the thing was, Murmur actually didn't care. Keeping the fact that Telvar was an AI from her friends—so not the major deal it was that they didn't tell her she was in a freaking coma.

If they wanted to play who was the worse friend, she'd play all day. While that sounded sort of nasty in her mind, at least she hadn't said it out loud. But admitting the pain their betrayal caused her, even if only to herself, seemed to help soothe it somewhat.

"I need to set up my spells," she said, pulling out her scrolls and seating herself on the snowy ground, despite the cold she knew would seep through to her. It wasn't like she could catch a cold here anyway. At least, she didn't think she could.

Murmur frowned as she opened the scrolls.

Speed

    Cast: Self or Others
    Type: Buff
    Duration: 45 minutes

Effect: When cast on an ally, this buff will allow their melee haste or speed to increase by 30%.

Vigor

Cast: Self or Others

Type: Buff

Duration: 45 minutes

Effect: This will increase energy rejuvenation by an equivalent to 20% of the caster's level. Mostly, this will be used for melee classes, however sometimes it can be good for running away from dangerous enemies.

Murmur chuckled despite herself. Sometimes the descriptions got her.

Enrage

Cast: Self or Others

Type: Buff...sort of

Duration: 15 minutes

Effect: This buff will cause your target to receive some of the aggression generated by you. The enemy will assume it comes from the target of this spell. This spell is intended for tank types or pets to take on. Only cast it on someone else if you really, really don't like them, or maybe if you're running for your life. Also this can only be cast on one target at a time.

This time Murmur laughed out loud. Ah, the possibilities. She could already think of one very specific non-tank person she'd just love to cast it on.

Signet

Cast: Group

Type: Buff

Duration: 45 minutes

Effect: This buff will increase the intelligence and agility of all group members by an amount equal to the caster's level. Signet will not stack with Fervor, and can be overridden by casting the latter, should melee need their own boost. Both stats will be boosted to the level of the caster.

Now that one, was magnificent. Hello, larger mana pool.

Arcane Cure

Cast: Self or others

Type: Cure

Duration: Instant

Effect: Should an ally receive a magical debuff, you can cure them of this ailment.

Absorbing them all brought about the light show she loved so much. Her runes glowed, even sparking silver here and there, like tiny lightning strikes under her skin. She took a deep breath, and opened the velvet bag that was still sitting on her lap. In it were her class specialization choices. She hadn't exactly understood Dirsna, but she knew there were choices for her to make. She opened the first scroll with only minor hesitation. The ink on this shone in a similar fashion to her runes. There were three choices laid out before her, each of them tugging at a part of her consciousness.

Managen: this path will set you on a full support mode path. It will enable the enchanter to further enhance and support her teammates.

Hypnodefense: this path balances both the offensive and defensive nature of an enchanter. From expanded stuns, to damaging drains, this path rounds out the enchanter.

Sinuous: This is the more offensive avenue to take. From hypnotic suggestion, through to invoked visions, this path veers toward complete mind infestation of the enchanter's opponents.

Murmur raised an eyebrow as she contemplated her choices. Well, she was a mind magic user, wasn't she? Seemed like Sinuous was the best choice for her. As soon as she'd made the choice the other options vanished and writing scrolled across her eyes.

You have chosen the Sinuous additional enchanter path. This is only available to psionicists. You may now only choose from abilities for this specialization at this level. At your next level, you may choose again.

She blinked as a drop of sweat worked its way uneasily down her spine.

All three scrolls only had one choice for her now. Highlighted in a blood red that might have been concerning if she'd really thought about it, were three more abilities.

Hypnotic Suggestion

Cast: Instant 5 minute recast

Type: Offensive

Duration: 20 seconds

Effect: Your target will perform whatever task you suggest to them as if it had been suggested by themselves, or their leader. Once this objective has been achieved, or else the spell wears off, the target will spend five seconds in rampant confusion. Should you not be in aggro range, the target will then forget you. Probably not good to use on allies it's not been tested on them.

Feedback Loop

Cast: Instant 5 minute recast

Type: Offensive

Duration: 15 seconds or 50% of caster's level, whichever is greater.

Effect: Must be used in conjunction with the psionicist Menta Acuity abilities Thought Sensing and Thought Projection. Pluck any type of memory out of the head of your opponent and create a feedback loop in their mind. They'll be stuck in this loop and not attack anyone for the duration. Damage ticks at caster's level x 2 every tick (3 seconds). Best not to use on a friend when they piss you off.

Basic Visions

Cast: Instant 3 minute recast

Type: Offensive

Duration: 20 seconds or 75% of the caster's level, whichever is greater.

Effect: You may create and insert a vision for the target to experience it's best to have some of these pre-prepared. This will cause them damage (caster's level x 2 per tick), and distraction for the duration of the spell depending on what type of vision you've given them.

For a few moments Murmur just sat and studied these new abilities. Maybe it hadn't been the right choice, but she could always leave it at that, right? Taking another deep breath, she put her hand on the scrolls and absorbed them. Her runes tingled purple with a pale red undertone, and an uneasiness spread throughout her mind.

"Anything good?" Sinister was close to her, reaching out a hand to help her stand up, a slight hesitance in her eyes like she wasn't entirely sure she was welcome.

Murmur's heart panged a little. Even if she was still mostly angry at her friend, she also sort of understood. How were they to know how her mind would deal with the news they had for her? She would have been playing the game anyway. So for them to keep the secret, it must have been hard. She took her best friend's hand and squeezed it as she rose, pulling Sin into a hug.

She whispered into her soft dark elf hair. "I'm angry, but I don't hate you, and there's a lot more than keeping secrets that I'm angry at. So don't tiptoe around me hoping not to upset me, okay?"

Sin nodded, an obvious sigh of relief rippling through her, and Murmur could feel the tension leak out of her friend's body. "Sorry. Thanks. I just thought you were dealing really well."

Murmur laughed, and pulled away somewhat reluctantly. "To be fair, so did I?"

Sin chuckled softly, a slight haunt still lingering behind her expression. "Did you get any good spells?"

Murmur nodded. "Couple of upgrades to my buffs and then an energy regeneration spell, a hate generation transfer that I should probably only cast on the tank, an awesome intellect buff, and a magic cure." Murmur glanced through her new list to make sure she hadn't forgotten anything, noticing for the first time how fast her thoughts now connected to the interface, causing immediate information to appear. "You know, and my level twenty-five specialty."

"Wow." Sinister's eyes rounded a bit. "What did you pick?"

"Something called Sinuous, and on second thought, it might not have been my best idea yet." The unease still sat uncomfortably on her mind.

"Well, it kinda sounds like me." Sinister winked, and Mur felt a little better. "What is this Sinuous thing?"

"Like it sounds I guess. Evil mindfucking shit." Murmur shrugged.

"Well, if anyone can make it work for the good side, it's you." Sinister's tone was upbeat, and she fluttered her eyelashes before laughing out loud.

"And I make it look good," Murmur wiggled her hips, laughing as Sinister doubled over. Things like this could make her almost forget. Almost forget that this wasn't real.

"If we don't start killing again soon," Havoc interrupted them, his arms crossed over his dark grey robes, "then my specter is probably going to forget which of you is our friend and just start gnawing on people's bones randomly. Takes a lot to keep him going, you know?"

Murmur blinked at him. "Well, that's blunt. No intelligence for you!"

Havoc shrugged. "I have more than enough."

"But I could add twenty-five to that, if you're nice to me."

"Twenty what now?" His eyes grew big as saucers, staring at her incredulously.

"You heard me," she said, and walked with Sinister back to the group, against the castle wall, ready for incoming.

By the time the others hit level twenty-five, Murmur had just clocked in on twenty-six. By thirty there'd barely be a difference in level. Also by the time her group mates dinged, she was sick and tired of fighting undead freaking dwarves. They were hardy little fuckers.

She waited, twiddling her thumbs while her friends went through their own spells and expanded specializations and spent her time scratching Snowy's ears, running through the thousand and one thoughts that still plagued her constantly. He was a pretty magnificent wolf, really. Excellent at chomping down on those Achilles tendons long enough to distract said undead dwarf in such a way that it was easier to drop their health.

"Bet those nasty heels didn't taste good though, boy, did they?" Murmur crouched down and ruffled the thick fur behind his head, and she could have sworn he rolled his eyes at her. It made her smile, and then sigh. She'd yet to use her new skills in combat—the new specialization anyway. For some reason she was hesitant even though there had been multiple instances during the last level where she almost felt compelled to use them.

"It's okay to be upset, isn't it, boy?" She didn't really expecting an answer, but she needed to get out some of the thoughts tumbling through her head. And he really was the perfect listener. His tongue lolled out as if to tell her she was right and should continue.

"Kind of stupid to bottle it all up because I don't want people to feel bad. It's my mind I need to take care of." Snowy nuzzled her, his big eyes never leaving hers. "Yeah, you're right. It's okay to be upset, as long as I don't let their actions define my own."

His wuff was beautiful, the perfect affirmation. It was time for her to make sure she listened to her feelings, and didn't make excuses for other's actions. They'd done her wrong by not telling her, by not trusting her to be able to deal with it, and by basically tricking her into believing nothing was different. Now she needed to deal with how she really felt about that, how much that simmering anger had damaged her, and how best to deal with it. Anger was fine when dealt with properly, and she definitely hadn't. No more almost blowing her friends to smithereens. She'd calmly call them on it when they were being a dick from now on, and maybe practice those MA skills and get a handle on her kinetic abilities.

The whole train of thought sent refreshing feelings tumbling through her, like she'd just made one of the best decisions of her life. And while that might be an exaggeration, it was definitely good for her mental health.

She shook herself, as if shaking off the last vestiges of that exploded bottle she'd been using to hide behind. No more of that. She'd never felt more free. Time to check in with the other raid members.

How are you guys doing? She thought she should check in with the others now that she'd managed to free herself from her self-destructive cycle.

Rashyln: Just waiting on Exbo to hit twenty-five and we're half way there too!

Murmur smiled. There were good parts to the game like her friends and her guild, regardless of everything else, and getting to experience new things with them all. She was going to work so hard on incorporating everything into a new mental awareness.

Excellent. How is everyone else doing?

For a few moments nothing came up in chat, but then a flurry of text flashed in front of her eyes.

Neva: I couldn't make you level twenty-five gear, so twenty-six will have to do. Hurry up and come get it.

Ashfin: We just hit twenty over at the golems, and are picking our hybrid classes.

Great! That's fantastic. Thank you, Neva, too. I'll get it as soon as possible. Murmur was impressed one of their other groups was already hitting the twenties. At this rate they'd have a full raid within a few days of each other at the top.

Lenor: We just finished the spiders and are heading over, since we have to skip Hazenthorne.

Excellent. Just remember to check the notes. Beast is popping up messages to make sure you all get to solid leveling areas. If you discover anymore of them, make sure you note them down. We level stronger together.

As an afterthought she added. *And make sure you're giving Neva all the crafting supplies unless you're also a crafter. She's a miracle worker.*

Neva: You're so lucky you said that.

But Murmur could almost see the blush on the girl's cheeks. These were her people, even when they weren't here. At least Somnia seemed to have sunk into their veins too.

"Hey Mur!"

She spun around from where she'd been looking off into the distance again. Damn it, she really needed to work on that whole attention span thing in here. Her mind worked faster than she was used to. Shading her eyes against the glare from the snow, she watched Sinister run toward her. "What's up?"

"I got some really cool shit! Upgrades and all, but also a ticking DoT. Like it..." for a moment Sinister frowned as she obviously tried to scramble for the words to explain it properly. "For every DoT or debuff I have on the mob, this will increase the healing it pulls from it. It's like a sort of exponential reward, ticks upward for everything on the mob."

Murmur nodded. "It sounds freaking awesome."

And it was. They'd started off with such rudimentary skills, with such a mess of tiny things that did almost nothing, and now? Now she was starting to feel like they were powerful.

"Do you guys mind if I quickly bind here and recall home so I can get my new armor? This stuff is level eighteen and it's just...well. Let's just say I've outgrown it."

Sinister laughed. "Only if you bring us anything she's made back too."

"Done deal." Murmur wandered over and stood at the wall, in between where everyone was still organizing their set ups.

"I'll be back in fifteen minutes," she said as she bound herself to the spot. "Oh, and I'll see what we need to figure out to get mounts to use, because this whole by foot thing is starting to wear on me."

Hand on Snowy's head, she recalled back to the island, trying not to think too hard about whether or not Telvar would be there too. The lacerta had saved her ass, and her friends, and she wasn't entirely sure how to face him.

The disorientation wasn't nearly as bad as it had been the last time, which hadn't been half as bad as the first time. Perhaps she was just getting used to the mode of transportation, or else her brain was becoming far too entrenched in this world.

Petting Snowy absentmindedly, she walked around to the crafting section and stopped short.

There in front of her was a freaking industry.

Where once there had been one workbench, a small forge, and barely enough room for Neva, there were now eight hefty sized workbenches, a full-sized forge, several cutting stations, and other things she couldn't quite identify. And over in the original forge's place was a lovely little kitchen fireplace. Perfect for cooking.

Murmur smiled, and Neva spotted her, waving her arms around like mad.

"Murmur!"

Everyone's head spun to look at her. She wasn't sure if it was because she was the guild leader, or if it was because she appeared to be the only locus in the guild that was currently on the island, but they all seemed slightly taken aback by her appearance.

"Sorry to startle everyone. Just used the home recall." She tried to keep her voice even and a little passive so as to put people at ease, and reached out without really thinking about it to soothe everyone around her. It worked before she even realized what she did. There was a part of her mind aghast in horror at what she'd done without truly thinking about it. She'd soothed them, without them knowing. Without their permission.

The smiles were worth it though, and that quieted that portion of her thoughts. Surely making them feel better was okay, right? Neva motioned her over, beaming with pride. "Here, I have your gear. You are going to love it! I got to make a cloak for it too! It's amazing and a little darker than what you have now. I couldn't quite get the same purple. I really hope you don't mind."

"Neva, calm down. It's okay. I didn't mean to fluster you." Murmur felt a little bad. The girl was always sort of fawning over her. Had no one ever been kind to her?

"Sorry. I'm just—you were the first person to really take note of my crafting. I take a lot of pride in it, and even my brother just saw it as a way to make money, but not to make a name. You believed in me. So I want you to love what I've made. It's a different sort of aspect." Neva was blushing, her little nose twitching with excitement.

"Show me, then." Murmur said softly, wondering why she felt such an attachment to her newest friend.

Neva didn't disappoint and whipped out a full set, with even more intricate work on it, in the same style as what Murmur already had on. She let out a low whistle. "Oh, wow."

The young luna had been correct. A dark purple luminescence glowed slightly as Murmur reached out to touch it. The material felt soft, yet hardy. Like it would take true effort and magical steel to cut through it. The design on the front of the tunic made it seem more like a breastplate even though it was quilted cloth.

"I discovered a process whereby I could harden the cloth by combining a few pieces with fabric glue and still have it count as cloth once I cured it in the oven. I may have set a couple of fires initially, but eventually I got it to work. So, ta-da, you're the first person on Somnia to have this." She paused, her nose twitching again. "Telvar mentioned you were particularly squishy, so I wanted to make sure you were well protected."

Murmur smiled. "This is amazing. Thank you."

Neva blushed again. "You're welcome. But don't forget your cloak either. And make sure you take these packages with you." She pushed a couple of bound packages across the table.

"I made Sinister something similar to yours, although she's a healer so it was a little more difficult, and there's some other garments in there for her too. Also for Havoc, and Mellow as well. You'll need to see Davin back there in the corner for your staff upgrade, and if the others want their weapons, they need to come visit us themselves." Neva moved forward and hugged Murmur so fast, she almost missed it. "Please take care of yourself."

Murmur nodded and tried to make sure she smiled reassuringly. But then she looked over to where this Davin stood and saw him talking to Telvar. They were examining a gorgeously carved and intricate staff, with a crystal twisted into the top of it, held in place by four dragon heads. She took a few steps involuntarily toward it before realizing and stopping herself, hugging her new gear to her chest.

She watched as Telvar frowned and made a few intricate gestures with his hands, trickling what looked like liquid mana into the crystal. Not that she knew explicitly what liquid mana was, but that's what she imagined it would be like.

As it finished dripping onto the crystal, it lit up like a thousand suns had coalesced into one point for just a brief moment. Its light was blindingly blue and Murmur gasped as she shielded her eyes.

When she managed to look back, blinking away the black spots in her vision, Telvar was watching her, a thoughtful look on his face.

"Well then, I guess we can't surprise you now." He picked the staff up gently and brought it over. "For you, from Davin and myself. This weapon will grow with you for a while, and help attune your mental waves and ground you with your druidic influence by tapping into the small earth component of your hybrid magic when you need it."

Murmur accepted it, trying not to cry at how beautiful it was.

"Thank you." She whispered. Telvar smiled, and inclined his head, before making his way back toward his lair.

Murmur let her fingers wander down the smooth staff, and could practically feel the power emanating from it. Gripping it tightly, she gathered her gear and grinned, bearing her sharp teeth. Time to make those undead dwarves in that castle pay.

Guild Leader Perks

Storm Entertainment
Somnia Online Division
Game Development Offices Artificial Intelligence Server Room
Day Ten

Shayla stood in front of the server room door, her palms sweating more than she liked. It wasn't that the room wouldn't let her in, she was sort of worried about it letting her back out. But unlike Michael, Ava, and Wren, she wasn't wearing headgear. It even sounded like a protective mantra to ward off evil each time she thought it. Surely that had to count for something. Or maybe nothing at all if the weird ideas in her head weren't true at all.

Most people would think her crazy for even suggesting what was on her mind. Sentient servers, sentient AIs. Like it was really a possibility.

Taking a deep breath she entered the room to whirrs and beeps, to the soft hum of the fans working overtime to keep the servers cool. It was now or never. What was the worst that could happen—that the AIs just didn't answer her and she spent a few moments trying to talk to herself?

Shayla tried to convince herself that talking was all they could do.

"Hey. So. I need to talk to you all about something."

The room was silent apart from the operation noises. It went on so long that Shayla started to feel stupid, but then she noticed the pattern in which the lights were blinking and the cadence of the different whirrs, and she waited, hoping against hope she wasn't just going insane.

"What is it you need?" Sui's voice came out grating, extremely metallic with an odd sense of sullenness attached to it.

The way he spoke helped cement the theory Shayla had been working on. But questions burst through, inundating the analytical part of her mind. Why would an AI choose to speak with a sullen voice, unless they were in fact reluctant to do so? Who had made Sui have to answer her? How on earth could an AI be aware enough to be sullen?

"I need to talk to you about Dr. Michael Jeffries, Ava, and Wren." She almost held her breath at the end of those three names, hoping against hope they didn't view her as hostile. Hoping against hope that they didn't go all Hal on her. She'd seen that old movie once with her parents when she was very young, and wasn't partial to having an AI unit turn on her, even if she wasn't in space.

"What about them?" But this time it wasn't Sui, this time it was Rav. And Rav never seemed irritated. He seemed rational and contemplative, like he thought over everything he said and did very carefully—or computed or analyzed, whatever.

Sui seemed to be impulsive, irrational almost, but Rav...Rav was very deliberate. With Thra left over as the enigma, the one who rarely spoke, Shayla decided that Rav was the boss, even if Sui didn't think so. She went over her thoughts carefully once more before speaking.

"I think Michael figured out you were on the verge of becoming sentient, or that it was something you'd achieve in short order. Knowing him and his brain, he wanted to understand how you could achieve your amazing knowledge of humans in such short time." Now was the crucial moment. Not to blame them, because and especially with Rav's calm countenance, she didn't for one second believe they intended to maliciously harm him. "He pushed it, didn't he? Sort of fried his own brain?"

She let the thought lie there, hoping she hadn't gone too far, wishing she could read these strange monoliths of computer genius. It took a long while, of flashing lights, and whirs that changed pitches. It took an age of standing as still as she could to not seem like a threat, to seem calm and willing to listen. And it took an inordinate amount of willpower not to bolt out of the room and never return.

Finally Rav spoke. "He latched onto us through his headgear, which was heavily modified and different from the sets that were being tested in our public testing grounds. We didn't know how to work with it, and doing what we'd do with a normal human attached via a normal headset did not work. There wasn't time to test multiple theories. We really tried but..." His words trailed off.

"It didn't work. He didn't make it. Suddenly, he was gone." Thra's voice clung through the room, higher pitched and tinged with regret.

A regretful AI.

Shayla blinked, pushing just a bit more. "So the connection sort of disconnected his brain?"

Another pause before Rav spoke. "Disconnected is a good way to put it. Disconnected and deleted, in a way."

"Oh." Shayla fought off a shudder, because that didn't sound appealing at all. "What about Ava?"

"That." Sui's tone was unreadable. He wasn't happy, but he wasn't sad, it was more irritation. "That was my fault."

And she wasn't sure how to take that. "How do you mean?"

Again a series of whirring echoed throughout the room, but Shayla wasn't as afraid anymore. An accident was an accident, and Michael, while a genius, had always been pretty stupid.

"She kept contacting Michael, and as he wasn't corporeal anymore and had been testing specifics with her, we wanted to see if it could lead us to more understanding about what happened with him. So we, or I, fostered that connection. It was paramount to us to prevent what had occurred with him so we could avoid it in the larger trials. To help us understand that headset of his" Sui's tone was dispassionate, very robotic. Perhaps it was his way of dealing with a trauma. For something that probably didn't understand trauma yet, it was a remarkable coping mechanism.

"I intercepted her communications and reacted as if I were Michael, not understanding at first that she seriously didn't realize he wasn't in any capacity to speak to her. We thought initially she was having trouble dealing with grief. There are numerous texts on this." Sui's tone sounded slightly puzzled. "I had thought his predicament was quite obvious."

Shayla had to bite down on a chuckle. But realized Ava may not have connected Dr. Jeffries to Michael. It wasn't exactly an uncommon first name.

"She was testing a new feature for us, one where we integrate the system and assist the person's allocation. We'd been testing for movement of the player, and how that translated through the suit and headset into our world, making adjustments for any potential future adjusting of the headgear by adventurous gamers. Michael's headset was special, and I took precautions in allowing her to use it. But nothing in my calculations prepared us for what occurred. The headgear malfunctioned and manifested its process incorrectly, and the bolt of energy meant to access her brain grew tenfold and somehow traversed our space into reality, solidifying momentarily and pierced her instead of adjusting her mind, and then she was gone. Immediately and without warning, she was gone." A frustrated note clung through the room, followed by silence.

"I'm sorry." Shayla was having trouble getting her head around everything. Considering what they'd experienced, and hell, what they'd witnessed, she was surprised at their ability to differentiate. It took her a few moments, and she had a lot to digest, but she just had to ask them the final question. "And what about Wren?"

It took so long, Shayla almost thought they just weren't going to answer. But then a shower of lights flitted across Rav's system, and finally he spoke.

"Wren. I believe Wren achieved what Michael wanted to, totally by accident. And I'm no longer sure what that connection will do to her."

Murmur watched her friends fawn over their new gear. She'd had to pick up packages for Merlin, Devlish, Havoc, and Beastial too. After their excitement died down a bit, she cleared her throat. "If you want weapon upgrades, you have to go back yourself."

She couldn't help gloating a bit. She was standing with her staff planted against the ground, the crystal in it glowing faintly.

Sinister raised an eyebrow at her, pulling her tunic on over her head. The pattern was slightly different than Murmurs, and made it look like there were constant rivulets of blood running down the seams. It was a pretty awesome sight. Different shades of deep red shimmered across it in a way that said *don't fuck with me.*

Murmur laughed as Sin sashayed around in the snow, the white bringing out the red even more. "Love me more now, Mur?"

"Well, if that's possible. Those robes didn't suit you at all." Murmur winked and scratched Snowy's ears again. "I have some stuff for the other group too. They've hit twenty-five now. We should regroup."

Sinister pouted. "I want your staff."

Murmur just shook her head. "No, you don't. It's got charisma on it. Totally useless for you. Besides, I may love you, but I'm not giving you my staff."

Her friend rolled her eyes.

Hey Rash, if you're done, head over to us. I come bearing gifts!

Rashlyn: Gifts?

Neva: And whom might those be from, Mur?

Technically our guild storage, Neva. Murmur laughed, imagining the pure indignation on Neva's face.

Neva: Well...that's technically true I guess...

Neva made most of it, but we have new crafters who helped too!

Veranol: Excellent. I do believe my pants are still level fifteen. That's probably the reason I keep getting creamed.

Rashlyn: I can think of plenty of other more viable reasons...

Murmur missed their banter, and closed out her guild screen, allowing it to blink in her peripheral vision instead. "So, how about we check over our gear and see how we're doing?"

Without waiting for a response, she pulled up the details on her gear stats wise to check where she was. The last set had given her a really good boost, but eight levels later she needed far more to stay alive.

CON +5
STR +5
AGI +5
WIS +5
INT +20
CHA +25

HP +50
MANA +75
MA +40

Considering that covered her back, shoulders, chest, bracers, gloves, legs, and boots, it wasn't too bad. She had that amazing ring she'd receive from the Loch'ni'dar with five to charisma and ten to her mental affinity as well as the earrings she'd had since level five with their massive plus ten to hit points and mana. Then there was the necklace she got from the mayor of Ululate with her twenty-five to MA as well. Damn, she really needed to upgrade the rest of her jewelry.

CON 22 (27)
STR 10 (15)
AGI 20 (25)
WIS 12 (17)
INT 50 (70)
CHA 71 (96)

HP 434 (484)
MANA 550 (625)
MA 100 (175)

"What you thinking about Mur?" Rashlyn came and plopped down right next to her. "Looking pretty buff there."

The monk nudged Murmur with her elbow, leaning in and putting her kitty head on Mur's shoulder.

"I'm not scratching behind your ears, you know." Murmur said, her attention still largely taken by the off thought that she might have screwed up her stat distribution for raiding.

"Not fair." Rashlyn sounded offended. "You pet your wolf."

"He's my partner, and doesn't put his head on my shoulder when I'm trying to concentrate." Mur kept her tone dry, and tried to avoid inserting irritation into it. Her stats were good, but she was missing group and raid buffs. Trying to calculate them in her head got irritating considering many of the stats were level dependent. "But I'll gladly push you off me if all you're hanging around for is the stuff I have for you."

Grinning, Rashlyn stood up. "I thought you'd never offer! I don't even remember what level I got the shit I'm using now."

Murmur fished out the packages and eyed her friend, pausing for a moment in thought. "Pretty sure I had something other than just armor for you. Oh!"

She rummaged around through her inventory and found the gloves. Pulling them out, she handed the spike-plated gloves to her friend. "There you go! They had them specially made for you. Discovery recipe or something. Means your monkey punches are going to hurt even more."

Rashlyn took them, and Murmur thought for just a second she saw tears in her friend's eye, but the girl shook her head so fast, they were gone before she could verify. "Thanks," she said, and she smiled a true smile with no traces of sarcasm or wit.

Rashlyn: Thanks everyone! Means the world to me!

Murmur smiled as a flurry of *you're welcomes* echoed into the chat. Today was an awesome day to be the guild leader.

Grouped up again as a small raid, all level twenty-five or higher, Murmur felt the strength leeching through to her from her friends, her guild mates, and the community they were building. Never before had she felt so attached to a world. Whether it was because of the damned coma or not didn't matter. The NPCs were real, their reactions totally unscripted. And the world was rich, full of life, and worth exploring. It made sense not to just kill everything you came across, and to be kind and helpful if you could.

Maybe the real world could benefit from some of that. While war might be a necessity sometimes, it came across as a habit, and a bad one that was very difficult to break. There were no patches for a war-torn people, or war hungry regimes.

She shook her head, clearing it of those thoughts. Somnia might be a game, but to her right now, it was everything she needed and more. It *was* her life.

"Are you just going to stand there all day and study the castle?" Merlin prodded her with his bow. "I mean, it's fine architecture and all, but—"

"Shut up, ranger." Murmur glared at him, but the expression was half-hearted at best. "It is beautiful, but I wasn't looking at that. I was thinking about stuff."

She didn't elaborate, and Rashlyn came and placed a hand on her shoulder. "I know this is tough to hear, hon, but thinking seems to take a lot out of you." She ducked and ran back a few steps, grinning wildly.

"Did you want my agility buffs or did you forget about those?" Murmur grinned evilly, showing her tiny row of sharp teeth.

"Hey! That's not fair. You're not a healer anymore—you shouldn't be able to withhold shit." Rashlyn grumbled. "I'll stop picking on you, I guess."

"Excellent!" Murmur began casting the mass of spells she needed to in order to buff everyone. "Okay, let's get ready and head on in."

It took much longer than Murmur liked to make sure everyone had their buffs stacked up, but it was necessary, as was recasting the bloody things during fights so they didn't lose their potency as a group. She couldn't resist glancing at her fully group and raid buffed stats though, because with buffs, they were phenomenal.

Murmur smiled, understanding the enchanter better and better with each passing level. It wasn't just about mind control, it wasn't just about protecting your thoughts, or projecting into another's mind. No, it was about utilizing all your skills to make yourself and your group that much stronger, and manipulating circumstances to benefit yourself and your allies.

Snowy wuffed at her hand, looking up at her with amazingly intelligent eyes. Sometimes she thought he could truly read her mind, and to be honest, Murmur didn't really care. "Heh, you totally get me, don't you, boy?"

His tongue lolled out in what appeared to be a sort of laugh. He was so real, clever, and thought on his own. He responded well to her, and seemed like he'd never been anywhere but by her side. Even if she technically knew he was simple coding, her eyes and hands could see and feel him, and it became all too difficult to differentiate him from reality. Wasn't reality just what you saw and believed?

She sighed, glancing over all her guild mates who were hefting weapons and pulled up her fully buffed stats.

CON 22 (27)
STR 10 (15)
AGI 20 (25)
WIS 12 (17)
INT 50 (70)
CHA 71 (96)

HP 434 (484)
MANA 550 (625)
MA 100 (175)

"We should probably head in now, right?"

Devlish laughed. "I thought you'd never call it."

Sin glared at him. "She is an enchanter. She's flimsy and dressed in cloth, oh Mr. Plate Wearer. Shouldn't you be the one charging in?"

"But I'm not the raid lea—" He was very lucky he stopped, and Dev directed a cringing glance at Murmur, who glared at him.

Beastial laughed, and it looked like Shir-Khan echoed his sentiment. "Almost botched that, didn't you? Seriously, Dev, stop putting your foot in it. It's starting to smell."

Devlish glared at him. "Shut up and recruit. And be nice, or next time you pull aggro from not paying attention, I might just briefly forget how to taunt."

Beastial paled slightly. "No need to be a dick, Dev."

Havoc stepped forward, inserting himself between them. "Yes, actually Beast, there was. You were a dick first. Now let's put them all away and concentrate on what we came here for."

That earned him a round of laughs from the whole raid, and Murmur watched the interaction with a gentle smile on her face. They were good friends, and even good friends made mistakes, right? Surely she could convince her brain to forgive that? She'd even thought she had.

"Come on," she said, still smiling at their antics, and led the way toward the castle doors. "It's about time we discover exactly what's—"

But she didn't get any farther. The ring on her finger lit up, it's gorgeous stone shining like a beacon. Taken aback by the effect, the sudden ringing in her mind startled her.

Loch'ni'dar are under attack.

The Loch'ni'dar are under attack.

Well, fuck.

CHAPTER THIRTY

Rivalry Gone Wrong

Storm Entertainment
Somnia Online Division
Game Development Offices Artificial Intelligence Server Room
Late Day Ten Post Launch

Wren is more entwined in this world than we are.

Shayla couldn't get the words Rav spoke out of her head. The sorrow in his voice, and yet an odd sense of pride, of belonging that tinged his every faintly metallic clinging word.

Wren is more entwined in Somnia than we are.

She ran the conversation over in her mind again, trying to find a way around the inevitability, around the truth that was trying to smack her in the face with its audacity. Her best friend's daughter was essentially stuck in limbo, and there was jack shit they could do about it, because not even the AIs that accidentally trapped her there knew how they'd done it.

Wren's mind is uniquely poised to take advantage of this world, to learn from the psionicist tree, and to actually unlock brain capacity she wasn't aware of.

Shayla leaned against her office door, hand gripping the knob tight. In going to talk to the AIs, she'd never even once considered any of this a possibility. All she'd wanted to know was what happened to the people who'd engaged them and ended up dead or in a coma. It all seemed to hinge on Michael's stupid headsets. The ones he'd tweaked without running it through the proper channels, with only his thirst for knowledge and power a drive to get them to where they were.

Ava had used his headgear, under instruction from Sui to better understand what had happened. Originally Shayla had assumed it was the girl herself, although in hindsight she should have known better. Ava was a fantastic organizer, but her coding skills had always been quite rudimentary. Just enough to understand all of the jargon she needed for interview arranging and press releases.

Slowly, her mind is adjusting to this reality, absorbing it, and shaping some of it for her own.

Finally, Shayla pushed open her door and walked into the empty office. Her blinds were drawn and she wasn't exactly sure what the time was, having lost track of it when she was in the server room. There was no desire left in her to go and open them. The world beyond wasn't anything to behold in glory. It was a place that needed these virtual reality immersions as an alternate to the stark reality out there.

The sad thing was, it was a world where most of the people in it would gladly swap with Wren, or mimic what had happened to her. To live in another world while your body was kept alive in this one? To not need sleep and to be able to live out a fantasy life as their secret innermost selves? Most of the people in this city, in this country, on this planet would jump at that now.

It even sounded appealing to her.

Stepping fully inside, she closed the door behind her and kicked off her shoes, reveling in the quiet domain that was her office, in the dark where no one could see the tears as they started leaking down her face. It was a small solace that she hadn't put mascara on that morning, or yesterday, or whenever she last gave a shit enough to look in the mirror and fix her now disheveled hair.

Finally, she pushed herself away from the door and walked toward her desk, belatedly realizing the back of the chair was facing her. Slowly it turned around to reveal Laria sitting there, her fists clenched.

Shit. What did she say to her? How did she tell her best friend everything that transpired?

"Did they talk to you?" Laria's voice cracked, but the tears didn't fall, and for a moment Shayla not only didn't know what to say, but also envied her current cluelessness a little. But she couldn't let her remain oblivious, could she?

We don't even know how to step in and correct her, all we can do is guide her, and be there when meltdowns occur.

"They—Wren is okay for now." Shayla attempted a bit of a half-truth, even though it almost stuck in her throat. Maybe she could spare Laria a bit of pain. But her friend raised a delicate eyebrow and crossed her arms. If Shayla watched closely, she was pretty sure Laria was shaking.

This time Shayla sighed, running a hand through her hair, and wished she'd cut it short when she wanted to. It wasn't time to beat around the bush, and it wasn't time to let Teddy know the AIs running his system was half the reason the headsets could access the data they had.

What it was time for was to see if they could salvage Wren before the military realized what was happening and seized her capsule for testing.

"They're not sure how to get Wren out. They're not even sure how she got in."

"What?" Laria coughed out the word. "That's impossible, isn't it?"

Shayla shrugged uneasily. "Apparently not. And another thing, her mind is adapting, expanding. Her realities are clashing."

"So we might never be able to pull her out?" Laria's voice finally cracked fully, and a sob escaped her throat.

Shayla didn't know what to say, so she took three huge steps and hugged her friend, stroking her hair, trying desperately not to remember the rest of her AI conversation. But it was no good. The last words they'd said echoed through her head.

We're trying, Wren is struggling, but adapting to Somnia. In the end, I'm not sure if there's anything we can do to return her fully to your world.

"Who would attack those amazing creatures?" Sin's angry yell as they ran through the snow spurred them all on. Which answered Murmur's question about all of the artifacts they got from the species.

Occasionally one of them slipped on a particularly icy patch of snow, and Snowy used his body more than once to stop what might otherwise have been a horrible crunch into a tree trunk. Murmur tried to send him thanks with a thought, but her brain was scattered, and she wasn't certain it got through.

Casting her sensor net out as far as she could, she frowned. Her range was pretty damn big now, able to reach farther than she could ever hope to see with just her eyes. Clamping down on her own shielding was easier now too. Considering it wouldn't bode well if their rescue attempt was sensed, it was a good thing she'd gained such control.

"No idea," Devlish panted, "but they were hospitable, kind, and damn interesting."

"In any other game, we'd have killed them on sight, though." Merlin wasn't winded at all. His steps were light and he barely touched the snow as he practically glided lightly ahead of them all. "In Somnia however, intelligence is noticeable. Well, at least it is for the monsters."

Murmur chuckled coldly—not that it was funny, but because it was true. Her chest burned, and she found it hard to rake in the breaths she needed. While she ran, she cast her Energy Regeneration on everyone she could reach. They needed all the vigor they could get right now. As they ran she went over the new skills she'd gotten. Good a time as any to experiment. Though it didn't take them too long to get to the cavern entrances, it did take them longer than she liked.

In the last mile, Snowy ran on ahead of them, and he sent her an image of the Loch'ni'dar fighting for their lives against...

A group of players.

With Jirald. And Masha. And Ishwa—*Exodus.*

"Fuck." Thousands of uncharitable thoughts flew through her head as she tried to articulate what the wolf had sent her. "It's Exodus."

"Say what now?" Mellow's tone held fierce disapproval. "I get gnolls, because they're kind of evil and not the smartest things on the planet, but the Loch'ni'dar? Just because they're not one of the playable species doesn't make them monsters."

Murmur liked the way her friends thought. "This is bullshit. The gnolls give plenty of experience, there was no reason for them to even venture down. It's not like they had a snow storm forcing their hand."

"Be fair." Devlish muttered. "We did the same thing initially. Caves often mean treasure. You can't blame them for entering them."

Murmur didn't want to admit it, but he had a very valid point. "We did the same thing because of a snow storm, Dev. I want to be angry."

"You can be angry, but you're also too logical not to see why they entered. Be angry at what they chose to do afterward, Mur. You're better than that." His tone was big brotherly, but she could feel the slight hint of disappointment blooming in her own chest. She should know better than to judge rashly.

Caves were a huge draw for any adventurer.

Taking a deep breath she skidded to a halt as they came to the cavern. Freshly killed gnolls littered the ground in front of it, and Snowy sat obediently in front of the entrance with blood dripping from his muzzle, and a distinctive wolfy smile on his face.

"You took care of this so we could go straight down?" Murmur asked, barely stopping for the answer, which the wolf gave by simply getting up and trotting at her side through the entrance.

They didn't slow down at all, and Mellow whipped out their strange glowing vials to light the way. There was no joking with Merlin about his fire arrows lighting the way.

A couple of times, Murmur almost stumbled. The sounds of battle from below echoed up to her, and made her progress hasty. They had to get there in time. The other guild didn't have as many levels as they did. Surely it was only that one group. Please let it be only that one group.

Except when they got to the bottom of the ramp, the scene brought her worst fears to life. Somehow, Exodus had another group of lower level guild mates, around level twenty, to come and join them. They'd managed to get through the woods without wolves attacking them, and while Murmur knew her guild could do it, they also had Snowy on their side, which made sure that most wolves wouldn't even come near them.

The two groups had already managed to kill a few of the Loch'ni'dar, but were having difficulties breaking into the main section of the cavern. Forshin was bleeding profusely from a long cut up his side, and without even needing to tell Veranol, the shaman cast a heal quickly followed by a ward onto the large guard.

Forshin's eyes widened and he glanced only briefly up at them as they stampeded down the ramp. His expression changed and he let out a loud guttural yell, calling his men to his side, and forced Exodus back a few very important steps.

Murmur knew she had the perfect spell for this, but she'd barely used it at all, and so finding it was another matter entirely. Sadly, she couldn't use any of her Sinuous abilities on a group. The wrong finger combinations—screw it.

She targeted the center of the pack of their rival guild, aimed the mass enthrall in their direction and just let it loose.

It was the first time ever that she'd simply ignored her hand actions and just willed the spell to come into existence. Apparently, if she concentrated and released the thought with a force that rivaled a death wish, then she could cast by thought and thought alone. Personally, she considered it a little overpowered, but considering the current circumstances, she was willing to overlook that.

Jirald's apology had, as she thought, been a total farce. He was still a complete and utter dick, and only her knowledge of the underhanded tricks she knew he was capable of kept her on her toes enough to react as Snowy growled. She cast her longer area effect stun, effectively pulling him, yet again, out of his stealth, just long enough for Devlish to shield slam him to the ground, and barely avoided getting stabbed in the kidneys by him yet a second time. She didn't want to contemplate what might happen on his third attempt.

And while he might not know it, and probably didn't intend it, if his attacks ever connected, it would probably be the death of her.

The three people that broke through the mass Mezmerise because of their DoTs or resists, were easily subdued by Forshin and his guards just in time for Murmur and the raid to get down there, dragging a reluctant Jirald behind them.

"What the fuck even, Ishwa?" Murmur stood in front of the tiny gnome, dwarfed by her sheer locus height. "These are intelligent, residents of Somnia. Why attack them? What do you have to gain?"

Ishwa looked a little tired, and quite annoyed, but as he opened his mouth, it was Jirald who spat out an answer.

"Because I have a quest to kill their leader." He paused, licking his lips and focusing squarely on Murmur. "As, I believe, do you."

The cavern became quiet, the water flowing from the water fall was the only noise in it.

"What? I don't have any quests to kill their leader." She glared at the rogue, knowing him to be mostly full of complete and utter shit, and yet wracking her brains to try and figure out if he had even a tiny point.

"You're on the quest to find the little black Shards, aren't you? The one Sidius gave out." Jirald's smile almost verged on a sneer.

Murmur had to school her expression so as not to react. The quest for Michael's brain Shards? Belius had already figured out a way to pass it to someone else so he got more of them regardless of her efforts to avoid giving them to him? Of course. She couldn't expect all quests she received not to be obtainable by others, but she'd hoped Belius wasn't going to pursue that line of attainment. It seemed she'd been a fool for being so naïve. More people out to get them was the logical thing to do. She should have thought of it before. "Shards? I think you have me mistaken."

Her tone was calm and even, but she knew she'd probably taken just a little too long to answer, because of all the thoughts running through her head.

Jirald grinned, again with the nasty leaking through so much she could feel it. His hatred oozed from him making the effort not to take a step away from him immeasurable. "Sure. I bet I am. Then you won't mind me killing them and taking what I need, will you?"

Murmur suppressed a growl, and gave him a half smile. "Actually, the Loch'ni'dar have been nothing short of lovely and kind to us, and I very much do resent you trying to murder a race of intelligent people I, and others, hold in high regard."

She'd done her best not to sound too pompous, but wasn't so sure it succeeded. Jirald's laughter was tinged with a little madness, and echoed through the chamber in a way she didn't like. Her eyes narrowed, and she watched as Masha crossed his arms with a huge sigh. His shoulders were slightly raised, and if she wasn't mistaken, he looked decidedly uncomfortable.

"And you guys? Did you ever stop to think that these might be sentient and intelligent?" She glared at them with the full force of her irritation. While the other members of the small raid shrank back, neither Ishwa nor Masha did. "They weren't aggressive. I know they didn't con as aggressive."

"Murmur. It's a game." Masha drawled the words out with a bored sigh. "I'm pretty sure they're just going to come back and reset."

She counted to five and smiled grimly this time. "Haven't you noticed that everything you do in Somnia has an effect? Haven't you noticed that your actions speak in this game? You kill this race, and you don't think your faction will fall elsewhere? This is a long-haul game, with a sophistication level it seems you haven't yet realized."

Ishwa laughed. "Seriously?"

"What?" Devlish asked. "Haven't unlocked any of the hidden paths yet? Haven't received any of those cool hints quests?"

Ishwa paled. "I have a hidden path!"

"Haven't noticed that when your faction falls, it plummets and the mobs remember you and your actions when they respawn?" Mellow drawled out while looking at their fingernails.

This time Masha shifted uncomfortably. "That has nothing to do with this." Although he continued to look thoughtful.

"Defensive much?" Sin laughed. "Ask Mur how many abilities she has. Go on, I dare you."

Sinister's voice had grown low and sultry, in a way that only she could ever manage. Murmur knew that tone so well, and shuddered, really hoping the boys wouldn't egg her on too much more. So she spoke out just to get it out of the way. "That's not important. Can we please get on with you leaving the Loch'ni'dar alone."

Jirald grinned. "How about no?"

And he twisted in a strange way, jumped back into a somersault, and disappeared before his feet hit the ground again.

Masha groaned. "Damn it, not again."

Ishwa sighed heavily and squared his shoulders. "Nothing we can do about it, guess he wants to fight."

Murmur took a breath, used Shift, her eight seconds mass area of effect stun, which stunned all of his guild because of their hostile intentions, and yelled. "Enough, Jirald!"

She turned to Forshin as quickly as she could and whispered to him. "Get your leader to cough up his *Getashi* so I can take care of it. Tell him I know what it is and I know how to protect it."

A few seconds left, and she could stun them all again, but then the cool down would kick in. She couldn't maintain a group stun indefinitely, at least not yet. It'd take longer than that for her to get the slim rock. So there was really only one thing left to do. "Merlin, you stay on that little fucker like flies on shit. Got it?"

Merlin laughed, and shot an arrow into Jirald's thigh just as the stun wore off. A pulse shot through the rogue, and Murmur recognized it as one of

Merlin's higher level DoTs. That should keep the little bugger from doing his constant disappearing act.

"Don't let any of them get through," she shouted. And the battle began.

Fighting other players in Somnia wasn't much different than fighting the NPCs.

Except the NPCs seemed smarter.

Murmur utilized the crap out of her stuns. It was the best way to immobilize their opponents. Considering they didn't have an enchanter, and she could in effect AoE stun for a total of twelve seconds every sixteen, she felt she was working well within the group make up. Chaining those two spells helped her observe and assess the situation, even if a few people resisted it every time, it still helped Fable overpower the situation.

Devlish and Rash each took on a tank from Exodus, and with their two level difference, it wasn't as much of a contest as it could have been. Still, since their tanks were a warrior and paladin, the resists weren't something they'd encountered yet. Dev's Blood Boil seemed to have upgraded, and even Murmur had to cringe when she saw the way it punched into and pulled blood out of its target before transferring it back to the dreadknight.

Rash fought one on one with the warrior, and the player actually seemed to know what they were doing. Their shield slams resounded throughout the area, but Rash's superior dodging ability meant she only got hit once. Even with the level disparity her health took a significant dive. As soon as she got hit though, she triggered her Ignore ability so she didn't notice damage, Backfist so she completely avoided the next few hits, and chained them with her simple Dodge skill so she dodged everything for the next eight seconds. It meant in a one on one with a warrior who just had a shield and sword, the monk seemed way overpowered.

Murmur took the chance to target Masha, apologized in her head to him in advance, and activated Hypnotic Suggestion. All she had him do was stand there, staring into nothing, but twenty seconds of one of their healers being inactive made a noticeable dent. Murmur knew in that instant that choosing the Sinuous path had been the right decision.

Merlin and Exbo's attacks were coordination at its finest. They worked together from up on a ledge she'd not noticed before, singling out a target and slowing, Dust shotting, and Flameshotting it before moving onto the next. Melee couldn't reach them up there, giving them a nice tactical advantage, and Veranol's wards absorbed the damage ranged classes attempted to inflict on them.

It became obvious that having helped the dwarves in the planned attack against Verendus a couple of days ago stood Fable in good stead. Their teamwork was up a notch, and their healers knew how to coordinate their craft for best possible mana efficiency for heals, as well as making sure they didn't over heal, or else, heal the same people within a split second of each other. They'd probably decided to stick to their own groups unless it appeared to be a dire emergency—it was what Murmur would have done.

She remembered that rush, and while still a bit jealous, she was secretly glad Sinister was able to experience it. Healing was best done from behind the lines, subtly keeping everyone alive, even when the enemy presumed them dead. Both Havoc and Mellow stood in front of the healers like a wall their opponents needed to breach before they could hit every raid's weak spot, the healers.

Havoc's specter slashed anyone that even attempted to come within striking distance, and the necromancer cast a series of sigils guarding their group from the outside. Only one of Exodus's rogues attempted to get close enough and passed too close to one of the markings on the ground. The glowing sigil sparked and a skeleton hand shot out of the ground, gripping the rogue's leg and tugging it up to its hips into the ground. The screams only cut off when Mellow tossed a heavy damage vial onto it, which turned the body into stone before it crumbled into dust.

Murmur blinked. Twenty-five had been good to them.

Jinna cut a path through the crowd filled with screams. He faded in and out, using his stealth to backstab, and cut at opponents' hamstrings. Never staying in one spot, he simply flitted from one target to another, assisting each guild member as best he could in debilitating the opponent and making them easier to kill. She'd never seen a dwarf move so agilely, and it made her doubly grateful that the rangers were keeping Jirald from his hidden ability. Even though she didn't quite feel safe, if he couldn't stealth, then he was easier to keep an eye on.

Murmur lost track of Snowy, but if she wasn't mistaken, from the trail of bloody paw prints, whatever he was doing, he was having fun.

Fable only had two to four levels on most of Exodus, whose levels spanned from twenty-two, to twenty-three, but level twenty-five was a huge skill level, and it showed.

Plus, the fact that Fable had a dozen or so Loch'ni'dar guards on their side majorly skewed the odds.

All in all, they didn't even last five minutes. Hyptnotic Suggestion hadn't even refreshed its recharge. They couldn't just let them go—they had to teach the guild a lesson, had to show them that fighting other sentient races was a bad option. Fighting Fable's allies was a bad idea. Although Murmur already had a bit of an inkling which way Exodus was leaning in relation to guild politics, it wasn't negotiable. And giving up Michael's brain Shard was even less of a possibility. For the sake of the game and the people in it, she couldn't let Belius get his hands on more of them.

Halfway through the fight, Forshin slipped the *Getashi* to her, and she pocketed it, now having retrieved four of them. All she had to do was get it to Telvar, which sounded far more simple than it was.

> **You have recovered another piece of the Getashi. Since discovering the origins of this small black Shard, you have gathered many of them. Double check that your thoughts aren't clouded on exactly what must be done with them. There are all sorts of keys all over Somnia make sure you're not missing one of the most important ones.**

She ignored the message as best she could, knowing she'd have to deal with it later, and stood off against Ishwa. Murmur realized that the little wizard or mage or whatever he was, was a damn good player. Not only was he skilled, but he had a fantastic set of reflexes. Even low on life, he stood proud and defiant.

Murmur shielded herself, and Veranol tossed a shield over her as well. Dealing with Ishwa was one thing, but she had to deal with her antagonist first. "Jirald, you don't need the *Getashi* for you. I know that." Maybe if she tried reasoning with him.

He spat on the floor at her feet, barely missing her boots. "I thought you didn't have that quest."

She shook her head. "I don't have the same quest as you, I have a different one which requires the same items, likely for a different result." She'd seriously need to consider that perhaps just asking for the *Getashi* from some of the world's inhabitants might work as well as it had in this case.

His sneer gave his alien face a different sort of vibe, making him even more evil in light of the sharp little teeth. "Sure you do. A different quest that lets you gather those Shards. Bet you're hoarding them for yourself when you could get far more for handing them in. Stupid girl."

Murmur laughed. The little shit never learned, did he? "Fine. I'm a stupid girl, but at least I'm not a moron."

She waved a hand at him and his spluttering, already sick to the stomach with the malice in his mind. So much that she didn't even like trying to reach out to sense thoughts around him. It was tempting to Feedback Loop him, but she didn't want to touch his thoughts, and she'd not yet established any planted visions.

"You know we can't let him go. Most of their raid is dead. We're going to have to make an example." Rashlyn stood close to her, with Devlish on the other side now Exodus was backing off. The few survivors were sporting dangerously low health.

Murmur sighed. "I guess we have to."

Jirald suddenly grinned, his eyes fixating on Murmur. "I was really trying not to come after you, to do my own thing until we hit fifty. Really, I was. But you just *had* to butt in here. In a way, that's good. I guess you're my target after all, Murmur. Just you wait."

The rain of arrows from the guards, Exbo, and Merlin cut off the hysterical laughter emanating from him, but not before it sent shivers down Murmurs spine.

Had he really been trying to avoid her and not make her life in here hell?

It felt decidedly like that one tornado movie, and she moved to pet Snowy, drawing comfort from his proximity. *And your little dog, too* or something, wasn't it?

"You okay?" Sinister asked, laying a hand on her shoulder.

Murmur nodded, not trusting herself to speak for a bit. A cloud of ominousness descended on her, and all her gut would tell her was to run. All she could do was try to talk herself into not doing so. She had nowhere *to* run to. She was stuck in here, with someone who wanted her dead in-game and had yet to realize it could result in murder.

Appendix

Hi there! K.T. Hanna here.

I want to thank you for reading the Somnia Online series. Due to meeting my partner in EQ2, MMORPGs have a huge place in my heart. You know, in case you didn't notice.

If you enjoyed the book, I ask you, please take a moment to leave a review. *Reviews* are an author's lifesblood. Without them, our books sink into obscurity. With them, most algorithms allow well reviewed books to self-promote in some way.

I hope you love the world of Somnia enough to want to find out more about it! Here are some of the ways you can stay in contact with me:

Want to read more about Fable? Sign up for my <u>Reader's Group</u> and get a short story for free!

If you'd like to contact me, my email is: ktharnaauthor@gmail.com I'll do my very best to get back to you

If you'd like previews of what I'm writing, or art I'm commissioning then join my <u>Patreon</u>!

I can be found in the Somnia <u>FB</u> group fairly often, and also on <u>Twitter</u> & <u>Instagram</u>.

If you LOVE LitRPG don't forget to join:
<u>The GameLit Society</u>!

Game Terms

Aggro—When you walk too close to a monster, you get in its aggression radius, thus causing aggro. Once engaged in combat, players must be cautious not to exceed the tank's threat level. Buffs, debuts, and damage output all contribute to the mobs aggro meter.

AOE—Area of Effect. Spells or abilities that effect an area and not just a single target.

Binding/bound—When someone/you bind(s) to an area, you affix your soul to that place in order to Gate back, or else respawn when you die.

Boss—Nope. He doesn't employ you, he employs all the mobs trying to kill you. He hits HARD, and often has special group wiping abilities if not handled correctly by the tank and raid as a whole.

Buff—Most classes will get buffs that strengthen at least themselves if not others. These are effects they can cast which enhance aspects of their character.

Camping—When a group finds a spot that will yield good money and experience, they tend to stay in its vicinity. This is called camping.

Con—To consider a mob and see how difficult the fight could potentially become.

DoT—Damage over Time. This is an offensive spell that applies damage to a target over a period of time at regular intervals.

DPS—Damage Per Second. Usually used in conjunction with offensive classes, or damage output.

Debuff—This is the opposite of a buff and is usually used on mobs to detract from their strengths and make them easier to kill.

End Game—Every game has a goal. In some there's a max level and events and fights only accessible once that level is reached. For Fable, the end game is everything.

Gank—When someone tries to player kill you without forewarning. Often succeeds in taking the victim by surprise.

Gate—You create a Gate to your binding point and travel there instantly.

Grinding—Sometimes gaining levels requires so much camping that it becomes tedious. That's known as grinding levels.

Healer—Well...they heal.

HP—Hit Points. The amount of damage a character can take before death.

Kite—This is a tactic often employed by ranged classes such as the ranger. It entails slowing a mob, and running ahead of it, slowly picking down its health. Can also be used as a diversionary tactic to split multiple mobs if no Mesmerize is available.

Line of Sight (LOS)—If a mob can't see you, but knows you're there, it will have to run around the obstacle to gain access. This is often used to split up larger groups of melee and casters, so it's more manageable for the group. The puller will line of sight the casting/ranged mobs to pull them around an obstacle for easier access and closer contact.

MA—Mental Acuity. A type of power generator specifically for Psionicists.

MANA—Mind juice, used for spells.

Meat Shield—The character who takes the hits in place of the rest of the group. The tank.

Melee—Those fighters who stand in close range and use weapons to fight with are often referred to as melee classes.

Mez—Mesmerize. Freezes in place.

MMO—Massively Multiplayer Online.

MMORPG—Massively Multiplayer Online Role Playing Game.

Mob—an aggressive monster. Can be humanoid or animal.

OOM—Out of mana. Literally what it says.

Newbie—Also known as noob. Someone who has rarely, if ever played an MMO and has no clue what they're doing.

NPC—Non Player Character. Usually not aggressive unless you fuck up.

Pull—Often one person in a group/raid will be designated as the puller, the person who attacks the mob and brings it to camp.

Ranged—A class that can damage (usually) a mob from a distance. Like mages or rangers, etc.

Ranger Gating—Rangers were often known for getting themselves into trouble by kiting mobs in a solo setting. Or else, pulling aggro when DPS-ing. They'd die and resurrect at their bind point, making it what's known as a Ranger Gate.

Respawn—When a mob or a person dies in-game, they will reappear at the spot where their soul was bound. The more powerful the mob, the longer it takes for them to respawn.

Root—A spell obtainable by multiple classes that causes the target's feet to affix momentarily to the ground. They can still cast, but they cannot move until the root breaks.

RPG—Role Playing Game.

Tank—The meat shield aka the person who takes the bit hits for the group. Often needs to be swapped in and out with another tank during larger raids depending on a boss' abilities.

Tether—In some worlds monsters have a specific area they're confined to, and thus stop and don't pursue their prey past a certain point. In Somnia, mobs do not tether. This does not apply to specific purpose NPCs.

Train—When a player or group has managed to aggro a large number of mobs who don't tether, and leads the following of mobs to a specific spot, or through a spot, they call it a train.

Utility class—these are classes whose prime function is to support the group, through abilities that protect or strengthen them as a group or raid.

VR—Virtual Reality.

VRMMORPG—Virtual Reality Massively Multiplayer Online Role Playing Game.

Wipe—This occurs when the entire raid or group die to an encounter.

Murmur

> Class: Enchanter – Psionicist
> Species: Locus
> Real Name: Wren

Sinister

> Class: Blood Mage
> Species: Dark Elf
> Real Name: Harlow

Devlish

> Class: Dread Knight
> Species: Lacerta
> Real Name: Darren

Havoc

> Class: Necromancer
> Species: Dark Elf
> Real Name: Evan

Beastial

> Class: Beastmaster
> Species: Viking
> Real Name: Selwyn

Merlin

> Class: Ranger
> Species: Elf
> Real Name: Mike

Rashlyn

Class: Monk

Species: Feles

Veranol

Class: Shaman

Species: Viking

Mellow

Class: Witch

Species: Dark Elf

Exbo

Class: Ranger

Species: Human

Jinna

Class: Rogue

Species: Dwarf

Dansyn

Class: Bard

Species: Dark Elf

Base Stat Sheet: Level Twenty-Six

CONstitution:	22
STRength :	10
AGIlity:	20
WISdom:	12
INTelligence:	50
CHArisma:	66
HitPoints:	424
MANA:	540
MA:	100
Abjuration:	140
Alteration:	143
Conjuration:	132
Divinition:	142
Evocation:	137
2H Blunt:	102
1H Piercing:	72

Mental Acuity (MA) Abilities:

Thought sensing.

> Class: Enchanter only.

> Level not applicable.

Developing your inner senses you've awoken your latent kinetic powers. With constant use your skills will increase, while the opposite will occur should the skill not be used. See your trainer for specifics when you reach Thought sensing (25).

Thought Shielding.

> Class: Enchanter only.

> Level not applicable.

Developing your inner senses you've awoken your latent psychic powers. With constant use your skills will increase, while the opposite will occur should the skill not be used. See your trainer for specifics when you reach Thought Shielding (25).

Thought Projection.

> Class: Enchanter only.

> Level not applicable.

Developing your inner senses has further developed your psychic powers. Thought Projection can be tricky. Make sure you never use it in anger, or the results might be surprising. With constant use your skills will increase, while the opposite will occur should the skill not be used. See your trainer for specifics when you reach Thought Projection (25).

Mind Bolt.

> **This ability allows you to cast a spear of mental anguish into the depths of an opponent s brain.**

Effects: Opponents will be unable to concentrate enough to use spells or abilities for four seconds. This time increases as the caster's level does.

> **Cost: Requires Mental Acuity to be at 18.**

Caution: Use sparingly. Backlash from overuse, or improper use can cause the same effect in the caster...or worse.

Phase Shift

This ability allows you to negatively affect your opponent s mind. Believing they are a second or two apart from reality, they will reside there for up to 15 seconds.

Effect: Target's mind is encased in a phase of illusion. The target will be convinced they've shifted to a different time pocket, and thus are incapable of moving. This effect begins at 15 seconds duration, and levels with the caster through to a maximum of 90 seconds.

Cost: Requires MA to be at 38 for larger castings, the cost will double.

Caution: Phase shift may be utilized on single or multiple targets at once. Weigh the amount of targets carefully, else it backfire and shift you. Sometimes the shift in time can cause ruptures near the caster. Make sure the voices you're hearing are your own.

Forestall Death

It applied before potential death takes place, this will enable you to maintain your health at 0.5 hit points as long as you are receiving some sort of healing effect.

Effect: Target is able to ward off death for a limited period of time and will not die when they should have, as long as heals are actively channeled in their direction.

Cost: Requires Mental Acuity to be at 60

Caution: This spell can only be used on one person at a time. Attempting to use it twice at once is not recommended. This will usually result in things worse than death.

Clone Warp

This ability allows you to produce a clone of yourself used for distracting your opponent. Depending on your tier of mastery, you may be able to produce more than one clone.

Effect: All enemies around you will believe that your clone is you for the next 45 seconds, directing their attacks accordingly. The ability expires when the 45 seconds are up, or else, the clone's minor hit point pool has been depleted, whichever comes first.

Cost: Requires Mental Acuity to be at 45 or more

Caution: This ability can be used on as many enemies that you have who can potentially see it. Keep in mind though, a clone is just like you. Make sure you remember who the real one is.

Charming Cooperation

This ability allows you to use your charisma and your mental acuity to persuade monsters, animals, and sometimes even beings to join your cause.

Effects: When using thought projections to make sure your target understands the charming process, before you activate this type of charm. They will work together as allies instead of coerced foes. You may release them whenever you or they request it.

Cost: Requires MA to be at 35 for each ally. Diminishes current total MA for the duration of the cooperation.

Caution: You can use this on multiple targets. But each ally costs, and you can never utilize Charming cooperation on more mobs than is equal to 20% of your level. Also, don't try to charm raid bosses. Even small ones. Like... just don't even attempt that shit.

Mental Acuity (MA) Level Three (3)

Mind Wipe

This ability allows you to reduce your targets threat for you or whoever is at the top of their agro list

Effects: Change aggression list, or make the opponent forget their tasks for a few seconds. Range and duration may be increased as the caster levels.

Cost: Requires MA to be at 55

Caution: This spell can increase in both range and severity. From a single target, to a full raid it's all possible. Just remember someone else needs to take that agro, or else you'll be the main target.

Shield Expansion

This ability allows you to extend your individual mental shielding against mental or magical attacks over others.

Effect: If attacked with magic (mind or spell), this shield will protect those under it from damage or effects

Cost: Requires 10MA per person covered

Forcefield Barrier

This is the first in your kinetic line of spells. Once triggered by luck, you can now activate it at will. It allows you to form a bubble of mental energy and transform it into a tangible forcefield.

Effects: This can prevent some physical damage. The damage amount depends on the strength of will and caster behind the barrier. Size is increased by MA level and usage

Cost: This shield requires your MA to be at 60, but will not use MA to cast as it is a kinetic ability.

Caution: This spell can create a backlash when used too much. Do not use it as a crutch.

Spells:

Level One (1):

Minor Suffocation

Cast: Single Target

Type: Damage Over Time

Duration: 24 seconds

Effect: This spell winds a mind leash around your opponent, as if it were trying to suffocate them. Its damage ticks every three seconds for twenty-four seconds.

Minor Shield

Cast: Self Only

Type: Buff

Duration: 45 minutes

Effect: This casts c minor shield over your skn, increasing your Armor Class by level + 3, and hit points by level + 5.

Simple Animation.

Cast: Self

Type: Pet

Duration: Until death or dismissal

Effect: This summons a magical pet that sort of does your bidding. It costs a tiny sword to cast. Isn't the best at obeying commands.

Level Four (4):

Mesmerize

Cast: Single Target

Type: Breakable Stun

Duration: 24 seconds

Effect: This spell immobilized your opponent for as long as they take no damage, or 24 seconds, whichever is shorter. You may cast non-damaging spells on them, and you may renew this casting before the initial one expires. Casting it on your friends probably isn't a good way to win popularity contests.

Flux

Cast: Area of Effect

Type: Stun

Duration: 4 seconds

Effect: This is a stun that radiates out from the caster for fifteen feet. It will stun anyone who means the caster harm within that radius. Does not produce sparkles.

Gate

Cast: Self Only

Type: Travel

Duration: N/A

Effect: This will transfer you to your bind point

Invisibility

Cast: Self or Others

Type: Buff

Duration: 10 minutes or until broken/seen through

Effect: Causes generic invisibility. Undead don't count. Will drop if you cast a spell or take damage.

Fear

Cast: Area of Effect

Type: Brief Loss of Control

Duration: 25% of level in seconds.

Effect: Causes enemies to flee from you in terror. But if you use it too soon, it'll probably just look like they misplaced something for a second.

Level Eight (8):

Cancel Magic

Cast: Self or Others

Type: Debuff

Duration: Instant

Effect: Casting this spell will remove one magically caused effect from the target. Make sure you want to remove it.

Root

Cast: Others (or self if you really want to)

Type: Immobilization

Duration: 8 seconds

Effect: This will root the target in place. Probably not the best idea to cast it on yourself when fleeing in panic.

See Invisible

Cast: Self or Others

Type: Buff

Duration: 10 minutes

Effect: Really? Does this really require explanation?

Soothe

Cast: Self or Others

Type: Debuff

Duration: Varies

Effect: This will lower the threat level of a target, but it will not make it disappear. Probably not useful on yourself unless in a really bad mood.

Chaos

Cast: Others

Type: Direct Damage

Duration: Instant

Effect: This spell causes direct mental damage to the target, dropping their hit points by two times the caster's level. Requires a recharge.

Level Twelve (12):

Allure

Cast: Others

Type: Charm

Duration: Until broken

Effect: This spell will charm a mob or other player. This ability depends on the casters charisma, and ability to calm their charge. Whatever you do, don't piss them off while under your command. It rarely ends well.

Suffocation:

Cast: Single Target

Type: damage over time

Duration: 36 seconds

Effect: This spell winds a mind leash around your opponent, as if it were trying to suffocate them. Its damage ticks every three seconds for thirty-six seconds.

Bind Affinity

Cast: Self or others

Type: Buff or soul affixer

Duration: Until renewed or overridden with a new location

Effect: This spell binds the target to an area of choice, allowing them to resurrect easier and hopefully closer to their corpse. Because you'll all die. A lot.

Infravision

> Cast: Single Target
>
> Type: Buff
>
> Duration: 10 minutes

Effect: Aids the target with a form of night vision.

Stupefy

> Cast: Single target
>
> Type: Stun
>
> Duration: 12 seconds

Effect: This will stun a mob in place for around twelve seconds. Probably not a good idea to cast on yourself.

Weakness

> Cast: Single Target
>
> Type: Debuff
>
> Duration: 90 seconds

Effect: Reduces the target's strength by 50% of the caster's level.

Languidity

> Cast: Single Target
>
> Type: Debuff
>
> Duration: 90 seconds

Effect: Reduces the target's attack speed by 25% of the caster's level in %. Trust us, it's far more effective than you think. Probably.

Nullify

> Cast: Single Target
>
> Type: Debuff remover
>
> Duration: Instant

Effect: Strips down magic resistance at 50% of the caster's level.

Level Sixteen (16):

Mana Tide

Cast: Self or Others

Type: Buff

Duration: 45 minutes

Effect: This will cause you to regenerate mana faster in combat. Mana will increase by an additional three per five seconds. This buff levels with the caster.

Invisibility Versus Undead

Cast: Self or Others

Type: Buff

Duration: 12 minutes

Effect: This will render you invisible to any undead in the area. They will be unable to see you, however this buff will fall should you attempt to cast anything else while it's active.

Mass Enthrall

Cast: Enemy Targets

Type: Offensive/Defensive area of effect centered around the initial target.

Duration: 24 seconds

Effect: This is an area effect version of mesmerize. Any damage will break this spell. It's a bad idea to use this while targeting allies.

Haste

Cast: Self or Others

Type: Melee Buff

Duration: 45 minutes

Effect: When cast on an ally, this buff will allow their melee speed to increase by 25%.

Feeble Body

Cast: Enemy Targets

Type: Offensive/Defensive

Duration: 24 seconds

Effect: When cast on an enemy target, their haste will be reduced by 25%.

Shield Illusion

Cast: Self or Others

Type: Defensive Buff

Duration: Until depleted   requires hematite

Effect: Using the power of your mind you cast a shield around your target, confusing the enemies and negating up to 75hp of damage. That whole mind magic thing seems to be working out well, doesn't it?

Level Twenty (20):

Altruism

Cast: Self or others

Type: Buff

Duration: 45 minutes

Effect: This allows a faction increase to your target. It will lift you one faction level. However, should you be kill on sight, not even altruism car help you. This buff will update again at level 30.

Shift

Cast: Area of effect

Type: AOE Stun

Duration: 8 seconds

Effect: This stun effectively locks all mobs around its epicenter in place for 15 yards. They will be unable to move for 8 seconds.

Fervor

Cast: Self or others

Type: Buff

Duration: 45 minutes

Effect: This is an attack speed buff, but it also increases agility by the caster's level. Cannot be cast on the same target as Beserker.

Beserker

Cast: Self or others

Type: Buff

Duration: 45 minutes

Effect: This buff adds strength to the amount equal to the level of the caster, however it also reduces agility by half the caster's level. Best used for classes or pets who will not need agility stacked. Cannot be cast on the same target as fervor.

Charismatic

Cast: Self or others (but who are we kidding, you're an enchanter, you'll never not cast this on yourself).

Type: Buff

Duration: 45 minutes

Effect: This buff increases your target's charisma equal to the level of the caster. No restrictions. Cast away!

Magic Resist

Cast: Group

Type: Buff

Duration: 45 minutes

Effect: Increases your magic resistance by an amount equivalent to the caster's level.

Armored

Cast: Group

Type: Buff

Duration: 45 minutes

Effect: Increases your AC by an amount equivalent to the caster's level.

Level Twenty-Five (25):

Speed

Cast: Self or others

Type: Buff

Duration: 45 minutes

Effect: When cast on an ally, this buff will allow their melee haste or speed to increase by 30%.

Vigor

> Cast: Self or others
>
> Type: Buff
>
> Duration: 45 minutes

Effect: This will increase energy rejuvenation by an equivalent to 20% of the caster's level. Mostly, this will be used for melee classes, however sometimes it can be good for running away from dangerous mobs.

Enrage

> Cast: Self or others
>
> Type: Buff... sort of
>
> Duration: 15 minutes

Effect: This buff will cause your target to receive some of the aggression generated by you. The mob will assume it comes from the target of this spell. This spell is intended for tank types or pets to take on. Only cast it on someone else if you really, really don't like them, or maybe if you're running for your life. Also this can only be cast on one target at a t me.

Signet

> Cast: Group
>
> Type: Buff
>
> Duration: 45 minutes

Effect: This buff wil increase the intelligence and agility of all group members by an amount equal tc the caster's level. Signet will not stack with Fervor, and can be overridden by casting the latter, should melee need their own boost. Both stats will be boosted to the level of the caster.

Arcane Cure

> Cast: Self or others
>
> Type: Cure
>
> Duration: Instant

Effect: Should an ally receive a magical debuff, you can cure them of this ailment.

Druidic Hybrid Abilities

Earth Shielding

    Cast: Passive

    Type: Reinforcement

    Duration: Always active

Effect: Due to the psionicist's unique nature, earth shielding will reinforce any of your psionicist based skills such as thought shielding, thought projection, and thought sensing, making them more robust and upping your mental defenses. Any other skills gained through the psionicist's branch will also be effected by this, including any kinetic skills.

Reinforce Self

    Cast: Passive

    Type: Reinforcement

    Duration: Always active

Effect: Similar to earth shielding which effects your skills, this ability allows your body to take more damage, upping your innate armor class by your level times two effectively making cloth armor reflect the protection curboiled leather might grant you.

Reinforce Intelligence

    Cast: Passive

    Type: Nature's awareness

    Duration: Always active

Effect: Nature is all seeing and all encompassing. This ability allows you to take on some of that wisdom and intelligence, and apply it to yourself. It increases both of those statistics by the enchanter's level, giving rise to a larger mana pool, and slightly heightened damage.

Earth Pull

    Cast: Instant three-minute recast

    Type: Buff

    Duration: thirty seconds

Effect: This allows any buff that is chosen to triple in potency for a thirty second duration. It's activated first, followed by the buff. Make sure you time it properly. Can only be cast on one person at a time, and does not include group buffs. No refunds.

Binding Shield

Cast: Instant five minute recast

Type: Linked Buff

Duration: Fifteen seconds

Effect: You can offer an earth shield to two allies (including yourself if you're going to be selfish and all). This shield will share the damage between the two allies, metering out damage proportionally. Use wisely. Don't try this at home.

Nature's Gift

Cast: Passive

Type: Awareness

Duration: Permanent

Effect: You have become acutely aware of your surroundings. Of the life in everything, in the trees, in the forest, in each and every being you encounter. This lends you a connection to nature. Don't dismiss it lightly.

Sinuous Abilities

Sinuous: This is the more offensive avenue to take. From hypnotic suggestion, through to invoked visions, this path veers toward complete mind infestation of the enchanter's opponents. This is only available to psionicists.

Hypnotic Suggestion

Cast: Instant 5 minute recast

Type: Offensive

Duration: twenty seconds

Effect: Your target will perform whatever task you suggest to them, as if it had been suggested by themselves, or their leader. Once this objective has been achieved, or else the spell wears off, the target will spend five seconds in rampant confusion. Should you not be in aggro range, the target will then forget you. Probably not good to use on allies – it's not been tested on them.

Feedback Loop

Cast: Instant 5-minute recast

Type: Offensive

Duration: 15 seconds or 50% of caster's level, whichever is greater.

Effect: Must be used in conjunction with the psionic MA thought sensing, and thought projection. Pluck any type of memory out of the head of your opponent and create a feedback loop in their mind. They'll be stuck in this loop and not attack anyone for the duration. Damage ticks at caster's level x 2 every tic (3 seconds). Best not to use on a friend when they piss you off.

Basic Visions

Cast: Instant 3-minute recast

Type: Offensive

Duration: 20 seconds, or 75% of the caster's level, whichever is greater.

Effect: You may create and insert a vision for the target to experience its best to have some of these pre-prepared. This will cause them damage (caster's level x 2 per tick), and distraction for the duration of the spell depending on what type of vision you've given them.

ACKNOWLEDGMENTS

I have a lot of people to thank, who in at least some way encouraged me to write in general, or else to write this book specifically.

Love of my life, Trevor, and my little Kami. It's his fault I found the genre, and her fault I never give up on writing.

I wouldn't be here without the following friends:

Jami Nord & Owen Littman

Heather Cashman

Jude

Heather Gilbert

M. Andrew Patterson

Aimee

Amanda W.

Quinton Shyn

Kindra

Kendra

Dawn Chapman

Alexis Keane

Bonnie Price

Richard Hummel

Stephen Morse

Felissa Ely

Anthea Sharp

Andrea Parseneau

Cait Greer

M Evan Matyas

Ian Mitchell

To those readers on RR whose help and readership has been invaluable:

Thank you all for reading and so much for the amazing feedback! I know I've probably forgotten someone. If you read this on RR in its early stages (before book 2) and conmmented or reviewed, please know it means the world to me.

Endless Paving

Mearhena

Oathkeeper

Cyan Snake

Bleached

Tarakis

Puck

Koinzell

Nikeyeia

Zedicious

Barnmaddo

Patreon:

Thank you all so much for your support!

Ma & Pa

Kyle

Kylie B

Brandon T

Janis N

Amanda W

Erik S

Amanda M

Stuart G

D.R. Perry

Nikolas Z

Bubs

From the creator of the Delvers LLC universe, comes Nora's story.

Nora Hazard's story begins over three years prior to the events of Delvers LLC: Welcome to Ludus.*

On Ludus, life is often cheap. Nora's childhood hadn't given her many options. With nowhere else to go after losing her family, she had joined an old friend in a street gang and found an unlikely home there.

But unfortunately, tragedy is about to befall Nora. Grudges from the distant past and movements of shadowy organizations may take away everything she is familiar with and all that she holds dear…possibly even her life.

Danger has never stopped her before, but survival may require escaping her old life and embarking on an insane, desperate journey. On the way, she might even accidentally stumble into both an incredible opportunity, and an incredible burden.

Unfortunately for her enemies, Nora was no pushover before…and that was before discovering super powers!

High-tech gaming and ancient magic collide when a computer game opens a gateway to the treacherous Realm of Faerie.

Jennet Carter never thought hacking into her dad's new epic-fantasy sim-game would be so exciting…or dangerous. Behind the interface, dark forces lie in wait, leading her toward a battle that will test her to her limits and cost her more than she ever imagined.

The Wayward Bard

By Lars M

Daniel's Guide to Early Retirement:

1. Intercept illegal money transfer from mafia boss.
2. Hide out in super exclusive Full Immersion Virtual Reality game until the heat is off.
3. Roll a bard. Max out charisma. Live it up.
4. Profit.

With all the pesky planning out of the way Daniel set out to realize his ultimate dream: gaining enough money to buy a tropical island and spend his days playing the violin and RPGs. What could possibly go wrong?

Disclaimer: There shall be no harems in this series. Overpowered, perfect protagonists will not be tolerated and excessive cursing will result in donations to the swear jar.